THE LAND WAS THEIRS
FOR THE TAKING. . . .

ELIZABETH ROLFSON—In the midst of danger, she dared to stand alone. In the face of all odds, she gave her heart to a turbulent love in a savage, strife-torn land.

LANCE TALLWORTH—His half-Indian blood bound him to a dark, vengeful past. Only Elizabeth could lead him out of the wilderness into a new world of his own making.

J. J. GRANGER—An American tycoon. Insatiable in his greed for power, he would stop at nothing to destroy Elizabeth and seize the Rolfson empire.

ERIC STARBANE—A powerful speculator with a will of iron. He alone held the secret of Elizabeth's past . . . and the key to her future.

THEIR FUTURE WAS A NATION
IN THE MAKING

Books by Vanessa Royall

FLAMES OF DESIRE
COME FAITH, COME FIRE
FIREBRAND'S WOMAN
WILD WIND WESTWARD
SEIZE THE DAWN

Seize
the Dawn

Vanessa Royall

A DELL BOOK

Published by
Dell Publishing Co., Inc.
1 Dag Hammarskjold Plaza
New York, New York 10017

Dell ® TM 681510, Dell Publishing Co., Inc.

ISBN: 0-440-17788-X

Printed in the United States of America

First printing—January 1983

To the editors of Vanessa's books,
with great appreciation.

Beverly Lewis
Kate Duffy
Andrea Cirillo
Kathy Sagan

Part One

GENEVA, SWITZERLAND • 1885

Elizabeth Rolfson, almost twenty-one, stood on the lofty balcony of the St. Ada's College library, waiting for graduation—and waiting for her life to begin. A warm spring breeze moved in off the Alps, across Lake Geneva, and over the towers of this ancient mountain-encircled city. The heart of a chance passerby on the road below quickened to wistfulness when he saw Elizabeth there, her lovely face turned up to the sun, the wind caressing her long auburn hair and pressing the neat school uniform against her slender, ripe, high-breasted young body.

Elizabeth watched the road for her uncle, Gustav Rolfson, who was expected to arrive momentarily. Uncle Gustav lived in Oslo, Norway, where Elizabeth had grown up, and since he was the closest thing to a parent that she had, it was only fitting that he attend her graduation. Gustav had constantly encouraged her to study very hard.

"I have great plans for you," he always said.

Elizabeth wondered what they were. She looked out over lake and city, and pressed her skirts down against the billowing wind. Very soon, she imagined, she would have no more use for this drab St. Ada's outfit, but would wear instead gowns of silk, sweeping to the floor. Silver shoes, if she wished. Bright dresses, tucked at the midriff to display her small waist, and gowns for the night, cut low and teasing at the bosom. A few more classes to attend, and after that the world awaited. No more schoolgirl woolens, but gleaming high-throated blouses with pearl buttons and ruffled cuffs. No more sensible black pumps, but instead high leather boots to lace up. No more St. Ada's, and gossipy classmates, but . . .

Who?

Time will answer that, Elizabeth reflected. And as she did, another realization came to her as well: *Time will answer all questions, even those memory is not keen enough to ask.*

She was just about to turn away when the spinning wheels of a carriage caught her eye. A fine charabanc drawn by two glossy bays, it came up the mountain road and turned into St. Ada's main gate. The uniformed liveryman blocked her view of the passenger for a moment, but Elizabeth already knew who it was. So when the carriage drew closer and pulled into the school's wide cobblestone courtyard, she was not at all surprised to see Gustav Rolfson riding in it, the livid crisscross of scar upon his ruddy face visible from where he stood.

Thank God he had not brought his mistress, Thea Thorsdatter, along with him.

"I had to wait half an hour for a hack," grumbled Gustav to Elizabeth when she met him in St. Ada's courtyard.

"I'm sorry, Uncle," she replied, studying him. He was as solid in build as ever and his broad face had the ruddy hue she remembered so well, but his coloration was different now. It was not the spring sun that had turned his complexion red, but rather the pressure of bad blood beneath his flesh.

He regarded her in his turn. "My, you have . . . grown," he huffed, climbing heavily from the carriage. "I hope you have not been wasting *your* time."

"No, Uncle."

"Good. Very good. And you have continued to do well in your studies?"

"Yes," she said proudly. "I am at the head of my class."

The driver and horses waited. Gustav squinted around St. Ada's, making sure everything was in its proper place. He glanced toward the main building, where he had first encountered Headmaster Vandevere and taught him a thing or two about proper education. Gustav considered himself an expert in everything. He frowned, seized by a spate of dry coughing. Gustav had never invited or inspired affection and, try as she might, Elizabeth had been able to feel but little toward him, in spite of the life and education he had given her. But she was genuinely alarmed to see him bent over in the courtyard, hanging on to the carriage for support, a victim of the spasms of his lungs. At length he recovered.

"I am afraid I've felt better in my day," he admitted, gasping. Even the liveryman was looking on with concern. "My *God*. What a life. My father lived to be eighty-four, fit as a fiddle until the very end. And here I am, a score years younger and . . ." He broke off. "Well, you have ended your expensive education, almost, so you will be ready to carry on now."

"Carry on what?"

"That is what I have come to discuss with you. That is also why Thea is not with me. We must speak alone. I fear that Thea is going to cause trouble for us."

"I don't understand," said Elizabeth.

Gustav coughed a little more. "Come, girl, and get in the buggy . . ."

Elizabeth noted that he had promoted her from "child" to "girl." Couldn't he see that she was a woman?

". . . and let us drive down along the lake, where the air is good. I need it. It has been a hard winter."

Gustav managed to struggle up into the buggy, ignoring the driver's proffered aid. Elizabeth climbed up beside him. She never felt as far away from Uncle Gustav as when she was near him, and she recalled the words of her gossipy

11

friends: "Elizabeth does not look as if she really *belongs* to him. . . ." Perhaps she did not. Gustav was always so glibly evasive about the past, as if it held secrets he would prefer to keep from her.

For as long as she could remember, Elizabeth had experienced a recurring dream, a memory that was as vague as a vision. In the dream, she was at play on a green lawn. A great white house stood above the lawn, and at the edge of the grass, beyond a thicket, flowed a wide blue river. She and a golden-haired little boy were at play on the grass, in the thicket . . .

"Uncle, did I ever have a brother?" she asked him bluntly.

The brick-red hue of his face seemed to lighten ever so slightly. "Why do you ask?" he said.

"I'm . . . I'm not sure." She did not want to tell him about her dream-memory.

"But there must be a reason for your asking?"

"You've told me many times that my parents were murdered," she said, as they rode through the city, between tall hotels and office buildings, "and I think I'm old enough now to know the details."

"I guess you are right," sighed Gustav. "Do not blame me for not telling you everything before. I was only trying to spare you unpleasantness."

Was it true that he had a heart after all?

"We were all in America then," he began, wheezing a little. "I was living in Chicago, of course, where my business offices were situated, and you were with your parents in Minnesota, a part of America on the north central plains. It is very rich in iron ore, which, even now, I am trying to lay my hands on. A hard struggle, I tell you. But more of that later. You wish to know of your parents. So be it."

"You *are* my father's brother?" Elizabeth asked. She

knew that he had told her this before, but she felt compelled to ask the question anyway.

"What do you think?" he said curtly. "That I would take in off the street a child totally unknown to me?"

No, you would certainly not do that, Elizabeth thought to herself.

"And my father's name was Olav?"

"Olav Rolfson, yes. My dear brother. And your mother was . . . was called Hilda."

"Was she beautiful?"

"Well, now that I think upon it . . . well, yes, she was more than commonly attractive. At least my . . . brother thought so."

Gustav harrumphed, and coughed a little more. The driver turned the buggy onto the street that ran along the quay. Lake boats glided in toward the docks or moved slowly out upon the water, carrying tourists on excursions. The people were happy and gaily dressed, waving and calling to one another. The ambience was one of celebration, cheer, good feeling. In the carriage, however, Gustav Rolfson spoke of death.

"My brother, Olav, was the . . . well, he was the less successful of us two," Gustav admitted. "He lived a good but unprofitable life in Minnesota . . ."

No big white house on the riverbank? Elizabeth wondered.

". . . with you and your mother . . ."

No little boy who had played with me and called me "Beth"?

". . . but he often wrote me for money to tide him over. And I always sent it, even though I was wrapped up in many a business struggle in those days. Now, I had this particular competitor. His name was . . . his name was . . ."

Gustav seemed to be having trouble pronouncing the name. His face flamed in anger; his features tightened, twisted. "His name was Gunnarson," Gustav spat. "As

13

common as a guttersnipe, as common as a barmaid's rag . . ."

Aware that he was losing a measure of control, and wishing above all else to project an appearance of command, Gustav gathered himself. "At any rate, this Gunnarson, who was competing with me for a chance at iron ore in northern Minnesota, learned that my poor brother was in need of money. Gunnarson was from Minnesota too, you see. A great number of us Scandinavians are settling there. Now, at the time, I was thoroughly besting this Gunnarson in our struggle for access leases to the iron ranges. I was besting him and so he chose to strike at me through my . . . my poor brother."

"How did he do that? Was my father involved in the business?"

"No, no," Gustav answered quickly. "Of course not. Any mercantile brains you have, you get from me. But Gunnarson knew that by embarrassing my brother, he could also take a blow at my own reputation. Times are changing somewhat, but on the American frontier, word is bond and family more than blood. Everyone knew everyone else. Gunnarson went to Olav with the offer of a loan, and Olav, God rest his soul, took it. He did not tell me. And when the note came due, he could not pay it back. He did not tell me this either. He was ashamed . . ."

Elizabeth felt a shrinking feeling. This "Olav" had been her father? This man who was poor? Who borrowed badly? Who could not meet his obligations? *No, I won't believe it*, she thought, even as Gustav went on speaking.

". . . he was ashamed that he had brought opprobrium down upon our name."

"But I don't recall any of this," Elizabeth said.

"You were too young. And then, too, you could not help being shocked out of your wits by what happened."

"*What* happened?"

Gustav gave her a look that, for him, seemed sympathetic, even mournful. "To make a long story short," he said, as if attempting to spare her feelings, "Gunnarson came to your home to demand his money. Your mother and father were there, and you as well. Your mother had not known of the loan either. Olav was desperate to make the appearance of a successful man. Gunnarson asked for his payment. Olav said none was due. Gunnarson began to explain the affair to Hilda, seeking to humiliate your father in front of your mother . . ."

Mystified, Elizabeth searched the farthest, darkest reaches of her mind. She could not recall anything remotely similar to what Uncle Gustav was telling her. But she realized why she might well have wanted to forget when Gustav said, in his abrupt manner:

". . . Olav pulled his gun and fired. He missed. In defense, Gunnarson drew his own weapon. His aim was better. But your mother threw herself in front of your father, seeking to protect him. She failed. Gunnarson's bullet killed them both. . . ."

Elizabeth felt helpless, and terribly angry. Her past, which Uncle Gustav had reluctantly revealed in response to her demand, was common and even tawdry. The only nobility in it was the fact that her mother, this woman named Hilda, had tried to shield her father from a bullet. And her mother had not only failed, but had been killed in the process.

"And I was there in the house when that happened?" Elizabeth asked in a small voice.

Gustav nodded, coughing. He waited a moment, as the carriage rolled along the quay, letting Elizabeth become accustomed to what he had related.

"So I sent for you," he told her, "and had you brought to my home in Chicago. You were in a bad state, but I saw your promise immediately. I took you home to Europe, and since then have endeavored to give you a style of life second to none, and certainly a life superior to that of brawling America. Although now I expect you will be ready for it . . ."

"Ready for it? Am I to go to America?" Elizabeth was confused. Still trying to sort out and absorb the welter of emotions Gustav had evoked, she now realized that he was talking about her future. Was this a part of the "plan" he had always spoken of, so consistently but so vaguely?

"Perhaps," her uncle replied. "But there is Thea to be considered." He frowned, and coughed. "You know, my fine girl, once I *thought* Thea was a lot like me, and took delight in the fact. Now I realize that she *is* just like me, probably more so. My health, as any fool can see, is fading fast, so I want to make sure you are taken care of, that my plan is put into effect, before Thea . . ."

The thought seemed to agitate him. He bent over in the buggy seat, gasping. Elizabeth felt the shadow of death in the face of thriving life. Bright flags waved from the buildings of Geneva, from the masts of boats along the lakefront. Children waved colored balloons, while organ grinders sent brittle but charming melodies into the air. People walked about, talking and laughing, bent upon pleasure and relaxation. But in the carriage with Uncle Gustav, Elizabeth was in the presence of death, past death and future death, together as one. The contrast between a happy day and a dark tale was disconcerting.

"What plan do you have for me?" she heard herself asking her uncle.

He lifted his arm limply, as if to wave aside her query.

"Tell me," he asked, "how do you feel about this man Gunnarson, of whom I spoke?"

Elizabeth had hated no one in her entire life, not even Thea Thorsdatter when that woman had—mistakenly, she later claimed—locked Elizabeth in the wine cellar of the Oslo mansion for the space of a winter day. Elizabeth remembered the darkness and the cold, and recalled the impregnability of the door against her tiny, pounding fists.

She still felt a black loneliness when recalling her child's weakness and impotent rage.

But she was no longer a child, and had grown to learn —from her own experience as well as from the books she loved—that destiny, large or small, belongs only to those who seek and grasp it, those who *feel*.

"Whoever this Gunnarson is," she told her uncle, "I hate him. I hate him for killing my parents, no matter what the provocation."

Did she actually see on Gustav Rolfson's face then the cold wintry flicker of a smile?

Now the carriage approached a small waterfront park, with swaths of green grass, sidewalks, and benches. Vendors peddled ices and sweets, and children waited excitedly along the pier, as a lake boat filled with tourists eased slowly toward the dock.

"*Now* we shall talk about the future," declared Gustav, as if he had finally heard in Elizabeth's words that for which he had been waiting. "Driver, stop here. We shall descend and take the air for a time."

The liveryman obeyed, reining the bays and drawing the charabanc to a halt.

Gustav managed to clamber down from the buggy, and Elizabeth followed, watching him. She was appalled by the obviously dangerous decline in his health, a concern that diminished not at all when he burst into another spasm of coughing while walking toward a park bench.

"Uncle Gustav!"

He lurched toward the bench, like a jittery swimmer floundering after a length of floating wood.

The lake boat had docked now, and the crowd of passengers was disembarking, their laughing voices like chimes in the mountain air.

Fear rose in Elizabeth's breast. Gustav was clearly in the grip of some attack, and she did not know what to do. Moreover, no one seemed to pay any attention.

Gustav reached the bench and flopped down upon it. He was red-faced, choking, waving his arms, like a swimmer going down for the third time, unable even to croak for help.

"Uncle!" Elizabeth went toward him and bent down. He was clawing at his cravat, his shirt collar. Yes, that was it. Undo the tie, the stud. She did this as quickly as she could, but Gustav's color was darkening alarmingly. In a panic she looked around for someone to help.

A man was hurrying toward her, looking beyond her at Gustav, already appraising the situation. Elizabeth saw, in that moment of panic and need, that the man was tall and strong, with black, intense eyes. Then she turned back toward her uncle, bending over him. The man came up beside her, and knelt down, studying Gustav. She had time to glance at him. He was quite young, certainly not thirty, and very tan. She felt a delicious surge in her body, in spite of the circumstances.

"This man is having a seizure," said Elizabeth's benefactor, in a quiet but resonant voice that touched an unknown chord inside her. He looked at her. He had eyes that were . . . "We must get him to a doctor at once."

"Yes," said Elizabeth.

"Are you familiar with Geneva?" he asked.

The liveryman, having finally noted the disturbance, was striding toward the bench.

"Yes, I am. There is a hospital . . ."

Gustav seemed in the grip of a convulsive spasm, which repeated itself intermittently as he struggled for breath.

"Good." The young man stood up and saw the uniformed driver. "You," he said commandingly, "bring that carriage over here immediately."

The driver rushed back for the buggy, and Elizabeth stood aside as the young man bent down, slid his arms beneath Gustav, and lifted him up. Gustav Rolfson was a man who had treated his body to much red wine, rich meat,

18

and sweets. His favorite meal consisted of devouring, all by himself, a roast suckling pig stuffed with barley and brown sugar. A large man to begin with, he weighed considerably more than he should have, but the black-haired young man in the elegant pearl-gray suit lifted him as though he were no burden at all.

"Let's go," he told Elizabeth, glancing at her over his shoulder as he carried Gustav to the buggy and lifted him up into the seat. Gustav's color was dangerously dark now, with tints of blue in his face. The young man helped Elizabeth up into the seat, and climbed up himself.

"Driver, go," he ordered.

The liveryman, pale and shaken in the presence of an emergency, clucked to the horses, and eased the bays out into the stream of heavy traffic. Pedestrians swarmed along the quay, and the street was filled with buggies and wagons, horses and humanity. The going would be slow.

"How far to the hospital?" the man asked Elizabeth, looking at her with those unusual eyes, which were hard but not hard, opaque but penetrating at the same time.

"Perhaps . . . a kilometer . . ."

"We'll never get there in time," the man decided, looking at Gustav. "At least not at this speed . . ."

Elizabeth barely believed what she saw then. In a series of moves so graceful they seemed to flow into one another, the man swung out of the carriage with tremendous balance and speed, swept the reins from the driver's shaking grasp, and leaped from the front of the buggy onto the back of the horse on the left. The startled beast seemed about to rear, but the young man leaned forward momentarily, patting its neck, seeming to speak to it. Then he slapped its flanks with the ends of the leather reins, did likewise to the right wheelhorse, and the carriage leaped forward. Elizabeth was thrown back against the cushions and the perplexed driver almost tumbled from his seat. Even Gustav was surprised enough to draw a good deep breath.

Along the quay, everyone turned to watch. Seldom had a sight like it been seen in sedate Geneva: a carriage streaking hell-for-leather along the main thoroughfare, driven by a man on the back of one of the horses. Coolly and skillfully, the young man guided the team through the heavy traffic, riding as if he had been born on horseback. In the carriage, Elizabeth was conscious of people, horses, buggies, buildings flashing past on either side, conscious of onlookers staring open-mouthed in surprise. And she was aware, too, of the man on the horse, aware deeply within herself, conscious with a part of herself that had never been alive until now. The very manner in which he rode the horse seemed elemental, like power or wind or fire, and the sight touched something inside her being that was elemental as well. She saw the manner in which the beast moved, and how he moved upon it as he rode. A sharp current flared deep in Elizabeth's flesh, an awakening of primeval impulse, the ancient memory of blood and brood. Watching this man's body move upon the horse, Elizabeth was born as a woman. All dreamy schoolgirl desire slipped away. For the first time in her life, the knife of mature need and desire pressed its blade into her being, withdrew, and left her hollow-hungry, aching with want. She did not understand it yet—there was no time to study it now—but she knew it. Oh, but she knew it.

Then, with the horses flashing at full gallop down the Rue Chambon, he turned and called, "What street do we take to the hospital?"

Elizabeth took her bearings, and judged her surroundings in the blur of speed. "There," she shouted back to him, pointing to where the Rue Dennis came down the hill toward the quay. "Turn right by that hostelry."

Uncle Gustav seemed close to unconsciousness now, his eyes glazed and his breath rattling. "I'm getting off this thing," the liveryman moaned. And when the buggy slowed slightly to turn into the Rue Dennis, he leaped out, rolling along the cobblestones like a sack of straw in uniform and boots. Up the hill the carriage flew, the horses straining, pounding along in tandem. The strange young man moved with the horses, and it seemed to Elizabeth almost as if, by a principle of existence unknown to her, he conveyed his own strength and resolution to the beasts. *Never*, she reflected, *have I seen anyone like him.*

The hospital was tall, narrow, and white. Run by the Sisters of Mercy, a large crucifix stood atop a pedestal of marble in a small courtyard paved with Belgian blocks. The young man guided the horses expertly off the street and into the courtyard, wheeled around the crucifix, and reined in the horses by the hospital entrance. The clatter of hoof and wheel was still reverberating in the air when he dashed back to the carriage and lifted Gustav into his arms again. For a moment, before turning to carry her uncle into the hospital, the man smiled at Elizabeth, as if to say, *Don't worry about anything, I shall see that all will be well.* His smile was dazzling, and Elizabeth felt as if a portion of her breath had been taken away. But there was a quality to his smile, just as there was a shadow in his eyes, that seemed tensile as well as tender, and wholly enigmatic. In spite of the situation, Elizabeth was intrigued. He was not a man easy to read, nor one to let himself be read.

She put the issue out of her mind now, and raced after him, as he carried Gustav Rolfson into the hospital. A sister, in her white coif and long spotless habit, glided to meet them.

Gustav had gone limp, his face bluish-pink, his breath stertorous or wheezing by turns.

"This way," said the sister, "follow me. Sister Candide," she called to another nun behind a desk near the front door, "summon Doctor Louis at once."

Gustav was placed on a narrow white bed in a bright white room. He lay unmoving, although his nostrils flared slightly when the nun held spirits of ammonia before him.

He might die, Elizabeth realized. She was disturbed, but not frightened. Beside her, she felt the presence of the man in the pearl-gray suit, and she knew without knowing why that she had no cause to fear anything when he was with her.

Dr. Louis, a shortish man with an air of fatigue, entered the room as the sister was expertly cutting away Gustav's clothing. He set his black bag down next to the bed and lifted Gustav's wrist, reading his pulse even as he studied the patient carefully.

"An injection of strychnine," he said to the nun. "Prepare it immediately. When did the attack begin?" he asked, leaning slightly toward Elizabeth.

"About . . . about ten minutes ago," she faltered.

Dr. Louis administered the injection, not directly into the heart, as Elizabeth had suspected he might, but into a vein in Rolfson's neck.

"It is not as serious as it might have seemed," he said to Elizabeth, "but it is serious enough. Our patient would most likely have recovered consciousness in due course. *This* time," he added emphatically. "I shall speak to him sternly regarding his living habits when he comes round. The man is vastly overweight, and I fear fat is threatening the arteries leading to his heart."

On the bed, Gustav groaned.

"Sir," barked Dr. Louis, "you're in hospital. You're all right."

After assuring himself that he was, indeed, alive, Gustav grunted and took his bearings. "Must be your thin mountain air that did this to me. Elizabeth, my clothes are ruined. You must send to my hotel and fetch more."

Dr. Louis disagreed. "Sir, I believe you ought to stay abed and rest, for several days at least. You're not a well man."

"Brilliant of you," returned Rolfson, pulling a sheet over

himself. "It is a wonder how much medical knowledge even a doctor can assimilate."

Dr. Louis held his temper.

"Send for my clothing," Gustav ordered Elizabeth again, "and let's get out of here." He grimaced toward the doctor and the nun. "You'll both be paid, I assure you," he oozed. "I am Gustav Rolfson, of Rolfson Industries. Worldwide," he added. "I know the Krupps."

"It is my duty to tell you, sir," Dr. Louis said in strained but measured terms, "that you must rest. At least for a week. In bed. And at once, you must cease consuming red meat, alcohol in any form, and sweets. They are blocking your arteries and killing you."

"Yes, yes," responded Gustav with irritation. "I shall consider that." He managed to sit up. "Hurry now, Elizabeth," he said. "Send round a messenger to fetch my things. I'm stopping at the Continental Hotel."

The doctor shrugged, closed his bag, and left the room.

"I shall pray for you, sir," offered the nun.

"Save your breath, sister," said Gustav.

Appalled, the good sister backed away from the bed and out the door.

"And who in the hell are you?" demanded Gustav, turning to measure the young man standing next to Elizabeth.

She was ready to explain how her samaritan had helped her get Gustav to the hospital, but he spoke for himself.

"My name is Lance Tallworth. I'm an American. I saw you in distress, and I chose to help."

Elizabeth loved the timbre of his voice, the way he stood, even the manner in which he looked straight at Gustav and said, "I chose to help," as if he might have chosen otherwise.

"Humph," grunted Rolfson. "I suppose you'll want money like the rest of them, like that quack doctor and the nuns . . ."

"I don't think you ought to speak that way," Lance Tallworth said quietly.

Gustav's eyes widened, and his color rose dangerously once again. It had been a long, long time since anyone had contradicted him, admonished him, even given him a hard look.

"So you're rich, eh?" he asked Tallworth, with a canny glance.

"Why do you say that?"

"Well, you don't want money. You must be one of those rich young men from America, here in Europe on a frolic."

Elizabeth turned toward Mr. Tallworth, meaning to apologize for her uncle's rudeness. But the expression in his eyes as he looked at Gustav silenced her. Lance was amused in a dark—and somehow dangerous—way. He did not laugh. But he smiled. Gustav grew polite when he saw the smile.

"Well, I do thank you, young man. That is the truth. For helping my niece and me. I only meant to suggest that a reward would be fitting. . . ."

"It is unnecessary, I assure you."

The three of them were speaking in French, and Elizabeth had noted in Tallworth's accent intonations of the southern provinces. This was unusual, since he'd said he was from America. She sensed, in a manner that went beyond mere understanding, that he possessed reserves, even mysteries, not because he wished to but because they were a part of his very nature. That nature was sparking her own, in a way she had never known before. She felt an impulse to shiver.

"I can't thank you enough, Mr. Tallworth," she said.

He looked down at her suddenly with his black, enigmatic eyes and chiseled face. He was not French, nor Italian, nor Spanish. He was neither Scandinavian nor English. Strains of blood had somehow come together to fashion such perfection. Elizabeth knew what he was not, but not what he was. She shivered.

"Are you all right?" Lance Tallworth asked, putting his hand on her shoulder.

She felt a fool for having shuddered, but she did not want him to take his hand away.

"Yes. The tension of what happened . . ." She faltered.

"I understand." He took his hand away. "Perhaps I might see you to your home?" Lance looked at Gustav, not to seek his permission but to tell him how things were going to be.

"My niece attends St. Ada's College. On the hill. But remember, she must fetch my clothing at the Continental Hotel."

"I am stopping at the Continental Hotel," Lance told him. "I shall attend to your garments."

"I want her back at the college within the hour," Gustav rallied, as Lance left the room with Elizabeth.

Outside the hospital, when he helped her into the carriage, when he climbed up into the seat beside her, Elizabeth could not help but think, *This feels so right! This is what I must have been waiting for!*

Yet how could that be? She did not even know this man, and there seemed to be forces in him that might be unknowable.

Wouldn't it be fine to try and learn them! But what if he wasn't interested in her at all?

"You must forgive my uncle. He has his good points. Few, I'll admit, but . . ."

"I am not interested in your uncle." He smiled, and flicked the horses with the ends of the reins. The carriage moved forward, down toward the city and the hotel.

Elizabeth considered his answer and allowed herself a moment of hope. Perhaps he *was* interested in her. He didn't say anything else, however, so she tried again.

"What part of America are you from?"

"Montana."

Elizabeth was a good student of geography. "That's in the West. I myself was born in Minnesota. My parents . . . died there."

Lance turned toward her abruptly. His wary reserve had flown in an instant. On his face she saw . . . she did not know what she saw. "What is it?" she asked, a little frightened. "Did I say something to startle you?"

He looked at her for a long moment, then decided to speak.

"My own parents died in Minnesota," he said. "I left the state five years ago. I shall never return."

In his eyes was something far deeper than bitterness, as if the two of them were joined in a secret bond of tragedy.

He didn't seem to want to talk about it, and she did not know why. Had he been unhappy there? Was that why he had come to Europe? Again, he projected that unmistakable aura of secrets, even perhaps of travail.

It would have been impolite to ask him what he was doing here in Switzerland, but she could certainly ask him if he was enjoying it.

"Not especially, until now," he said.

Elizabeth's heart quickened. Only much later, after she had answered in the emphatic affirmative, did she recall how he had phrased his question.

"It may not be right," he asked, "but would you dine with me tonight?"

Dr. Vandevere of St. Ada's strictly enforced the prohibition against meetings with the opposite sex without benefit of a chaperone. A woman could lose her degree for violating that precept. But Elizabeth could not bear the thought of sharing this man with someone *else*.

"There are certain rules at our college prohibiting us from socializing unchaperoned," she told Lance Tallworth, "but I will meet you at the Continental Hotel this evening anyway."

He studied her for what seemed a long time, as the

carriage moved along the lakefront. "I'm very glad," he said then, softly.

The words excited Elizabeth, until she realized that perhaps he had not known many things in life to be glad about.

Until now, she vowed.

2

"Headmaster Vandevere," said Elizabeth, "I want to request special permission to leave campus this evening."

Vandevere squinted at her through his monocle, and blinked in astonishment. There were no scheduled social activities during this period of final examinations and it was highly irregular for a St. Ada's woman to venture out at night.

Vandevere placed his hands palms-down on a gleaming teak desk.

"And why do you make this request?" he demanded.

"This afternoon my uncle suffered a seizure, and a stranger from one of the lake boats came to our aid and rushed him to hospital. I did not have the opportunity to thank the gentleman properly, and so I should like to make inquiry after him at one of the hotels."

"Why does your uncle not express his own gratitude?"

"He has taken to his bed. Doctor's orders."

"Quite ill, eh?" asked Vandevere.

"Yes, sir."

"Well, how do you know this stranger is even staying at one of the Geneva hotels?"

Elizabeth had carefully prepared her explanation. "He was on a tourist boat," she said, "and the cut of his clothes was foreign. Also, his French was accented."

"Ah! What nature of accent?"

"I could not be certain."

"He helped your uncle, and then disappeared. Is that what I am to understand?"

"Yes." More or less.

"Well, then it is quite obvious he does not wish gratitude."

"But if you have taught us anything at St. Ada's, sir," Elizabeth replied, "it is that there are obligations in life that must be met, and I think this is one such obligation I must fulfill."

She was studying Vandevere's face. He looked very dubious. She suspected that he was going to refuse her request outright. The knowledge convinced her all the more that she *must* find a way out of St. Ada's tonight.

"Why not wait until morning?" he asked, leaning forward. "What is the compulsion behind this, anyway?"

To herself, Elizabeth answered, *Because I must see him again.* To Headmaster Vandevere she said, "If he is on a journey, he may leave Geneva before I have the opportunity to thank him."

Vandevere pondered the matter. "No," he decided finally. "It is a somewhat special circumstance, but insufficient in importance for me to approve a variation in the rules. This is a matter for your uncle, not for you. Discuss it with him in the morning."

Vandevere stood. So did Elizabeth. She showed no disappointment. She was already considering another course of action.

"This is unlike you, Elizabeth," Vandevere tut-tutted. "Asking for special favors!"

He showed her to the door.

"Yes, sir. Thank you, sir," Elizabeth agreed.

But darkness found her in an alcove near the school chapel. Every evening after dinner, the girls of St. Ada's were expected to attend chapel for a brief prayer service. Elizabeth had never missed once in four years. Her absence would probably be noticed tonight. Even so, this was the only safe time to leave St. Ada's and walk down into the city. With everyone in chapel, there was little chance of being observed. She would face her punishment later.

As soon as the chapel bells ceased ringing, Elizabeth eased out the door, around the corner of the building, and down across the edge of the main courtyard, heavily obscured by shadows. She slipped out the main gate, and walked swiftly down the hill. The lights of Geneva glittered below, and a breeze clear as new snow came in off the lake. She felt a bit unusual: this was the first time she had ever broken school rules. But the freedom of the night, the crystal wind, and the thought of the man she was meeting all combined to give her the same heady feeling she had experienced before only from a glass of wine at holiday dinner. By the time she reached the city, all thought of St. Ada's had flown. It was, she realized, probably the first time she had been totally on her own in her entire twenty-one years! She felt wonderful. Everything was changed. Even these stones beneath her feet, which she had trod for years, were altered, soft and springy to speed her on her way. She thought of Lance Tallworth, and the feeling she had had this afternoon returned. It was not a single sensation, nothing she could grasp with her mind, but instead a yearning, tempting, pulsing hollow of body and soul combined, hot, dangerous, and infinitely exciting. How many times had her classmates whispered and giggled and tried to imagine the precise *feel* of desire? Too many times to count. There had also been times when, courted and kissed by young men who studied here at the university in Geneva, Elizabeth had pretended or tried to pretend that what she felt matched the soaring descriptions of her friends. Yet she had always known, even with Arndt Stryker, who loved her very much, even with Jorge Lora, who said he worshipped her, that her feelings for them would never compare to an expectation she could not put into words.

Until now.

Arndt Stryker and Jorge Lora and the others were mere boys. Lance Tallworth was a man. Until today, she told herself, she had been but a girl. Now she was a woman. Walking down toward the city, toward Lance, her heart beat with a woman's strength and need, and a desire that was no longer obscure made her body flow. And soon she would possess everything for which God had created her. Love, everything . . .

The thought was incomplete. Why? Elizabeth picked her way as swiftly as she could down the cobblestoned hill from St. Ada's to the Continental Hotel. She had the odd feeling that she knew exactly what she was doing and, on the other hand, no real idea what she was doing at all.

Rue Florence, which led down to the Rue Chambon, was empty at this time of the evening. Most people were inside their dwellings having dinner; the night life of the city had not yet begun. So when Elizabeth heard the clatter of team and carriage coming down the hill behind her, she was startled. Ducking behind the gatepost of a streetside house, she watched the horses go by, and saw Professor Vandevere in the buggy. Elizabeth was sure he had not seen her, and she congratulated herself on wearing, not her St. Ada's uniform, but a cloak of dark green that set off her hair and eyes even as it tended to deflect attention in the gathering darkness. Beneath the cloak, she wore an azure dress of silk, high-necked and exceedingly chaste, although some might have considered it more uplifting and supportive of her bosom than was essential. Quickly she descended, and came out of the Rue Florence onto the wide flat sweep of the Rue Chambon, busy at all times, save very early in the morning.

Upon reaching the Continental Hotel, Elizabeth took a deep breath, and walked into the lobby. A small part of her heart turned to stone. The great chandelier sparkled, fire and diamonds and ice. The marble pillars were reflected in mirrors, and glowed in pink-shaded lamplight. Woodwork gleamed, and thick patterned rugs looked expensive and exotic. All of those things were fine. The sudden chill she felt was caused by the sight of Headmaster Vandevere speaking to a hotel officer at the desk. The clerk wore an unctuous expression and a red carnation in his lapel. He turned toward Elizabeth when she entered, even as he continued to speak with Vandevere.

". . . only the best of quarters," she heard Vandevere telling the other man, ". . . must make St. Ada's appear to be above reproach in all matters . . ."

What was this? The clerk had turned back to Vandevere, intent upon his words. There seemed something shoddy in their congress, wholly at odds with Vandevere's half-obsequious, half-autocratic attitude. *Only the best of quarters? Absolutely above reproach?* wondered Elizabeth.

Then Headmaster Vandevere turned away from the desk. He looked right at her! How could he not *see* her? But the doughty academician screwed his monocle into an eye-socket, and walked across the glittering lobby toward the dining room. Elizabeth heaved a sigh of relief. But what was she to do now? Should she have Mr. Tallworth paged? But with Headmaster Vandevere in the hotel, the chances of him seeing her were still too great. Perhaps she should go back to St. Ada's. No, as long as you are here, *do* something, she told herself. *Don't agonize. Act.* Always Uncle Gustav's motto, Elizabeth decided it made quite a lot of sense. She walked determinedly toward the desk.

"Mademoiselle?" oozed the desk clerk.

"I'm . . . I'm here for Mr. Tallworth. He's expecting me."

The clerk smirked. "You're here *for* him?"

"Would you please be so kind as to have him paged," Elizabeth said coldly.

"Mr. Tallworth is right behind you, Mademoiselle."

Elizabeth spun around to see Lance Tallworth striding toward her across the hotel lobby. His very gait touched a chord in her. She felt as she had upon seeing him atop the carriage horse this afternoon. The powerfully fluid rhythm of his body, which she perceived with her very flesh, sparked within her a fine, strange symphony of pulsing fire. She breathed, her breasts rose and fell, but there seemed suddenly to be no sustenance in air. The sensation was threatening, but also glorious. Because Elizabeth knew, in a way she could never have studied or learned, that he would give her air to breathe, and flesh to be strong, and nectar to drink until she was full and more than full and running over in splendor.

He seemed dolefully unaware of her piercing bliss, however.

"Miss Rolfson. Forgive me." He offered his arm. "Shall we go into the dining room?"

He was looking down at her, again with those dark, depthless eyes. He did not make her shiver this time. He made her glow.

But he looked unhappy. Perhaps, seeing her again, he had changed his mind. Perhaps he had reconsidered his earlier desire for her company. The possibility distressed her. And there was another problem. Lance was already taking her toward the restaurant entrance.

"Mr. Tallworth?" She wanted to call him Lance, but couldn't yet. He possessed a formidableness that was both magnetic and remote.

"Yes?"

"The headmaster of my college is dining in that restaurant."

"I see." Without breaking stride, he took her past the entrance, through the lobby, and out onto the street. Night had fallen, and the lights of the city sparkled in the hills. Without speaking, he led her down the street to a small cafe, comfortable but inelegant, and took her inside.

"I like this place much better than the hotel restaurant anyway," he said, as they were seated.

Elizabeth was surprised. He looked like the kind of man who would be at ease in the most refined of surroundings. She herself had been coached by Uncle Gustav to avoid a cafe like this one. It was decent and clean, but it was—as Gustav would have said—"Quite common, my child."

Yet, having expressed his regard for this little place, Lance Tallworth did not seem to be enjoying it very much. Or was it that he did not care for his companion?

Elizabeth smiled and tried to make small talk about school, Geneva, even the weather, as a waitress brought them a bottle of white Bordeaux, bowls of fish chowder, and crusty bread. Lance Tallworth did not seem interested in St. Ada's, Geneva, or the weather. He drank, ate slowly, and looked at her from time to time with an expression she could not read, but which roused a tenderness that lived in the very base of Elizabeth's soul. Until now, she had not known it was there in such intensity.

The tenderness did not seem to be of much use to Mr. Tallworth, however. He seemed ten thousand miles away.

Perhaps he is, Elizabeth thought. Exasperated, tired of carrying both ends of this engagement—which *he* had requested!—she set her soup spoon down on the edge of the plate and faced him.

"What's the matter?" she asked.

He looked at her as if he didn't understand her words.

"What's wrong?" she tried again.

He looked bewildered. "Why, nothing . . ." he began.

"No. Something must be. You helped me this afternoon, and I thank you for that. You have asked me to dine, and here I am. Happy to be here, I might add. What *is* the matter? If it's something I've done or said . . ."

Lance put up his hands briefly and smiled. He did not look bewildered now. Instead, he seemed amazed. Her outburst, low-keyed as it was, seemed to have touched a secret place in him. Something passed between them then, a current of affinity and understanding, which, if it was as yet intangible, was no less powerful for that. Elizabeth felt it to the core of her being. Lance seemed to feel it as well. He moved as if to touch her, but he did not. Not quite.

"My mind was on other things," he apologized. "I'm sorry."

"What other things?" she asked softly.

"Problems I am going to have to resolve in the least harmful way."

Did this have something to do with his reason for being in Europe? Or—and Elizabeth felt cold to think of it—was he referring to *someone else*? She had never been attracted to a man this way before—she had never really known a *man* before!—and the sudden, irrational bile of jealousy that surged within her produced a shadowy nausea. She could not face the possibility of *another woman*, so she addressed the other question.

"Do these problems have anything to do with your trip to Europe?" she asked.

He was looking at her again with that expression of perplexity.

"What's wrong now?"

Lance shook his head slowly. "If I seem amazed, it is that I am not used to speaking like this, speaking about what I am thinking. At home, I haven't the opportunity . . ." He broke off. "I find that it is not so easy to express myself," he said. "Not yet," he added.

Elizabeth felt wonderful. Now she was certain, not only that he was attracted to her, but also that he had found in her something he had long sought, and that he needed.

Strangely, however, Lance continued to be quite reticent throughout the rest of the meal. He did tell her that he was a rancher in Montana, and had come to Europe to examine a new hybrid type of hardy cattle in Gascony that might be of use to him. He seemed astounded at her interest,

although she could not understand why. He also said he had
decided that he must see what the larger world was like.
Lance said this in a way that made Elizabeth think he had
been starving, or drowning, for a change of scene.

"You don't like Montana?" she asked.

"No, I love it. I must go back to it. But not soon," he
added quickly, looking her in the eyes. "First I must . . ."

The weight of some unnameable problem sat upon his
wide shoulders.

Elizabeth decided not to ask him any more questions this
evening. She didn't want words anymore, either. She
wanted to hold him and be held by him, a passionate desire
new and wonderful to her, whose life had been—admit it
—so dull so long. But time was running and she had to get
back to the college and sneak in without being seen.

What a stranger I have become to myself in one day! she
reflected, astonished. *Or am I simply meeting myself for the
first time?*

As they set out on the walk back up the hill toward St.
Ada's, Lance Tallworth, his face hidden in darkness, said
something that would excuse forever the taciturn part of his
nature.

"I have never met anyone like you, nor dreamed of it," he
said. "Until now, I have not known enough to imagine
you."

Now it was Elizabeth who could not find words, overwhelmed by the magic of this man, a magic in which her
own tender sorcery had played such a part.

They walked in silence for a time, and then she felt his
arm around her waist, exactly the way some of the college
boys walked with their favorite girls. She had always
thought such displays a bit . . . well, a bit overmuch. Now
she understood, and pressed close to Lance.

"I must see you tomorrow," he was saying. "May I call
for you?"

Elizabeth wanted to tell him how much he had touched

her, wanted to tell him how he seemed to her the lost part of their twin soul, which she had sought forever. She believed, too, that she sensed not only his readiness, his capacity, to accept the love she felt, but also a desire to give a secret part of himself to her.

From behind them, a team of horses pulling a carriage came clattering up the hill.

Vandevere, returning from his dinner! Why was he haunting Elizabeth on the first night of freedom in her entire life?

"I'm afraid it's my headmaster again, coming back to the school," she whispered urgently to Lance.

He glanced back down the roadway, and saw the horses approaching. His look, when he met her eyes again, was as matter-of-fact as the glance of Uncle Gustav when he decided to run a poor man out of business.

"Do you want me to see that he doesn't harass you?" Lance Tallworth asked.

Elizabeth started, and her eyes opened wide. Her tender feelings toward him did not melt away, not at all, but she realized how foolish she had been to invent in her mind an idealized nature for him, when she barely knew him at all, or the forces that had forged his soul.

"No, there's no need to hurt him," she laughed quietly. "Here!"

Seizing his hand, Elizabeth drew him along after her. They were walking beside a high stone wall, which shielded the garden of a hillside house. Behind them, Vandevere's buggy kept coming, but just ahead were the twin gateposts marking the entrance to garden and house. There were only a few scattered streetlamps in this part of Geneva, and Elizabeth was almost sure Vandevere would take little interest in two strollers. But she wanted to be on the safe side, just in case. Now, if the gate was open . . .

It was, and it gave way as she pushed through, with Lance following. Light showed in a few windows of the house, but the garden was quiet and dark. The earth had already been spaded to receive spring seeds, and its smell by night was cool and fecund. Vandevere's carriage rolled past. The gate was easing shut of its own accord. She saw Vandevere glance in their direction. To shield her from the headmaster, Lance stepped before her and pressed her against the stone gatepost.

From that instant, everything became wild as wind, natural as night. Elizabeth felt his hard body all along the length of her own. *Be careful*, she warned herself fleetingly.

But Elizabeth forgot her own warning, possessed immediately of a wild need. Her knees seemed about to buckle, and she felt her body flow in response to Lance. Not a word had been spoken, but there was no need of speech, save for the speech of the flesh. Outlined darkly against the paler darkness of the sky, she saw his head bend down to her for a kiss, sensed his lips trembling close to her own, almost as if questioning. But then she pressed upward slightly and her lips met his, and then they were caught in a voluptuous frenzy Elizabeth had never dreamed and could not name. The twin parts of their divided soul, meeting for the first time, burst into flame.

The lone and lovely animal he was rose up to lose himself in her, and she knew from the moment she felt his kiss that anything he wanted she would give, that everything she had or would ever have was at his command. Everything was right: the time, the night, Geneva, even the gatepost for a bed. He swept aside her green cloak, to feel her more keenly against him, and his hands were at her breasts, tenderly at her breasts, hers seeking and clutching the staff that gave him his nature. His strong, gentle hands slipped up and away from her body the delicate dress she wore, tore off her undergarments as if they were no more than shreds of cloud. Elizabeth felt the cool night air against her skin, wild as nature. His hand was on her now, at the center of her being, and she felt for the first time in her life an exultant pressure building at the base of her spine. The force became intensely, unbearably keen, shooting all along her body, upward along her spine, and her mind dimmed in ecstasy and wonder. She could hear her breath come gasping, far away, yet very near, and his too. They were two wild things together for all time, racing together away from the savage, lonely places of the earth. She would never be lonely again, nor would Lance, and Elizabeth knew it beyond doubt when the cool air against her skin was replaced by his hot, demanding nakedness.

It is not supposed to be this way, she thought disjointedly, recalling fragments of fantasy. She had always imagined a softly lighted room, and a canopied bed in which some faceless man took her gently for the first time. *But this is the way it is!* she told herself joyously, as he lifted her up, the gatepost still against her back, and spread her wide to take her for himself. Half-mad, she opened and closed around him, opened so widely she felt she would never be complete again, knowing in an instant how false her fear had been, closing about him to keep and hold for as long as it would last, which had to be forever. He was plunging to the roots of her body and soul, and in her mind tiny patterns of light dazzled and flickered. It seemed she could not breathe, could not get breath, but that could not be true because she heard herself gasping and one needed breath to gasp. The pressure in her body, where he explored and caressed and pinioned her, just grew and grew and grew until, unable to bear it any longer, Elizabeth writhed upon his staff, and cried out in glorious unintelligible syllables to the mountains and the sky. She thought she heard him moan as well, and the sound gave her joy, and then she did hear him moan, and felt inside her being a mighty, throbbing current of heat, filling and flooding her, tides alive to wash the living walls of her desire.

"Iiiiiiiiiii," he gasped, holding her more tightly than

ever, in the steely wrap of his arms, which she never wanted to leave. Nor did she wish to be lifted and removed from him. She felt him inside her like a tower, was held and possessed by him even as she surrounded and possessed him in her turn.

She was trying to catch her breath when he began to move again, more gently this time. The cells of her body and brain, already shot through with wonder, forced her to cry out in glory at this new assault, and at the promise of more pleasure to come. Suddenly she was engulfed and lifted up and away, swept beyond consciousness, in the consummation of sensation, and another cry, primal and inarticulate, was torn from the core of her being.

Her cry carried into the night air. A window was thrown open in the house, and a wedge of light fell upon the garden, partially illuminating the lovers at the gatepost.

"Mein Gott im Himmel!" raged a nightcapped figure in the window. "Have you no shame?"

Calmly, Lance lifted Elizabeth from himself and lowered her to the earth.

"No, why should we?" he called back. "Now close that window and go away."

The man at the window closed it and withdrew. Something in Lance's tone suggested that retreat was a wise course.

Elizabeth's body was still in the soft grip of fading splendor. Her thoughts were coming slowly over a great distance, and it did not seem necessary that they ever arrive at all. She felt open, now that he had left her. His length and form and shape had carved an indelible niche in her being, which he alone could fill. He was gone. She began to realize it. And even his seed was seeping away, like fruit never to blossom and ripen. Elizabeth felt sad, all of a sudden.

They left the garden and began to climb again toward St. Ada's. His arm was around her, and she leaned close to him as they walked. But near as he was, it seemed he was far away. She hated the feeling, and it made her a little afraid. What had happened to her in that garden? What had happened to them both? In a day and a night, her entire life had changed. Hope and joy gave way to uncertainty; life seemed more wonderful and more dangerous than it ever had before.

At the college gate, Elizabeth and Lance parted with a kiss. A soft kiss, and gentle, yet it provoked in her a new surge of fiery need for the glory she had known such a short time ago.

"We shall meet tomorrow," Lance said, holding her close to him so that she could feel his own renewed desire.

"I'll come down to the hotel after my morning examination," she whispered, wondering why the exam no longer seemed important, even wondering whether she ought to sit for it or not.

She slipped through the gate, saw no one about, and watched her lover—*I have a lover! I am a lover!* she reflected in wonder—walk back down toward the city. Then she stole across campus, into her building, and to her room. No one had seen her, she believed.

In the morning, she sat for her examination in political philosophy, one of her favorite subjects. But the ponderous questions seemed ludicrous, and Elizabeth was barely aware of the answers she composed. How could the thoughts of dead men compete with the desires of a living body? After finishing the exam, she left St. Ada's, once again without permission, and met Lance Tallworth in front of the Continental Hotel. Thrilled when she noted that his usual somber nature was not evident, Elizabeth leaned against him in the carriage seat, content just to be with him. They drove up into the mountains above the city.

"I have decided something," he told her, as she laid out the picnic lunch he had purchased at the hotel, "and I must discuss it with you."

Lance was seated on the sun-warmed grass and she came down beside him, putting her fingers to his lips. She, who had sought words from him just yesterday, did not want to hear them now. "Later," she told him, opening her mouth for his kiss and her being for his love. She did not know, this lovely, newly wild young woman, that other lovers had entwined passionately on meadow grass in the high mountains. The emotion of love can be analyzed and stored away, studied and savored, but not love's sensation. The feeling is new each time that lovers meet, and the splendor of bodily sensation is never the same. Lovers create, again and again, each new day on this ancient earth, and thus did Lance and Elizabeth mingle and meld. Elizabeth closed her eyes to shut out all but sensation. The sunlight on her eyelids ignited flashing patterns of colored light in her mind. Lance's caresses on her breasts and body, gentle at first, then more urgent, triggered wild need in her flesh. He stripped her and she felt sunlight and cool mountain air on her bare skin. Then she felt his hard nakedness against her, the gorgeous long hardness of him taking her, becoming her, as she became him, until it was all mixed up, and her legs were pulled up high alongside his riding body, at one with her in motion and being, and whether she was riding him, or he her, who knew?

"Now tell me what it was?" she heard herself asking him, long afterward, in the naked drowsy afternoon, every pleasure in life tasted and eaten, save for the picnic lunch. "What did you want to tell me?"

But Lance was reluctant to rediscover the words he had intended to tell her earlier. Something in the madness of long lovemaking had touched and troubled him in a way Elizabeth could not interpret.

"It was all so clear and true to me this morning," he said. "What was?"

"I'm not even certain anymore." He looked out over the mountains. "This place is beautiful, but it is not mine."

Elizabeth sensed that he was going to ask her to go with him to America. She imagined herself arguing the matter with Uncle Gustav. But Lance did not ask. Yet he had as much as told her he could not remain here, and she already knew that he loved and belonged to another place. Montana.

Aware that there were elements of him she would not understand until he explained them, Elizabeth resolved to remain calm.

"I want to be with you," she told him. "That's all I know right now."

He nodded and drew her to himself, their bodies flaring again as skin touched skin. The afternoon passed in love, not words. Love seemed to come much easier to him than words, and Elizabeth herself forgot all language, and lost herself in scathing splendor.

With nothing resolved but the immense fact of their love, Elizabeth and Lance returned to the Continental Hotel at nightfall. A liveryman sprang forward to grip the horse's bridle, and the doorman waved an envelope.

"Message for you, Mr. Tallworth, sir. Just arrived this afternoon."

The doorman handed over the envelope. Elizabeth noted foreign stamps on it, and several arrows and readdressings. The missive had been pursuing Lance for some time. His eyes narrowed. Taking it, he ripped the envelope open, unfolded and read the message inside. Elizabeth could not make out the words on the page, but she saw Lance's reaction. His peerless dark-gold skin paled and his eyes seemed to dim and hollow.

"*Ycripsicu*," he groaned. Then he looked at her. "I must leave Geneva immediately," he said. "Come, let me take you back to your college."

Leave Geneva? Now? Elizabeth felt weak, sick. And she saw that Lance seemed close to despair.

"They are *not* going to take it away from me," he said.

43

Ycripsicu? Elizabeth wondered. A place? A thing?

Lance was lost in thought. Then he remembered her, and turned to her. He saw that she had been as stricken watching him as he had been stricken reading the message. Elizabeth could see him draw upon a reserve of strength and steel, as he gathered himself.

"It is nothing," he said. "Let us go to your school now."

Elizabeth did not move. During her twenty-one years, she had witnessed very few people in trouble, in suffering, in need. She could not recall her early years clearly. Gustav and Thea Thorsdatter were cold and self-sufficient. Her classmates at St. Ada's and their families were wealthy, the cream of Europe. In contrast, she had just witnessed Lance Tallworth stricken to the core of his guarded but fierce nature.

"Let me help," she said instinctively. He was her man and would always be. She would do what she could.

"Impossible. Come, I must take you home."

They drove back up the hill to St. Ada's College. "Will you wait for me?" he asked her, as they neared the entrance. "I would ask you to come with me now to America, but there is great danger and . . . certain things that must be resolved. But if you will wait, I shall return for you."

"Of course," she replied, as how could she not? He was her world and future now.

"But what is *ycripsicu*?" she asked.

"Me," he said.

Lance drove the carriage through the gate and into the college courtyard. Elizabeth did not care. What did it matter who saw her with Lance, or who saw him take her into his arms and kiss her good-bye? Her past life was dead, set aside, put behind her. The future waited.

"I will return for you. We are meant to be together," he vowed.

"But I shall not be here! My uncle has plans for me, which he has not yet revealed. You will always be able to

44

reach me, however, by writing the house of Gustav Rolfson, in Oslo. I shall go there directly after graduation."

"My darling," he said, and kissed her again.

And then he drove away.

"Who was *that*?" asked Simone Pellier, a classmate, who had observed the parting. "You know, I'm certain that Headmaster Vandevere saw you kissing that man. What on earth has gotten *into* you, Elizabeth? None of us has ever understood you at all."

You will when you fall in love, Elizabeth thought.

3.

Elizabeth went to bed that night bereft and crestfallen. The man she would love forever—the only man she would ever love—was gone. All of the hard work she had done at St. Ada's was worth naught to her if Vandevere would not permit her to graduate. And if the news got out to the other girls—which scintillating news invariably did—wouldn't that give them something to gossip about, though!

Elizabeth went to bed feeling desolate. But something had touched her—Lance Tallworth had touched her—and she awoke the next morning with an altered perspective on her situation and prospects. Her body, so willingly given and gloriously well-used by the strangely compelling American, felt radiant, as if she fully possessed it, fully *owned* it for the first time in her life. And she realized another thing as well: very subtly, her thoughts were on the future now as well as on the past. A woman did not simply meet and know ecstasy with a man by accident. No, there was something fated about her melding with Lance, the destiny and outcome of which waited to be fulfilled in the future. She knew it.

In the bed beside her, Simone Pellier came awake, stretched, and yawned.

"You're in trouble for missing chapel the night before last," said Simone.

"Is that right?"

"Yes," said Simone. She was deeply puzzled. Elizabeth,

usually so predictable, was not behaving characteristically, not in the least.

"Who was the handsome man?" she asked, skipping the preliminaries and getting to the heart of the matter.

"An American named Lance Tallworth," answered Elizabeth, going off to dress. "And, by the way, I shan't be at breakfast this morning either. I must go down to the Continental Hotel. My uncle has left the hospital. I must see him."

After she had made her toilette and dressed, Elizabeth calmly left St. Ada's and walked down the Rue Florence toward the Continental. Passing the gateposts behind which she had first known love, she felt a peculiar trembling throughout her body.

At the hotel, she asked for Gustav Rolfson, and while a bellboy went upstairs with her message, she inquired as casually as she could after "Mr. Tallworth," and learned that he had departed on the previous evening.

Gustav summoned her upstairs. Dressed in a crimson robe that matched his scar, he was eating breakfast when Elizabeth knocked and entered the suite. He looked puffy, tired and pale, but his condition had not prevented him from ordering his usual gargantuan breakfast. The aroma from a pot of strong coffee rode the air, and his plate was heaped with broiled kidneys, thick sausages, and a half dozen eggs fried in butter. Heavily sugared rolls, onto which Gustav had smeared slabs of butter, rested on a second plate beside his coffee cup. He ate methodically: kidney-egg-bread-sausage-egg-bread-coffee, repeating the sequence time after time. Three bottles with pills also were on the table, next to his coffeepot.

"Uncle," Elizabeth cried, somewhat alarmed, "ought you to be eating such a large meal? I thought Dr. Louis had told you to alter your habits. . . ."

"Nothing wrong with me," Gustav grunted, his mouth full of kidney, egg, and bread. "Nothing wrong with me the good air of Norway won't cure. Geneva is all right, but it's too close to France and Italy. Everything is rotten in those countries, and I include the populations thereof."

"What about your pills?"

"To hell with my pills. You want them?" He speared three fat lengths of sausage with his fork and stuffed them into his grinding mouth.

"But yesterday you were . . ."

"I was just a little tired from the trip. That's all. Nothing to it. I feel fine today. Here, you want some of this?" he offered, waving his hand at the food. "I'll have a boy fetch china and silver."

Elizabeth shook her head.

"Can't eat, eh? That's bad. Very bad. What's the point in living if you can't eat, and a young girl like you, just getting ripe, can't let herself get skinny."

Gustav leered and went on chewing. Elizabeth felt blood rush to her face, not only because of his customary crudity, but because the memory of yesterday, of being held and loved hard, was evoked by his remarks.

She decided to come right to the point. "Uncle, as you know, the man who helped get you to the hospital had not been properly thanked. So I asked *Herr Doktor* Vandevere for permission to leave St. Ada's . . ."

Briefly, she told of Vandevere's refusal, her own dis-obedience, her trek down to the Continental. Gustav seemed surprised, and not at all displeased, that she had flouted the headmaster's orders.

"And so, after I thanked Mr. Tallworth on behalf of us both," she concluded, "he walked with me back up to the school, because it was dark. Vandevere may have seen us, and my graduation might be in jeopardy."

Gustav set down his fork. There was fire in his eyes.

"Vandevere is nothing but a schoolmaster," he roared. "You shall graduate or I'll have him drawn and quartered. It's unfortunate they don't draw and quarter people anymore. A good method of execution and an excellent deterrent to crime. But you need not worry. I have plans for you, and headmaster or no, Vandevere is not going to stand in the way of the honored graduation you've earned."

"What plans, Uncle?" asked Elizabeth, thinking he might reveal them to her now, since he was being so loquacious.

But he waved away her query. "Later," he said, "later."

Gustav bent to attack a last mound of eggs. Elizabeth rose to leave. Gustav looked up. "Where are you going?"

"Back to school."

"Sit down," he ordered. "You stay with me. We'll both go up to call on Vandevere, but only when we're good and ready. In truth, this little adventure of yours is fortuitous because it provides me with an opportunity to show you how to go about dealing with and destroying an adversary."

Elizabeth was a little alarmed. She did not wish to "destroy" Vandevere, merely to make certain he would not punish her unduly.

"Now first," Gustav demanded, giving her that hard look she had seen him use so often on his employees, servants, and those he considered to be his social inferiors, "are you sure you're telling me the whole story?"

Elizabeth balked. How *could* she tell him about Lance Tallworth? The night in the garden, and the day in the mountains.

"I have told you the truth," she told her uncle, nervously assured that at least this was not a lie. The problem was that she had not told the *whole* truth.

Gustav Rolfson was not a man inclined to split hairs over such things anyway. He moved from step one to step two and on to the end of a problem with the inexorable determination of a tyrant.

"Trouble is," he was saying, slurping the last of his coffee, "Vandevere is rather well regarded here in Geneva. At least I think so. Now, if this were Oslo, I'd know everything about him, and you can be sure I'd know some dirt that would embarrass him enough to give me anything I wanted." He winked crudely. "Even his wife for a night, if I wanted her. No, that's right, *Herr Doktor* isn't married. Hmmmmm, I wonder if he's vulnerable there . . ."

Before she was fully aware of what he was saying, Elizabeth said, "Last night I overheard the headmaster talking to the desk clerk, and he was saying something about keeping St. Ada's above reproach . . ."

Gustav's eyes glinted with quick, happy suspicion.

"I thought St. Ada's *was* above reproach," he said, with narrow eyes. "What else did he say?"

"The only other phrase I heard had to do with 'best of quarters.' 'Only the best of quarters,' that was what he said."

"And this has something to do with keeping St. Ada's 'above reproach'?"

"I guess so," Elizabeth said.

Gustav looked around. "Well, the suites on this floor are obviously the best quarters in the hotel. All occupied by parents of St. Ada's girls, by the way. You know Denmark?" he asked suddenly.

"Yes, of course . . ."

"You know what I think of Italy and France?"

"Certainly, but . . ."

"Well, something is rotten in Denmark too."

Elizabeth was perplexed.

"Literature," cried Gustav, getting up heavily from his breakfast table. "I have a little education too. 'Something rotten in Denmark' is a famous phrase by this Frenchie, Voltaire. It means where there's smoke there's fire, do you see? Now, you wait here. I must speak to the hotel manager, or perhaps bully him would be a more accurate way of putting it. And then I may summon some bankers. But I smell smoke, and I doubt you will have to worry about Vandevere again."

Late that afternoon, just as the girls of St. Ada's, dismissed from classes, were filling the walkways and strolling across the courtyard, Gustav and Elizabeth arrived on campus in the most elegant hack Gustav could find for hire. "Always make the impression of power and wealth," he said. "It never fails. That is, it almost never fails. In America, I knew a modest little Godster who did pretty well. John D. Rockefeller was his name. But I beat him."

The hack pulled up and stopped in front of the main palace, in which the headmaster's office was located. Gustav got out slowly. He looked, for a second, weak and woozy, but it passed. He held Elizabeth's arm as she descended. Gustav was in high spirits, and apparently he had managed to learn something designed to cow Vandevere, but he declined to tell Elizabeth what it was. "A surprise for your graduation," he'd said, "just one of several."

Some of Elizabeth's classmates, seeing her there, rushed over.

"Elizabeth!" exclaimed little Donnabella Trinacria, "wherever have you been?" She lowered her voice and stepped closer, as a dozen girls gathered around. They stood a bit apart from Elizabeth, as if she were a celebrity or a renegade. "There is a story making the rounds," Donnabella went on, "that you ran away with a man!" She glanced up at Gustav, who glared at her. "But I see that's not true," Donnabella faltered.

"With the wit God gave you," Gustav told the Italian girl cuttingly, "try not to make as many babies as your country-women do."

"Uncle!" said Elizabeth, blanching.

"Come along," he told her, "we must now teach Vandevere an important lesson. He must learn how events proceed in the real world."

With an uncertain glance at her gaping classmates, Elizabeth followed her uncle into the building.

"It's late," she said, "and the headmaster may not be here."

Gustav barreled down a wide, carpeted corridor, like a bull heading for a herd of heifers. He was wheezing mightily, but his blood was up. Fighting kills some men and lets other men live longer than they might. Gustav Rolfson was one of the latter.

"Vandevere'll be here, don't you worry," he told her. "I sent a message. That's another lesson, girl. Make your enemy wait on you."

"But is he really an en—?"

Foolish question. To Gustav, the merest hint of recalcitrance in the face of his desires was enmity and perfidy and betrayal.

Gustav shouldered through the door into the suite that held the headmaster's offices.

"Herr Rolfson," greeted a male secretary, standing up behind his desk at the doorway to Vandevere's office, "please be seated, and I will announce you . . ."

"I'll announce myself," Gustav sneered at the pale young man, and pushed through the door. Elizabeth had little choice but to follow.

There was the headmaster, a little man behind a big desk. His blood was up, just like Gustav's. He was quite angry. A tic flickered rhythmically on his cheek, possibly caused by the ferocity with which he had screwed in his monocle.

Vandevere attacked first. "The girl must leave," he said.

Gustav gave Elizabeth one of his I'll-show-you-how-to-run-things looks. "Sit down here, Elizabeth," he told her, gesturing to a chair in front of Vandevere's desk. He took one beside it, and settled down.

Elizabeth would just as soon have left the office, but she was afraid of what *Herr Doktor* would bring up in her absence. Obviously, he was uncowed by Gustav's aggressiveness.

"So be it," said Vandevere, bowing to the situation. "But she shan't be here at St. Ada's very much longer."

"You are correct," Gustav replied. "She will leave directly after commencement."

"I am afraid it will be a bit earlier," Vandevere grinned frigidly. "Sad to say, in view of Elizabeth's otherwise excellent record; but she must have been deceiving us about her true nature for the past four years. Now we know. And, Rolfson, I promise you that, at St. Ada's, we do not graduate disobedient, loose, *immoral* women, no matter how brilliant they may be!"

Rolfson descended, with no difficulty at all, to the vernacular. "What in hell are you talking about, you pompous little glass-eyed shitheel?"

"Ah! Always charmed to converse with a master of language," Vandevere retorted in a mocking voice. "The other night, at a very late hour," he continued, in a voice that could have driven slow nails into a coffin, "I happened to return to the campus by carriage, having dined in the city. On the way up the Rue Florence, I *thought* I saw a man and a woman ducking behind a stone wall. I was almost certain, sir, that it was your niece, whom I had forbidden to leave the school that night . . ."

"Why did you forbid it?" Gustav demanded, attempting to take control.

"I run this school, and everything here is my responsibility," snapped Vandevere piously.

The headmaster, pleased to be in apparent dominance, did not notice the slow, snakelike malevolence with which Gustav agreed. "Yes, *everything*," he said, showing a grin that was icier than a fjord in winter.

"And upon my arrival at the campus," Vandevere was orating, "I went back to close the gate for the night. My responsibility again, you see, and I saw your niece kissing and embracing a man. Yesterday she returned with him—in a carriage!—and they kissed again. Therefore," Vandevere pronounced, "I shall endeavor to spare you and the young lady further embarrassment. Leave now. Her education here is at an end. I assure you that her things will be packed and shipped posthaste to Oslo."

"I'm sorry," retorted Gustav, in a parody of sweet politeness, "but you are quite mistaken. As I said at the outset of this friendly little chat, Elizabeth will take the honors she has won. Only after graduation will she depart St. Ada's. So she left the campus? Is that so bad? You are the one who ought to be ashamed, forbidding her to thank a good samaritan . . ."

Now Vandevere smiled with anticipation and delight. "But there is a measure of shame in the matter, because I think a surpassing amount of gratitude was also dispensed. The manner in which they held on to one another suggested undeniable carnality!"

Vandevere was smirking, waiting for Gustav to fly into a rage and denounce Elizabeth for immorality.

Vandevere did not know, however, that Gustav Rolfson possessed no code of morality at all. Indeed, Elizabeth's uncle, his face red and his eyes watery, began to laugh. Vandevere gaped and Elizabeth looked on in some alarm as Gustav wheezed and laughed, rocking back and forth in the chair, enjoying himself immensely. "Just . . . like . . . Kristin . . ." Gustav groaned in glee, "just like her . . . that will make my plan even better."

Like Kristin? Elizabeth thought. The words and actions of Uncle Gustav were making very little sense.

"I fail to see cause for amusement," snapped Vandevere with sanctimony.

"Close your mouth and listen," ordered Gustav in a sharp voice. He had regained control of himself, although tears of laughter still rolled across his cheeks and down along the crater of his scar, as if it were the channel of a river.

54

Then Gustav asked a series of sharp questions.

"What relationship does St. Ada's have with the Continental Hotel? Why are you so concerned that the parents of St. Ada's girls have only the best quarters? How does the headmaster of a school, albeit a fine school, find it possible to invest two hundred and fifty thousand francs in Geneva businesses, including the hotel, when his salary is less than half that sum? And what does such a headmaster do when the investments fail to earn what he supposed they might? And when, in certain cases, the money was irretrievably lost in unwise speculation?"

Now Elizabeth realized why Gustav had been consulting with Geneva businessmen and bankers for a good part of the day. He had been setting a trap, spinning a web, for the hitherto arrogant headmaster. Vandevere looked pathetic now, the more so as Gustav went on speaking.

"You used money from the school, didn't you?" Gustav demanded. "You took funds and fees given the school by parents and invested them to feather your own nest, didn't you? But it hasn't worked. You have lost money. Your books could not stand an audit, nor your reputation scrutiny. And so you must go to extremes to make an impression, mustn't you?"

"I don't know what you're talking about," Vandevere managed.

Gustav started laughing again, but mirthlessly now.

"Deny any damn thing you want," he said. Then, winking at Elizabeth to signal the sagacity of the course he had chosen, he leaned toward the hapless schoolman. "You made your own muck," Gustav told Vandevere, "and that's your business. You think that I, a world-renowned entrepreneur, would stoop to telling tales of your folly? You think *I* would wish to dirty my hands in your petty little pool of deceit? Hah!" he cried, astounded at the absurdity of such a prospect. Then his eyes narrowed and that characteristic icy glint came into them. "Of course, I will feel compelled to do exactly that if my niece is not permitted to graduate."

Vandevere got the point. "I understand your proposition, sir," he told Gustav, trying to hold on to what small dignity he had left.

"I suppose you do. Come now, Elizabeth, let us go. This has been a most enjoyable and profitable visit."

"Will you tell the authorities about Headmaster Vandervere?" asked Elizabeth, as she and Gustav went outside and stood beside the hack. He would ride back down to the hotel, and she would return to her room.

"Not unless he gives you further trouble."

"But . . . but in a way, is it not your responsibility to report something like this? You have knowledge of affairs that are against the law."

"Well, so I do," Gustav grinned. "But let all of this be a lesson to you. You may have need of such wisdom sooner than you think. What you want to attain in conflict is leverage over your enemy. That is what I achieved by my inquiries with the bankers this morning. Secondly, make use of your leverage to beat and humiliate your adversary. Rub his face in the muck, as I did to Vandevere. Make him see that he has been outgunned all down the line, and that resistance is useless. Finally," he said, coughing a little, "finally, make sure you leave a sword hanging over his head, just in case he begins to develop fantasies of revenge. See, I have left over Vandevere's head the possibility that *at some future time* I may go to the law. So he had better behave himself and do as I insist. No, girl, we shall have no further trouble with Headmaster Vandevere."

He climbed up into the cab, and looked down at her. He was smiling with pure amusement again.

"Who was the man?" he asked.

Elizabeth felt heat rise in her face. "An American," she answered.

"You found him a . . . a *good* man," Gustav snickered.

Elizabeth nodded.

"Then I suppose he has done both of us a favor. He got me to a hospital bed, which I needed badly at the time, and he got you to another kind of bed, which you badly need at your age."

"Uncle," she interrupted. He was treating the matter so lightly, as if it meant nothing. That was not true at all. It meant *everything*. She did not want him to make sport of it. "Uncle, why did you say, while we were with the headmaster, that I am just like Kristin?"

"Oh, did I?"

"Yes."

"Who is Kristin?" Elizabeth asked.

Momentarily, a look of inexpressible bitterness crossed his face. "Someone I once knew," he said curtly. "Now, get back to work. I shall see you on the morrow." With that, he tapped the driver on the shoulder, the driver snapped his whip, and the carriage rolled out of the courtyard, through the gate, and away. Elizabeth stood there watching for a moment, with a mingled feeling of relief and unease. The crisis with Vandevere was over, but it had been mean-spirited, even vicious, and she could not take pleasure in it. Was the world truly the way her uncle believed it to be? If so, it was a forbidding place indeed. Or, she reflected, entertaining a sanguine possibility, perhaps each person made a world in his or her own image. Certainly she never wanted to consider others as enemies, never wanted to outmaneuver and humiliate them as Gustav had done to Vandevere.

But what if it should ever be necessary? she asked herself.

It never will be, she answered. With the confrontation ended, her mind moved back to love and Lance Tallworth again.

Donnabella Trinacria accosted Elizabeth on the steps in

front of the library. Her eyes were red. She had been crying and, even now, sobbed a little.

"Your uncle is a mean man!" Donnabella cried. "He said I had no wit, he said I . . ."

"Come now," Elizabeth replied, putting her arms around the diminutive Italian girl, "he meant nothing. It is just his way. His health is bad," she temporized, "and he is worried about it."

"Still . . ." sniffed Donnabella. Then she remembered the gossip. "What happened? What happened when you saw the headmaster?"

"Why, what was supposed to happen?" asked Elizabeth in return, feigning surprise. "My uncle merely called on our headmaster as a matter of courtesy. That is all."

Donnabella looked quite disappointed. "But I thought . . . I mean, everyone is saying . . . that . . ."

"Yes?"

Donnabella looked around furtively, and lowered her voice. "Everyone is saying that you *have been with* a man, an extraordinarily handsome foreigner . . ."

"That is quite true," Elizabeth told her sweetly, and left Donnabella dancing with curiosity on St. Ada's library steps.

4

On commencement day the diplomas were awarded—*Herr Doktor* Vandevere managing a weak smile when he handed Elizabeth hers—and then, just like that, Elizabeth was leaving St. Ada's. She had spent the last four years of her life at the school, and now it was over. The change was sharp and sudden; it took a bit of getting used to.

"You must always be on guard," exuded Gustav, in the mountainside inn to which he had taken her for celebration. "I demonstrated to you, just the other day, how the world works. There you had old Vandevere, who had known you *for four whole years*. And the first time something happens to put your reputation in doubt, he immediately turned against you. I have seen it happen a thousand times. One must always protect oneself. Always. And with every quiver of wit at your command. I have plans for you. . . ."

"I have been waiting to hear what those plans are." She was worried about Lance being able to contact her by letter.

"Here tonight, as we dine, you shall."

The waiter approached, and Gustav flourished his napkin as if it were a cape.

"Oysters first," he commanded, "with Beaujolais Blanc. Triple butter with the oysters, please, and aquavit to clear the palate. Then we shall have pressed pheasant with truffles and marmalade, and accompanying that I should like a bottle of champagne. Make it your best, you hear, and don't try and trick me. I know the taste. None of this switching labels on me!"

The poor waiter, offended, stepped back a bit. Elizabeth gave him a smile to indicate that this was the way it always was with Gustav Rolfson.

"Then," Gustav continued, "we'll have two suckling pigs. Serve Chateauneuf du Pape with them . . ."

"I don't think I can eat a suckling pig, Uncle," Elizabeth said quietly.

"Bring two anyway," he addressed the waiter, "I'll finish what she can't."

The waiter bowed and prepared to move off. "And plenty of bread," Gustav called after him. "Plenty of bread and . . ."

He began to cough, fending off the attack.

"Damn thin air up here," he complained. "I need some wine in me."

Elizabeth sighed.

The oysters were served, and Gustav stuffed his mouth with a half dozen of them. "Let me tell you something," he said, "you must forget about that American. Your 'Noble Savage,' as it were. You have read too much Rousseau. Ought to have stuck to Machiavelli."

For a long moment, Elizabeth felt numb. Gustav spoke with such authority that it almost seemed as if he had known Lance Tallworth, as if he had hired Lance to "give the young girl a lesson in what the world is like."

To her consternation, Elizabeth learned that her uncle had a very crude interpretation of love. "Men get what they can," he told her. "Forget him. He got what he wanted, and you'll never see him again. Not a chance."

Yes, I shall, Elizabeth vowed. *Lance felt for me as I felt for him!* She had to believe it.

"As long as he made the first time good for you," Gustav pronounced, giving yet another part of his vision of love, "he did well by you, and you should thank him for it."

Thus did Gustav expound upon numerous mysteries of life as the dinner progressed. By the time the suckling pigs were served—little crackling-brown carcasses with their feet in the air and roasted pears, not apples, in their mouths —he seemed dazed and drowsy. But still hungry. With a quick flick of his knife, he severed the head of a pig, ducked it in his goblet of Chateauneuf du Pape, and slurped wine from the tiny snout of the piglet.

"Now for my plan," he said, leaning forward. Elizabeth was listening. She could not have eaten another bite of anything, certainly not of this pig.

"You are going to go with me to America," Gustav hissed, swaying a little drunkenly in his chair. "We are going to get revenge on Gunnarson. Because he killed your parents. And," he added extravagantly, "you think this dinner is your graduation gift, do you? Well, it's not. It's nothing! I have decided to give you all my American holdings! Yes! Everything will be yours. The Chicago real estate. My interest in the railroads. The little bit I have left in oil"—he frowned, as if he had not meant to say this— "and the great future we have in Minnesota iron ore. Thea, of course, will not be too pleased with my decision, but . . . but *you* are my instrument of revenge." He lifted his glass and gulped wine, as if a toast had been made. "And to hell with Thea Thorsdatter anyway! When I changed my will . . . when I changed my will, she said she'd . . . ."

Gustav Rolfson, bits of pig in his mouth, wine in his gullet, stopped talking and blinked once. He and Elizabeth were dining on an open verandah that looked down a steep slope. A meadow ran to the edge of the slope, where a line of pine trees broke the sweep of flower and grass. Twilight was upon the mountains now. Nothing could be seen amid the pines. And yet Gustav blinked and stared off toward the treeline as if he had spotted something there, something ghastly and dangerous.

"No . . ." he gulped, his hand grabbing at his breast.

"Uncle Gustav, what is it?"

Elizabeth was looking at him, and he at her. He loomed preternatural and fantastic in her vision. Peripherally, in a vague haze, she saw the distant waiter turn toward them, alerted by Gustav's cry. The old man's eyes were still fixed on the dark curtain of pine trees.

"It's there!" he shrieked, in a strangled voice. "I see it . . ."

"What? *What?*" Elizabeth looked toward the trees but could see nothing.

Gustav's eyes were wild, and he grabbed feebly at his cravat and shirt collar. "Can't you see it?" he rasped in terror. "Here it comes!"

Gustav tried to rise, but could not. His eyes, widening, widening more, were still fixed across the darkening meadow. *"Here it comes!"* he wailed, and threw up his arms to defend himself against the inescapable. Elizabeth, getting up and moving around the table to help him, glanced once more at the forest but saw nothing. Yet in Gustav's death-bound, fear-maddened eyes, she was almost certain that she perceived for an instant the spectre he saw all too clearly, the phantasm of an implacable, fire-eyed wolf.

Death came to Gustav Rolfson, and its face was his own.

5.

DO NOT DELAY STOP BRING BODY HOME OSLO STOP BE
PREPARED.

THEA

Be prepared for what? Elizabeth wondered. She had had
her uncle's body embalmed, had purchased a coffin, and
had arranged rail transport for herself and the burden all the
way to Bremerhaven. From there they would go by ship to
Oslo, and to Thea. Elizabeth had long known her uncle's
failings and frailties, his cruelties and his cunning, and in
her heart she could not mourn him as if he had been a good
man. Yet she knew that, for some reason buried in his black
soul, he had—in his way, for his own purposes—been as
kind to her as it was in his nature to be. She felt more
bewildered than stricken, less sorrowful than simply disem-
bodied.

And now there was Thea to face, and her cryptic BE
PREPARED.

For what? Elizabeth asked herself again.

The train would leave Geneva for Bremerhaven on the
following morning, and everything was in order. Then,
walking once more the uphill route she had taken with
Lance, Elizabeth thought of a remaining detail. Turning
back down toward the city, she made her way swiftly
toward the University of Geneva and sought the aid of a

scholar in linguistics. He was an older man, who seemed unnerved and enchanted by her beauty.

"*Ycripsicu*?" he asked, puzzled. "You say it is an American word?"

"I believe so."

"Well, it certainly is not English. Nor Spanish, French, or Dutch. Perhaps it is Native."

"Native?"

"The American savage, Mademoiselle . . ."

Savage? thought Elizabeth. Spinning fragments of memory and perception circled one another in her mind. Lance Tallworth was certainly not a savage. He was a civilized, even elegant man. Yet there had been something about his profile, his attitude, that reminded her of the past, of her dream of the house on the riverbank and the dark man who had been playing with her on a fateful day . .

"Mademoiselle?" the scholar was asking. "Mademoiselle?"

"Oh, I'm so sorry. I was thinking of something."

"Shall we try certain of the Native tongues? We do not have all of them glossaried by any means, but . . ."

"If you would be so kind."

The experience proved fascinating for Elizabeth. Now that Uncle Gustav was dead, she was no longer certain of the plan to go to America. But she had been born there—it was her land of origin—and she studied the vast map spread out upon the library table, tracing with her fingertips borders and coastlines, rivers and lakes, thrilling subtly to the poetry of names: Huron and Nantucket and Dakota, Missouri and Montana and Chicago . . .

Chicago was at the southwestern tip of long Lake Michigan.

A wisp of memory came to her then.

The lake. Days on water, long days. No, those days had been spent on the Atlantic, going toward Norway. Had they not?

She remembered a man and a woman, talking: "We'll be in Chicago in a couple of hours . . ."

The memory drifted away.

The library scholar, who had already attempted to locate the mysterious word in dictionaries devoted to the Seminole, the Creek, and the Matinecock, now decided to try a different tack.

"It is possible the word is not listed anywhere," he said. "Work is only beginning among those people . . ."

But undaunted, he sought *ycripsicu* in Ute, Paiute, Navajo, Blackfoot, and Sioux . . .

"Here it is!" he cried, as delighted with his discovery as any global explorer would have been at discovering an uncharted continent. Elizabeth leaned over the book and read.

Ycripsicu. *ē-krip'-să-kū*. Revenge. Noun. *Orig.*, Sioux nation of North American plains.

Revenge? thought Elizabeth, mystified and a little fearful. Lance had spoken the word as though it were a place, a geographical location, *himself! "They are not going to take it away from me."*

Take away revenge?

And certainly he was no Indian, although he might have some of that blood. Nothing added up. More puzzled than ever—hurt, too, because Lance was not here with her and she wanted him—Elizabeth thanked the scholar and left the university library. She spent the evening in Gustav's suite at the Continental Hotel, deep in thought. Even in his absence, Lance Tallworth had a hold over her being. He had awakened in her a throbbing, undeniable need, and she was sure—in spite of his guarded nature—that she had affected him in the same way. And now he was gone.

Gone back to the maelstrom out of which he had

emerged, in which he had met and known and been molded by forces she could not imagine.

But he had said that he would find her again, and Elizabeth believed him.

Expecting that a letter from Lance Tallworth would be awaiting her upon arrival in Oslo, Elizabeth saw her uncle's coffin placed in the baggage car, then boarded the wagon-lit for the journey north through Germany, north toward Norway, home.

But was Oslo home, now that Gustav was dead? Had the forbidding Rolfson mansion there ever been home?

Settling into sleep that night, Elizabeth dozed and drifted and dreamed . . .

. . . and the water was blue that day, which she saw from a high place, yes, from a window in a big white house. The house was very, very big because she had to stand on tiptoes to see the river over the windowsill. The river was wide, very blue, and moved slowly beyond the thick green leaves of trees along the shore. If someone held her around the waist and lifted her, she could see not only the river and the trees but also the green lawn that ran down from the white house to the riverbank. She had played on that lawn and along that riverbank. She lived in the big white house. She had ridden in canoes and been rowed in boats upon that river. She knew this. But who had played with her, and rowed her on the river? And who was lifting her now, so that she could see over the windowsill?

It was a boy, a child not much older than she was, and he said, "Can you see? Can you see the boats on the river now, Beth?"

Beth. She had been called that. Elizabeth had been called that, or dreamed she had been called that. In another life.

"I can see them. I can see them. Let's go down. Let's go down there now and play, please?"

The memory went blank there. She remembered the boy lifting her, recalled herself asking to go down to the riverbank to play, but the name by which she called the boy was lost forever.

Uncle Gustav said the name was lost because there had never been any boy, let alone a house and river.

But then the boy held tightly to her hand as they descended a grand staircase, and she knew she would not fall because he loved her and he held her fast. Oh, she knew that sometimes his mood would change suddenly, and he was apt to thrust a frog in her face, or put mud in her hair, but that was only when he was acting badly. He didn't mean it. Boys were that way. And he always held her safely and made sure she did not fall when they went down the great staircase of the white house.

Had she ever *been* in such a house? She was not sure. Perhaps not. She barely remembered Uncle Gustav's house in Chicago, to which he had taken her after her parents had been killed, but she knew it was not like the house in her "dream." Nor was Gustav's mansion in Oslo, which was dark and gloomy, its richness revealed only when, in candlelight, gold and silver glinted in reflection off polished mahogany and teak. Her uncle, Elizabeth knew all too well, did not fit in the white house of her memory.

But the man and the woman did.

Elizabeth came down the staircase, holding tightly the hand of her little friend, and at the bottom of the steps a man and a woman were waiting. The woman had golden hair, and so did the man, and they were laughing happily at the two of them as they came down the stairs. Elizabeth remembered laughing too, but she had the feeling that the man was going away. Not going away forever, but going just then, for a short time. She did not want him to go. She stopped laughing happily when she realized he was about to leave, but he noticed her mood, read the expression on her face, and lifted her into his arms. "I'll never leave you, honey," *he said,* "you don't have to worry about that," *and hoisted her onto his shoulders, which were as wide and broad and strong as the maple bench on the lawn in back of the house.*

Then the man lowered her gently from his shoulders and onto a gleaming floor. The blond woman, shining like an angel, bent down then and gathered Elizabeth and the boy beside her into her arms for a moment, kissing them. She said something that Elizabeth could not remember; the boy also spoke, and then the big man called to someone else. . . .

In the thick bushes, among the leafy branches by the riverbank, Elizabeth and her friend were playing. Hunting. They were hunting someone or something, or it was hunting them. Yes, it was a bronze man. Elizabeth caught a glimpse of his dark scowl between the green leaves. He was coming. She squealed and hid from him. Why? She did not know, but there was no danger. It was fun. "Hide! Hide and be very quiet!" *the boy told her.*

Down by the water, it was slow and moist and hot. Boats and canoes moved up- and downstream, and as Elizabeth tried not to giggle, waiting for the bronze man to find her as he always did— How did she know he always found her? How did she *know* that?*—she was startled by the muffled slap of a canoe paddle, just offshore. And as suddenly as if it had been Death himself, a canoe carrying two men hissed swiftly through the water and touched upon the riverbank.*
. . .

Whatever had happened after that could not be abided, nor remembered, not even in a dream.

Elizabeth slept. The train streaked across Bavaria, beyond green mountains, northward onto the German plain, carrying her on the first leg of a great journey back toward the white house and the blue river, back into her past.

Part Two

MINNESOTA AND MONTANA ⸱ 1863–1885

1

Father told me to show no fear, the boy exhorted himself, *and so I shall not. I am Sioux. He told me to show neither sadness nor sorrow, and I shall not. I am Sioux. And he told me not to feel harshly toward Mother, when she gives way to tears. She is a white woman, after all, and a good woman too. But I am Sioux, I am Sioux, I am Sioux!*

The boy was awake at dawn. He felt the cold earth beneath his buckskin, and saw the thin vapor of his mother's slow sleeping breath in the dazzled air. A low mournful mutter rose from the squaws and children asleep all around, and the easy wind was sweet with scents of dew-wet prairie grass and sunflower. The young sun grew warm on the boy's face, and he saw the circle of blue-coated horsemen guarding the bound braves. The white man's strange killing machine framed the dawn, platform and beam and loops of rope.

They called it a gallows.

The Sioux nation had made war against the white men, once and forever to drive them from Minnesota, this land of forest and green plain, water and sky. But the white men possessed a mighty army, with tubes bellowing thunder and fire and death. The Sioux nation had lost, and now, in 1862, it must move west, into dry Dakota and faraway Montana, into places unknown and unseen. But first those who would be allowed to leave must witness the deaths of their chiefs on the gallows.

The boy's father, Tall Lance, was a chieftain. He lay on the ground now, legs chained, arms pinioned, within the circle of the blue-coated horsemen.

"Do not mourn me when I die," he told the boy. *"Be proud. I die a warrior's death. But protect your mother. Perhaps I was wrong to marry a white woman and bring her into our ways, which she does not fully understand. But I loved her and I love her still. Someday you will know the force of such a devotion. Now, give me your vow as a brave that you will look after her."*

"I give you my vow," the boy promised.

Later that morning, when the sun was climbing and the birds were calling, Tall Lance was led to the gallows. He refused the blindfold and stood very straight, looking down at the boy. The hangman had to stand on tiptoe to loop the noose over his head.

The boy's mother, standing beside him, began softly to weep.

The boy was embarrassed.

One of the bluecoats, who wore golden stars on his clothing, looked up at Tall Lance. "Do you have any last words?" he asked.

Tall Lance nodded. "That which is unjust must be avenged," he said.

The bluecoat shrugged. The Indians were silent. But the boy was very proud. He and his father held eyes until his father's eyes rolled up.

The boy's mother could not stop crying. He felt sorry for her. But she was not Sioux, and that was her way.

As the boy and his mother were packing their few belongings, preparing to move west with the nation, a missionary priest approached them.

"I am Father Pierre LaPointe," he said to the boy's mother. "I have heard of your terrible plight. You must come with me, and bring your son too. Do not take him west with these savages, but come to my mission and he will be schooled in a Christian manner."

The boy flung himself at the priest, grabbing him around the knees, trying to trip him, trying to sink his little teeth through the priest's thick woolen cassock, and into the priest's legs.

The boy felt a fist on the side of his head. He spun through the air and landed, breathless and panting, in the trampled grass of the encampment. He did not cry.

"I don't know," his mother was telling Father LaPointe. "I don't know what to do."

The priest was not so undecided. "You were born a Christian," he told her, "and so it is my duty to make up your mind for you." So saying, he took her hard by the wrist and began to drag her away. Blue-coated soldiers watched, bearing guns. The boy stood up in the dust, ran after his mother, and tried to break the priest's grip on her arm.

Again he felt a blow, and again he was lying in the dust.

"What is his name?" he heard the priest asking.

"Lance Tall One. He is named in the manner of his father."

The boy picked himself up out of the dirt and charged again at the priest, hurling his pitifully inadequate child's body at the bulky missionary.

Father LaPointe cuffed him again and knocked him flying.

"The child is a warrior!" exclaimed Father LaPointe, not without wonder.

Father Pierre LaPointe, born and educated in southern France, was in charge of the Indian mission at Portage la Croix between Upper Red Lake and Lake of the Woods in northern Minnesota. He had also been appointed chief agent of the sprawling Red Lake Indian Reservation in that area. Father LaPointe, an intelligent, troubled man, was strong-willed, passionately single-minded, and merciless when he did not get his way. "God has told me what is right," he often said, "and that is what I must do."

God had instructed Father LaPointe to take Lance Tall One and his mother and hundreds more Sioux northward to the Red Lake Reservation. Lance's mother, Teresa-Starflower, was a beautiful woman, but not strong. The trek north was difficult for her, and when her feet bled, she had to be carried in a litter. Her life had already been harsh enough. Her childhood home near the village of Red Wing had been burned and her family killed by a Sioux war party. Teresa was dragged back to the Sioux village, a war captive intended for the pleasure of victorious braves. But a current of tenderness passed between the lovely white woman and the Sioux chieftain, Tall Lance. He shielded her from the others, protected her. After a time, he took her to wife. Teresa was a gentle creature, and the warrior treated her like a fragile starflower, which became her tribal name. In 1859, Starflower bore Tall Lance a son with his father's dark, watchful eyes and his mother's glowing Nordic skin.

Life seemed happy and full of promise. Tall Lance could not have dreamed that in three years his gentle wife and little son would be consigned to a remote reservation, victims of history and prisoners of fate.

At Red Lake, the boy and his mother lived not in familiar teepees but in crude wooden boxes with high-angled roofs. Firesmoke rose in a stone column, and the fire was used for cooking. But the fire was not a good fire, nor did the stone chimney draw well. The hut, as it was called, became intolerably hot in the summer. During winter, they lay shivering and freezing within it. But they survived.

The boy watched and waited. He had vowed to his father that he would protect his mother. And that was what he would do, no matter the pain or sacrifice. He often thought, too, lying in his blankets in front of a dying fire, of his father's last words. *That which is unjust must be avenged.*

One day, after mother and child had been at Red Lake for

a year, Father LaPointe sent for them both. He had forced the Indians to build a church along the shores of the lake, and next to the church he had also ordered built a large, ugly house with huge, square rooms. The boy was uncomfortable the moment he set foot inside. Nature possessed few shapes that were square and enclosed. Young Lance Tall One hated Father LaPointe's house as much as he hated the smoke-stinking hut in which he had to live.

On the wall in every room of the house hung a cross of wood, and upon that cross hung a naked man with his head lolling to one side and an arrow in his chest. Such a cross, in larger form, was also in the church. On many an evening, out in the night and the darkness, Lance Tall One had peered through the windows of the church to see Father LaPointe on his knees in front of the cross.

Father LaPointe entered the room, wearing his strange dark ankle-length garment. He greeted mother and child and bade them be seated. He stood before them, smiling, but in his hand he held a length of pine bough, thin and supple.

"Teresa," he said, "kneel so that I may bless you."

The woman knelt on the foor, and the priest crossed his hands above her and murmured alien words.

"Now, son, you kneel."

The boy did not move.

The priest, without prelude or warning, struck out with the pine bough, lashing the boy across the shoulders, sending him forward onto the floor. The blow hurt like fire, but the boy made no sound.

As if he were somewhat surprised, even ashamed, at his own anger, LaPointe's voice was soothing. "Obedience," he told child and mother, "is a hard thing to come by. Well do I know. But you, boy, are the son of a Christian woman, and it is my duty to see that you be raised as a Christian. You ought to be baptized with a decent, godly name."

"I am Lance Tall One," said the boy, looking up with his piercing, implacable eyes at the bulky, towering priest.

LaPointe raised the bough to strike again. The boy bent, bracing for the blow. But his mother, so docile and distracted since her husband's death, leaped forward, and stood weeping between the child and the priest.

Lance Tall One was ashamed to see his mother crying —he would as soon have borne a hundred blows—but in response to the woman's tears, the priest did a strange thing. He lowered his weapon. Lance Tall One saw in LaPointe's eyes a dark glimmer that he did not understand.

"All right," he told the woman, wrapping his arm around her and leading her back to the chair, "I will be merciful. *This* time. Your son is obviously willful and will be slow in learning the ways of Christianity. You and I, Teresa, must teach him those ways. And I am sure you will be most cooperative, will you not?"

To Lance Tall One's chagrin, his mother nodded vigorously, still weeping.

The boy studied the priest's eyes. He did not like at all the expectant gleam in them.

"I need a woman for my house," the priest said then. He held out his open hand, palm up. "Life can be most pleasant for the both of you," he said. Then he made his hand into a fist. "Or life can be very difficult."

"I can cook and sew," Teresa-Starflower hastened to offer. "I can bake and knit."

"Yes," smiled Father LaPointe with great satisfaction. "And in return for performing those humble but necessary tasks, I shall provide you and your son with bed and board. And," he added, glancing at Lance, "should the boy show promise, I shall endeavor to give him an education. I long to speak the language of my homeland once again, and a touch of the civilized world may befall the boy if I teach him a noble tongue."

Lance glared up at the priest.

"Now, you two go back to your hut. Bring your belongings here. A wonderful new life is about to begin."

Lance did not believe him. He wanted to run away, to flee the reservation, to travel beyond these pine forests until he found a place that gave body ease, heart peace. But he had promised his father that he would protect his mother, and he already knew—more with his blood than his mind—that she was not safe in the house of Pierre LaPointe.

Ayarota was the word for enemy. Pierre LaPointe was *ayarota*.

2

Twenty-one years old in 1880, Joseph stood as straight as a young maple tree, and he stood alone, a thing unto himself. His Christian name, bestowed by Father LaPointe, had been adopted too by the Indians of the Red Lake Reservation, and Joseph, the priest's houseboy, was set apart from those he had once considered his true brothers. Setting him apart from them still more was the fact that he had lived with his mother all these years in LaPointe's rectory, and had acquired there knowledge sufficient to remove him forever from the ancient ways of his father's people.

Father LaPointe believed that his years of effort with the somber, watchful boy had borne fruit. Joseph was obedient now, he did as he was told. When white strangers came to the mission, either on business or while making the portage from Red Lake to Lake of the Woods, Joseph was able to serve them their dinner as well as converse with them in French or English. Joseph had a good mind—thanks to the tutelage of Father LaPointe—and he was able to discuss geography or agriculture or the recent presidential election of James Garfield. True, Joseph showed little enthusiasm or spirit. What spark he possessed lay behind those brooding black eyes, but his singular appearance, that tall, strong body and striking profile, emanated an aura that never failed to impress those who met him.

"Well, Father LaPointe," guests were wont to pronounce after meeting and speaking with young Joseph, "you have indeed accomplished the impossible. You have fashioned a civilized man out of a savage. How on earth did you do it?"

The priest beamed in appreciation of such praise. "Learning and the lash, that's all. Learning and the lash. Yes, Joseph is civilized now. He's not a worthless pagan anymore."

In the rectory kitchen, helping his mother clean up after the white men's meal, Lance Tall One would have smiled, had he ever learned how to do so.

"Yes, he's broken now, for sure," LaPointe boasted to his guests.

Lance Tall One knew better. *I shall never be broken.*

His mother, on the other hand, had long since become inured to her position. It was as if she were no longer his mother at all; the priest's strong will had broken what little spirit was left in her. LaPointe's powerful, erratic nature had forged an indelible mark upon her soul, and she belonged to him. Lance understood now, all too clearly, the evil gleam that had been in the priest's eyes on that long-ago day. That glimmer had signified LaPointe's recognition of souls to be molded, human spirit to be bent to his will, which was also God's will. So LaPointe had learned in the seminary at Marseille, and so he proceeded at his mission, which he dominated with a heavy hand.

Teresa was stripped of her Indian name, Starflower, as arrogantly as Lance was christened Joseph, and Father LaPointe set about his task of "breaking" them. Constant criticism and unremitting labor proved sufficient to turn Teresa into a scurrying drudge, but Joseph proved both more resilient and more recalcitrant than any boy LaPointe had ever known. Lashings with the pine branch had no effect on him, although LaPointe persisted in laying on this punishment even as Lance grew to manhood. Forcing the boy to pray was no good whatever; Joseph would spit at the holy symbols and flee into the woods.

But he would always return, and LaPointe knew why.

The boy was bound to his mother. LaPointe understood this readily enough, although he was unaware of the vow Lance had made to his father. He did not know, however, that Lance had long been planning to flee the mission.

The burden of remaining at Portage la Croix grew heavier as Lance got older. When he reached Sioux manhood at thirteen, the time at which he would have become a brave had his people not been enslaved, he went to his mother.

"Let us go from here," he pleaded. "I will care for you. Let us leave the reservation and go where we can be free."

"And where is that?" Teresa mourned. "No, I haven't the strength for it. Life has been too sad. Let me live out my days here. Perhaps the God of whom Father LaPointe speaks will reward me after I die."

Many more times in the following years Lance asked his mother to flee with him, but always the reply was the same. So Lance remained at the mission. He had made a vow. *Someday*, he vowed, *someday I shall have* ycripsicu *for all that has been done*. *Ycripsicu* was the word for revenge, and it was right under God and the sun that injustice be avenged.

Father LaPointe had a special phrase: "Offer it up." When Teresa bent under her burden of work, when Joseph's back burned under the lash, LaPointe would say, "Offer it up. Offer the pain you suffer to Our Lord, and when you die he will give you a high place in heaven."

"Do not be so contemptuous of me that you think I would believe that," Lance told him. He did not offer up his suffering. He saved it, and remembered. And waited.

At breakfast one warm morning in May 1880, while consuming his usual vast quantities of porridge and cream, bread and honey, Father LaPointe addressed his houseboy.

"I'll be expecting you to stay near the rectory all day," the priest declared. "The Government Inspection Detachment ought to be arriving at any time, and I'll want you to wait on them."

Each year, once after the ice on the rivers had broken in the spring, and once just before snow fell in the fall, soldiers came north to the reservation and met for several days with LaPointe. Lance had overheard their conversations many times. The priest gave them descriptions of conditions on the reservation, details as to shelter and food and population. Always the priest would exaggerate the number of Indians at Red Lake, and always he would extol his ability to provide adequate food and fine shelter on the minimal sums given him to do so.

Lance, listening, knew that these were lies. The poor Indians could count on LaPointe only to tell them how hot hell would be. For the most part, they foraged or hunted their food, and built their pitiful huts from whatever materials could be found. Yet LaPointe spoke to the soldiers as if, by his effort and charity alone, a whole nation enjoyed safe haven.

Teresa had stayed in bed that morning, complaining of severe stomach pain, and so it fell to Lance to get LaPointe's breakfast. After washing the dishes, he opened the back door and tossed LaPointe's uneaten bread crusts to the chickens. Leaning against the birch behind the rectory was Fleet Fawn, one of the Sioux girls. Lance was surprised to see her there, because the Indians seldom approached the rectory unless they had to.

"You'll have much work today, Joseph," she said drowsily, arching her back and then relaxing against the birch. "Pale Horse and Two Birds were fishing yesterday. They saw the soldiers coming north on the lake in canoes."

Lance stepped out of the house and walked toward her. Fleet Fawn excited him. She had a way of staring into his eyes, then dropping her eyes to her breasts, which were full beneath a buckskin jacket. Fawn did this now, arching her back upon the tree.

"My name is Lance Tall One," he told her. "Anyway, the soldiers are not here yet." He glanced about to make sure

LaPointe was not within earshot. "I planned to do some fishing myself today."

Fawn smiled with sure knowledge and looked up from her breasts. "I fish very well. Even my father has told me so. What do you seek?"

"Trout. Where the Tamarack River enters Upper Red Lake."

"A good place," observed Fleet Fawn, moving away languidly. Lance Tall One could not keep his eyes off her hips swaying beneath the buckskin skirt.

At noon that day, Lance stood knee-deep in the icy water of the Tamarack, and cast his hook into the blue pool above the fall and the rapids. He had stripped to a breechcloth and the sun, beating down through the trees, was warm upon his shoulders. The waterfall pounded in his ears, blotting out the sounds of birds and forest animals, and Lance squinted against the sharp, dancing light of the rapids. He felt an inquisitive tug at the end of his line, felt it again, anticipated the third tug and yanked hard. Hooked, the silvery trout leaped from the water into the air, spun and arched and fell. Bracing himself against the riverbed rocks, Lance pulled in the line. The fish came, leaping and fighting all the way. Lance pulled it in, walked back to the shore, and lay peacefully on the sunny riverbank wondering if one fish would be enough for his midday meal.

"That's all you've caught?" teased Fleet Fawn, as she stepped out of the forest and into the clearing. "One fish?"

Lance was not surprised to see her. Instantly, he was excited. His eyes, his face showed nothing, but Fawn read his body well.

"Why do you spend so much time alone?" she asked, sitting down beside him. "Everyone talks about you."

"They must have very little to do." He noted that Fawn had eschewed her jacket and wore a loose white blouse onto which beads had been sewn. The blouse looked suspiciously like one of Father LaPointe's shirts with the sleeves removed. She had probably stolen it from the wash line. Fawn's breasts pressed against the thin fabric, her nipples like twin brown beads. Lance felt something like hunger take hold of his body.

"Where did you get that garment?"

"Do you like it?" she asked, leaning back on her hands and showing her breasts the more.

The hunger clamped its vise of need upon his soul, and Lance reached for the maiden. Fawn laughed lightly, coyly, and made a small show of trying to fend him off. But Lance was neither to be dissuaded nor delayed. The urgency of need was beyond his control.

"Slow," murmured Fleet Fawn now, having abandoned her display of coy resistance, "go slow . . ."

But Lance did not hear her. Fervently, wildly, he pressed his mouth to hers, and his hands moved over her, tearing off her clothing, so that he might feel her bare skin next to his own. Awed by the force and splendor of the need inside him, Lance gave himself up to that need. So, after an appreciative, calculating glance at the mood of her stallion, did Fleet Fawn. She had known many a young man, in many a way, and she had come here today seeking to amuse herself with what she presumed to be the "priestboy's" timidity. But Fawn did not know the complexity of buried emotions in Lance. Hers was a sometimes playful, sometimes sentimental nature, but she was not inquiring or imaginative. She had come to an appreciation of one thing in life, however, and as Lance stripped her bare and poised for a delicious instant above her, Fawn knew she was about to revel, with an intensity never known before, in that one thing.

To Lance, it was as if he were in a land of freedom and pleasure as he melded with Fleet Fawn. Yet Lance knew, even as he moved into her, even as he felt the hot folds of her body envelop him, that it was something more, something other than Fawn he desired, something exceeding even the pleasure she generously gave. He had never known a feeling like it, the deft slippery clutch and pull of one body against another, so natural and so enchanting that he could not tell for moments on end whether it was his body moving or hers.

Fawn's deep breasts were beneath his chest. His face was pressed down into her soft neck. Beneath her was the sweet, pine-needled bank of the Tamarack River. The sun burned down on Lance's back, and his loins burned too with swelling need. Now Fawn reached down to fondle him in a way he had never felt, and it seemed as if a rainbow of colored lights like the aurora borealis exploded all the way up the length of his spine and into his mind and soul. She continued to caress him with her fingertips where he was outside her, and where he was inside she flowed and curled about him like the fragrant forest flower embracing its prey. Lance thought he felt Fawn moving faster beneath him, but he could not be sure. His mind seemed no longer a part of him. The air in the world was beginning to thin, as if he had run hard for an hour through the woods. Patterns of red and black began to throb behind his closed eyes, and at the base of his spine a pressure of nectar built. Fawn's subtle fingertips touched and caressed, prodded and squeezed the glowing gourd that was himself. It seemed he could bear it no more, stand it no more, yet the glow built and built. Until—it was true; there was an end to all things—the force burst from beneath her fingertips and surged, as if through his entire body and brain, up him and along him and out of him, into her.

Fawn was moaning as if hurt. Lance lay upon her, warm and dazed, but his mind was cold again, fixed upon the priest. *This* was the feeling against which LaPointe always railed, the feeling that would drive those who sought it into the blasting red fires of hell.

"Joseph," Fleet Fawn sighed, "how wrong I was about you!"

"How wrong you were." He slid out of her, the mere act of withdrawal sparking twinges of pleasure at the end of him.

"Don't go!" she cried. He caught the pleading note in her voice, and looked at her closely. There in her dark eyes he saw softness now and not guile. He had made her feel something with his lovemaking that she had not envisioned and he had not imagined. *She loves me*, he realized slowly. He knew he had loved the pleasure with her, but that he did not feel toward her what she felt toward him. Fawn sent him a rapt glance more tender than playful now, vulnerable even. Her eyes were like the eyes of an abandoned fawn, shaky on new legs in the dew-wet thicket. "Don't go," she pleaded.

Lance, who had known much suffering, found that he could not bear to cause or witness it.

"I am not leaving," he said. His breechcloth, torn off in haste, lay near the edge of the water. He did not go to get it, but stretched out on his back beside her and turned his face to the sun. Fawn moved beside him, close, naked too. She seemed different now, the brassy glint gone from her eye.

"Do you know what you said?" Fawn was asking.

"I said I am not leaving. I am here, aren't I?"

"No. What you said when you were at the height. Inside me."

Lance could not remember that he had said anything at all. "What was it?"

"You said *'Iiiiiiiiiiiii!'* "

"I did? What does it signify?"

"Nothing," she laughed. "It is just what you said. People say many things then. Or so I have *heard*," she added hastily, glancing anxiously at Lance.

He laughed. It was a strange sound to him. He could not, ever, remember laughing. So this enchanting pleasure of bodies caused unexpected results afterward, did it?

Certainly that was the case with Fleet Fawn. She was

caressing him and pressing against him, her once mocking eyes slow and dreamy.

"Why are you called 'Joseph'?"

"The priest gave me that name. 'Joseph, born in bondage.' The name is an abomination, as is the fat book from which he took the name. I was born in freedom, and soon I shall be free again."

Fleet Fawn sat up and studied him, crossing her arms beneath firm, brown breasts.

"You are thinking of running away from the reservation?" she asked, with a combination of fear and respect. "It is against the law."

"White man's law!"

"They might hunt you down. Throw you in prison. Even kill you."

"Not if I get out of Minnesota. And I do not look like an Indian."

"That is true. But the Sioux is in your eyes, and in your heart. When they see it, people will know it for what it is."

"Then I shall not let anyone see it."

"That is impossible if someone is close to you." She snuggled close to him again. "Someone close to you will see the Sioux, even if they do not understand it at first."

"Good," said Lance, "then they shall know to be prepared for *ycripsicu.*"

Fawn's body stiffened against him. He had uttered the word for revenge. Not for simple revenge, but a vengeance complete, ritualistic, and terrible.

Lance sensed her unease. "Do not let it trouble your mind. It may be years away. It may never happen. For now, I must think of my mother."

"It is understood that she wishes to remain here," Fleet Fawn said.

"It is more complicated than that. She cannot see her way clear to leave here. There is a difference."

"What will you do?"

"I will take her with me. I am strong. She cannot resist."

Fawn was silent for a moment, thinking. She pressed her body very close to his, all along the length of him, and tenderly fingered the vessels of his manhood. "Please take me with you too," she asked.

Lance knew that she was serious. "You are lovely," he said, "and I have enjoyed that which we shared. But we are very different. I would distress you, sooner or later. You are happy and content. I am not. There are things I want . . ."

"Want? What do you want?" Fawn sounded hurt, as if she expected to be all that Lance would need.

"I don't know yet. Many things, to fill an emptiness I do not understand. It will take time."

"It is *I* who do not understand," Fawn said, ceasing to caress him.

"You see what I mean?" he asked her. "Already, you are hurt by what you think you cannot give me, even though my need has nothing to do with you. . . ."

"I want to hear no more about it," declared Fawn sharply. She had already decided to go along with him, no matter what she would have to do in order to arrange it.

"I would end up causing you distress," Lance told her again. "Knowing that I distressed you would cause me pain, and then we would both be in pain. It would not be right. You are not a woman made for pain."

Fawn was quiet for a long time.

The sun was very warm now. Lance began to feel two kinds of hunger. Downriver, waterfall and rapids spoke unceasingly to the sky.

"Where will you go?" Fawn asked at length.

"West. Far west."

There was another long silence.

"Take me with you," Fleet Fawn asked. "For when you have need of peace and pleasure, I shall give it."

Lance sighed, and reached for her again. Pleasure she did give, pleasure that held and devoured and lifted his body to savage, splendid heights. But sadly, he knew she could not lift his soul, which had to be transformed if he were ever to know peace.

After they had made love again, they caught more trout and cooked them over an open fire, eating them happily and quietly beside the river. Then Lance spotted the canoes of the soldiers on the lake, making their way to Portage la Croix.

"I must return to the rectory," he said, rising and putting on his breechcloth. "They will want food and drink."

"Don't go. Let your mother tend to her duties."

"She is ill."

Fawn pouted a bit, but there was nothing she could do to change his mind, not even offering herself, which she attempted yet again. Lance preceded her through the forest, and they separated near the mission, Fawn back to her hut and Lance to the rectory. The soldiers had already reached shore, and were pulling their canoes high up on the bank. Supplies and bedrolls were piled along the shore. Father LaPointe was conversing with an officer who wore more ribbons than any other.

"You, Joseph," railed the priest upon catching sight of Lance, "get down here and carry these things up to the house."

"My men can do it," advised the officer, one Major Renner, who seemed more civil than most of the soldiers Lance had seen in previous years.

"No, no," protested LaPointe, "he must obey in all things or the little good I have done him will be lost."

Renner scowled but acquiesced. Lance worked for an hour taking up to the rectory supplies the soldiers could have transported in ten minutes. When he entered the rectory, he could hear the men talking, laughing, and drinking in the parlor. Teresa was lying on the kitchen floor, doubled up and grasping her abdomen. Her face was pale and contorted.

"What is it?" Lance asked anxiously. "You were in bed. What are you doing here?"

"He . . . he made me get up . . . to prepare the food . . ." his mother managed, before another bolt of pain traced an evil pattern within her body.

Anger possessed Lance Tall One, like a tainted mushroom growing and growing in the dark wet furrows of his mind.

"You go back to your bed," he told the woman. "A doctor must be summoned." Lance knew this would be of no immediate help. The nearest doctor practiced in Grand Rapids, a hundred miles to the southeast. The Chippewa had a medicine man on the reservation, and several squaws who were said to be skillful with herbs, but Teresa's condition seemed too serious for ground pine-root and essence of ivy. Lance carried Teresa upstairs to her room.

Lance was sliding pans of bread dough into the big wood-fired oven when Father LaPointe entered the kitchen. His thick face was red, and he carried an empty bottle of apple brandy.

"Where is your mother?" he barked, looking around. LaPointe always acted obsequiously toward the soldiers, but made up for it by being doubly severe to Lance and his mother.

"She has returned to her bed. You must send for the doctor."

LaPointe ignored this. "Get her down here at once. Who will cook dinner for the government representatives?"

"I will," said Lance.

"I want a fine dinner," scoffed the priest, "not scraps thrown together." He put down the brandy bottle and started toward the stairs, meaning to force Teresa back to work. Lance sprang forward and grabbed the priest around the neck. He was taller than LaPointe now, and as strong. He held the blade of a butcher knife to the priest's throat, just beneath the jawline where blood pulsed in the carotid.

"She stays in bed. You will send for a doctor."

Amazed, LaPointe looked at Lance out of the corner of his eye, his head and neck immobilized by the grip in which he found himself. Stealthy time has a way of sneaking up on one. Everything remains the same for years, but then one day a person looks around and realizes that the whole world is different and has been different for a long time. LaPointe tried to reason with the young man. "We have guests," he pleaded, tilting his head slightly toward the parlor, "and it is to our advantage that they not be upset."

"They are your guests," shrugged Lance, pressing the knife blade just slightly into the priest's fat neck.

"You will be beaten for this," growled the priest threateningly. "I know you are not stupid enough to kill me here."

"I will never be beaten again," Lance told him. "Now, send a messenger for the doctor."

"My guests . . ."

"Send the messenger, then go to them. I shall cook your precious dinner. You must promise."

LaPointe, with great struggle, might have broken Lance's grip on him. But the effort would have caused a terrifying melee, and he did not wish to signal the soldiers that anything was amiss at Portage la Croix.

"I promise," he said to Lance, who released him.

Immediately, the priest was scornful. "When you find out what I will do to you, you will wish you had slit my throat. Why didn't you kill me when you had the chance?"

"It is as you say," Lance told him coldly. "I am not stupid. My mother lives, and I must watch out for her."

LaPointe touched a fingertip to his throat, checking for blood.

"Send a messenger for the doctor," Lance demanded again.

LaPointe, who alone had authority to empower departures from the reservation, had a better idea.

"Major Renner and his men will be leaving in the morning. I shall ask him to carry the message."

Somewhat doubtful, Lance nonetheless acquiesced. A doctor summoned by an Indian might take his own sweet time about getting to Red Lake. Or might not even come at all. A soldier would carry greater authority.

"Have we a bargain then?" LaPointe asked acidly. "All right, you do the dinner now, and I'll look in on your mother later."

LaPointe and the men laughed and drank while Lance prepared rabbit and venison stew. It was a simple, hearty dish, one he had seen his mother cook many times. When he served it, the men ate with relish, mopping up the thick gravy with slabs of freshly baked bread.

"Thought you said you had a woman servant," said one of the soldiers, a slow dolt with a dull eye and a low brow.

"Yes, but she's ill."

"The woman is not seriously ill, I hope?" inquired Major Renner.

"No," answered Father LaPointe, with a glance in Joseph's direction.

"Yes," contradicted Lance, pouring coffee.

"Much pain?" asked the major.

LaPointe was silent this time. "Yes," said Lance, again.

"We always carry laudanum on long treks," Major Renner observed. "If the woman is in great pain . . ."

"Please," said Lance. The word startled him. He did not use it often.

Renner stepped outside to get the saddlebag in which he kept medical supplies during trips through the wilderness. Laudanum was no good as a cure, but it would ease the pain of a man dying from rattlesnake bite or arrow, help him bear the jostling of a stretcher if he had to be moved with a broken leg.

"You do not know the hell I am going to mete out to you," LaPointe told the young man while the major was gone.

"I am afraid it is the other way around," Lance informed the priest.

Then Renner reentered the house with his saddlebag. LaPointe led the way upstairs, and the other two men followed him.

Teresa lay doubled up and perspiring profusely on a bed in a small room just down the hall from LaPointe's own. Her face was twisted in agony, and she seemed scarcely to notice Renner, Lance, or the priest. The major, shocked at her appearance, knelt beside the bed, felt her forehead, and began to count her pulse. He had had plenty of experience with the sick and wounded during the Civil War.

"This woman is in a *very* bad way," he said to LaPointe, with a note of reproach in his voice.

"It has come on quite suddenly," LaPointe responded. "Why, only yesterday she was about her duties. . . ."

Gently, Renner rolled back the sweat-stained blankets covering the woman. She wore a heavy, sweat-soaked nightdress. The pillow on which her head rested was also stained darkly with perspiration. Another pillow, thrust between her legs, was stained with blood.

"It may be a ruptured tumor," guessed the major. "This poor woman must have been in pain for years!"

The soldier's sharp concern conveyed to Lance an irrefutable sense of imminent tragedy. "Can you do anything?" he asked Renner, with a tone almost of pleading in his voice—he who had never begged bounty or mercy.

Abruptly, the major stood up beside the bed. "I shall try," he said. "First, we will try to mitigate the pain. Get me a glass half filled with water."

Lance did as he was instructed. The major stirred a

considerable quantity of white powder into the water, lifted Teresa's head beneath his blue-uniformed arm, and helped her drink the milky compound. He was staring curiously at Father LaPointe.

"Yes?" asked the priest, almost fearfully.

"Well? You are a priest, aren't you? What about the last rites of your kind? You said she was Christian, didn't you?"

My mother is going to die, thought Lance. He remembered the dark day in 1862 when Father LaPointe had claimed them, had taken his mother and himself from under the gallows on which Tall Lance twisted in the wind. Pierre LaPointe had much to answer for in the years since that day.

As if a minute's haste might somehow exculpate the result of his tyranny, LaPointe raced to fetch holy oils for the last rites.

Lance looked down at his mother. Her eyes closed, opened, closed, and flickered open again. Drug, pain, and approaching death distanced her from the world, but her eyes found his.

"It is over," she said.

"I am going to report this!" Major Renner declared. "Your mother has been ill for a long, long time, and it is obvious that her fingers have been worked to the bone. And by a priest!"

Father LaPointe returned to the bedroom, red-faced and sweating. He held a crucifix in one hand and a small vial of oil in the other.

Lance stepped between the priest and the deathbed, facing LaPointe. "No," he said.

"What?" cried the priest, outraged, when he understood Lance's meaning. "She must be anointed or her soul will burn in everlasting torment."

The major stepped back, watching. Affairs of the spirit were beyond his bailiwick.

"You touch her and you die," said Lance, utterly calm.

LaPointe did not move forward. "She will suffer . . ."

"She has already suffered all there is to suffer at your hands. This is Starflower, my mother, the wife of a Sioux chieftain. She will have in death the dignity you would not permit her in life, the dignity I have struggled to keep since first I laid eyes on your face."

3

Lance washed Starflower's body, adorned her in tribal dress, and carried her far into the pine forest north of Red Lake. The women of the reservation had provided the garments, and would have gone willingly to the burial, as would have the braves, but Lance did not want their company. Working throughout most of the day, he shaped a mound for Starflower and placed with her in the feral red earth of the wilderness those items which would be of use. A bowl and spoon, a cup, a blanket. A necklace of agates to signify that she had been the wife of a great warrior. Lance, who had lived between two ways of life, believed as little in the agates as he did in LaPointe's ubiquitous dead-man cross and fat black book.

He covered his mother with sadness and with earth.

Standing for a last moment over Starflower's mound, he heard a rustling in the trees behind him, and turned quickly.

"I . . . I did not mean to surprise you," said Fleet Fawn, stepping forward. She walked from the underbrush and studied him. "You should not bear this alone."

"And how is it different from anything else that must be borne?"

"I don't understand what you mean."

"No matter. Thank you, anyway, for coming."

"What are you going to do now?"

"Go back to the mission, gather my belongings, and leave."

"Leave? Go away? Tonight?"

Lance nodded, and began to walk back through the woods toward Portage la Croix.

"What will the priest say?" Fawn asked worriedly.

"I do not care."

"What if he tries to stop you?"

"Then I shall kill him."

Lance was striding swiftly and Fawn had a hard time keeping pace.

"But not *ycripsicu*?" she asked breathlessly.

"*Ycripsicu* is too special a thing to waste on him," Lance said.

"Where shall I meet you?" Fawn asked.

"Meet me?"

"When you leave, I shall be with you."

Lance halted, turned to her, and put his arms on her shoulders. "We have talked of this before," he told her, his voice gentle. "You are a young girl, and a fine and beautiful one, but our souls are not alike."

"Our souls don't have to be, it doesn't matter," Fawn protested, resolutely holding back a tear.

Lance left her on the pathway close to her hut, and hurried to the rectory. Darkness was falling, and he could see the light of an oil lamp burning in Father LaPointe's upstairs bedroom.

He went into the ugly house and climbed the stairs to his own room.

"Joseph? Joseph, is that you? Come in here at once!"

The priest's speech was thick and slurred. He had been drinking.

Lance pushed open LaPointe's bedroom door and stood there. The priest was lying on the bed, holding a bottle of apple brandy. An empty brandy bottle lay on the floor. The oil lamp burned on a table beside the bed.

"Joseph, fix my supper," commanded the priest.

"No."

"No?" LaPointe tried to rise, but could not.

"I am leaving. Good-bye."

Lance's peremptory tone further enraged the already angry cleric. "You leave?" he asked scornfully. "Hah! I have many lashes to deal you, boy. You'll stay for them, too, and for much else, for whatever I say. That soldier, Major Renner, will report me to his superiors as being an unsatisfactory Indian agent. It's your fault, all the fuss you caused. Teresa would have died anyway . . ."

Lance turned to go to his room.

"I'm not finished talking to you," screamed the drunken priest, trying again to rise. "Anyway, you can't leave. It's against the law to leave. You'll be hunted down and brought back here in chains. . . ."

"No, I won't," said Lance, turning back toward La-Pointe. "Never. And you can go straight to that hell you are always talking about . . ."

LaPointe could not bear the insolence. He half-rose, reached out, grabbed the burning oil lamp, and hurled it at Lance.

The lamp was in the air, flashing fire, bound for Lance's head. He grabbed the doorknob and pulled the door shut. A moment later he heard the lamp smash against the wood. He heard the flashing *whoosh* of spreading flame and felt the blast of heat on his ankles when it shot through the narrow slit at the bottom of the door. He heard Pierre LaPointe scream.

"Save me! Please save me! Oh, God, I'm trapped. I can't move. . . ."

Now you know how it feels, Lance thought. *Ycripsicu would be far worse. You are lucky.*

He hurried to his room and gathered his belongings, then ran downstairs and stuffed as much food as he could into saddlebags. LaPointe's bellows had been swallowed now in the greater roar of the spreading fire.

Lance let the fire consume everything that belonged to his

identity as Joseph, and fled the rectory and Portage la Croix forever.

Waiting beneath a hoary three-trunked maple on a low range of hills west of Portage la Croix, Fleet Fawn saw an unusual flicker of light along the shore of Upper Red Lake. She had been resting against the old tree, waiting for Lance Tall One to come. If he left the reservation, he would ride this way. Only with subterfuge and difficulty had Fawn managed to slip out of her hut, and she had been here for hours. Perhaps Lance had changed his mind. She might as well go back to the hut, sneak inside, and try to sleep.

The odd spate and flutter of light by the lakeshore attracted her attention, however, and she stood up to get a better view. The night was dark. A thin rind of moon hung in the sky, intermittently obscured by the fleece of a swift cloud. Red Lake rested in the distance, a flat black mirror. Then the light Fawn had glimpsed suddenly bloomed like a giant orange flower.

"It cannot be!" Fawn cried aloud in disbelief. Father LaPointe's house was aflame. And Lance Tall One lived in that house. Instantly, she began to run down the hill to the forest trail leading back through the reservation to the mission. Her body trembled, and she knew it would be impossible to reach the burning house in time to save those asleep inside. But yet she ran, because Lance Tall One was her whole world now.

Fawn ran with the speed for which she had been named, racing beneath pine boughs, between the fragrant buds of spring thickets. She was not aware that someone was approaching her on the trail until, rounding a bend between brook and rock, Father LaPointe's stallion whinnied and reared in her path.

Startled, Fawn fell backward. Her hand found a sharp rock to hurl. She hated LaPointe, as did all the Indians. Then the chestnut stallion calmed and settled to earth, prancing. Fawn saw Lance Tall One upon the back of the horse. He looked, in the thin moonlight, wild and radiant. She picked herself up from the damp nighttime earth. Then she saw a second horse behind Lance, and saw bulging saddlebags on both mounts. Lance held a rifle in his hand. Several more fire-weapons were fastened to the saddle of the horse he rode.

"All right," Lance said to her. "I have told you how it will be."

Fleet Fawn did not ask where they were bound. She said nothing at all, just swung up onto the back of the second horse, a brownish-gold mare. Lance made a clucking sound and the horses moved up the trail to the top of the hill.

"What is in these saddlebags?" asked Fawn, feeling the weight of them against her legs.

"Food," he said.

Questions settled like a flock of jabbering birds on the edge of Fawn's tongue. But she asked him nothing, not then. They reached the three-trunked maple, and Lance turned back toward the lake. So did Fawn. They stared out over the treetops.

Fawn wanted to ask him what had happened, but did not. She already knew that he would tell her only what he wanted, when he wanted. Lance was still water, dark forest, brilliant snow. He was the truth of these, and the watchful power of these, and the beauty of these. She was in his hands and she exulted.

Along the shore of Red Lake flamed the rectory, pyre for Pierre LaPointe, antechamber of the hell he had created and earned.

Lance and Fleet Fawn watched on horseback from the hill as the flame burned house and church. When the big cross on the church caught fire and toppled into the lake, sending a great hissing roar that was audible to them in spite of the distance, Lance pulled taut the reins of his mount, and turned away from Portage la Croix. Against the bright blaze of the conflagration, which was like daylight for fully a hundred yards from the site, he had seen not one figure, not one Indian, come to view the debacle, much less to mount a rescue.

They rode all through the night and the next day, slowly so as not to fatigue the horses, but steadily to cover distance. In the evening, they reached the Red River.

"We will spend the night here," Lance said. He tethered the horses, and went to scout the terrain. Fleet Fawn did as a wife must do—she thought of herself as Lance's wife—and unpacked the saddlebags, laid out the bedrolls, and prepared to light a fire for the meal.

Lance returned. "No fire," he said quietly, "no smoke, no trail. I shall pass without a trace out of this Minnesota, and I shall never return."

Fleet Fawn obeyed. They ate dried beef from LaPointe's kitchen, and bread and dried apples. They drank from the Red River. Before sleep, Fawn gave pleasure to her man, and he delight to her.

"Where are we going?" Fawn asked, just before Lance fell asleep in her arms.

"Far away."

On the evening of the second day, she asked the same question. They were camped at Sweetwater Lake in Dakota.

"Farther," he said.

Each night, after loving him, Fawn asked the only question of her day. And each time he responded in a similar fashion. "A great distance." "Farther." "Westward."

Finally, camped along the shores of Medicine Lake, in Montana, filled again with his seed, filled with the warmth and sounds of the June night all about, Fawn asked her question again.

This time Lance's answer was different. "It will not be too long now," he said. "In a few more weeks, we ought to have reached the high country."

"The high country?"

"Many men passed through the priest's house while I was there, and I listened to everything they had to say. If we keep going west, we will come upon a wondrous place where the land leaps out of the sky, where fat cattle graze in the shade of tall blue hills."

"There is such a place?" Fleet Fawn asked dubiously.

"There are many places, and I have heard and remembered. There are vast seas that take three months to sail across, with great cities and strange peoples living there . . ."

Fawn's eyes were wide.

"Someday I shall go to those places too, but now I seek the golden plains beneath the mountains, where grass stands as tall as a man."

"And what will you do when we get there?" Fleet Fawn wondered.

"I shall take a piece of it and make it my own," Lance said.

Fawn felt that she was falling away from him. She understood neither his strange ambitions nor the dark forces that gave rise to them. But she did understand his body, and it sanctified her to make him throb and quiver with delight. They traveled southwest across Montana. Like a miracle, like the Promised Land of which Father LaPointe had so often spoken, the land Lance had promised Fleet Fawn came into view: green-golden plains rolling on toward rearing purple peaks. Lance seemed happy and Fawn was happy and Fawn was with child on the day they rode out upon this holy ground.

It would have been paradise if the others had not already been there.

4

The town of Black Forks, on the Madison River, served as center to the high cattle country of southwestern Montana, offering a telegraph office, general store, combination hotel-saloon-cafe, and a handful of clapboard houses no more sturdy than the other buildings. Black Forks had existed for less than a dozen years, and it could not exist for that many more unless the railroad came. The iron horse already spanned the continent, but did so far to the south, across the Great Plains. Here in the north, the mighty Rockies had thus far hindered empire building.

Few people were about Black Forks on the afternoon Lance and Fleet Fawn rode into the town. A woman wearing a drooping sunbonnet and a gingham dress came out of the store carrying a gunnysack full of merchandise. Panting with effort, she lifted the sack up onto the back of a buckboard, while the scrawny pony to which the buckboard was hitched flicked his tail spasmodically in a useless defense against a cloud of angry flies. Several horses were tied to the hitching rail in front of the hotel, likewise battling pests, and a ragged child next to the telegraph office tried to interest a yellow mutt in the pursuit and retrieval of a stick. But the dog sought shade beneath the porch of the store, the woman in the buckboard rode out of town, and the horses at the hitching rail kept flicking flies.

Lance guided his horse up to the hitching rail. Fawn and her mount followed. The boy walked over, curious. A sunburned towhead to whom strangers were not an every-day occurrence, he stared frankly at the tall man in a flat-crowned broad-brimmed hat and travel-stained white shirt. His eyes opened the more when he saw Lance's many rifles in scabbards hanging from the saddle, and it was with a kind of fear that he regarded the young woman in her buckskins. *An Indian woman!*

The boy turned and dashed into the saloon, its weather-beaten wooden doors flapping behind him.

Lance looked at Fawn and saw that she was ill at ease in this strange place. Oh yes, all the stories had come back to the reservation: stories about Indians caught alone in the white man's world and lynched on the spot, about Indian women raped and degraded for the sport of white renegades. These stories were true.

"It will be all right," he told her, dismounting. Since leaving Minnesota, Lance had felt a power to shape his own destiny. On the long ride across Dakota and Montana, he had also reviewed all the things he had learned—voluntarily or inadvertently—at Portage la Croix. The world outside Portage la Croix was as rich in promise as the mission itself had been ineffably bleak.

Lance helped Fawn down from her horse. Faces in the dust-streaked windows of the cafe-saloon were peering out at them now, pale faces flat and distorted against the crude, wavy glass.

"It is only that they are not used to seeing strangers," said Lance. He had a knife in his belt, and so left the rifles on the horse. No danger threatened on such a quiet day in this tiny town.

Lance and Fleet Fawn went through the swinging doors and into the gloomy half-light of the saloon and cafe. Raw, unpainted wood made up the entire place, walls and bar, tables and chairs, even the narrow stairway leading to the hotel rooms upstairs. As his eyes adjusted to the light, Lance saw a burly man behind the bar along with a kid who

was washing dishes. Three men—one of them in a good suit
—were drinking beer at the bar, and four or five cowboys
were shooting dice at one of the tables. The dice clicked,
rolled, and stopped. "Damn," said one of the cowboys.
Then he turned, along with everyone else, to stare at the
strangers.

The man in the suit, a big rangy fellow whose cold smile
showed yellow teeth, nodded to the bartender.

"What can I do fer yuh?" the bartender asked Lance. He
was staring at Fleet Fawn. His words had neither warmth
nor inflection.

"Food, drink, and land."

There was a long silence. The bartender looked at
Yellow-teeth, waiting for him to make some kind of
decision. Already Lance hated both men, the bartender for
his lack of will, and Yellow-teeth because he approximated
LaPointe's smug, arrogant manner of authority. Finally, the
man shrugged. Half-turning toward Lance, with everyone
watching warily, he let his hand fall to the butt of the gun on
his hip, easily and naturally, as if no threat at all were
intended.

"Got money?" he grunted.

"I will work."

"For food and drink and land?"

Lance nodded.

"Injun?"

"What?"

"I asked if you was Injun?" He studied Lance, then stared
again at Fawn.

In some well of his soul, from time beyond memory,
Lance seemed always to have known that someday this
scene would be played, this question would be put to him.
Coldly, he kept his eyes locked on those of Yellow-teeth.

"Part Sioux," he answered.

The men stared dumbly at him, and then Yellow-teeth
laughed. No man, except a fool, would admit to Injun blood

in these parts. This tall young fellow must have an odd sense of humor! For sure, he didn't look like no Injun. But then, he did have him that there squaw in tow.

"Got a name?" Yellow-teeth demanded.

"Have you?" Lance shot back.

Dumbfounded at Lance's temerity, the bartender spoke again.

"You want I should teach him some manners, Mister Whitlock?"

But Yellow-teeth shook his head and lifted a casual hand. "Any man who wants to buy land is a man who interests me. I ain't one for enemies. Unless it can't be helped. I'm Schuyler Whitlock," he told Lance, nodding as if to say, *Now it's your turn.*

No longer "Joseph, born in bondage," as LaPointe had called him, and no longer "worthless" either, Lance was ready.

"I am Lance Tallworth," he said.

"I knew it," Whitlock observed sagely. "I knew you wasn't no Injun, and certainly not with a name like that. Sure, come on in an' grab a table an' chair. Only thing is you got to leave the squaw outside."

Lance shook his head. Behind him, slightly to his left, he could sense Fleet Fawn's fear. The cowboys at the dice table, so quiet during Lance's exchange with Whitlock, now shuffled uneasily. If Lance was no Injun, all right. But the woman *was* redskin, an' no buts about it. Trouble, so recently eluded, seemed sure now.

"We don't give neither eat nor drink to Injuns in this town, Tallworth," the bartender said. "It's just the way things is. Nobody told you to tie up with a redskin squaw, an' that's your business. An' nobody can tell me to let one of 'em in here, an' that's *my* affair."

"Not anymore," Lance said.

Whitlock was studying Lance now, not just looking at him but *measuring* him, surprised and astounded too. The bartender glanced at Whitlock, but found no guidance there. The dice players stepped back and away from their table, and the other men at the bar eased toward the side of the room.

"Get out of here, you an' the bitch," the bartender ordered.

Lance shook his head. He saw a twitch in the bartender's shoulder, and knew. When the black barrel of the pistol came up over the edge of the bar, Lance had the tip of his knife between his fingertips. The bartender, set to fire fast and point-blank, was slightly distracted by the quick flashing arc of Lance's arm. The bartender's hand, holding the gun, lifted slightly, enough to serve Lance as a target. The flashing knife caught the bartender's hand just as the gun exploded, reverberating off the wooden walls, and then the bartender spun around, flung backward, his hand pinned by the knife to the wall behind him.

Hand pinned against wood. It reminded Lance of the crucifixes in Father LaPointe's rectory.

The bartender was howling in pain, and everyone was looking at him. Lance, realizing that he was defenseless without his knife in a roomful of gun-bearing men, leaped forward, grabbed Whitlock around the neck, and took his pistol from its holster. He did not raise the weapon against anyone, however, just held it and held Whitlock. He could smell the stink of the big man's rotting teeth.

The bartender was still howling, pinned to the wall.

Carefully, without a word, Lance released Whitlock.

Fleet Fawn was still standing by the door, apprehensive but admiring.

Whitlock brushed himself off, and glared at Lance. He also glared at the others in the room, and Lance sensed something that he had not realized earlier. With the exception of the bartender, everybody else hated Yellow-teeth.

Whitlock left and the bartender went to bandage himself. Lance and Fawn sat down at one of the tables and ordered food from the kid behind the bar. The men at the bar drifted out of the saloon, and all the dice players too except one, a wiry, grimy little man who went to the bar and drank beer after beer, now and then glancing over at Lance and Fawn with an appraising eye.

After staring awhile, the little man approached the table, beer mug in one hand, his other hand outstretched. "Name's Rowdy Jenner," he said. "See yer finished chowin' down, so I'd liketa offer my congratulations. Never yet seen me a man who'd face down Schuyler Whitlock."

"Why," asked Lance, "does Whitlock seem to be so powerful around here?"

"Hell, because he *is*. He owns him huge chunks of land, and holds mortgages on lots more. About the only thing he don't have is the Tatum spread, out on the approach to the Bitterroot."

"The what?"

"Bitterroot Pass. Gateway through the Rockies in this part of the good old U S of A. Land there is high and not as good for grazin' cattle as some of the stuff Whitlock bought himself early on. But now, with these surveyors comin' through and trackin' possible routes for the railroads, the Bitterroot could turn into a gold mine." He grinned and shook his head. "Or it could turn into the dry hole old man Tatum is makin' of it."

"So the land you are telling me about is already owned."

"As of this mornin' it was. If old man Tatum ain't contrived some way to foul that up too."

"Is it for sale?"

"Is it for sale!" Rowdy shook his head and growled. "Hell, you've seen Mr. Whitlock. Such as he is. An' he has been pressin' to buy it for as long as I can recall. He is no dumbbell, an' he can read a terrain map as well as anybody else. But Tatum hates his guts—as we all do, heh-heh—so no sale so far. But Tatum is tirin' of the West. He come out here thinkin' it was gonna be all romantic and everything.

109

Now he wants to cash in his chips. If you're lookin' to buy land, you might be interested."

"I am, but I don't have any money."

"That is sort of a problem when you want to buy something," Rowdy Jenner said.

Fleet Fawn listened to the conversation as best she could. The little English she had reluctantly learned at LaPointe's mission school did not suffice even to understand the words passing between Lance and this curious little cowboy. Had she been able to understand the words, the meaning of the conversation might not have been so lost on her, but she would have been in difficulty nonetheless.

"What are you speaking of?" she asked Lance in the tongue of her people.

"Something I want," he told her in English. So she sat at the table listening, thinking of all the distance between Black Forks and Minnesota, and all the love spent along the journey. Fawn felt suddenly chill, alien, excluded. She wanted to touch her husband, just to make sure he was here, but she did not have the nerve.

Lance himself was assaulted by the burdens of newness and stress. He had learned many things from the visitors and travelers at LaPointe's house, and he knew that he wanted land of his own, but apart from that he would have to go where his wits led, and the terrain sketched by Rowdy Jenner was wildly unfamiliar.

"You a rancher?" Jenner was asking.

"I will be. I like the look of this high country."

Jenner peered at him. "If you don't mind my saying so, you don't much look the cowhand type. And you got no money. Also, you're real young. Your daddy had a ranch and lost it? Or you figured to head out on your own?"

Lance nodded. "How many men work for Mr. Tatum?" he asked.

"About thirty, thirty-five during the summer. Drops to

110

maybe twenty in the winter. That's the regular crew. I'm the foreman. Or I will be until Mr. Tatum sells out."

"Will you take me to him?"

"Beg pardon?"

"Will you take me to Mr. Tatum?"

Lance knew that Schuyler Whitlock was his enemy, and Rowdy Jenner had told him that Tatum and Whitlock were enemies. He knew little of ranching, but he knew that he wanted to live in this country, where blue air bathed the mountaintops in eerie light, and the sky was still. And he knew that one's enemy's enemy is a friend. At least for a while.

Jenner, Lance, and Fawn rode west out of Black Forks to Tatum's ranch, the Lazy T, fifteen miles from the village, on the high plains up along Bitterroot Pass, once used as a thoroughfare by wagon trains on their way through the Rockies to Oregon.

"Tell me, Mr. Jenner . . ." Lance began.

"Name's Rowdy. That's all I go by."

"Tell me, Rowdy, why do you think your boss, Tatum, is failing?"

Rowdy leaned sideways in his saddle and spit tobacco juice onto the gray dust of the trail. "Lot of reasons," he said. "Firstways, he never bothered to learn anything about cattle. Secondways, he got tired of putting money and effort into the place. He don't have that love of land you got to have. Thirdways, he never cooperated with any of the other ranchers."

"How would that have helped?"

"Everybody was looking to him, at least when he first come out here, to sort of ally up with 'em against Whitlock. Instead of that, he kept to hisself. It didn't sit well, not a'tall."

"How about the men who work for you? What do they think of Tatum?"

"Well, he's paid 'em so far, and that's more'n can be said

for some spreads. But most of the boys just shake their heads when they see what Tatum's doin' to the ranch. It isn't the best grazing land, true. But it could be a lot better than it is."

"What's needed most of all?"

"More stock! We got to get us more cattle. But Tatum's lost interest. He's lookin' to move back east. And"— Rowdy shot Lance a look—"you ain't got no money."

Lance did have two important things, however. He had an idea, and he had nothing to lose.

They rode along the pass for a time, in which the Bitterroot River gleamed like a thin ribbon of glass, and then down toward the white buildings of the Lazy T. Tatum had liked his comfort, and the ranch itself was clean and attractive.

Rowdy glanced back at Fawn, who was riding behind the men.

"Maybe it's not such a good idea for her to come in with us. No offense, you understand."

"No," Lance told him. "She comes with me. You and I will talk to Tatum. She will not interfere."

Fleet Fawn, who heard what was said, felt a shrinking in her heart. But she made her face impassive, and showed nothing.

Lloyd Tatum barely noticed Fawn anyway. Upon learning from Rowdy that Lance might be a purchaser, he unburdened himself of a long litany of frustrations and discontents. He must have been mad to have wanted to live way out here in the first place. The summers burned you to death, and the winters froze your soul. Cattle died, there were no profits, and there was no one to talk to. Schuyler Whitlock was always maneuvering for this advantage or that, and the other ranchers ran their herds across Tatum's range all summer.

"Why is that?" Lance asked.

"Gets mighty dry out here in the summer. Cattle need

water, so they're driven across my rangeland to the river in the pass. It causes me no end of difficulty with my so-called neighbors, and there isn't any law around here worth mentioning. The final drawback is that we have to drive our herd all the way north to the railhead in Helena if we want to sell them, and they lose so much weight on the trail that it's hardly worth the trip."

Tatum, a gray-haired man with a soft body and smooth face, looked straight at Lance and asked his question.

"How much are you willing to put down?"

"How much do you want for the ranch? Stock included?"

"It's all of ten thousand acres, and after spring calving the herd comes to about three thousand head. I'm asking fifty thousand dollars for the whole shooting match."

"I'll pay you over a five-year period," Lance told him, as Rowdy Jenner gaped. This bold young stranger had just said he had no money.

"All right. We'll get it all done legal with that lawyer, Steinbronn, over in Black Forks. And I'll want ten percent down."

"I'll guarantee that by the fall," Lance said. "After we take the cattle to market."

"What in hell? I never came close to making that kind of money in one season . . ."

"But I will. I plan to get more cattle."

"Oh, I see," said Tatum slowly, with what he presumed to be shrewdness. "A big operator, hey?"

"And," said Lance, "in the paper that we sign, I will include words to the effect that I shall never bargain or deal with Schuyler Whitlock in any manner. This ranch will remain intact."

Tatum looked at the young man for a long time. "Deal," he said, and held out his hand.

"Boss," worried Rowdy, after Tatum had moved back east and Lance had taken over the ranch, "the boys is behind you all the way so far, but you ain't never goin' to make five thousand dollars without more cattle."

"I told you that I am going to get more cattle."

"But, boss, you said you was broke."

"I don't need money."

With Rowdy alongside him, Lance visited all the ranchers in the area, and offered them passage across his land throughout the summer. Any rancher might water his stock in the Bitterroot River, with no trouble at all and no payment required—if they agreed, at summer's end, to turn over to Lance a percentage of their herds, based upon size of the herd and number of trips made across the Tallworth ranch. When the deals had been made, the ranch was renamed the High Y. Only Lance knew why.

5

It was a hot summer. Countless water holes dried up, and Lance's herd was greatly increased when it came time to market the cattle that October.

Lance made his first payment on *Ycripsicu.*

Fleet Fawn gave birth to a baby girl early in 1881, and named the child Sostana, which meant peace. Lance doted on his daughter, and sometimes it made Fawn jealous to see him holding her, talking to her in meaningless, affectionate syllables. Fawn loved her husband, and she knew that he was trying to love her. But he had been right when he'd told her of the difference in their natures. She did not understand why he worked so hard during the summer, out on the range with the men and the cattle, when he could just as well stay at the ranch with her. Nor did she see the point of his ordering all those books and pamphlets in the mail, reading and studying them all winter long.

"I want to make the ranch better," he explained to her. "I want to improve the herd. I want to learn things that I don't know."

Fawn was perplexed. What did he mean? What was he talking about? Didn't he already know enough to live a sweet life with her? Didn't she already know enough to live a fine life with him?

Didn't he think so?

She felt troubled in her heart, but it was not a feeling she could form into words.

Time passed. The ranch thrived. Sostana grew. By the spring of 1885, Lance was on the verge of paying off Tatum in full. The herd was strong, and there was every prospect of a good season. But Lance was restless. Fleet Fawn had allowed herself to hope that, when the ranch was finally paid up, he would change, relax, let slip away the strange intensity she could not fathom. Instead, when the season was at hand, he grew more puzzling to her.

What bothered her most was that he never talked to her about what he was thinking. True, he had tried to do this a few times at the beginning of their life together, but she hadn't been able to follow. Her mind had wandered. He would be discussing his plans for the ranch, and that was very nice. He would tell her how he felt in his heart about having the land, owning it, possessing it, in order one day to pass it on to his children. That was very nice, too, but ought she to have rabbit or beef for supper, and weren't there pretty beads in the general store in Black Forks?

But Fleet Fawn paid attention to a conversation between her husband and Rowdy Jenner, in March of 1885.

"Rowdy, I've read of a new breed of beef cattle developed in Gascony," Lance said. "I have an idea that if we could get hold of a few and crossbreed them with our longhorns, something might come of it."

Rowdy asked the question that was on Fleet Fawn's mind.

"Where's Gascony?"

"In France," Lance answered.

Rowdy seemed to know where France was, but Fleet Fawn didn't.

Later, in bed that night, Fawn wished to impress her husband. "France is in Gascony," she told him.

"The other way around," he replied. "Anyway, I'm going there."

Fawn sat bolt upright in bed, frightened.

He put his hand on her warm thigh. "Not forever," he

soothed. "Just for a while, to look at a new breed of cattle that might help the ranch."

"The ranch," she repeated, almost bitterly. Always the ranch and Sostana. What about Fleet Fawn? "Where is France?" she asked, realizing too late that she must again appear stupid to him, and angry because why should—how *could*—she be anything but what she was?

And that was not enough for him, although he would never tell her.

Now, tonight, he held her close, and they made love, almost as well as they had made it long ago, on the shores of Red Lake.

Afterward, he was silent and unsleeping beside her, thinking things, dreaming things, wanting things that she would never understand. Fawn wanted to weep but she did not know why she wanted to weep.

Lance would go away to this place called France.

He would return.

And everything would be the same as it had been.

Part Three

NORWAY AND CHICAGO • *1885–1886*

1

Rain fell upon Oslo the day Gustav Rolfson was laid to rest. All morning long the skies were gray and threatening, and during the funeral services the clouds opened up. It was, Elizabeth thought, as if Gustav's inability to draw tears from those who came to his burial caused an embarrassed heaven to make a show of grief.

Heaven wept alone. No one in the cemetery of Saint Olav troubled to make an effort.

The Rolfson family plot comprised a huge square of grass in the far corner of the cemetery, as remote and exclusive as Gustav might have wished. The great cathedral could scarcely be glimpsed through thick dripping leaves, and Oslo in the distance was but a shadowy phantasm in rain and fog. A towering marble obelisk stood at the center of the plot, the beautiful veined stone rendered thick and phallic according to the wish of old Adolphus, Gustav's father, dead now for almost twenty years. The old man had come out of a tiny village near Trondheim in the North, to build a mercantile empire and acquire a vast fortune. In keeping with his ambitions, this huge cemetery plot was purchased to receive the remains of generations of Rolfsons. Yet, until this rainy morning, Adolphus's bones had rested here alone. His wife had been buried fifty years ago in the home churchyard, and his second son, Olav, Elizabeth's father, had been killed and buried in America, according to Gustav's account.

Elizabeth wept a little then, for the father she could remember only as the big blond man who'd carried her on his shoulders, and for this green rectangle of Norwegian earth.

The bronze coffin rested on the bottom of the new grave, and Rector Mortenson prayed sonorously over it. "Commit him to the glories of Your realm," the churchman boomed, "and give Your faithful servant, Gustav, a part of the business of heaven to administer, for we are confident he will do as well in heaven as he did on earth . . ."

Thea Thorsdatter, Gustav's longtime mistress and companion, coughed behind her black veil. Thea had barely succeeded in suppressing a laugh, her response to Mortenson's pious hyperbole. Thea needed her veil today; she had been in great good spirits ever since Elizabeth had returned to Oslo with Gustav's body.

"Well, my dear," she had said, greeting Elizabeth in the mansion, which displayed no wreaths of mourning, "so your schooling is concluded. Have you found a husband yet?"

Learning of Elizabeth's failure in this regard, she was undiscouraged. "Don't worry your pretty little head," she had promised, "I know plenty of fine young men who would jump at the chance to . . ."

Her appraising eye swept the younger woman. "Hmm-mmmm. Your hair, with that nice auburn color, is extraordinary, and your eyes too. We Nordics *must* have blue eyes. Your bosom is good, but, really, you ought to pick up a few pounds in the derriere . . ."

This was practically the same thing Gustav had tried to tell her!

". . . because a man wants something *there*. You do know what I mean, don't you?"

"I had not really thought of matrimony just yet . . ." Elizabeth had protested.

"What? *What?* Nonsense. You just leave it to me."

Thea Thorsdatter had been in high spirits, had been so helpful, so *kind* since Elizabeth's return to Norway. What on earth had become of the Thea who had "accidentally" locked young Elizabeth in the wine cellar, who had spent years reviling the child as an orphan, usurper, and pest?

Elizabeth looked at Thea now, as the older woman stood by the grave, gazing down at Gustav's coffin. Thea was a bit fleshy, but lush, a woman who managed to convey sensuality and hard indomitability at the same time. Gustav's kind of woman.

Elizabeth saw Thea looking at her from behind the veil. She saw a brief white flash of the woman's teeth.

"The immediate family may now come forward for a final farewell," Rector Mortenson intoned.

Insofar as Elizabeth had been able to determine, the funeral party of perhaps a hundred people consisted mainly of high-level Rolfson employees and Thea's acquaintances. So there ought to have been only two people stepping forward to the grave, Elizabeth and Thea. But when Elizabeth did pick her way through the loose earth and stacked squares of sod, she was surprised to find a man accompanying Thea, and even more stunned to feel another man's hand on her elbow. At first she thought he must be a member of the mortuary staff, keeping her from pitching forward into the grave. But she looked at him and saw instead a fine-looking young man with rich, chestnut-colored hair, lean body, and blue shining eyes. He was looking back at her raptly, and in his glance she saw Arndt Stryker and Jorge Lora and the other boys of Geneva. *Thea the matchmaker!* Elizabeth thought. *Perhaps she feels a responsibility to find a husband for me.*

Upon her arrival in Oslo, Elizabeth had anxiously inquired if there had been a letter for her. "Why, of course not," lied Thea easily, recalling the letter from Cherbourg, a letter filled with words of love, apparently from an American Elizabeth had met in Geneva. Thea had destroyed the letter. An American in love with Elizabeth did not fit into Thea's schemes.

Steadying Thea at graveside was a man Elizabeth recognized immediately, although he had grown much balder and much stouter during the years she had been in Switzerland. Lars Thorsen, once a modest solicitor and attorney in the village of Lesja, from which the mineral deposits of Rolfson Industries were mined, had long been Uncle Gustav's chief legal advisor in Oslo. As his hair thinned, the thickness of his red beard increased, until now it snarled in thick curls about his shirtfront and his vest.

"Rest in peace and may Our Dear Saviour greet you at the gates!" Mortenson proclaimed. He bent down and picked up a clod of loose earth and handed it to Elizabeth. It felt cold and slimy in her hand. Mortenson nodded toward the grave, and Elizabeth cast the clod down onto Gustav's coffin top where it broke with a dull thock into a thousand tiny particles.

"Ashes to ashes, dust to dust," the rector intoned, bidding Elizabeth and Thea to throw more earth into the grave. They obeyed, and even Lars Thorsen tossed down a couple of clumps. The ritual might have continued for some time but Thea muttered, "Hell, that's enough," and Mortenson, looking a bit amazed, gave a final blessing, the gist of which was that Gustav would thrive in heaven's marketplace. Then the crowd formed a line, filing past Elizabeth and Thea and offering condolences. Finally, it was over. With the young man still at her elbow, Elizabeth made her way toward the carriage at the cemetery gate, Thea and Lars Thorsen right behind. She could hear the workmen grunt as they spaded dirt into Gustav's rapidly filling grave.

Thick Lars huffed forward and helped Elizabeth into the carriage, which was serenely adorned with crepe. Thea climbed in without aid and took the seat across from Elizabeth.

"I shall see you this evening," said Thorsen, bowing

slightly as he closed the carriage door. The young man stood behind him, shifting from foot to foot, his adoring eyes still on Elizabeth.

"Don't you think he's absolutely charming?" asked Thea, as the carriage rolled away from the cemetery gate. She pushed up her veil, sighed with relief, and unpinned the plain black hat she wore. Her smile was wide and full and utterly empty.

"Who?" asked Elizabeth coldly.

Thea laughed, a sound like chunks of ice rattling in a barrel. "Come, my dear, life belongs to the living. I could see at a glance that Harald was absolutely enchanted with you."

Elizabeth felt vastly discouraged. The funeral itself, with all its ambience of sorrow and termination, futility and obscure woe, weighed upon her, whose body and mind were still concentrated upon Lance Tallworth. To have this callow, unknown Harald propelled upon her by Thea was ludicrous. It was like . . . it was like inviting a clown to a funeral!

"Harald Fardahl is of a fine, wealthy family," Thea was saying. "You could not do much better and you could do a lot worse."

I could not do much worse and I have done a lot better, Elizabeth thought. "He is quite nice looking," she said absently, for Thea Thorsdatter's benefit.

"Ah! You see!"

"Is he what you meant when you cabled me to 'be prepared'?"

"Well, yes. That, and other things too. For instance, tonight at the house there will be the reading of Gustav's will . . ."

"Is that what Solicitor Thorsen was referring to?"

"Of course. He will be at the house to read the will. He was Gustav's attorney and business advisor. You know that."

"Do these things customarily take place so soon after . . ."

"It depends. But in this case, we must proceed posthaste. Gustav has not been in America for a long time, and word from there gives us indication that his enterprises are not going well. Not well at all. A firm hand must be applied as soon as possible."

Elizabeth had more than an inkling that Thea wanted other things to happen quickly as well.

"Harald Fardahl will be at the house tonight too?"

"Why, of course, my dear. I want you two young people to get to know each other. Didn't you *see* the way he was looking at you?"

Thea, the romantic? The picture was not right. Thea was the last person on earth Elizabeth would have picked to be a romantic, much less a matchmaker. She was working on some scheme, some plan. No point in asking her what it was. Elizabeth would simply have to wait and see.

"I have no intention of marrying for a long time," she did manage to say, so Thea might be able to convey the true state of affairs to this Fardahl boy.

"Tut-tut, my dear. Don't be silly. Your uncle's death has been an awful shock, but you will get over it . . ."

"It's not that . . ."

"And what else *can* you do? Young girls get married and start families, and so shall you!"

Elizabeth was too dispirited at that moment to argue with Thea, besides which, what good would it have done? The woman was not to be resisted. Still, Elizabeth was certain enough of herself to know that she would resist Thea if necessary. And it would be necessary, but only at the right time. She would first have to wait and get her bearings. She would have to learn what was going on.

It was still raining heavily when they reached the Rolfson mansion, a huge gray blocky affair on a hill overlooking Oslo harbor. The place was solid and dull and expensive, cold as the stone from which its walls were made. Every room boasted a huge fireplace, but somehow the house was always chill and drafty. Elizabeth's earliest memories of life here were midnight searches for more quilts and comforters to pile on her bed. If a house could truly reflect the heart of its owner, Gustav Rolfson had succeeded in building it.

The driver helped them down from the vehicle and the butler, ancient Ellison, met them inside the door and took their wraps. One of the few servants with a touch of warmth in him, he gave Elizabeth a smile. "You'll be wanting some refreshments?" he asked.

"No, thank you, Ellison. I think I'll go up to my room and rest."

"Very wise," Thea declared, handing the butler her sopping cloak. "We have a busy and important night prepared."

Elizabeth went upstairs wondering how Thea would react when she learned that Gustav had changed his will, leaving all of his American holdings to "the usurper."

Just as Elizabeth remembered, it was cold in her room in spite of the roaring fire, and even a long hot bath did not warm her very much. Bundled in a soft thick robe of Shetland wool, she stood at the window, watching night fall upon Oslo, the strange northern night of high summer, when even from midnight to morning a bright eerie glow fills the sky. The rain ceased at sunset, and the harbor, previously obscured by mist, became visible. Ships of a dozen lands rode gently at the piers, and the water in the harbor glinted blue and gold, with gray patches here and there where spates of rain still fell. Elizabeth leaned against the windowsill and tried to put things into perspective.

Her thoughts went to Lance and instantly the pleasure she recalled within her made her blush. Where was he now? Was he safe? She wished he was with her to help her through this gloomy ordeal.

Elizabeth remembered with an uncontrollable shudder Lance's touch upon her bare skin, his hard yet strangely tender kiss upon her mouth, upon her body. She recalled how it had felt to open herself for him, to feel his long, searching shape easing in and going out and coming in, the pleasure building like a hollow tunnel of fire, slowly filling, filling, and her wild need to be ridden and riven and filled . . .

Elizabeth turned away from the window, flushed and excited. Lance had left with her a mystic essence of himself, which she would never lose, not ever; nor would he lose or forget the mark of her soul upon his. For the first time in her life, she believed that tides of whirling stars touched the fragile human shapes upon the earth, and made them wondrous and divine.

She believed it because she had to. Lance was not with her. There was nothing else in which to believe.

Presently, there was a knock at the door.

"Come in."

It was Ellison, the butler, in his formal frockcoat.

"Dinner will be served in an hour," he announced stiffly, looking her over. He had not seen her for quite some time, true, but there was more than mere appraisal in his expression. He seemed sad, as if he wanted to tell her something, but did not know whether to do so or not. It was unusual for him to come up and announce dinner. That was a job for one of the houseboys or a maid.

"You were with Uncle Gustav a long time," she said, to make conversation.

He stood just inside the door, nodding slowly, lean and sallow and bent. "And with his father before him, Miss. Yes, I go back a long time . . ."

His voice trailed off. He *did* want to tell her something.

"What is it, Ellison?"

"I'm . . . I'm not quite sure, Miss Rolfson. Lord knows, I've never done a thing like this before in all my life, to talk out of school, so to speak. But I think there's a plan afoot that's not designed to do you any good. And it's not fair that they try to pull it on an innocent girl like yourself."

He turned toward the door, preparing to leave.

"What kind of a plan?" Elizabeth blurted. She had had the same insight riding home from the cemetery, an inkling that Thea was spinning a clever web.

"I've already said more than I ought," returned the butler, "and, anyway, I don't know. I just have my suspicions. Might only be the maunderings of an old man, but you never can tell. It's best to be on guard."

Ellison opened the door and prepared to step out into the hallway. It had been most kind of him to warn her in this manner but, as he had said, he'd never done anything before to compromise the propriety of his position. Wasn't that, in itself, a bit odd?

"Ellison, why are you telling me this?" she asked him frankly.

Again, he hesitated before speaking. "Because I just want to see you get your rightful share," he told her quietly. Then, closing the door soundlessly, he was gone.

"Just want to see you get your rightful share?" Elizabeth wondered. What a nice old man! But there was nothing to worry about. Uncle Gustav had already told her about the will. She dressed for dinner, choosing a demure gown of dark blue satin, high at the throat and loose at bodice and hips, in case the panting Harald Fardahl should make an appearance. And he probably would. Elizabeth knew that Thea, once set upon a course of action, was virtually as immovable as stone. Elizabeth decided against wearing a fragrance of any kind—once again acknowledging Harald —but, as usual, brushed her long beautiful hair until it gleamed like old gold. Descending the stairs for dinner, she was already making tentative plans to go to America. Thea had said Gustav's affairs there needed a firm hand, and she

had learned a great deal of practical worth at St.
Ada's . . .

The staircase swept down in a great spiral to the main
floor of the mansion, a huge hall three stories high, along
one wall of which hung a gigantic Norwegian flag, a
white-bordered St. Olav's cross of blue on a field of red.
Gustav, for all his pomp and pretension, had been genuinely
proud of his nationality, even though he had not been
patriotic in the least. The library, in which guests were
often received, opened off the foyer to the left, and the
dining room was on the right. Elizabeth had come down a
bit early, to be on hand when the guests arrived, and so she
was a little surprised to hear voices in the library. And she
was even more startled to overhear Thea Thorsdatter say, in
an insinuating, teasing voice, "Not here, you fool!"

Already alerted to the possibility of the unexpected, both
by Ellison and by Thea's "be prepared" telegram, Elizabeth
could not resist turning toward the library. Walking quickly
on tiptoe to keep the heels of her pumps from clicking on
the marble, she hurried across the foyer and paused outside
the big double doors of mahogany. They were closed.

A gasping, strangled voice said, "Thea, *please*," a plea
followed by the sounds of a subdued scuffle. Through the
partially opened doors on the opposite side of the foyer,
Elizabeth saw a servant placing silverware on the dinner
table.

Inside the library, Thea giggled. Someone groaned.

Deciding, Elizabeth reached out and took the door latch
in her hand. She pressed gently down all the way and eased
the door open to see what was happening inside.

Thea Thorsdatter was half-seated, half-sprawled on one
end of the big leather divan in front of the fireplace, her
long hair tangled and the hem of her expensive white gown
up around her thick solid thighs. Solicitor Thorsen, kneel-
ing on the floor at her feet, was bent to her breasts, trying to
kiss them through the fabric, his shiny bald pate twisting
this way and that. One of his hands was thrust up and out of

130

sight between Thea's thighs. Thea was laughing and panting, her face red from a combination of passion and mirth, and Lars Thorsen panted with desire into his red beard and Thea's silk-shielded bosom.

"Oh, do *stop* it!" she said then, pushing his head away. "Our guests will be here any minute, and we have to remain perfectly composed all evening . . ."

"Yes, Thea, but . . ."

Reluctantly, Thorsen stood up. He was in a state of advanced tumescence, which Thea playfully caressed, pretending to calm the pulsing angry bulge inside Thorsen's trousers. He moaned, and made as if to fall to his knees again, but she stood up abruptly and stepped away.

"I mean it, Lars. Nothing must go wrong." Thea smoothed her gown and, borrowing the comb he used for his beard, began to get her hair in order.

"There won't be any problems," Thorsen told her, still agitated but resigned to temporary carnal frustration. "She is just an innocent young thing . . ."

"Hush. Voices carry in this big old place. And I'm not so sure about this 'innocence.' She's matured . . ."

They are talking about me, Elizabeth realized.

". . . and I've a pretty good eye for things like this. The girl who came back is not the jejune little thing Gustav sent to Switzerland years ago. I suspect she's even had a man."

"Oh, Thea, come! She's a baby."

"So were we all once." Thea stared lustfully at Thorsen, and he could not resist coming to her. He was a few inches shorter than she, but much broader. "But no," she went on, breaking away from him, "she's had some experience. I can tell. And she's smart as a whip. We'd best do this right."

"What about Fardahl?"

"Harald is smitten. He will play right into our hands. One look at her, and he was a dead duck."

"She doesn't like him, though."

"She will. She will, and I've given him some advice on how to proceed with a young girl."

Lars Thorsen looked dubious.

"Well, I was a young girl myself, not so long ago." Thea added abruptly. "And if you think I'm too old now, well, you can just forget about me and walk out the door."

"Oh, no," cried Thorsen piteously, "I didn't mean to imply . . ."

Whatever it was that the solicitor had not meant to suggest was lost to Elizabeth, because the big gong at the front door sounded, heralding the arrival of guests. She managed to get back across the foyer to the bottom of the staircase, and it seemed to Ellison, as he shuffled toward the door, that Elizabeth had just come down from her room.

"Why, good evening, Elizabeth," Thea called cheerfully, coming out of the library with Thorsen at her side, "did you have a nice rest?"

Eager Harald Fardahl arrived first, accompanied by a prosperous-looking older man from whom he had clearly inherited his good looks, and a soft simpering woman from whom he had learned traits of character. The elder Fardahls were as fully taken with Elizabeth as their son had been.

Thea directed that sherry be served in the library, which the guests entered upon their arrival at the mansion, to express their condolences, to sip and chat. It seemed almost a festive occasion. Theobald Norstrem was there, chief executive of Gustav Rolfson's European enterprises. He had come with his wife, a henna-haired woman broad of grin and beam, who greeted Elizabeth with excessive cheer and then retreated to hiss and whisper with Ursula Thainson, a wisp of a girl who was as strong as copper wire and married to Gunnar Thainson, treasurer of Rolfson Industries. Other executives there with wives were Paulus Tillstrom, Lief Dittersdahl, and Friedrich Kayrslatter, whose attempt to deny his German roots was a thing to behold.

Elizabeth watched them drinking sherry, moving about,

and noted that not one representative of Rolfson Industries in America was present. But then, there would not have been time for any of them to cross the Atlantic on such short notice. She felt, however, a slight twinge of alarm. The American holdings were to be hers. Yet she knew nothing about them.

Despite her best efforts, Harald Fardahl succeeded in cornering Elizabeth at the fireplace. He smiled with casual aplomb when he saw how red her face was, attributing to himself the flush a pile of burning logs had caused.

"Elizabeth," he cried, "how are you bearing up, old girl?"

Old girl? Harald was swaggering a bit and working hard on his insouciance. *This* was the winning advice Thea had given him? To be grand and casual and to use a sporting tone? He did seem bolder, though.

"After dinner," he intoned, almost but not quite looking her in the eye, "I think we ought to go for a stroll in the garden."

"It rained today," Elizabeth said.

"But it stopped some time ago."

"Everything is still wet out there, and I so dislike walking in a wet garden."

"Oh, yes, I know exactly what you mean," he responded instantly. "We'll find some other place to be alone."

He smiled at her in a way that was meant to appear sage and knowing, as though he and she were conspirators.

It was all Elizabeth could do to keep her composure. After the piercing love she had known with Lance, the thought of another man holding her, wanting to hold her, even wanting to be close to her, was obscene. Could not Harald see that she belonged to another and always would? Had not her body, her very being, been scorched forever by the sacred brand of Lance upon her? Would that that were so, for all the world to see and know. And to leave her alone until she could be with Lance again.

But why had Lance not written her, as he had promised? Every day she waited for the post, and every day she was disappointed. She would already have written him herself, written him a hundred times. But *ycripsicu* was not an address, was it?

Across the room, where she was talking earnestly to Norstrem and Thainson, Elizabeth saw Thea keeping her eyes on everything and everyone in the room. She looked in some indefinable way *triumphant*. Lars Thorsen, strutting and pawing at her side, appeared no less self-satisfied. Then Elizabeth learned that Harald Fardahl was to be her dinner partner.

Perhaps I am being unfair, she thought, as he held her chair for her. *Do I have an actual reason for disliking him?*

Yes, she answered herself. *He fawns and swaggers. He is a good-looking rich boy who has grown up without maturing. Mama's delight. Papa's instrument. And,* she added, naming the worst thing, *for some reason he thinks he already owns me.*

Thea Thorsdatter was probably the reason for young Harald's presumption.

But to what purpose were these orchestrations designed?

The dinner—cream of sorrel soup, lobster boiled in beer, filet of young doe—was excellent, and the guests, while extravagant in praise, were quite sincere. But Elizabeth was unable to enjoy the meal. Harald Fardahl kept after her, asking her to "tell me about Geneva, old girl," and "well, old girl, I should tell you that very soon I'm taking on major responsibilities. Makes a man think of his future, know what I mean?" He tried hard to give her one of the commanding looks Thea must have coached him to use, but behind the thin veil of false confidence there was only sweet-faced, handsome Harald who would probably say he'd die to kiss her once. Elizabeth felt the eyes of the Fardahl parents on her too, but fleetingly, obliquely. She did not like them any better than she did Harald! In fact, as she listened to Harald and puzzled about his parents, she began to feel that old Ellison had been right. All these people, Thea and the Fardahls and the others, were about to use her unfairly. She glanced around the table, saw them eating prodigiously, saw their eyes glittering with avarice and fine wine, and knew she did not know anyone at the dinner who could help her, should she need aid.

Then she analyzed her situation again, and realized that she had been wrong. There *was* one person she could use!

"You know, old girl, I've never been inside the Rolfson place before," Harald boomed in his emptily jovial tone after Thea had announced that coffee and brandy would be served in the library prior to the reading of Gustav's will. "Perhaps you might be good enough to give me a gander at it."

"Why, of *course!*" exclaimed Elizabeth, sweetly enthusiastic, as if she had been waiting for years just to hear him make this suggestion. "Let us dawdle behind a little until the others are in the library."

Harald looked astounded at his great good fortune. He cooperated beautifully, hanging back, and when Thea had shepherded her guests from dining room to library, barely glancing back at the youngsters, he was all suavity and charm.

"Where shall we go first?" he asked, bowing and offering a gallant arm.

"Let's see the garden."

"What? But I thought you said . . ."

"I just love the garden when it's dripping wet after rain, don't you?"

"Oh, yes!" he cried. "Nothing better!"

Elizabeth had decided on the garden because, with the servants and guests inside the house, the chances of being seen or overheard were minimal.

Gustav Rolfson's garden was overlarge, overdone. The hedges were too thick and too high. The statuary of Viking

135

warriors around the pool was excessively aggressive and martial. Even the flowers had been planted too closely together, and in bloom they looked haphazard, unaesthetic. Harald did not notice.

Halfway down the path from house to pool, Harald got his courage up and reached for Elizabeth's hand. She let him have it, casting down her eyes modestly, keeping an eye on her conquest with an occasional discreet glance. She had expected him to say something, to make some portentous gesture or declaration by now, but he seemed satisfied just to sigh and be with her. Could it be that she had made a big mistake? Had she been a fool who divined a plot where there was none?

Harald surprised her. "Well, I expect you've been told," he giggled.

Elizabeth calculated for a split second. "Oh, yes," she said cheerfully.

"I couldn't be happier."

"I'm so glad."

"I know you'll make me a wonderful wife . . ."

What on earth?

"Mama and Papa," Harald babbled on, "will love you like the parents you never had. Of course, it's all very advantageous for them, no denying that, but it's a great financial boon for us as well . . ."

Money, thought Elizabeth. *Thea and Gustav's money, and the will.*

". . . and you'll come to love me, I know."

Harald stopped, there on the path, and pulled her to him, kissing her clumsily at a spot slightly below her lower lip and slightly above her chin. He pressed close to her and she felt his excitement. She could not decide whether to laugh or push him away, and so did neither. Eventually, he stopped kissing her jawbone and sighed, gazing into her eyes like a moonstruck calf.

"Harald," she asked softly, bringing up her hands and

putting them flat on his chest, "do you know how I feel about you?"

"Oh, yes!" he exulted. "And I promise I'll be . . ."

"No, please listen. I went to college, as you know, but there are many things on this earth that I don't understand."

He fairly shivered with worldliness and knowledge. "I'll teach you."

"For example," Elizabeth continued, hoping that he knew as much as he thought he did, hoping he was lulled enough to reveal things she needed to know, "I don't *quite* understand how this business about that silly old will relates to your family. To *us*," she amended with emphasis.

Harald, never perspicacious at the best of times, and hardly cunning even at the worst, was overwhelmed by her sweet humility in the face of his wisdom.

"Why, it's so advantageous to everyone, as I've said," he declared, maneuvering to kiss her again. "And Thea Thorsdatter has fashioned a plan to help us all."

"She *has*?" exclaimed Elizabeth, putting up a hand to fend him off.

Harald became hurried and explicit, wanting to move on to another kiss. "Yes," he told her, "it all works so well. Thea is a genius. We Fardahls are of the nobility, which you Rolfsons are not. You Rolfsons are wealthy, which —quite frankly—some of us old nobles aren't. The dowry Thea is providing for you shall be a fair exchange for the title you will gain! Moreover, I shall make you a fine husband . . ."

So that was it. Elizabeth had been right in her earlier surmise. Thea had every intention of marrying her off, of getting her out of the way. But Thea had best think again! Elizabeth, as soon as possible, would go to America and, with the fortune Gustav had left her, take up a new life. Good-bye and farewell, Harald Fardahl! Still, there was one thoroughly mystifying aspect to Harald's breathless dissertation.

"Why on earth does Thea feel she has to provide me with a dowry?" Elizabeth asked.

"Come now, old girl. You needn't play the proud one with me." Harald pressed down energetically for his kiss, and with reciprocal strength befitting the occasion, Elizabeth pushed back. "You don't have to be ashamed," he babbled. "Penuriousness is no great taint, if one has class and title . . ."

"What *are* you talking about?" she demanded, sharply enough to give Harald pause. He ceased his attempt to press his mouth down on whatever part of her he might find.

"Oh!" he cried, alarmed. "You haven't been informed of the contents of the will? And here I've been . . . God, I'm sorry. But you'd have found out presently anyway, so perhaps it's best that your future husband tells you. Gustav left you nothing, old girl. You are poor as a church mouse."

Harald mistook for anguish the sudden surge of anger in Elizabeth's eyes.

"Poor as of now," he clarified, "but with the dowry Thea will provide when we marry, everything will be fine. I promise you. I might even take a position of some kind. Later in life. Right now, I want to spend all my time making you happy."

2

Elizabeth took her seat in the library for the reading of Gustav Rolfson's will. Harald, tender and solicitous, sat down beside her. His shocking news about Thea's machinations had upset Elizabeth, but she forced herself to remain calm. It was possible, after all, that Harald did not know what he was talking about; no one would think to accuse him of wide experience in the more practical affairs of life. Wills did not become magically altered, especially not after the deaths of their authors, but there were always lots of rumors upon the demise of a wealthy man. Wistful, dreamy Harald Fardahl might have forged fantasy out of fragment. On the other hand—and Elizabeth could not safely ignore this likelihood—Thea might have learned all too well the lessons that Gustav had taught.

In battle against his enemies, Gustav had always delighted in creating crushing dilemmas with which to vex and madden and destroy. "Always give the bastards a choice," he had said ad nauseam, "but make sure it's a choice between the devil and the deep blue." Elizabeth could not help but feel additional wariness toward Thea, whose years at Gustav's elbow and in his bed had not been spent without profit. *"Be prepared,"* Thea had cabled. The dilemma: Elizabeth could choose to be penniless and alone, or she could choose Harald and a dowry. In either case, she would be out of Thea's hair. And out of money to which she felt entitled.

Elizabeth was sure Thea would not be overly generous with a dowry, at least not when it was measured against the worth of Gustav's American wealth.

She felt Harald's hot hand settle on her arm, and started slightly.

"You'll always have me," he whispered, as the others were finding seats on sofas and comfortable chairs. Lars Thorsen, seated at the big desk, was taking a bundle of papers from his calfskin briefcase. Thea watched eagerly from a chair in front of the desk. She looked triumphant already.

Elizabeth felt Harald's eyes on her. Turning toward him, and seeing his woebegone look, she realized he meant well, but she felt a twinge of pity for him.

"Harald," she told him, while the Thainsons and the Tillstroms and the Norstrems got settled, "I think I am going to need your aid very soon . . ."

"Oh, Elizabeth, yes . . ."

". . . and my request will surely cause you a great deal of trouble, perhaps even . . ."

"Shall we now proceed?" Lars Thorsen boomed, stroking his red beard, getting to his feet behind the desk.

"Perhaps even what?" whispered Harald, with wide eyes.

"The disapproval of everyone you know," Elizabeth finished.

Harald regarded her with wonder. No one had *ever* disapproved of him. He had difficulty imagining how such a thing could be. He took his hand away from her arm.

Everybody quieted expectantly, and Solicitor Thorsen chose to reminisce a little. "At a time like this," he began, "one cannot help but think of the past. I remember, as if it were yesterday, the time Adolphus and his young son Gustav came riding into the village of Lesja, up north, to survey the mountains for mineral wealth. I was a humble village official then, but I knew at a glance that those two strong, forthright men were going to change my life. And, yes, I was right. Within a couple of years, they had taken over an entire mountain range. Iron, lead, copper, and nickel poured out of those mountains, thousands upon thousands of tons, to forge the cannon and the shells, the ships and the trains, the rails and the towers of modern Europe. Yes, the Lesja Range has served us . . . ah, the Rolfsons, well, but now it is . . ."

Thea seemed to give him a sharp look, almost of warning. Thorsen was a lawyer, though, and his mouth did not miss a beat.

". . . time to look to the future."

In response, there was nodding and nervous coughing. Beside her, Elizabeth could tell that Harald was still puzzling over what she had just said to him. He *was* more than willing to help her, true. But he was not at all sure he wanted to suffer the disapprobation that might result.

"After I read this document," Thorsen said, "you are all invited to examine it. Gustav signed it just before he left to attend our dear Elizabeth's graduation at St. Ada's in Switzerland."

Now Thorsen laid the papers down in a row on the desk.

"I, Gustav Adolphus Rolfson," the solicitor read, "being of sound mind and body, hereby effect my last will and testament . . ."

There followed a discourse of a personal nature, in which Gustav detailed the great amounts of wealth he had amassed, and the beneficent quality of his presence on earth. Then:

". . . to my dear friend and companion, Thea Thorsdatter, I do give and bequeath my home in Oslo, in which she now resides; my chateau on the Rhine near Saverne, in France; my mansion on Fifth Avenue in New York City . . ."

Elizabeth straightened slightly, bracing herself. A house in New York was American property, and Gustav had told her she would receive *all* his American holdings.

". . . as well as my summer retreat in Newport, Rhode Island; my home on Lakeshore Drive, in Chicago; and my country place in Lake Geneva, Wisconsin."

Thorsen paused. No one in the group said anything. Thea kept her eyes blank. Mrs. Thainson turned to Mrs. Dittersdahl and made some dolorous hissing noises, in which the sound of sympathy for poor Elizabeth could be discerned.

Elizabeth forced herself to sit bolt upright, and to show no emotion whatever. She was a little afraid, but far more furious than beleaguered. *They are not going to do this to me*, she vowed.

"To my servants in all these places," Thorsen was reading again, "I offer employment and residence so long as my prime beneficiary deems appropriate.

"To my only other beneficiary, Elizabeth Rolfson, to whom out of the goodness of my heart I have provided housing and education over the years, I offer residence in my Oslo home for as long as my prime beneficiary deems appropriate. Furthermore, I designate said prime beneficiary, Thea Thorsdatter, as legal guardian of Elizabeth until she should reach her majority of twenty-one years."

Elizabeth groaned inwardly. She was almost twenty-one, but almost was not good enough.

Elizabeth listened for items relating to trust funds, stocks and bonds, bank accounts, and other private caches of wealth. There were many of these, both in Europe and America. But, according to the will Thorsen was reading, they had all been left to Thea.

Elizabeth started to keep track of the figures, especially the American figures. Lake Shore Realty Holding Company, Chicago, Illinois, net worth $3.5 million; preferred stock, Baltimore and Ohio Railroad, net worth $1.3 million; U.S. Government Treasury notes, $700,000; and on and on until Minnesota Mesabi Mining, net worth uncertain.

And Thea had been saying how *bad* the American situation was!

By comparison, Gustav's fortunes in Europe were rapidly falling, and Elizabeth thought she was beginning to understand why that should be so. The Lesja Range had been mined empty. Oh, there was no doubt that Gustav Rolfson would have been rich, given his European interests alone, but the *source* of that wealth was drying up. The future of Rolfson Industries lay in America.

"First thing I would do," observed Harald's father laconically, "is sell off that Minnesota Mesabi Mining operation."

Thainson and Rolfson, Tillstrom and Norstrem, Dittersdahl and Kayrslatter looked at Fardahl as if he were mad, or at least the befogged nobleman he was.

"In America," Thorsen offered diplomatically, "they are just getting started on iron mining. From the look of it, no greater deposit has ever been found, quite likely never will be found, upon the face of the earth. He who controls the Mesabi controls the next hundred years of construction. Gustav and a few others are just beginning to fight for mining rights. Or, rather, Gustav *was* beginning to fight . . ."

"Who are the others?" Elizabeth asked.

"The others?" replied Thorsen.

"Yes. The other men who are interested in getting hold of all that iron. Who are they?"

Thorsen shrugged. "One fellow by the name of Granger, James J. Granger. And a second man known to your uncle as Gunnarson . . ."

"Gunnarson!" cried Elizabeth, not able to restrain herself.

Everyone stared at her. Harald jumped in surprise.

"You have heard of him?" Thorsen was asking.

Elizabeth saw that Thea was looking at her in an odd manner.

Best not to betray too much here. She did not even know

143

half of what was going on. "I . . . I thought I might have," she said lamely.

"Then if you will be so kind as to permit me to conclude . . ." Thorsen oozed.

Very little of the will remained to be read. Thea had been bequeathed everything, right down to the interest in Minnesota Mesabi Mining. Moreover, she had control over Elizabeth, as her legal guardian, at least for a little while.

"How are you feeling?" Harald was asking Elizabeth anxiously, as Rolfson stacked the papers neatly and prepared to return them to his briefcase. Other eyes were on her too, as if she might faint. Even Thea Thorsdatter glanced over inquiringly.

"I feel fine," Elizabeth told her presumed future husband. "Mr. Thorsen, wait," she said, getting to her feet.

She could see the solicitor brace himself. Now he expected her angry outburst, her accusations, her tears.

"Yes, Elizabeth?"

"Sir, I question the authenticity of that will," she said coolly. "In Switzerland, just prior to his death, Uncle Gustav told me what his will specified, and what he told me bears precious little similarity to what you have just read here today."

Lars Thorsen lost at least three shades of color in the space of a second. Thea Thorsdatter, in the same amount of time, gained five shades.

"You poor desperate girl," snarled Thea.

"I am neither poor nor desperate," Elizabeth shot back. "I say that will is not authentic, and I intend to contest it."

"Contest it?" sputtered Rolfson. "How do you know . . . what do you know of things such as that?"

"I did not spend my time at St. Ada's embroidering slipcovers and learning how to walk," she answered. "Uncle Gustav said he had a 'plan' for me, and so he encouraged me to study. Perhaps it was good that I took his advice."

"Now let's talk this over calmly," Thainson said.

"Let cool heads prevail," agreed Dittersdahl.

"Oh, dear, oh my goodness," mourned Harald Fardahl, beginning to see just what aid Elizabeth might ask of him.

"Let us all calm down," declared Thea, smiling and surprisingly calm. "This is much ado over very little, don't you see?"

"But Madame," protested Herr Kayrslatter, "I hardly think that judgment does justice . . ."

Thea lifted a hand and waved away his Teutonic concern. "Much ado about *nothing*," she amended. "No minor may bring suit in our courts unless he or she is sponsored by a person who has reached majority."

Thorsen heartily affirmed this sanguine statute.

"Unless there are any further questions," Thorsen called out, "I declare this proceeding ended."

Thea invited everyone to go back to the dining room, where a snack of herring and caviar, smoked salmon and pickled eggs, had been laid out, along with icy aquavit. There was to be a celebration. Scarcely looking in Elizabeth's direction, everybody left the library, and left her there. Only Harald Fardahl remained behind. He did not seem to want to, really, but he did not seem to have the courage to leave, either.

"It's all for the best, Elizabeth," he kept saying, "it's all for the best."

She turned to him, and gave him the warmest smile she could summon.

"Harald," she asked sweetly, "how old did you say you were?"

3

Thea may win, Elizabeth told herself, *but she is going to know she's been in a fight.*

Berobed and bewigged, the King's magistrate strode into the trial chamber, climbed a short flight of wooden steps, and took his seat behind the high bench. "The matter of Rolfson versus Thorsdatter will now commence," he said in a bored voice, looking at some papers before him. "Will counsel please approach me?"

Lars Thorsen got up and shuffled to the magistrate's perch. His red beard was showing streaks of gray now. Elizabeth smiled. Thorsen had earned the gray. Just behind Lars Thorsen, and a little to his left, walked Bjorn Tennerson, Elizabeth's representative. Bjorn was barely out of university, a feisty little fellow with a nose as sharp as his tongue. He was the only lawyer in Norway who would take Elizabeth's case; and the fact that he risked fighting for her at all was due to Harald Fardahl.

There were not too many people in the courtroom, and Elizabeth thought she knew why. Whether or not she won the case over Gustav's will, Thea and Lars would not want known the extent to which they had colluded with each other. *Nor*, reasoned Elizabeth, *will they want others to see how they are going to have to lie in this court.*

She was certain they would lie about everything.

Hadn't they done so already?

None of the Rolfson executives could be counted in

attendance today, except for Alois Smedley of Chicago, Illinois, in the United States. Smedley had been summoned across the Atlantic by Bjorn Tennerson, not as a witness on Elizabeth's behalf particularly. "I don't think you can trust anyone, Elizabeth," Tennerson had said. Smedley was present since, as Rolfson's longtime executive officer in Chicago, he presumably knew the entire picture regarding American operations. Smedley was as sleek and slick as his black oiled-down hair.

Harald Fardahl sat on a bench near Elizabeth.

Bjorn and Lars Thorsen had now concluded their sotto voce conference with the magistrate, a conversation having to do with procedure. Lars went back to his seat, and Bjorn Tennerson sat down beside Elizabeth.

"How do things appear?" she asked him, just a trifle anxiously.

He shrugged, but there was a kind of enthusiasm even in this pedestrian gesture. "This is my first case, and I don't intend to lose it," he said cheerfully. "No sense worrying about it. Lars Thorsen and Thea have the will in their possession, an actual document, and that's a very powerful persuader. We have nothing but suspicion, based on the word of a dead man whose word was not very good even when he was alive. Our only chance lies in unearthing the other will."

"The other will?" asked Harald Fardahl, leaning forward to confer with them. "What other will?"

"It's this way," Tennerson explained. "If the will Lars Thorsen possesses, the one leaving everything to Thea, is indeed forged, then what became of the true one that Gustav signed?"

"Lars and Thea would have destroyed it," answered Elizabeth.

"I don't think they'd take that risk," Bjorn stated.

"What risk?" Fardahl asked, wondering.

Then the magistrate banged his gavel, called upon King

and Country, Truth and Justice, and invited Bjorn Tennerson to step forward and make his case.

"My client's position is quite simple, Excellency," the little lawyer declared, striding before the bench with such assurance that it seemed he had been practicing for years. "Her uncle, Gustav Rolfson, recently died. He had verbally assured her that she would be left with a significant amount of his property, to wit, his land, goods, domiciles, and investments in America. However, when the will was read, she was left virtually nothing. It is her contention that the will is a fraud, that it is forged, and that it is the result of criminal conspiracy on the part of the defendants here seated, Lars Thorsen and Thea Thorsdatter. She seeks to have the present will declared null and void, and the restitution of what that fraudulent will has taken from her. You have a copy of the spurious will, Excellency, do you not?"

The magistrate scowled and looked down at his bench. He nodded. "How do you expect to prove this is a forged will?" he asked doubtfully. "It seems in order to me, down to the signature."

Lars Thorsen could not contain a small smirk of triumph.

"To begin," Tennerson said, "I shall call to the witness stand Mr. Alois Smedley."

Smedley, the American, stepped forward and swore to tell the truth. He had sharp, black eyes, and he regarded everyone with a mixture of suspicion and amusement. Elizabeth did not trust him, because of his sneaky smile and shifty eyes, but he was exactly the type of man who would have appealed to Gustav Rolfson. Perhaps he was adept in business and management.

"What do you do as a profession, Mr. Smedley?" Bjorn Tennerson asked.

"I am chief executive for Rolfson Industries in America."

At Tennerson's request, Smedley told of all the companies he had managed for Gustav Rolfson.

"And how would you judge the current state of those businesses, Mr. Smedley?"

"They are in excellent condition, sir."

Elizabeth looked over at Thea, who had said the American operations were in sad shape. Had Thea lied in order to give Elizabeth the impression that she would not be losing very much under the terms of the doctored will?

"How well did you know Gustav Rolfson?" Bjorn asked the American.

"Not . . . not well at all, in a personal sense. Mr. Rolfson believed in keeping a distance between himself and his employees. I was better acquainted with his business strategies, as I had to be in order to carry out his directives."

"So I would be correct in assuming that Gustav Rolfson did meet with you with some regularity, at least when he was in America, to discuss and plan and give direction to his enterprises?"

"Oh, yes, sir."

"Did he ever mention to you what he planned to do with his operations in the event of his death?"

"Yes, sir, he did."

"Would you relate his words for the benefit of this court?"

"I certainly shall. Mr. Rolfson told me he intended to leave everything to his niece, and that I would be called upon to train her."

"That is impossible!" cried Lars Thorsen, on his feet now. "In any event, this is total hearsay. There is absolutely no documentation to back it up . . ."

"Counsel will have opportunity in due course to question this witness," the magistrate ruled. "Mr. Tennerson, you may continue."

"Did your employer ever *write* you to the effect that Elizabeth Rolfson would be his beneficiary?"

"No, sir," said Smedley, "but I did receive a letter from him this past April, shortly before his death, indicating that he and Miss Rolfson would cross to America together. But then he died and . . ."

"Thank you, Mr. Smedley. Did you bring that letter with you?"

"Yes, I have it here." From his waistcoat pocket, Smedley took an envelope and handed it to Tennerson, who carried it to the peering magistrate.

"Inspect it closely, Excellency," said Bjorn acidly, looking at Lars Thorsen. "We must be sure the signature is authentic."

Reddening, Lars rose and came forward to view the letter himself, which the magistrate permitted him to do.

"This means nothing," he declared contemptuously, "except that Rolfson was taking his niece on a trip to America."

"Yes," countered Tennerson, "but I am attempting to show a pattern here of circumstance and intent on the part of the deceased. First, he *tells* his niece what she is to inherit. Then he *writes* his key officer that he and his niece are coming to Chicago. He has previously *told* this officer, Mr. Smedley, not only that he intends to bequeath his properties and business to her, but also that he, Mr. Smedley, will have to train her in business in the event of Rolfson's death . . ."

"Still circumstances," snapped Thorsen. "Nothing more to it than that."

"I suggest you leave that judgment to me," barked the magistrate, in some heat. "Lest you have forgotten, I have the sole authority to decide this matter."

Thorsen blanched. Arrogantly, he had overstepped his bounds, and he knew it. Even Thea glared at him when he shuffled back to his seat and sat down.

Tennerson thanked Smedley and excused him. When the American came by Elizabeth's chair, he gave her a wide ingratiating smile, but his eyes were cold. Something about him chilled her to the core, although his testimony had been most helpful to her case. Since Smedley had arrived just days ago, Elizabeth had not met with him yet, in addition to which Bjorn had stressed the impropriety of such a meeting prior to the court's decision on the will.

"Have you any other witnesses?" the magistrate wanted to know.

"Only one, Excellency. I call Lars Thorsen to the stand."

"What?" huffed the red-bearded solicitor in surprise. He was a defendant in the suit, and he was representing Thea. But protocol in this type of case required his acquiescence to such a call, and he took the stand, frowning formidably.

Bjorn Tennerson was quiet and disarming now. "In your long capacity as Gustav Rolfson's legal advisor, Mr. Thorsen, did you sometimes have occasion to effect his signature on business papers and such?"

"Why, of course I did. You ought to know that this is standard practice. An important man cannot sign every little thing . . ."

"Perhaps not his own will, either?"

Thorsen flared. "That, sir, is a damnable lie! Excellency, I protest . . ."

"You have been protesting quite a lot, haven't you, sir? Please be so kind as to answer the questions."

"I have but one more query, Excellency," Tennerson said, bowing toward the bench. "I should like to ask Mr. Thorsen whether he or his codefendant or any person known to and/or directed by them did either conceal or destroy the true will of Gustav Rolfson?"

So recently flustered, now Lars Thorsen exploded yet again, and Elizabeth recalled Bjorn's remark about the "other will." Was the diminutive solicitor on the right track?

Thorsen, however, vigorously upheld the authenticity of the will he had read in the library.

"I did not ask you whether that will was *legitimate*," Tennerson clarified. "I asked you if there is or was *another* will, the real one?"

"This is ridiculous," spat Thorsen. "Of course not," he added.

"That's all, Excellency," Tennerson said. "I rest my client's case."

Thorsen was stunned at the brevity of Tennerson's gambit, but attributed it to inexperience, if not incompetence. Soon he and Thea were chattering away together, pleased as punch.

For the next three days, in fact, Thorsen was in high good spirits as he paraded before the court a long array of witnesses. There were men and women to attest that Rolfson had, on countless occasions, told them of his intention to leave his worldly goods to his beloved Thea. More men and women came forward to swear that old Gustav had personally drafted parts of his will in their very presence. Lastly came three business employees and a ship's steward who vowed that Gustav, upon boarding ship for his journey to Switzerland, had worried about Elizabeth. "How will the poor girl react when I tell her Thea is getting everything?" Gustav was quoted as having said.

Through all this, Harald Fardahl fretted and Elizabeth herself went from anger to futility and back to anger again. Lies, lies, lies! The magistrate got so tired of listening to the ceaseless chorus of testimony, he fairly fell into a snooze at the bench. Even cold, imperturbable Alois Smedley was moved to approach Elizabeth.

"I certainly hope you win this, my dear," he assured her, with a thin, lopsided smile, "because if you lose, then so do I."

Elizabeth, occupied with the trial, did not give his remark much thought just then.

At long last, Thorsen rested his case.

"Do you wish to rebut?" the magistrate asked Bjorn Tennerson.

"No, Excellency," responded the little lawyer, his sharp

nose sniffing the courtroom air. "I should just like to recall Lars Thorsen to the stand."

When Thorsen had taken the stand, Tennerson fixed him with his gaze. "I have only one question," he said, "one I asked earlier: Where is the real will, since this one is a fraud?"

Lars Thorsen lost control of himself. *"There is no real will!"* he shrieked.

"You ought to have told us that three days ago," observed Tennerson drily.

Even the magistrate laughed.

On the morning of the fourth day, no longer amused, that luminary mounted to his bench to hand down a decision.

"Were I as wise as Solomon with the mothers and their babes," he began, "this would be easy. But I have been thinking of Solomon, indeed I have. For there are elements in his experience that apply to this case. A live will and a dead one? Perhaps. Who knows? But, in spite of my human frailty, it falls to me to judge. All I know is what has transpired in my courtroom. On the one hand, we have a young plaintiff who avers that she has a right to approximately half a legacy, which is being nefariously withheld from her. On the other hand, we have two defendants who maintain all of the inheritance is theirs, and who have mounted a magnificent campaign . . ."

Lars Thorsen swelled with pride. Thea Thorsdatter was wary; she did not like the direction of the magistrate's words.

". . . to prove their point. I have, I assure you, puzzled and pondered on this matter, and I have reached a decision. What our American, Mr. Smedley here, has told us about Gustav Rolfson must be judged as true. I myself had the acquaintance of the deceased, as did most men of affairs in Oslo. And Gustav Rolfson revealed of himself and of his plans only that which was necessary. It is unlikely—it is in fact unbelievable—that Rolfson would have told everyone from chimney sweep to upstairs maid what he intended to state in his testament."

Elizabeth felt a surge of good blood into her heart, and she turned to see her once-reluctant champion, Harald Fardahl, pressing away a tear.

Bjorn Tennerson showed nothing. He had the vague boredom of a man who has done an easy job well.

"And so," the magistrate concluded, "unless there exists another will, the true will, of Gustav Rolfson, with its specifics, I cannot but judge the document in question here to be false, and to award all of Gustav Rolfson's worldly goods to his niece, Elizabeth."

Harald Fardahl sprang forward and hugged Elizabeth, Elizabeth hugged him back and then hugged Bjorn, and then they all hugged one another.

"Excellency! Excellency!" Thea was shouting.

The room gradually quieted.

"You may speak," the magistrate told Thea.

Clearly discomfited, Thea screwed up her strong will. She projected her sensuality, the exotic effect of which was not lost on the court. "I am a frail woman," she pleaded, "and I was misled by this man"—she pointed to the hapless Thorsen—"who endeavored to lead me by strategies I did not understand, and about which he lied to me. Yes," she cried, "there is another will, the *real* will, and it leaves all of the European property to *me*, and the American holdings to . . . to that girl." Thea pointed abruptly at Elizabeth, as much a dismissal as a designation. Thea would retain her rightful share, at least, and Elizabeth could go and be damned for all Thea cared. "And I will bring this document to the court."

"No, no!" Lars Thorsen was begging, trying to pull her down, trying to stop her from speaking.

"Yes, you shall bring it!" boomed the magistrate.

"And will I get my share?" Thea implored, relaxing a little.

"Of course," the official assured her, "you will receive it as soon as the will is judged authentic and as soon as you are released from prison."

"Prison? *Prison?*" Thea staggered on her strong, splendid legs.

"Oh, I *told* you to keep your mouth shut," wailed Lars Thorsen.

"Conspiracy to commit felony and fraud!" declared Bjorn Tennerson. "I suspected it all along. You would not destroy the true will simply because, if you lost the contest over the false one, there would be no document to show your rights to anything at all."

"Solomon was actually *quite* wise," mused the magistrate. "In the Bible, the mother of the dead child behaved extravagantly, and in this case so did Thorsen and his companion. It was the excessive nature of their strategy that made me suspicious."

Pale and shaken, Lars Thorsen approached the bench and commenced bargaining so that he and Thea would not be consigned to prison forthwith. He needed time to prepare for the trial, he babbled; he needed time . . .

The magistrate awarded him a month to prepare, but held out little encouragement that a life of freedom and wealth waited.

"I must censure you, sir," he informed the trembling Thorsen. "You, a man of law, stooped to steal the rightful property of a lovely young girl. You are a disgrace to the law, to Norway, and to yourself."

"Yes, sir, yes, sir," Thorsen bleated.

Slumped in her chair, that magnificent body limp and impotent, Thea Thorsdatter seemed to be in a faint. Only the random, spasmodic flicker of her eyelids belied the appearance of unconsciousness.

When the magistrate had withdrawn and everyone was preparing to leave the courtroom, Alois Smedley stepped over to Elizabeth and offered his congratulations.

"I suggest we meet as soon as practicable," he said, "in order to discuss the general situation you will encounter when you reach America. I am at your service. As my new employer, your wish is my command."

He gave her his smooth, oily smile while speaking, and even as Elizabeth murmured her thanks for his good wishes, she could not keep herself from thinking that Smedley reminded her of a particularly obnoxious snake. Yet—she had already faced and accepted the fact—she needed him. Animals of the world! Gustav, with his wolf's eyes and his long flat vulpine nose, had taken as his chargé d'affaires a sleek serpent who smiled instead of hissing, and who proffered fealty with smooth words and a cold heart.

"I'm so glad you won this case," Smedley was telling her. "You'll never know how much, truly. Now, let us meet as soon as possible. I must get back to the United States and watch out for Granger and Starbane."

4

"Granger and *Starbane*?" inquired Elizabeth, when she held her formal business meeting with Smedley two days after the trial had ended.

"Yes, Ma'am," the executive replied. "J. J. Granger and Eric Starbane, both Minnesotans. They are battling us for mineral leasing rights in the Mesabi Range of northern Minnesota. That's what our Minnesota Mesabi Mining subsidiary is established to handle . . ."

Smedley went on, explaining how the interlocking Rolfson companies were organized, with headquarters in Chicago, Illinois, and corporate tentacles stretching all across America. Elizabeth listened with one ear. She had already learned most of what he was telling her through a detailed reading of materials in Uncle Gustav's Oslo offices. Yes, she listened to Smedley, but her mind was on something else. Someone else. *Gunnarson*. On the evening that Lars Thorsen read the false will, had not one of the executives —no, it had been the solicitor himself—told her that Granger and *Gunnarson* were the primary competitors in the Mesabi? And was this the same Gunnarson who had killed her mother and father? What was going on here? Who was Starbane?

The business conference was being held in Alois Smedley's stateroom on board the S.S. *Valkyrie*, which even as they conferred was getting up steam for passage to America. Winter passage. Cold going.

The stateroom had been chosen to please Smedley's taste. It was the very best the *Valkyrie* had to offer, with inlaid parquet flooring, teakwood moldings and doors, a grand mahogany desk of the Imperial style, and a small dining table of the same wood and type. The outer chamber, in which Elizabeth, Smedley, and Bjorn Tennerson conversed, seemed like a fine room in a great house, with only the portholes to give it away. Adjacent to the stateroom were Smedley's bedchamber, with a canopied four-poster anchored to the floor, and a grand bath with a tub of ivory-colored porcelain and gold fixtures.

"And when *do* you plan to arrive in Chicago?" she heard Smedley asking. She had the feeling he had already asked the question a time or two.

"Oh . . . oh, I'm sorry, I was thinking of . . . something. I plan to sail later this year. There are so many things to deal with here, now that Thorsen and Thea will probably go to prison . . ."

Bjorn Tennerson nodded.

". . . and so I shan't be in America until early next year," Elizabeth reiterated.

"Miss Rolfson will be in direct contact with you at all times," Tennerson said pointedly, "and we shall both expect a constant flow of messages."

"What if we receive, let us say, a lucrative offer to sell this or that company?" Smedley asked.

"Do you have any particular operation in mind?" Elizabeth shot back, more heatedly than she had intended.

"Oh, no, not at all." Smedley smiled. "I speak hypothetically, for my own information, you might say."

"I see," she said.

"If you have such offers, forward them here to Oslo," Bjorn told him.

Smedley was of another mind. "Sometimes one must act on the spur of the moment, in order to get the best advantage."

His voice had a subtly threatening note in it now, a tone Elizabeth did not like at all. It was another of the sinister nuances Smedley had learned from Uncle Gustav.

"You will take no major actions until I reach America," Elizabeth heard herself say.

Oh, my God, she had spoken too loudly! She had been too theatrically authoritative, thus revealing her own insecurity. The men—Smedley for certain and perhaps even Bjorn—would laugh at her now.

She braced herself for the ridicule of male snickers, but did not hear any.

Smedley's dark face had grown darker, and Bjorn Tennerson was regarding her with admiration.

"All major matters are to be held in abeyance until I arrive in Chicago," Elizabeth went on, pressing her advantage, "but before you sail, I must clear up something."

"Whatever you say, Ma'am," Smedley responded, thoroughly ingratiating again, as if their exchange, their preliminary test of wills, had never taken place. Yet it had. *I shall have trouble with him in America*, Elizabeth realized. And, she admitted, *I am not at all sure I can handle him as easily there as I did here*.

"Have you," she asked Smedley then, "ever heard of a man called Gunnarson? A man who may be after the same iron ore Rolfson Industries wants?"

"Gunnarson?" Smedley was genuinely puzzled.

"Uncle Gustav never mentioned a man named Gunnarson to you?"

Smedley thought it over. "No, I'm sure he didn't."

"Anything important, Elizabeth?" Bjorn interjected.

"I don't . . . I guess not," she answered. Yet it was not only important, it was also mystifying. Gustav had gone on and on about Gunnarson, the murderer, and Gustav's Norwegian officers seemed to think that same man, or another with the same name, was challenging Gustav in the American iron business. But Alois Smedley, who ought to know America if anyone did, had no knowledge of Gunnarson at all!

"Something you want me to do about it?" Smedley asked, with just the faintest trace of sarcasm.

"No. No, I think not."

The ship's whistle blew then, a high piercing blast that filled Oslo harbor and echoed off the far mountains.

"Time to sail," Smedley said, standing as if to dismiss them.

"What do you think?" Elizabeth asked Bjorn Tennerson, after the *Valkyrie* had sailed off into the February bleakness of the Skagerrak.

"About what?" The little lawyer seemed wistful. "I was actually thinking that I ought to go to America too."

"Oh, would you?" she exclaimed with delight.

"I can't right now. Parents. Too old to go. Responsibilities. Someday maybe."

She nodded, understanding.

"You're worried about Smedley, aren't you?" he said.

"Yes. Other things too."

"It is my profession to make words, but I can also listen to them."

Elizabeth felt a tightness in her throat. Her past, her youth, which had flown so quickly, was gone. She stood upon the awful precipice of her future. She was unafraid of that future; she welcomed it. But she knew keen anguish which, purified and distilled to its essence, emerged now in six rending words.

"I don't know who I am!" she told Bjorn Tennerson.

And then the tears came. Bjorn, who had thought that she was upset because of her exchange with Smedley, was taken aback for a moment. He had no idea what she was talking about. So he took her to a snug, warm dramshop that he knew, a rude place frequented by workingmen. Only a few people were there on this February afternoon, and that was good. The fire burned steadily, lighting the gloom, warming the room, and after Bjorn had gotten her to sip a couple of hot brandies, Elizabeth felt better. She had been talking through her tears, and he had listened. Now she fell silent. She had told him everything, everything she remembered from the dream-vision of the white house on the river right up to this present day, this very dramshop with fire roaring. She also told him about Lance.

"I cannot imagine what might have happened," she said tremulously. "When I was with him, it was . . . it was the sweetest, most overpowering feeling I have ever known. I cannot hope to know anything greater. He asked where he could contact me, and I gave him my address here in Oslo, but there has not been a word." She paused, and dabbed at her eyes with a silk handkerchief. "I know he would have written, if he were at all able to do so. And, if not . . ."

"You said that he had to go back to America to deal with something that was dangerous?" Bjorn asked.

"I try not to think of that," Elizabeth said. "I couldn't bear it if calamity has befallen him. God wouldn't give us a taste of paradise, would he? And then pull it away? He wouldn't offer us the experience of ecstasy, just to torment us by withdrawing it?"

"I hope not," Bjorn said.

"Well, that is what it seems to me now. Even if I do not know my own past, it would have been possible to live into the future with Lance. He would have been more than enough. But now I don't have him, either. I have got to find him, or he me . . ."

"You will," said Bjorn, to soothe and console her, "I know you will. I don't claim to know much about God's plans, but no one with a love as strong as yours will be allowed to remain apart from her beloved for too long."

"Oh, do you really think so?"

"Yes," Bjorn said, "I do. There, that makes two of us who have faith that you will find your Mr. Tallworth. The faith of two people is three times stronger than the faith of one."

"Three times stronger? How so?"

"Its effect is enhanced by the unity of believers."

Elizabeth smiled. Bjorn was so comradely, so encouraging, so sweet.

"You know the thing you desire above all," he told her, "the one goal which will shape and define your life, and that is already more than most people ever have. Destiny lies before you, and you *will* find your past again."

Elizabeth drank brandy, wiped her eyes, and began to feel a little embarrassed about her emotional display.

"Harald Fardahl, the nobleman's son, would marry you in a minute," Bjorn said, not to slight Harald but to cheer Elizabeth, "and you could have many others, with but a smile and a delicate glance. Oh, it's true, and you know it. So stop dwelling on the past. If it is meant that you discover hidden things, then you will. I think there is some kind of plan for all of us, and if we do not make too many mistakes along the way, we all find out what that plan is."

"I hope so," Elizabeth affirmed. "Oh, I hope it so much."

Lars Thorsen and Thea Thorsdatter were tried for felonious fraud and found guilty.

"I worked so long, so hard," Thea mourned. "I pretended to love Gustav, that animal, and then pretended to love Thorsen, that despicable weakling. Why must I go to prison? What have I done? Why can't I be rich too, like everyone else?"

But in spite of her appreciation of wealth, she was sentenced to ten years. She would be fifty-five years old upon her release. Her only consolation came with the knowledge that she would not be incarcerated in one of the harsh old-time jails, where the food was crude, the chains harsher, and beatings not infrequent, but rather in a new institution stressing the spiritual betterment of its inmates.

Lars Thorsen committed suicide on the night prior to his imprisonment by taking aquavit liberally spiked with arsenic. Elizabeth was sorry, but with Thea in prison and Thorsen's life concluded, Elizabeth turned to settling her affairs in Norway. Passage was booked on the magisterial S.S. *Odin*, the fleet new flagship of the transatlantic line. Given good weather conditions, she would arrive in New York in early or mid-January 1886.

Time passed quickly, what with seeing to the house and arranging baggage and material for her American voyage. Elizabeth was kept on edge too by a series of messages from Smedley in Chicago. She had best make haste, he kept writing. There was an American saying, he wrote, which adjured one to "strike while the iron is hot." The iron, he maintained, was sizzling.

But he was tantalizingly lacking in specifics. "It would be dangerous to go into particulars via correspondence," he wrote.

A Gustav Rolfson *manqué* to the soles of his expensive, high-topped boots, all he lacked was a dueling scar.

As her departure from Norway drew nearer and nearer, time seemed to accelerate for Elizabeth. Days flashed by, days filled with a hundred and one details. She began to realize what leaving meant: a complete break in the pattern of her life. America had been her birthplace, but Europe —Norway and then Switzerland—had seen her grow to maturity. She was leaving *home*, perhaps forever, and this knowledge struck her far more profoundly than had her departure from St. Ada's. Uncle Gustav's great house, whose rooms she had explored as a little girl, the corridors of which she knew like the back of her hand, would soon be transformed from reality to memory.

One gloomy day toward the end of 1885, with autumn long gone and the Christmas holidays still in the future, Elizabeth felt a bit of a cold coming on, and did not make her customary appearance at the Rolfson offices. Tennerson could see to whatever was necessary, or dispatch Harald Fardahl to handle this errand or that. But by late afternoon, she felt better. The evening stretched before her, an empty vista, trackless and drab.

"Would you like tea served here in your room?" inquired Ellison.

"No, thank you. I shan't have anything until dinner, and I do hope it's something light."

"Oh, yes indeed."

"Thank you, Ellison."

Elizabeth got out of bed and put on her robe. The air was gray and the city was gray and the sea was gray. She was gray, too, and so was the big house. Restless, she left her room and walked down the corridor, inspecting the house, taking a look at it as if for a final time. Gustav Rolfson had spared no expense to furnish his home, and even along the walls here in the hallway there were illuminated Russian icons, ornate wood carvings, and the splendid, if slightly grotesque, oils of Selezi, the Italian, and Yassir Bentpudlian, the modest Armenian.

Looking at the house she was leaving, Elizabeth wondered about the place in which she would live. Wouldn't it be fine to ship the best things here to America? No, she couldn't do that, it wouldn't be right. But the thought was intriguing, and she felt spirited for the first time all day. Descending half a flight, she entered Gustav's private gallery, in which he kept objets d'art he had considered too rare for the eyes of common guests and lesser men. A wealth of talent and hoarded beauty filled the room, from African statuary to Eygptian vases fully four thousand years old. Attenuated torsos of Greek models dead for millennia stood upon pedestals, and what Gustav had always claimed to be the true tapesty of Heloise hung on the far wall.

Just off the gallery was a combination workroom-storeroom, dusty but otherwise neat, with a workbench, stacks of frames, hooks, lighting fixtures, and a miscellany of random tools and furnishings. Lesser objects had been consigned here, and those replaced by more recent and more portentous acquisitions. With idle curiosity, Elizabeth examined a stack of paintings over which a canvas veil had been tossed. She removed the canvas and began to study the paintings, setting each one aside as she finished looking at it. There was a pedestrian still life of wine, fruit, and cheese, a painting of two girls in a canoe, and three formal portraits of men ferocious enough in aspect to have been Rolfson ancestors. And then there was, suddenly, the portrait of a woman so beautiful Elizabeth fairly gasped to behold her face. She would scarcely have been more stricken had she stumbled into the arms of a seraph. The woman's eyes were large and deep blue, with the mystic depths of a fjord in winter. Her wide fine cheekbones shaped an oval face, an exquisite face of strength mingled with delicate tenderness. A high-piled mass of thick, sun-colored hair conveyed an impression of gentility, yet left a hint of imminent abandon, of a wild spirit held in check until the time of release should come. Elizabeth could not take her eyes off the face for many minutes, and when she did it was to note the artist's signature. "Phipps, 1863."

Anyone at all familiar with painting knew that Percy Phipps, the American, was perhaps the most sought-after portraitist on either side of the Atlantic. But who on earth was this woman and what was her picture doing in Uncle Gustav's storeroom? Certainly, given the quality of the work, it ought to have been displayed along with the other prizes. How long had it been languishing here, under the canvas shroud? Elizabeth noted the date once more. 1863. It seemed sad to reflect that more than twenty-one years had gone by since this beauty had sat for Phipps. And yet she was timeless, immortal, captured by art.

Elizabeth gazed at the picture for a long time, admiring both the woman's face and the artist's workmanship. But the light was fading, so she carried the portrait out of the storeroom, through the gallery, and down the corridor to the main staircase, where she summoned Ellison with a tug on the bellpull.

"Ready for some chicken broth and bread, are you, Miss Elizabeth?" asked the old butler, coming to the bottom of the staircase.

"No, Ellison, I'm not ready to eat yet. I summoned you because . . ."

She had intended to call him upstairs to look at the picture, but her sudden perception of his age compelled a change of mind.

". . . because I wanted you to take a look at this portrait," Elizabeth continued, coming down the steps toward him. "I declare I've never seen a woman so lovely."

Ellison's face was carefully blank when Elizabeth reached the bottom of the staircase. He appeared to have braced himself for an obscure form of confrontation, and his glance was studied and casual as he looked at the painting in Elizabeth's hands.

"Do you know this woman?" she asked.

Ellison hesitated, and Elizabeth realized the incorruptible old butler was trying to decide whether or not to lie. Since the painting had been made two decades ago, she quickly altered her query.

"*Did* you know this woman?"

"Yes," he said. He swallowed and coughed nervously, avoiding her eyes, clearly caught in a situation he would much rather have evaded. But he was, at base, too honest to lie.

"That was Miss Kristin," he said.

"Kristin!" exclaimed Elizabeth. The name Gustav had uttered in Geneva.

"I don't know if she is still alive, or anything about her anymore. I last saw her in 1865."

"Where?"

"It was in New York."

166

Elizabeth made some quick calculations. Based on what Uncle Gustav had told her of his life and travels, he had lived in New York at that time. Ellison, as a servant, would have been with him there. And Percy Phipps, the portraitist, was an American.

Sensing his reluctance, and not wishing to put him on the spot further, Elizabeth altered her approach.

"You are hesitant to talk about this, aren't you, Ellison?"

The butler nodded.

"Why?"

"Because I was enjoined to secrecy, Miss Elizabeth."

The situation was growing more fascinating by the moment. The picture of a mysterious beauty, and a vow of secrecy as well. How much else lay buried in time?

"Did Uncle Gustav demand that promise of you?"

"Yes, he did."

"Again, might I ask why?"

"I presume it was because of his embarrassment, Miss Elizabeth."

Embarrassment? Elizabeth paused, looking once more at the face in the painting. "Ellison," she prodded, "you told me what Lars Thorsen and Thea were planning against me. I'm grateful, but in a sense your telling me about them transgressed the private bonds of your profession. Couldn't you possibly tell me just a little more about the woman in this portrait?"

He wanted to tell her. She knew that much. But there was a difference, which he explained.

"Thorsdatter and the solicitor," Ellison said, "meant to do you actual harm, and I could not countenance that."

"Then no harm can come to me from this woman?" asked Elizabeth.

"I honestly do not know," he answered, after a long moment of reflection. "I do not see how harm could possibly come about. As I said, I do not even know if Miss

Kristin is still alive. But when time is disturbed, who knows what consequences might ensue?"

"Thank you, Ellison. I respect that." Already Elizabeth was wondering of whom she might inquire next.

"Thank *you*, Miss Elizabeth. Would you care to dine presently?"

"Yes, that will be fine. I shall dress and come down shortly."

Elizabeth took the painting back to her room, and thought about the woman as she dressed. Given her confusion and lack of knowledge regarding her own past, the first wild thought that crossed her mind was that, somehow, this striking beauty was her own mother.

A white house on a hill by the river. Coming down the stairs. A boy wanting to play. A man who lifted me to his shoulders. Another dark man with a profile such as Lance had had. And a woman with golden hair . . .

No. How could it be? She took the painting to the mirror and examined the reflected image next to her own. They had blue eyes, both women in the glass, but the mysterious beauty looked upon the world with eyes of darkness. Elizabeth's, to the contrary, almost glittered from within, especially when she laughed. Both women had well-molded cheekbones and distinctive features, Elizabeth's being less oval and slightly more delicate of line. And Elizabeth's sun-touched auburn hair was her own.

It did not seem possible that she was this woman's daughter.

Elizabeth felt disappointed, though. Her old and familiar companion, the dream-vision, stood out at times with such lucidity that it seemed impossible she could have conceived it on her own. The essence of imagination, she knew, lay in reality far more than it did in whims and faery musings. Also contradicting her fleet hope of a bond with Phipps's prize—as well as negating the golden family in her dream —was Gustav Rolfson's dour version of Elizabeth's past.

The woman in the painting knew wealth and luxury. Ellison had known her in New York, he'd said. This could not be Hilda, wife of the debt-ridden Olav, who'd hurled herself in front of a gun in frontier Minnesota so many years ago.

When she went downstairs to dinner, Bjorn Tennerson and Harald Fardahl were waiting in the library. A message had been received from Smedley that very afternoon, in the mail pouch aboard the S.S. *Morgenstern*, or Morning Star, a German vessel just arrived in European waters from America. They wished to convey the contents of the letter to her, and discuss it. Since neither had plans for the evening, she asked them to dine with her. She had her broth and French bread, and the men cut heartily into juicy rare beef. Tennerson essayed the crux of Smedley's latest concern.

"This Mesabi Range business," he said, nodding to the servant for another goblet of Pinot Noir, "is truly heating up. What it amounts to is this: Rolfson Industries must set some strategy very soon, or else J. J. Granger and Eric Starbane will have the mineral rights all to themselves. Granger, Smedley reports, is unprincipled, devious, and ruthless to the core. Starbane, while a gentleman, is one of the most powerful men in the region. Smedley wants to know what to do."

Elizabeth spooned her broth, all the while regarding the roast beef with increasing appetite.

"It seems a way might be found," she offered, "to play Granger and Starbane off against each other?"

"Spoken like your uncle," said Harald Fardahl, laughing. "Blood will tell."

"I merely meant . . ." she began, in her own defense.

"Yes, and you are right," Tennerson said.

"What is the relationship between Granger and Starbane?" she asked. "Do we know this? What are the chances that they might form an alliance?"

"Never," said Tennerson. "According to Alois Smedley, their relationship is akin to that of two bull moose vying for the prize cow in the herd."

"Well," said Elizabeth then, "it seems Rolfson Industries might play the key role after all. And I am getting eager to sail!"

"The *Viking Serpent* has been refitted stem to stern," Fardahl commented. "I'm sure you'll have a good crossing."

The *Viking Serpent* was Gustav's oceangoing yacht, which had carried him to and from America many a time. Elizabeth had always intended to peruse the old logbooks for a record of Gustav's travels, but she had never found the time.

Dinner was completed with a serving of cherries and sweet cream, and the men rose to leave.

"One thing more before you go," Elizabeth said. She told a houseboy to bring down the Phipps painting and showed it to Bjorn and Harald.

"My goodness," exclaimed Fardahl in admiration. Bjorn let out a low murmur of undisguised appreciation.

"Who is she?" they asked in unison.

"I don't know." She told them how she had found the painting, how Ellison's reluctance to discuss it had served to whet her curiosity.

"Ask some of the other servants," Bjorn suggested.

"I doubt they'd be of much help. Most of them are quite young, in addition to which they've never been to America."

"1863, I see," observed Fardahl, noting the date on the painting.

"But I think this woman is Norwegian," Bjorn said. "There is a certain look. Thea might know," he added. "She, if anyone, was privy to as much of Rolfson's past as he felt moved to share. Why not ask her?"

"I shall. I must call on her at the prison before I sail, out of pity if nothing else. Although I must confess that I am loath to enter the place."

"Oh, it won't be that bad," Tennerson said encouragingly. "It is a modern prison of the new style."

"Still it is a prison," replied Elizabeth.

There were no high walls, nor was there sharp wire, but the formidable bulk of the gray stone building with iron bars on tall narrow windows made its function unmistakable. Elizabeth identified herself at the main entrance, a heavy iron gate with a small barred slot to communicate with the guards. Passing through this imposing barrier, she was led into the building. After passing two more intimidating gates, she was admitted to the office of the prison superintendent, a stout but hard-bodied woman, savage of eye.

"So you wish to see the prisoner Thorsdatter, do you?" she inquired, looking Elizabeth up and down as if she might be a felon herself.

"I was told it would be possible. That is, if it's no trouble . . ."

She hated the manner in which her voice faltered, but the very thought of being inside a place that existed to deprive people of freedom filled her with obscure terror, as if she herself had once been captive and powerless.

"Oh, it's no trouble," barked the superintendent, "no trouble at all. But I must tell you that the woman you are about to see is not quite the woman you knew."

"I'm . . . I'm afraid I don't understand."

"You will. Prisoner Thorsdatter is, how shall I put it, resisting the program designed for her spiritual betterment. It is a shame, but it is her own fault. You see, under the old ways, a person convicted and consigned here could expect one thing and one thing only. Punishment. *Harsh* punishment. But now, in these enlightened times a new philosophy is being employed. Rather than hard labor, or the withholding of food, we in the penal profession now attempt to bring convicts a greater knowledge of themselves, a sense of their own souls. Since they have committed crimes, there must be something in their natures that requires healing. But before evil can be healed, it must be identified. The only way such a success can be realized is through prayer and isolation."

Prayer? Thea Thorsdatter had never prayed in her life. And *isolation?* For a woman who thrived on the richness of her appetites, and on her relationships with others?

"Yes," said the superintendent, in response to Elizabeth's dubious expression, "this is the philosophy of the new way. Upon her arrival here, prisoner Thorsdatter was assigned to a small cell, there to reflect upon the perfidies of her past and thus come to a knowledge of her own failings. Through such knowledge comes wisdom, and from wisdom comes redemption. Once a week, once only, she is allowed to leave her cell and go to chapel to pray. Those who pray well, who give evidence of spiritual transformation, may eventually be released from the small cells."

"The next cells are larger?" Elizabeth asked.

"A little. It is a reward for spiritual improvement and self-knowledge. Eventually, the prisoner who behaves well may graduate to a cell with a window. Those who manifest true repentance for the evil acts that brought them here may, after a year or so, be allowed the company of other prisoners."

"They are permitted to see no one?" Elizabeth asked in astonishment.

"Only the guard who takes them, one at a time, to chapel. And the guard is forbidden to speak. Food is slid soundlessly into the cell through a slit in the door," the superintendent added. "This is the new way, and prisoner Thorsdatter is not responding well."

Such news did not surprise Elizabeth. What normal person would not be driven wild by such a regime?

"Before I take you to the prisoner," the superintendent

was saying, "I must ask you one thing. What is the purpose of your visit?"

"I am leaving for America," Elizabeth answered, "and I must ask her some questions."

"Such as?"

"About members of the family," Elizabeth temporized. "A great many Scandinavians have emigrated over the years. Perhaps Thea knows certain people who may be of help to me when I reach the new world."

The superintendent scowled, either doubting the worth of this intention or Thea's power to help. "All right, but I warned you," she decided, and led Elizabeth from her office, through more heavy, guarded gates, and down a long, long corridor with scores of locked doors narrowly spaced along the sides. Gloom pervaded. The sound of moans and sobs filled the air. "You are hearing the cries of those who are resisting their own impulses toward spiritual betterment," said the superintendent.

Then, far down the corridor, there rose a scream of hellish rage, followed by a long sob of despair and another wild shriek.

"We are nearing prisoner Thorsdatter's cell," the superintendent said.

Elizabeth was too horrified to reply.

Thea's next pathetic ululation was broken off when the superintendent rapped sharply on her cell door. Elizabeth heard a scrambling within, and then scratching, clawing sounds, like those of a trapped animal trying to get free.

"Thorsdatter! You have a visitor. Stand aside."

The scratching ceased, and the superintendent unlocked the door, easing it open.

Elizabeth stifled a cry of disbelief. Thea, clad in a faded smock and ragged felt boots without laces, stood in the middle of a room scarcely larger than a closet. There was no light, save for that which came in through cracks between the planking, and no furniture except a crude bunk on one wall. A thin blanket lay neatly folded upon it.

"The prisoners must not sit or lie down during daylight hours," explained the superintendent.

Thea was staring at Elizabeth as if she were an apparition from another world. As Elizabeth's eyes adjusted to the gloom, she noted long angry scars on the prisoner's cheeks.

"She savages herself in rage," said the superintendent. "Are you sure you wish to be alone with her?"

Elizabeth nodded.

"I'll be right outside," said the official, closing the door.

Now it was almost completely dark. Thea's eyes blazed, angry pinpoints of light.

"Thea, do you know me?" Elizabeth asked.

"Ah, Mother, I knew you'd come!"

Mother? Thea was mad.

"No, Thea, it's me, Elizabeth. Elizabeth Rolfson. Remember?"

Thea stepped forward and peered at Elizabeth's face. Her smock smelled of musk, and her breath of onions. "Ah, *Elizabeth!* Yes, I *know*! Oh, thank God you've come to get me out of here. Gustav must be angry at my disappearance."

Debating what to do, Elizabeth decided upon the truth. If Thea was truly gone in her mind, nothing could hurt. Certainly, the truth could do little damage now.

"Thea, Gustav is dead," she said.

"He is. Then who are you?"

This visit is hopeless, Elizabeth thought. Thea would be able to tell her nothing. Still, she was here and it was worth a try.

"Thea!" she said sharply. "Thea, I have something very important to ask you."

"Important?"

"The gallery in the house, Thea? Remember it?"

A long pause. "The gallery. Lovely things . . ."

"There is one picture, Thea, one picture of a woman. A beautiful blond woman, Thea. I found it under a canvas veil. It was painted by Percy Phipps in . . ."

"Yes!" hissed Thea. "It is *her*!"

So Thea did know something about the woman. "Kristin?" she prodded, using the name Ellison had provided.

"Kristin!" affirmed the prisoner. "Yes, and now you've come to get me out . . ." She seized Elizabeth's arm tightly, and shook it.

She had to keep Thea's mind on Kristin. "Did you know her, Thea? Did you know the woman in the painting?"

"What? What painting?"

"The painting of Kristin. In the gallery."

"The gallery. Lovely things . . ."

"Did Uncle Gustav know Kristin?" Elizabeth demanded, trying to pry loose Thea's fingers from her wrist.

"Kristin ran away from him!" said Thea abruptly, as if these words represented something new and interesting that she had never thought of before.

"Ran away from him?" Hadn't Ellison mentioned something to the effect that Gustav might have been "embarrassed" over Kristin?

"Yes," cackled Thea, as if warming to a pleasant memory. "His precious wife, his mountain jewel. Ha! He gave her everything and she hated him. What a fool he was. And all she had eyes for was that commoner, Gunnarson . . ."

"Gunnarson?" Elizabeth felt a combination of discovery and mystery. So Kristin had been married to Gustav, and had left him for the stranger . . .

"Quick now, let's flee," whispered Thea anxiously. "Let's get out now while they're not looking." She tried to push Elizabeth toward the door.

"Who *is* this Gunnarson?" Elizabeth asked.

Thea stopped pushing, and leaned close to Elizabeth. Her fiery eyes glowed.

"He is your father, my dear," answered Thea, with a wild, knowing chortle.

"So Kristin is my mother?" she asked.

"Kristin your mother?" howled Thea, with broken manic glee. "Ha! No, no . . ."

"Who was my mother? *Is* my mother?" asked Elizabeth, trying as deftly as she could to keep Thea's mind on the subject at hand.

Thea stopped laughing, and a long black pause filled the cell. "Dead," she pronounced.

Oh no, thought Elizabeth, *she has lapsed back into miasma.* "Kristin is dead?" she asked, deliberately confusing the issue to see if Thea might note the inconsistency and speak clearly again.

"No, *your mother is dead,*" pronounced the prisoner.

Had Gustav been telling the truth? Had that unknown woman, Hilda, been her mother? Hilda who had thrown herself in front of Gunnarson's pistol? Then Gunnarson might indeed have been her father, and Olav Rolfson, Hilda's husband, simply a cuckold. Gustav *would* have deemed the death of a brother cause for revenge. But why would the woman have taken a bullet for the husband she had wronged? It made no sense, and neither did Thea Thorsdatter.

Elizabeth decided that she could not rely absolutely upon anything Thea had said.

"Mother?" Thea was pleading now. "Please let's hurry and get out of here. They are awfully mean to me here, Mother . . ."

"Thea, I'm sorry but I can't. I would if I could, and that is the truth. Your share of the estate awaits you. There is just one more thing I want to ask you . . ."

"No! Don't leave! You can't leave me!" Thea screamed.

". . . the scar on Gustav's face? How did he get it?"

A simple question. She asked it out of curiosity, and also

176

to see if Thea could be forced back to the concrete world of small, hard facts.

Thea could not. Then, in response to Thea's last cry, the superintendent opened the cell door. Thea, glimpsing daylight and the silhouette of her tormentor, sprang forward and closed her hands around the superintendent's throat. But the official was strong, experienced, and prepared. She broke Thea's grip with savage twin chops to the wrists, grabbed the prisoner, and wrestled her back into the cell and down upon the bunk.

"Out," she commanded Elizabeth, springing up herself and retreating. The door slammed shut, and the superintendent locked it. Thea howled and scratched behind the wooden door. All along the corridor reverberated a hopeless wailing and pounding, the sounds of lost souls in a trackless section of hell.

"Did you get the answers you came for?" asked the superintendent, showing Elizabeth to the prison's main gate.

"No. Just more questions, I'm afraid."

"I hope they don't keep you up nights."

"Oh, but they will." Because Elizabeth had learned that, while time could never be reclaimed, neither could the facts of history be changed. Those facts could be altered and distorted, forgotten or lied about. But never changed.

5

Elizabeth arrived in Chicago on a bitterly cold morning in January of 1886. Cold she was used to, both in Norway and in the Alps, but here it was different. Wind roared in off Lake Michigan, a blasting icy wind that cut through leather and woolens and fur, cut through skin, too, and buried itself in the bones.

Alois Smedley, his fur hat pulled low over his sleek black head, was waiting for Elizabeth on the platform at Union Station when the long yellow cars of the Baltimore and Ohio rolled into the cavernous terminal. Great engines snorted and hissed, whistles hooted and keened, shrieking jets of steam shot from the exhausts, spreading out over the rails and up into the air, there to mingle with the breathy vapors of thousands, and with the steam that rose ceaselessly from the blanketed bodies of carriage horses.

"Miss Rolfson, how delightful," boomed Smedley without delight, offering his hand and helping her down from the private Pullman on which she had come from New York. "And I trust you had a pleasant trip?"

"Yes," answered Elizabeth. She could tell that Smedley was unhappy to see her. It was not that he displayed any sign of animosity, or even lack of ease. If anything, his manner was courteous to a fault. But she had an inkling that Rolfson Industries' chief executive was a man to be understood in opposites. No matter what he appeared to be, no matter what he said and with what conviction he said it, there was a good chance that the opposite was true.

"I'm so glad," Smedley told her now, leading her through the steamy, roaring din of Union Station, down from the platform to a waiting coach. "Winter passage on the Atlantic can be perilous. To say nothing of the experience you would have had if your train had been caught in a Pennsylvania blizzard."

"No," said Elizabeth, climbing up into the coach, where piles of furs and blankets awaited, "the *Viking Serpent* made excellent time, and from what I saw of America from the train windows, all I can say is that I love it already."

Smedley's eyebrows went up slightly. The most common reaction on the part of stylish Europeans who witnessed raw America for the first time was bewilderment, often seasoned with a touch of fear.

"Well, this is Chicago," Alois Smedley said, as the carriage lurched out of Union Station and joined the river of traffic on the icy city streets. Elizabeth looked eagerly out the window of the vehicle, all the while wrapping a fur blanket tightly around herself, and tried to absorb the spirit of her new home. Even in this cold, the streets were filled with people, and all of them seemed to be rushing somewhere. In Norway, heavy snow meant that the pace of life slowed naturally, but here people seemed to ignore the elements, going about their daily business with a kind of driven need. The buildings along State Street were raw and new, crowded close together so that not an inch of space would be wasted. The structures on Michigan Avenue were more elegant, and faced the gray frigid expanse of the lake.

"Everything is so new!" Elizabeth exclaimed.

Smedley laughed. "That's because, fourteen years ago this winter, the city almost burned to the ground. It had to be rebuilt from scratch."

"The entire city?"

"That's right."

"My goodness, how did it happen?" Elizabeth imagined a terrible holocaust, launched perhaps by some agent of revenge.

"Somebody's cow kicked over a lantern in a barn," Smedley told her. "The wind off Lake Michigan did the rest."

"It must have been terrible."

"Yes, that's true. But you will learn that we Americans are a very optimistic race. We *do* have a new city, and all because of one cow."

"Where exactly is Uncle Gustav's house?" Elizabeth asked, settling back into her seat and pulling down the isinglass curtain over the window to block out the cold wind. "I thought it was just north of the business district."

The coach was moving northward along Michigan Avenue now, where well-dressed men and women hastily exited hacks or coaches and rushed to the warmth of restaurants and glittering shops.

"Ah . . . yes," responded Smedley, with just a moment's hesitation, a delay to which Elizabeth paid no attention at the time, "the house is"—he pointed—"just a few blocks in that direction. But it's been shut down since your uncle left on his last trip to Europe. No coal or wood on hand for the furnace, I'm afraid. So I took the liberty of engaging a suite for you at the Blackstone Hotel. Finest in the city, you may be sure."

Elizabeth was sure. Smedley's tastes ran automatically to first class. She assumed he could afford the high life.

"Thank you," she said. "The hotel will be excellent for the time being. As long as it's nice and *warm*."

"You may be sure of that too."

"Tell me," she asked, thinking it wise to impress upon him immediately her intention of being taken seriously, "what is the current business situation?"

Did she glimpse the flicker of an indulgent smile on his

thin mouth? But, when he spoke, there was no hint in his tone that he was attempting to humor her.

"Grover Cleveland is President of the United States now," Smedley said. "A Democrat. That could be disadvantageous to our interests."

"How so?"

"He wishes to lower the tariffs, and remove some of them entirely. Many industries have been protected by tariffs against foreign competition. If the protections are lifted, it will be more difficult to turn a profit. Or to move in the direction we wish."

"The iron ore?"

"Yes. That's one of the products on Cleveland's list."

"What is the state of the Mesabi situation?"

Smedley gave her a straight look. "We shall soon see," he told her. "J. J. Granger arrived in Chicago two days ago, and he has asked for a meeting. I waited until you were here, but I would suggest we meet with him as soon as possible."

"Yes, we can do so this very afternoon. Isn't J. J. Granger the Minnesotan with the unsavory reputation who . . . ?"

Smedley nodded. "Yes, the man who is in competition with Starbane and ourselves. I see this as an opportunity to strike a blow in our own best interests. Granger is the devil, but if one must do business with the devil, then one must."

"Let us also approach Starbane," Elizabeth offered, thinking of her plan to drive a cunning wedge between the two competitors.

"Ah . . . no," Smedley disagreed, again with one of his quick, measuring glances in her direction. "I think it would be better to see what is on Granger's mind first. There will be time later . . ."

"All right. It will take me awhile to become familiar with the nuances anyway. First things first."

"You certainly do seem intent on getting involved in

every little thing," observed Smedley, in a tone of great warmth.

Yes, a man of opposites, Elizabeth realized. *He means the reverse of what he says.* "That I do," she said.

Smedley lapsed into a silence, but there was more that Elizabeth wanted to know.

"Where shall we meet with J. J. Granger?" she asked.

"I think the restaurant at the hotel would be a good place. Granger is a man of prodigious appetites. Fine food and drink—and the presence of a woman as lovely as yourself —may ameliorate some of his more barbaric tendencies."

"Yes, that will be fine. Please arrange for our dinner when we arrive."

"Very good."

"There is one more thing," she said.

"Yes?"

"I know this matter was brought up when you were in Oslo, but it may be important. Did Uncle Gustav ever mention to you a man named Gunnarson?"

"No," Smedley said.

"You're quite sure?"

"Why, yes."

He seemed to be telling the truth. "A business competitor?" she asked, trying again.

Smedley opened his palms. "Eric Starbane and J. J. Granger are our major competitors. What is this all about?"

"I don't know," Elizabeth said, feeling foolish. She didn't know anything. Gustav had told her that Gunnarson was responsible for the deaths of her parents. Yet, if Thea Thorsdatter's babblings were to be believed, Gunnarson *was* Elizabeth's father. Gustav had had a "plan," and it was a scheme for revenge, of that she was sure. A chilly current passed up Elizabeth's spine, and into her heart. In the bleak and savage caverns of his brain, had Gustav Rolfson spun a terrible web, a plot of bitter genius to gain revenge by sending daughter against father?

Certainly, these were private things. She would never confide them to Smedley, even if he seemed trustworthy, which he did not.

The coach rolled along northward toward the Blackstone Hotel. Elizabeth was lost in thought. Her early recollections of Uncle Gustav were faint, but one particular image had remained indelible down through the years. Whether the incident had occurred in America, when she was first brought to Gustav, or later in Norway, Elizabeth did not know. But she remembered the incident with startling clarity, because at the time it had impressed her so powerfully *with a sense of her own worth*! Elizabeth had been readied for bed by nurse or governess—or perhaps even by Thea—and brought down to bid Gustav good night. The great man sat in a chair by the fire, smoking one of the long cigars on which he doted, and blowing rings of thick blue smoke up toward the ceiling. She remembered standing before Gustav, just a drowsy little girl ready for bed. And she recalled him asking her something. She could not now remember exactly what it was he asked. Perhaps a poem she was to have memorized, or maybe something he had taught her for later recital, such as the names of the ships he owned. But, whatever it had been, she had responded correctly. And when she had spoken, after she had answered correctly, Elizabeth recalled the sudden beam of sheer pleasure on Gustav's face, and he had said: "This little girl is sharp as a tack. How smart she is! There'll be no stopping me now."

There'll be no stopping me now.

At the time, and for years afterward, Elizabeth had thought only of the pleasure Gustav had given with his compliment. When praise is involved, everyone is a child; wise bestowal of accolades can win loyalty for a lifetime.

Recalling the incident now, however, she thought of his words with quite a different perspective.

There'll be no stopping *me* now.

"Here we are!" exuded Smedley, as the coach pulled up in front of the Blackstone.

Smedley summoned a man to see to Elizabeth's luggage, and saw to her registration at the desk. Confirming their plan to dine with J. J. Granger, Smedley departed and Elizabeth went upstairs to her suite. It was warm and comfortable, as promised, and she took a long, luxurious bath. Now that the journey was over and she really was here in America, her thoughts turned to Lance. Was he in Montana? She must try and reach him. Had he attempted to send her a message, either to Switzerland or to Norway? It seemed forever since they last embraced, yet the memory of his kisses was as vivid as if it were just yesterday. Had something evil befallen him? When he'd left Geneva so hastily, he had told her that something "dangerous" awaited him. How dangerous?

She was frightened for a moment, but made herself relax. No, despite the long silence nothing had happened to him. And she sensed nothing would. Lance and Elizabeth were fated to be together. She would obliterate that quiet air of tragedy he wore, vanquish and erase it forever simply by loving him. Yes, she would. Thinking of him, heat flowed through her body, sweet flesh glorified and soaring. Lance was as real to her now as pleasure, as elemental and irreducible as fire or water or wind. They would be together again, and she would love him. Yes, she would!

Part Four

MONTANA • _1885–1886_

1

Lance Tallworth was summoned back from Europe by his ranch foreman, Rowdy Jenner. The message had been short, alarming, and brutal: *"There's a range war starting up and we're gonna get beat bad if we don't fight."*

It was a tribute to Lance's way of dealing with his men that Rowdy had instinctively used the word "we." He and the ranch hands felt at one in their effort with Lance. They were proud of what he had done with the High Y, and proud of themselves too. They were ready to fight.

Fomented by ruthless men, who could not be precisely identified, nor convicted with actual evidence, the range war threatened central and western Montana. A small army of well-armed riders would descend suddenly on ranch or farm, burn buildings, kill people—men, women, and children alike—and drive away livestock. If there were crops in the fields, these were torched. Soon the landscape of a great portion of Montana was devastated. Smoke from burning farms and ranches clouded the horizon like a blot of shame against the big sky, and each week the mysterious marauders moved farther toward the Rockies. In the meantime, people moved out, moved back east, sold out cheap when they could, or merely abandoned their land. "Better to be safe and poor," the saying went, "than the proud owner of six feet of Montana and a pine box."

Lance did not subscribe to this cautious maxim. Rushing back from Europe, he took the first train from New York, changed in Chicago, changed again in St. Paul, and shot on to Helena. In Helena, Lance bought a horse, rode south through Butte, and then on to Black Forks and *Ycripsicu*. During that headlong ride, he saw evidence of pillage and depradation: cattle dead on the ranges, rows of small white crosses beneath cottonwood trees, charred beams of burned homesteads standing against the sky, eerie and forlorn. Sometimes, against the horizon, he saw bands of dark riders, moving into the distance, like the black figures of a biblical plague.

But when he reached *Ycripsicu*, he found that it had not yet been attacked. Wordlessly, Fleet Fawn embraced him —Lance could see in her eyes that she had thought he would never return—and Rowdy Jenner was, for once, less than laconic.

"You got back here in the nick of time," Rowdy said, removing his battered Stetson and mopping a brow marked with worry and sweat.

"Who's behind all this?" Lance snapped.

"Don't nobody know for sure. Got to be somebody wants land awful bad."

"Schuyler Whitlock," Lance said, naming Yellow-teeth, the Black Forks tyrant.

"Don't seem likely," Rowdy Jenner demurred. "Whitlock's been tryin' hard to organize a defense in this area of Montana. Been out here hisself a coupla times, wantin' to see if we was prepared to fight."

Fleet Fawn nodded in tremulous corroboration.

"Hah!" cried Lance. "Whitlock was out here to find out if we are vulnerable. Come. Tell the men to saddle up. We're going to Black Forks."

"But that'll leave the ranch unguarded . . ."

"It won't matter. No one will touch the ranch."

Lance led twenty armed and mounted High Y hands at a gallop into Black Forks where they reined up in a cloud of dust before the saloon. Whitlock had an office in a room behind the bar. Lance strode purposefully toward the doorway. Kuffel, the bartender, began to reach for the revolver at his belt but thought the better of it, remembering what Lance's knife had done to his hand a few years before.

Throwing open the door, Lance found Schuyler Whitlock behind his desk, his booted feet on top of it, spurs raking the battered wood. Seeing Lance, he jerked himself to his feet, eyes narrowed, his mouth trying to find a smile.

"When did you get back. . . ?" he began.

Lance cut him off. "Do you want to buy *Ycripsicu*?" he asked.

Old Whitlock looked as if he hadn't heard right, couldn't believe this piece of luck. "Why sure, you know I do . . ."

"It's not for sale, and it never will be," Lance snapped, cutting him off. "Nor is it for the taking and it never will be."

Rowdy Jenner and a half dozen cowhands crowded into the little office.

Lance stepped toward Yellow-teeth, his movements a blur of savage speed. With one hand he seized the man at the throat, with the other at the groin, lifted him bodily into the air, and slammed him against the wooden wall. A mounted elk's head fell to the floor; an antler point snapped like a twig. Whitlock was moaning in agony, still pinned against the wall.

"I know you're behind what's been happening here," Lance told him, his voice perfectly cold, totally calm. "Aren't you?"

Whitlock's mouth was open in pain. Spittle formed on his long yellow teeth.

"Aren't you?" Lance demanded, squeezing both of Whitlock's hands.

Whitlock howled.

"*I* know," Lance said. "If one more ranch or farm is burned, if you *ever* dare to touch *Ycripsicu*, you will die. You will die for a long, long time."

Again, Lance squeezed, this time as hard as he could.

Schuyler Whitlock shrieked, shivered, turned white. Lance released him, and the man dropped unconscious to the floor.

"My God!" Rowdy Jenner breathed. Rowdy had known in his bones that "the boss" was capable of great resolve, great rage, but to see it loosed so suddenly was an eye-opener. The other cowboys looked upon the scene, astonished and a little pale themselves.

"But how did you know it was Whitlock all along?" Rowdy asked Lance, as they rode back toward the ranch.

"I didn't. But I've wanted to do something like that ever since he treated Fawn so badly on our first day in town." Indeed, Fawn had been on Lance's mind during the journey back from Europe.

"What do we do now?"

"Now we wait. If the attacks cease, then we will know for sure Whitlock was behind them."

"If the attacks do stop, then you've beaten Whitlock!" Rowdy Jenner exclaimed.

"Oh, no. He will wait for another time. Men like Whitlock always do."

"And what'll you do then, boss?"

"I shall kill him as I said. It is never good to break a promise, especially to one's enemy."

The attacks, the killings, the burnings did come to an end. The marauders left the territory as suddenly as they had come. Many months later, Schuyler Whitlock began to buy up land between Black Forks and Butte, and much more land stretching eastward from Black Forks to Billings, as if he had a specific plan in mind. There was no way to connect him directly to the range war, and soon he was riding high again.

After his return to the ranch, Lance lost himself in the usual frenzy of summer activity. The breeding stock he had purchased in Gascony arrived by rail, and the best of the longhorns had to be laboriously cut from the herd to graze with the new cattle. This, in addition to preparing for the fall roundup and the annual drive to market in Helena, filled Lance's days and many of his nights. He lost himself in the affairs of his ranch, and he was glad to lose himself.

Nevertheless, Elizabeth was always on his mind, and so was Fawn. That was the agony. On some days, he did not know how he could live without Elizabeth, and thought that he must leave again, immediately, and go to her. At other times, he would see his little daughter, Sostana, at play in the shade trees behind the ranch house, and understand his ties and responsibilities to Fawn. Ought he to have told Elizabeth that he was a husband and father? He had been meaning to, that day they'd picnicked in the mountains above Geneva. But the love she had given touched him so deeply, exalted him so much, that to have confessed his situation would have been too wounding, even sacrilegious. Would she be better off never to see him again? How could he leave Fawn? Other than Sostana, Fawn's simple devotion to her family was all she had, and all she wanted. It was as he had told Fawn in the beginning: the two of them were different and always would be.

In the mind of Fleet Fawn, the laws of the world and everything in the world were immutable. From the manner in which she brushed her hair, to the sequence of her daily activities, to the ritual by which she skinned a rabbit for the grill, nothing changed, not a movement was different from one time to the next. When she set out an arrangement of wild flowers, it was always the same, each sunflower, lilac, honeysuckle positioned *just so*.

Sometimes Lance found this amusing. Sometimes the mindless unchangeability maddened him. Once he altered the arrangement of the flowers, and waited to see what would happen. Later, when Fawn entered the room, she noticed the flowers and moved them back exactly as they had been, but without the slightest curiosity as to how they had come to be altered.

Yet, even when it seemed to Lance that he would perish for want of a woman to share his soul, he admonished himself for wanting the woman whose body he shared to be anything more than what she was. True, she had insisted on leaving Red Lake with him, but he had not turned away from her embrace. Out of that embrace had come Sostana, who was marked with her mother's beauty but her father's deep, thoughtful eyes and questing mind. Lance loved her passionately, in a way that, before her birth, he had not imagined, even as he had not envisioned, until he met her, the intense love he felt for Elizabeth.

Often he would ride far out to the high land by the Bitterroot Pass and wonder what to do. Never before had he been afflicted so remorselessly by the ferocious conflict of desire and responsibility. Was the fullness of love measured by the pain attendant upon it? Was fate an unyielding master?

These questions followed Lance as he rode out into the hills. If, upon completing his purchase of cattle in Gascony, he had decided to go back immediately to America, none of these thoughts would be on his mind. But he had had some time available, and he had grown curious to see the mountains of Europe and compare them to the Rockies. Because he had gotten aboard that train to Geneva, everything was changed.

At length, Lance reached the place where the Bitterroot Pass slashed through the Rockies. Here he dismounted and dropped the ends of the reins on the ground. His horse, a strong but gentle palomino, began chomping spring grass and sweet wild flowers. Wind blew down from the mountains, singing through the Bitterroot like the ethereal music of benign spirits, a sound that always reminded Lance of his father. "I am Sioux," he said to the mountains and the sky. He knew he was Sioux, but he had also learned that he was more. Holding Elizabeth, he had known it. Her touch, her presence, her very being had broken down an invisible barrier within, and Lance was now forever more than he had been.

For such knowledge, much pain. Love and pain again. They came together. But a man did not turn away from pain.

Then his sharp eyes caught an unusual movement far down in the pass. So attuned was he to the rhythm of the wilderness that anything out of the ordinary drew his attention. He dropped to the earth and gazed down at the pass. The eastern end of it, which Lance now scrutinized, was part of *Ycripsicu*. The rest of it was U.S. government property, unpurchased and unclaimed. Lance's section was valuable, both financially and strategically. Such worth seemed to be increasing by the moment, because as he watched, he saw two men standing down in the pass, waving to each other in a formalized ritual of signals. One of them held a stick or wand upright before him, its base stuck in the dirt. The other gazed through a small telescopic device set upon a tripod.

Surveyors!

Lance had seen them at work during his days in Portage la Croix. They charted and measured parcels of wilderness, divided the living earth into sections, and nothing was ever the same again.

What these two surveyors were doing on his land, Lance could not imagine. They might have been charting the unclaimed section, and then wandered by accident onto ranch territory, in which case they were certainly not very good at their profession. Or they were here deliberately, for reasons less than honest. Suspecting the latter, Lance crept along the grassy embankment over the Bitterroot until he reached a wooded slope leading down toward where the men were working. Calling upon the stealth that was a part of his Sioux blood, he moved from tree to tree, from ravine to bush, until he could hear the men talking.

"Bart, I got to tell you again. I'm getting that funny feeling. I don't like this one bit, not at all."

"Hell, you're too goddamn jittery, Pete. There. To your left a notch. Left, I said. For Christ's sake, didn't your ma teach you right from . . . there! Hold it."

"If we get caught in this, we're the ones'll haveta pay, not . . ."

"Shut up, Pete. Sound carries."

"I hear Tallworth is a mean bastard, an' we've been on his land since yestidday afternoon."

"Well, we'll be off it by nightfall, if you lock up your mouth and figure out which arm is which . . ."

Behind the trees, Lance considered what he was overhearing. The surveyors knew they were on the High Y, and had been sent by someone who had warned them against Lance himself. Obviously, their intentions were dishonest, perhaps criminal. Who had sent them, though? Whitlock?

He waited until the man with the tripod, Bart, hoisted his instrument onto his shoulders and set out for a new location, passing directly in front of Lance's concealed position. Slipping the revolver from its holster at his hip, Lance leaped through the greenery, sprang at the man, and slammed him to the earth. Then, with a knee on Bart's throat, he swung the muzzle of the gun toward Pete, the surveyor's assistant, who was stumbling up the pass.

"Don't move," Lance said.

Bart was wriggling and choking beneath him. Lance felt the man's Adam's apple jerking against his knee.

"Oh, Bart, I done *told* you . . ." Pete whined.

"Come over here." Lance motioned with the gun. Pete, hands raised, complied. Bart was still choking. "Aren't you gonna let him up? He'll croak."

When Pete got within ten paces, Lance leaped up easily and stood with his gun on both of the surveyors.

"What are you boys doing here?" he demanded.

Bart was gasping for breath, and Pete didn't want to say anything, lest it prove to be the wrong thing.

Bart recovered enough of his breath to croak, "Put down the gun, man. What the hell do you think you're doing?"

"I want to know what you two are doing. This is my land."

Bart acted as if the end of the world couldn't have surprised him as much.

"What?" he cried, in a bellowing growl caused by a partially squashed throat. "By God, what the hell, Pete, you dumb bastard, I told you you got us way off the line." Bart gave Lance a quick, evaluative glance. "Mister, my partner here ain't got the wit to protect his balls when he sees a rattler. God. We're on your land? Hell, I couldn't be sorrier." He started to get to his feet. "Let me apologize and we'll just go on back . . ."

"Hold it," Lance said.

Bart sat down again. Pete did not move, his arms still in the air.

"I happened to overhear a little of your conversation," Lance told them, smiling in a way they found most unsettling, "and you're lying to me now. Who are you working for?"

Bart looked at Pete, and Pete looked up at the sky.

"Schuyler Whitlock?" Lance asked.

Both men looked at him suddenly, as if surprised.

"Schuyler Whitlock?" Lance asked again.

Pete seemed flabbergasted, even amused. Bart opened his hands, palms up, as if to say, *"Look, man, we don't know who the hell you're talking about . . ."*

Lance fired, and the big lead slug of the Colt ripped off Bart's kneecap. Pete screamed reflexively, and Bart howled with pain, writhing in the dust.

"This is my land," Lance told them. "I've fought for it once, and I'll fight for it forever. Do you understand?"

Pete was nodding like a nervous bird, wings aloft.

Bart was howling, clutching his ruined knee. "Please," he pleaded, "get me a drink of whiskey, get me something. God, I can't stand it . . ."

"Schuyler Whitlock?" Lance asked again, aiming at Bart's other knee.

"Man, I ain't even *heard* of Schuyler Whitlock," begged Bart, trying to scuttle away in the dirt.

"That's right, sir," Pete put in. "Look, you got to help him, he's sufferin' and you . . ."

For a moment, Lance let down his guard. Had he been mistaken? There was Bart on the ground, wailing in pain, his leg permanently damaged. *I did that*, Lance thought with revulsion, *I did that because I hate Whitlock* . . .

"All right, get him some whiskey if you have it," Lance told Pete. He would get to the bottom of this presently anyway, and find out who had hired these feckless surveyors.

Pete walked back down the pass a short distance, leaned over, and picked up a pack from the grass. Holding the pack aloft, so that Lance might see there was no danger to it, he came up and set it down next to Bart.

"We done only got about half a pint left. . . ," he commented, opening the pack flaps.

Lance, watching, was also thinking about who had sent these fools. Either they had never heard of Whitlock, or they were a lot better liars than they were surveyors.

As he was thinking, Pete was yanking furiously at something in the pack. Lance caught a glimpse of metal. A flask, of course, because a glass bottle would break . . .

The metal in Pete's flashing hand was long and hollow at the end.

Lance fired. Pete fired. Bart lurched toward him. Lance fired again. The echoes of the explosions rolled off down the pass, reverberating like tides of thunder in a tunnel of doom.

196

Lance stood there in the pass. Waves of sound washed over him. Bart and Pete lay dead at his feet.

Fool, he accused himself. He had let down his guard for an instant; for an instant he had trusted a probable enemy. And now he was worse off than before. Not only had he killed two men on his own land, he didn't even know who had sent them. Sure, he suspected Whitlock, but what if Yellow-teeth were not behind the actions of these surveyors? Then who was? Lance could not learn the answer from dead men. *Fool!* he denounced himself.

What to do? He had to decide fast. Already, circling high up in the gorgeous blue sky of Montana was the pilot buzzard, its scent of dead flesh as keen as Schuyler Whitlock's penchant for power. Soon more of the scavengers would appear, to fill their stomachs on Bart and Pete, picking them clean but leaving the bones. Yet such a feast would take time, and time was what Lance did not have. Moreover, the bones must not be found. Deciding, he gave a long low whistle, and in minutes the palomino came sliding and stumbling down the embankment into the pass. Lance mounted, rode down the Bitterroot, and found there two horses and a pack mule, with which the surveyors had been traveling. Neither the horses nor the mule were branded, a fact that added to Lance's darkest suspicions. He took off the saddles and packs, then slapped the beasts smartly, sending them off into the wilds. Carrying the equipment back to the bodies of Pete and Bart, he buried it with them in the soft earth on the side of the Bitterroot. He dug as deeply as he could, and hoped the coyotes would not get the scent. Coyotes tunnel eagerly for sweet flesh.

In the sky, seven buzzards circled, grew discouraged, then limped away on their ratchety wings.

Lance rode back home.

Fleet Fawn found him even more withdrawn than usual that night, and after she thought he was asleep, she wept. Never having wept before in her life, over Lance or anything else, she was startled by the knowledge of her own heartache and soon she was sobbing uncontrollably.

Then he was awake and she was in his arms and he was loving her and for that night it was all right again.

2

The winter of 1885–86 marked a bleak run of luck on the western plains. Rowdy Jenner rode in one October day, fresh from a tour of the ranges.

"Boss, there's a blizzard comin'. I *smelt* the sucker when I bedded down last night up by Termagant Hole."

The cowhands scoffed, because it was just October. The cattle could graze a couple more weeks before roundup. Neighboring ranchers made no haste to corral their stock. But Lance shared his foreman's hunch. Weather was a woman of different fragrances: lilac for the low summer, sage for the high, green grass and wheat of spring, pine for the winter and oak of autumn. But a brewing blizzard had a smell all its own, a cold spark struck by an elk's hoof on rock, wet snow on an aspen leaf, chill wind fondling thickets in the high country.

"Round 'em up," ordered Lance.

Because he trusted his sensibilities and acted quickly, his herds were saved and his ranch was safe. Others were not so fortunate. Spring found tight-eyed ranchers pondering carcasses on the plains, where snowbound longhorns had floundered and died. Ranches failed. More people gave up and moved away than had succumbed to the marauders a year earlier.

Schuyler Whitlock offered hard cash for the land.

But this time Lance Tallworth offered more. A dearth of beef cattle due to the cruel winter resulted in a rise in meat prices. Buyers at the railhead in Helena paid top dollar for the meaty hybrid cattle of the High Y ranch. Lance had money and he spent it to buy land. Whitlock had already purchased a great deal of land, much more than he seemed able to manage. Yet—and Lance would have been among the first to declare this—Whitlock was far from being a stupid man. The one of yellow teeth had a wild card up his slick sleeve.

On the cattle drive to Helena, Lance learned what it was that Whitlock strove to attain.

He and Rowdy and the men had driven the cattle to the Helena railhead and sold them to buyers from meat-packing plants in St. Paul and Chicago. They were watching them being herded aboard cars for shipment to the burgeoning cities back east when one of the Minnesota buyers, Follansbee, stepped up to Lance and began to shoot the breeze.

"So, Tallworth, you managed to sell dear, eh?"

Lance nodded. Never one to make idle chatter, he did not especially care to listen to it either.

"Lucky, damn lucky. You got the best prices I ever heard of in my time. Coulda got more though."

Lance gave him a sharp look, as if the High Y had somehow been cheated.

"No, no," responded Follansbee, with a nervous laugh, "I didn't mean that. I just meant that your cattle lose weight during the drive up here to Helena from your ranch."

"This is the nearest railhead," said Lance.

"Might not be for long."

"What do you mean?"

"Thought you folks might have heard. Plenty of talk back east lately of another railroad, this one coming across southern Montana. Open up a whole new section of the country, it surely will."

Lance grasped all facets of the equation immediately. At present, the Grand Northern line was the sole road, striking up from St. Paul, through the Dakotas, into Helena, where it veered northward toward Canada and over the Rockies. A second road could be laid through Billings, and then to Butte. But there was only one point at which it might go through the mountains. Bitterroot Pass.

"A second railroad would be very helpful," he told the ebullient Follansbee, calculating how much land Schuyler Whitlock had purchased between Black Forks and Billings, Black Forks and Butte. He understood completely now why Whitlock had always been his enemy. Whoever built the second railroad would have to pay great sums for right-of-way, especially for access to Bitterroot Pass. Whoever sold those strategic parcels of land would become immensely rich.

"This second road," he asked, with as much disinterest as he could muster, "who's behind it?"

"Two outfits gearin' up to go after it hot and heavy right now," Follansbee expanded. "One of 'em's Granger, of Minnesota. You've heard of J. J. Granger?"

"Yes, I have." Few had not heard of him. The Minnesotan was involved in lumber, land speculation, timber rights, iron mining, and now—according to Follansbee—he would soon be in the railroad business too.

"And the other outfit?" Lance prodded. He was far more interested in railroading than he had been ten minutes earlier.

"Company out of Chicago. Guy by the name of Smedley seems to be . . ."

"What if Granger or this other organization fails to win right-of-way?" Lance asked casually.

Follansbee blinked with astonishment and then roared with laughter. He laughed so hard that the gold watch chain looped across his round belly quivered and shook.

". . . an' . . . an' . . . they say you Montanans don't have no sense of humor," he roared.

"What's so funny?"

Follansbee recovered. "Railroads is king in this country

now," he wheezed. "Don't you know that? Used to be it was cotton, but now it's the iron horse. You know how the Grand Northern got right-of-way, don't you? If not by the buck, then by the bullet. By God, that road is gonna come through here one of these years, like it or not."

"I don't know if I will," said Lance.

"What's that you say?"

"I said I don't know yet if I'll like it or not." Lance could not help but think of the bodies of those two surveyors, buried where the railbed would be dug and laid.

"That's what I said," chortled Follansbee, laughing again. "I always *told* everybody you Montanans had a great sense of humor."

Returned from Helena, Lance took little Sostana on a horseback ride. She had her own pony, but this time he put his daughter in the saddle on his own horse, and swung up behind her. She squealed with pride and delight as the palomino trotted easily away from the ranch and onto the high, rolling plains. Lance felt, when he was with the little girl, as if nothing bad had ever happened to him, and never would. He spoke to her without restraint, something that would have astounded anyone who knew him. Sostana understood very little of what he told her. She didn't care and neither did Lance. Love was behind the words, and love was all that had importance.

When they had ridden far up into the high country, Lance reined the horse. To the west stood the vaulting Rockies, and below lay Montana. A light breeze from the southwest billowed Sostana's little gingham skirt and bent back Lance's hat brim; above horse and riders arched a sky of cornflower blue.

"What do you like best?" father asked daughter. "The mountains, or the pass? The prairie or the sky?"

Soberly, Sostana thought it over. "I like you best, Daddy," she said.

"All right," he laughed, hugging her, "then what do you like second best?"

Again, she considered it, looking down from horseback upon this high ground, like a princess about to choose a kingdom.

"I like them all," she said, after a while. "I like everything."

Her answer, in its honest simplicity, delighted him.

"I'm glad," he told her, "and it's all yours too."

"Everything?" she asked, turning her little head and looking up at him with her black Sioux eyes.

"Everything."

Lance, overwhelmed with love for her, did not want the moment to end.

"Do you know something?" he said to Sostana.

"What, Daddy?"

"You and I will never die."

This she considered too, weighing it carefully as was her habit. "That's nice, Daddy," she said, "but what's die?"

"Something we never have to worry about," he answered.

They rode home toward the ranch, happy with each other, warm in the sun. Remembering his own savage childhood, colored by disruption and outrage and evil, Lance wished more than anything that Sostana might remember today especially, out of all the other days, when they had ridden out into the high country and he had given her the world.

A couple of miles west of the ranch, Lance pulled the palomino to a stop.

"Why aren't we going home, Daddy?"

"Hush. Just a minute."

Lance thought he had seen something unusual on the horizon in the direction of Black Forks, and he squinted against the bright sky, trying to get a better view. Then, holding the little girl tight, he spurred the horse and set off again toward the ranch, riding fast. Sostana wrapped her strong little fists in the horse's mane and chortled with delight.

Fawn, having seen the two of them galloping toward the house, came out onto the wide, white wooden-pillared porch to see what was going on. Her first thought was that something had happened, that somehow Sostana had gotten hurt, but when she saw the little girl safe and happy, Fawn relaxed.

"Perhaps you oughtn't to ride so fast with her," she said anyway, by way of gentle admonishment. Something *could* happen: things could always happen.

Lance edged the horse over to the porch railing, and handed Sostana down to her mother.

"Oh, Daddy, let's ride some more."

"I'm going over to Black Forks for a while," Lance informed his wife.

"Black Forks? Why?"

"I saw a lot of dust in the sky. Many riders. I want to know what it means."

"The marauders again?" asked Fawn, in an anxious voice. "Are you taking anyone with you?"

"No. The men are all out on the range with the herds. I'll ride over myself and find out what's going on."

"Maybe it's a stampede on one of the ranges," Fawn suggested. She did not want him to go. She knew the depth of bad blood between her husband and Schuyler Whitlock.

"I don't think so," he said. "I have a different feeling."

He rode away from the High Y, unwilling to tell Fawn that his glimpse of the dust in the sky had produced a premonitory shudder. The cloud of dust was like a smoke signal in the days of old, a portent in the sky heralding distress.

It was nearly sundown when Lance rode into town. At first, after having left his ranch, he could see the cloud of dust clearly, moving across the horizon, and for a time he even thought Fawn might have been right. A herd of stampeding cattle would make a cloud like that. But all of a sudden the dust settled and disappeared, precisely in the area of Black Forks. When Lance approached the village and urged his tired horse up the dusty street, he knew why. Hitching posts along the street tethered at least fifty horses, each of them harnessed and saddled in the same manner, all of their saddle blankets bearing the stamp U S ARMY.

Two soldiers, in blue, dust-covered uniforms, wearing broad-brimmed blue campaign hats and yellow bandanas at their throats, leaned against the saloon's facade, standing weary guard over the horses. Lance dismounted, tied the palomino at the town's water trough, and climbed the steps to Schuyler Whitlock's headquarters.

Soldiers stood all along the bar, sat at the tables, lounged along the wooden walls of the saloon, drinking beer from cold, dripping mugs. Whitlock, ever clever, cut huge blocks of ice from Winston Lake during the winter, preserving them in an ice house for use during the warmer months. Lance crossed to the bar, which Kuffel was wiping with a wet rag. The bartender looked at Lance with undisguised malice, but kept his tongue under control. "What'll it be?"

"Beer."

"What makes ya think I won't dope it on you?" This with an evil smirk.

"Because I'll watch you draw it. Because there would still be time to kill you if you did."

"Heh-heh," said Kuffel, tilting the mug beneath the tap, righting it just before it filled to make a white foamy head. He set the mug on the bar in front of Lance, who lifted it and drank half at a gulp.

Soldiers on either side of Lance were drinking too, and talking without animation. They'd ridden a long way, and they were tired. Lance wanted to find out why they were here. A truce had ended the Indian wars some years earlier, and the Army's presence in this region was rare. He identified five sergeants by the gold stripes on their sleeves, and several corporals. The rest were privates, troopers. He did not see an officer, but noticed that the door to Whitlock's office was shut.

Draining the rest of the beer, Lance shoved the mug to Kuffel, who filled it again.

"We white men generally pay for what we drink," growled the bartender.

Lance slapped a silver dollar down on the bar.

"That's what I like to see," Kuffel snorted. His curiosity got the better of him. "What brings the likes of you to town?" he asked.

Lance took a swallow of the beer, drinking more slowly now that his trail-thirst was quenched. "What brings these men here?" he said, gesturing toward the nearest soldiers.

"Why don't you ask 'em?" Kuffel shot back.

"I thought I'd give you a chance to show you know something."

The bartender reddened, but held his temper. "I wouldn't tell you."

"You mean, even if you knew you wouldn't tell me."

Scowling, Kuffel made change of the silver dollar. "You know, the boss ain't gonna put up with you forever. A word to the wise."

"It's the other way around. I'm not going to put up with your boss forever. That's a word *from* the wise."

Kuffel's eyes narrowed. "Think you're pretty goddamn smart, don'tcha?"

Lance ignored the taunt. "Where *is* Yellow-teeth, by the way?"

Kuffel inclined his head toward the office door.

"I think I'd like to see him," said Lance. "Haven't had a chance to pay a call in some time."

He was thinking that seeing Whitlock might be a good idea. Whitlock might fly off the handle and reveal what he knew about the coming of the iron horse. It was worth a chance.

Kuffel was of another mind, though. "He said he don't want to see you again until the day you ride out of town."

Lance laughed. "He'll have a long wait. So you *don't* know what the Army is doing here in Black Forks?"

Kuffel shook his head, and went to fill the mugs of some men down the bar, who were setting up a clamor for more brew.

Lance finished his beer, and headed toward the office door.

"Sorry, sir. Colonel's in there now."

One of the sergeants had spoken, a rough-looking man with a short, mean-bladed knife at his belt. His voice had been courteous, but he meant what he said.

Lance saw no reason to make trouble. "My mistake. I'll wait. Can I buy you a beer?"

"Sir, you're an honorable gentleman, an' that's a hard commodity to come by in this territory."

Lance signaled Kuffel, and in a moment he and the sergeant lifted glasses to each other.

"What unit is this?" Lance asked, indicating the soldiers.

"Detachment of the Twenty-third Cavalry."

"Indians on the warpath again?" asked Lance, as casually as he could.

"Hell no, the bloody red bastards! Looka this." He grabbed the knot of his yellow bandana and held it under Lance's eyes. A glass-encased broochlike clasp was pinned to the bandana, and under the glass Lance saw a shrunken but familiar object.

"Got this sucker when we fought Chief Joseph and the Nez Percé tribe in Idaho back in '80 . . ."

Lance flinched. He knew of the terrible fate that many tribes had suffered.

". . . cut the sucker out of a squaw, I did. Human eyeball. Gets a lot of conversations going."

"I'm sure it does," said Lance. The sergeant was talking now, and that might prove useful. "What brings you out here, then? If you can talk about it?"

"You a local settler?"

"Rancher. West of town."

"Hell, sure I can talk to you," the sergeant said expansively. "We're out here to protect you fellas."

"Oh?"

"Lot of folks been comin' back east and raising a big stink about how they was bein' burned out of their ranches and farms . . ."

Now Lance understood. The survivors of the marauders' raids had sounded an alarm, and now—much too late—the Army was here to protect the countryside.

"And then there's that other thing too," the soldier added, pausing to gulp some more beer. "You heard anything about it?"

"About what?"

"Well, seems there was these two surveyors. They was hired to come in here and do some surveyin'. And they disappeared off the face of the earth without leavin' so much as a fare-thee-well. Say, where'd you say your ranch was located?"

Lance, alarmed by what the man had said, drank some beer too, concealing his face and collecting his thoughts behind the upraised glass.

"Yep," the sergeant was saying, "they was hired by that Minnesota tycoon, J. J. Granger, to figure out a route for a railroad he's fixin' to lay through these parts, an' nothin' been heard of 'em since. Maybe through part of your ranch, hey? Where's it situated?"

"West of here," Lance answered, trying to sound enthusiastic. "I'll bet there's money to be made by those who own land along the route."

"Money! By God, I'll say so. Course, there's some who don't want to sell. Don't want their ranges cut up by a lot of iron and a big smoking engine coming through, know what I mean?"

"I know what you mean."

"Anyway, the colonel's in there now, talking to Mr. Whitlock, who seems to run things pretty much in these parts. J. J. Granger's got a lot of influence all the way to Washington, D.C., and he wants us to get to the bottom of this surveyor business . . ."

Lance experienced the dismal image of Bart and Pete, decaying in the earth of Bitterroot Pass. He imagined, too, the scene now being played behind Whitlock's closed door: the suspicions alive in Whitlock's quick mind, the deadly suggestions and innuendoes that would be rolling readily off his supple tongue. And he knew that Whitlock understood as well as he did that the key to any railroad in this part of the country—a fantastic expanse of territory stretching from Missouri and Minnesota to Montana, from Kansas City and St. Paul to Butte—lay at the west of *Ycripsicu*, in Bitterroot Pass.

3

Later that spring, Schuyler Whitlock called unannounced and alone at *Ycripsicu* ranch. Lance was not surprised to see him. He was down at the bunkhouse planning range assignments with Rowdy Jenner. Whitlock cantered toward them on a mud-spattered roan, and reined in. His pale face was wet, dripping with rain. Water seeped slowly into the impressions made by his horse's hoofs.

"Why, if it ain't the devil hisself," Rowdy Jenner said.

"Why, thank you," Whitlock responded, dismounting. "Tallworth, I think it's time you and I had a little talk."

"Get your ass back up on that horse," barked Rowdy, "an' ride out the way you came . . ."

"It's all right," said Lance, putting a restraining hand on his feisty foreman's shoulder. "Go on over to the tool shop and see if the men have those ropes fixed yet."

"Glad to see you so tractable," said Whitlock to Lance when Rowdy Jenner had gone. "Course, you got reason to be. Let's get in out of this rain."

Lance took the man into the bunkhouse. It smelled of bedding, leather, and the sweat of horse and man. But the iron stove had been lighted against the chill day, and the interior was pleasantly warm. Whitlock stripped off his poncho, shook the rain from it, and hung it on a peg near the stove. Then he sat down on the nearest bunk and showed Lance a large number of his discolored teeth.

"So what do you want to talk about?" Lance demanded.

"A deal."

"What kind of a deal?"

"A deal for railroad right-of-way. For Bitterroot Pass. You've got complete access to the western end of it, and I want half. Actually, I want it all, but I'd be willin' to settle for half."

Having known Whitlock for several years now, Lance was nonetheless astounded at the man's audacity.

"I ought to pin you against the wall," he said, "like I did that time in your office. Get out of here."

Whitlock just smiled his unnerving smile, and shook his head slowly. "Come on, Tallworth, I know I'm no match for you physically. Few men are. But I wouldn't go gettin' uppity till you hear me out. I was always real good in school when it came to addin' two and two."

He waited for Lance to respond. Lance just leaned against a wooden post and looked at him.

"So you give me half a share in the right-of-way across your ranch, and half a share in access to the Bitterroot, and we'll both make so much money there won't be any need to worry ourselves about . . ."

Lance laughed at him.

"I don't think I even *want* a railroad coming across my land," Lance said.

Whitlock was flabbergasted. He choked on cigarette smoke, and coughed for a minute. "Tallworth, now I know you're crazy," he said finally. "In less time than you think, cattle are gonna cost more money to raise than they'll be worth on the market. Whereas the railroad got to *pay* for right-of-way, and we can fix it so they got to *pay* every time they come through here. Why, the money . . ."

"I did not buy *Ycripsicu* to make money, but rather to have a place to live in peace."

"How'd you manage to get rid of those surveyors?" Whitlock asked bluntly, stubbing out his cigarette on the bunkhouse floor.

The unexpectedness of the question caught Lance off guard. Bart and Pete had knowingly trespassed on his land, true, but he had not meant to kill them . . .

Whitlock, with his shrewd and highly developed instinct for human weakness, noticed Lance's momentary discomfiture. "Whether those men are alive or dead," he drawled, "they are gonna cause somebody around here a heap of trouble."

"I don't know what you mean."

"You will, son. You will. Because just yesterday some of the Army men found one of the horses and a mule, both of 'em bearing the Granger brand."

The Granger brand? Bart and Pete had been surveying Bitterroot Pass for Granger, sure, but . . .

"Yep," Whitlock continued, "that Granger is one clever hombre. Brands his animals in little tiny letters up on the neck, under the mane. Interested in knowing where the horse and mule were found?"

"Not particularly."

"Well, you will be. On your ranch. Up north. They were runnin' with a herd of wild ponies."

"So what?" said Lance.

"So *what*? Where's the saddles? The equipment? Where's the *graves*? The Army's doing a tooth-and-comb search of the pass."

Whitlock looked Lance over, long and hard, trying to find a trace of the unease he'd witnessed moments before. But this time he was unsuccessful. Lance was braced, cold as stone.

"Well, be that as it may, I hope those soldiers don't find nothin'. It'll slow down the deal we aim to make."

"You don't give up, do you?"

"Why should I? Clint Granger is due out here any day now, and you and I got to be ready to bargain."

"Clint Granger?"

"J. J.'s boy. A real terror, from what I hear. He's the

advance party for his old man. They want to move fast and get rights-of-way sewed up, since a Chicago outfit is beginning to press toward a road too."

"Is that a fact," Lance said.

"That's right. Rolfson. Rolfson Industries."

"Rolfson!" cried Lance.

Whitlock looked at him suspiciously. "Say, you ain't been dickering with Rolfson, have you? That would complicate everything. J.J. is the man to deal with. He understands how to skin a cat and leave no traces, if you get my drift . . ."

Lance scarcely heard him. He was back in Switzerland now, hearing Elizabeth tell him about her uncle, a businessman with holdings in America. A sharp jolt passed through his body.

"No," he said, "I haven't dealt with anyone. But who is this Rolfson fellow?"

"Ain't no fellow. It's a gal, from what I heard tell . . ."

Lance could barely retain his cold facade. It had to be Elizabeth!

". . . an' you know no woman can possibly do these things right. Not to mention the problems involved if you were to deal with Rolfson, and me with Granger. See what I mean?" Whitlock reached for his tobacco pouch again, and started to roll another cigarette.

"Get out," Lance told him, very calmly. He felt as if the pattern of his life had suddenly changed, and everything was clear and hopeful. The rain battered hard on the bunkhouse roof, but for Lance the day had changed, the clouds were gone, there was bright sunshine all around.

"What the hell . . . ?" Whitlock exclaimed, getting halfway to his feet.

"I said get out. Now. There will be no deal. Not now, not ever."

He stepped forward, which Whitlock took as a threatening gesture. But Lance merely grabbed Yellow-teeth's dripping poncho from the peg and tossed it toward the man.

He would start making plans to go to Chicago. Yet what of Fawn and Sostana?

"You are a prime fool!" spat Whitlock, realizing that he was not going to be assaulted. "Well, you asked for it. I always get what I want, and I'll get it this time too."

He threw the garment over his shoulders, opened the bunkhouse door, and ducked out into the rain. Lance followed him, standing in the doorway as Whitlock mounted.

"Don't say I didn't warn you," Whitlock snarled, wheeling the horse and riding away. Great clods of red mud flew up from the horse's hoofs as Yellow-teeth galloped off into the rain.

All day it rained, more and more heavily. For a long time, Lance barely noticed. *Elizabeth is in Chicago*, he kept thinking. *Elizabeth is in Chicago. I must decide what to do.*

About an hour before nightfall, as Lance walked toward the house for the evening meal, Jasper Zenda rode in from the west range. Jasper, a slow-witted but very loyal hand, was pushing his panting mount at a dangerous pace over the slippery ground. Lance watched him come, and so did Rowdy Jenner and the men who had been working at the ranch site all day. Jasper pounded up in a flurry of rain, sweat, and mud.

"Boss . . ."

"What is it?" snapped Lance. Had Whitlock tried something already?

"It's the rain, boss. The herd's movin' an' we got too few men to hold 'em back."

Damn, thought Lance. He should have thought of it himself, and would have if his mind had not been on Elizabeth. During heavy storms, whether rain or snow, the herds sometimes began to move blindly, trying to get away from the fury of the elements. The wind and rain were battering in from the northeast, which meant the herd was moving toward the southwest, toward the ridges and cliffs over Bitterroot Pass. If they moved on into the darkness, the lead cows would stumble over the edge, taking the rest along with them. It was the nature of the beast. Like most congenital followers, cattle were not very bright.

"Any danger yet?" Lance asked Jasper.

"Not if we can get 'em turned before dark, but we got to have help."

"Saddle up," Rowdy Jenner yelled at his men, who gave up thoughts of a hot meal in the cookhouse and headed for the corral.

Satisfied that there was no immediate danger, Lance went on into the house for dinner, and Sostana read to him until she went to bed. She was five now, and very quick. Rowdy Jenner came back from the range and reported that the herd had been turned and was settled in for the night. It was still raining, however, and Rowdy also reported the probability of flooding in the pass. "Won't hurt nothin', though," he commented. "Wash away a lot of deadwood, is all."

Wash away a lot of deadwood . . .

"Isn't it time we had another child?" said Fleet Fawn, pressing naked against Lance in bed that night. "Wouldn't it be fine to have a son."

Lance felt the warmth flow, although in his heart he was torn. He loved another and would always love another, but Fawn wanted him, and knew how to make his body burn. He remembered her way of arching against the birches at Portage la Croix, showing her breasts. He remembered having her the first time, on the sun-drenched bank of Red Lake. She offered her breasts again now, arching her body, and he had her again, she who knew how to move slow and serpentlike, and then with fierce abandon, and a joyful keening deep in her throat when she felt him shuddering and shooting inside her.

Then Fawn slept, one arm beneath his neck, and the other over her eyes, an unconscious protective gesture. Lance could not sleep. He kept thinking of what Rowdy had said before riding back out to the men and the herd.

Wash away a lot of deadwood.

Lance pictured the tumbling waters in the pass, sweeping old logs along, washing the roots of trees, tearing up the smaller trees, digging massive furrows in the earth.

In which Bart and Pete, the surveyors, slept the long sleep.

When would the Army men begin their sweep of the pass?

No, he could not take a chance. Sliding quietly out of bed, Lance dressed, found a kerosene lantern, and went to the stable. There he saddled the palomino, mounted, and rode out into the high country. The going was slow, but by midnight he reined the palomino, peering down into Bitterroot Pass. The rain had lessened a little, and in spite of the clouds, the sky had acquired a dull luminosity that promised an end to the storm. Lance could hear water moving in the pass.

Dismounting, he lit the lantern in the shelter of bushes, and started down the embankment. He knew exactly where to look. The gravesite's location was burned into his memory, into his very soul.

The daylong downpour had swollen the Bitterroot River. Not very deep, it was nevertheless powerful, and had done considerable damage. Holding the lantern before him, Lance eased down the slope toward the bushes beneath which he had buried Bart and Pete. Coming upon the site, the flickering glow from the kerosene-fueled wick showed Lance that the shrubbery was gone, washed away. Bart and Pete were waiting for him, lying there bony and white in a water-filled hole. Lantern-light glinted on their gumless, grinning mouths, and outlined the black sockets where eyes had been. The saddles were still identifiable, although badly rotted, and the surveying equipment was rusty and grotesque, like a twisted iron insect.

Lance tried to decide what to do. If he left the skeletons here, the soldiers were certain to find them. His other choices were two: bury them again or move them. Cursing the moment Bart had grabbed for his gun in the saddlebag, Lance set the lantern down and began to scout the area for large rocks. Then he broke Bart's bones across his knee, stuffed them down into a small part of the original grave, and set a large boulder over them. He dragged Pete's skeleton through the tossing stream, dug a hole halfway up the opposite side of the pass, broke Pete's bones and concealed them behind a makeshift wall of carefully arranged stones. It was a gamble, but it was certainly safer than leaving Bart and Pete where they had been. Recrossing the stream, he inspected the old saddles, which fell apart under his touch. He tossed them into the water, watching them swirl away, out of sight in the tossing foam. Then he turned to the most difficult problem: the surveying tools. Bart and Pete were separated now, and their saddles would be pounded to smithereens in the water. But he must also get rid of the tools.

An idea struck him as he climbed back up to his horse. He would take the instruments back to the ranch with him and render them unidentifiable over the coals of the smithy's forge.

Lance started back home. The rain, in lucky portent, ceased as he rode, and the clouds, thin and fast moving, began to reveal patches of starry sky. Far away, cattle were lowing, and Lance could hear an occasional call from one of his men to another. The surveying tools, strapped to his saddle, were secure. Lance had spent a bitter night, but it was over.

The palomino cleared a last rise of rangeland, below which lay the white buildings of *Ycripsicu*. Tired but still alert, Lance scrutinized his pride as he rode toward it. He had come a long way to this special place, and it had a great hold on his heart.

By the house. In the shadows near the house. A figure running.

Along the foundation of the house, a single flashing flare.

Fire shot in a thin line along a wall and around a corner, then gathered itself and leaped all the way up one wall. Well laid, well lighted, the flames jumped triumphantly into the night, crawled up the wooden pillars of the porch, and onto the roof.

Whitlock! thought Lance, pounding the tired palomino with his spurs, whipping it with the ends of the leather reins. Thank God for Bart and Pete! If he had not gone out to the pass, Lance would be asleep now in the pyre of his house. As it was, he could reach it in time to save Fawn and Sostana. There would be time to deal with Whitlock later, and wouldn't he be surprised to see a dead man come for him?

Leaping from the horse while it ran, Lance raced between the burning porch pillars and crashed through the door into the house. No fire inside yet, and only minimal smoke. *Thank God*, he thought, *thank God, there is time . . .*

"Fawn!" he shouted, *"Fire!"*

Flashing past their shared bedroom, he saw her dark figure standing beside the bed. Good, she was awake.

"Get out!" he yelled to her. "I'll get Sostana."

He rushed into Sostana's nursery, the bright button-eyes of her stuffed toys shining in the light of the fire. There she was, asleep in her little bed. He slid his arms beneath her, lifted her onto his shoulder, and ran out of the room, catching a brief glimpse of Fawn coming out of the bedroom darkness toward the door. She was moving slowly, heavily, as if still half-asleep, or confused. He felt Sostana's hot tears on his neck.

"It's all right," he told her. "Come, Fawn, hurry! Get out!"

Lance rushed outside. The house was fully ablaze now, and soon the roof would collapse. The palomino was nowhere to be seen. Horses in the corral were neighing frenziedly, racing back and forth. Ranch hands would see the fire and gallop in from the range. All he had to do now was find the palomino with the surveying tools tied onto it . . .

"Darling, it's all right," Lance said to his daughter, whose tears streamed hot beneath his shirt and onto his skin. He held her away from him, smiling to assure her that she was safe.

Sostana stared back with blank, wide-open eyes, blood pouring from the black gash across her throat.

Holding her, howling with a supranatural grief, he spun back toward the house, wanting to hide Sostana's wound from Fawn. Yet it was not his wife who came out of the burning house, but Kuffel, Whitlock's sleazy bartender. Stricken though he was, Lance understood what had happened. Kuffel had gone inside to kill—to kill Fawn and Sostana and Lance himself. His partner, meanwhile, had laid and torched the fire. Confused at finding only two people in the building, Kuffel had delayed too long. Now, in panic and disbelief, he stared down at Lance from his position on the flaming porch, frozen in fear at the sight of Lance's terrible eyes.

Lance laid his little girl on the ground, and sprang up at the bartender, whose arms were raised for whatever defense he could muster. Lance ignored a few blows, seized Kuffel's thick neck in his two hands, and snapped it fast, one fist balled at the nape of the neck, the flat of his other hand ramming upward into Kuffel's chin. The bartender's body had not even hit the ground before Lance reached the flaring bedroom and gathered Fawn into his arms. He heard her groan, or sob. She was still alive. He carried her outside and laid her down next to Sostana.

Fawn's throat, too, had been cut. She was dying and she

knew it. Fawn could not speak, but she looked up at Lance Tall One, the mystery she had loved so well, and saw in his eyes the grief he bore. Fawn had awakened out of deep, after-love sleep to see a figure moving in the bedroom. For a moment, she had thought it was Lance. But her instincts told her no. Her arm reaching for Lance on the bed told her no. She saw the flash of fire and, against that fire, the figure of the man in the room. Kuffel! Whitlock's man. But before she could leap from the bed, or fight, or even speak, his knife had come slashing across her throat.

Lying on the earth now, fire all around, she looked up into Lance's eyes. It didn't matter about the house, nor did she care what had happened to Kuffel, but about Sostana she had to know. Placing her arms before her, she made a cradling, rocking motion. Lance understood.

"Sostana is safe," he lied. There were tears in his eyes. That was very odd, she thought. She had never seen tears from Lance.

Then Fawn lifted her arms—oh, God, it was so hard —and he bent down his neck. She placed her hands behind his head. She tried to speak, and her tongue moved, but the words were a gurgle of blood. *I love you*, she was trying to say. He was nodding. Yes, he was weeping. She could not believe it at first, but yes it was so.

"I will avenge you," he was saying. She heard him as from far away, as if she were here and he were calling to her from the Bitterroot.

No. She tried to move her head, to shake her head. *No. No vengeance*. He had Sostana to live for now, her name meant peace . . .

Lance had placed his head between her breasts, to hear her fading heartbeats. Fawn's arms felt as if she were lugging great pails of water again, as she had at Portage la Croix, but she slid them down around his neck, and linked her fingers so they would not loosen.

"I will avenge you," he was sobbing.

No. She tried to speak again, to lift his head so that he could look into her eyes, but it was all flowing away from her now, the blood, the strength, words, spirit, everything. She was aware of each particle of the living universe now, from the wet earth to the suddenly starry sky. Ah, there would she go and be, in but a moment . . .

Lance lifted his head and looked into her eyes. He looked startled, like an animal surprised in its shelter. He had heard what Fawn had already felt: the last heartbeat of her living body.

"No . . ." she heard him say.

But at that last moment, Fleet Fawn knew no grief. Her daughter was safe; Lance had told her so. And he was with her, his arms around her. If this was as it had to be, then it was good. Yes! She held his eyes and smiled. Lance was still water, dark forests, brilliant snow. He was the truth of these, and the watchful power of these, and the beauty of these. She was in his arms and she exulted!

When Fawn had died, Lance took Sostana's body and laid the little girl in her mother's arms, settling his wife and child so that they could look up at the sky. He had no more tears. His tears were gone. Lance remembered what his father had said to the gold-starred Army officer. *"That which is unjust must be avenged." Ycripsicu.*

And he recalled what he had told Sostana that day on the high plains.

"You and I will never die."

"I shall find a way to make your name live forever," he cried to the stars, where Sostana had gone to dwell in peace, until he should come to her.

4

Rowdy Jenner and a dozen of the cowhands galloped up to the burning house, which was too far gone to save. Lance was standing over the bodies of his wife and child, like an animal unable to grasp that death had come and gone. He was so still and silent. Eerie. The body of Kuffel lay next to the house, sparks from the fire beginning to smolder on his clothing.

"Oh, my God and Jesus Christ," Rowdy breathed, feeling himself in the presence of cold implacability when Lance turned to him and said, very quietly, "My horse is around here somewhere. Get him for me."

Rowdy knew that this was not the time for revenge. Those Army boys were all around! Schuyler Whitlock was a dead man, no doubt about it. But now was not the time.

"Hey, boss, I know there ain't nothin' we can do . . ."

"You can get my horse," Lance told him.

"Hey, boss, let's wait till mornin' and let's . . ."

"Schuyler Whitlock didn't wait," Lance said.

"But boss," interjected loyal old Jasper Zenda, "you'll jes' be ridin' into a trap."

"Those who set traps are caught in them," answered Lance, still with that same unearthly stillness.

Rowdy shrugged. "Couple you boys go hunt up the palomino," he said. "Rest of you get back to your jobs. Nothin' here but what a man's grief will have to do itself."

"Thank you," Lance said. "And when you find the horse,

bring it directly here." He was thinking of the surveying instruments. "Hunt up Kuffel's horse too," he added. "It can't be very far away."

Then, when the men had gone to obey his instructions, Lance fell to his knees on the ground beside the bodies of Fawn and his little girl. Tenderly, he pressed closed their eyes, and for a little while he was with them, as gone from the weary earth as they were gone. Fawn's last words had been a plea against revenge, but the feeling, the need, the very injustice was too much for him to bear. Now was the time for *ycripsicu*.

Rowdy Jenner came walking across the yard, leading the palomino. Lance stood up, and took the reins. Rowdy was looking at him warily.

"Boss, I wish I could tell you how sorry . . ."

"You cannot, and no one can, but you have always helped me, and been a true friend to me. So I know you will be likewise now. Many things must be done."

"Like I was sayin' before, boss, now may not be the time . . ."

"It is the time. Whitlock does not yet know that I am still alive. He does not even know what happened to Kuffel. And the Army men will be in their tents tonight, east of Black Forks. Now is exactly the time."

"Boss, what's this junk tied to your horse?"

"Schuyler Whitlock's tombstone," Lance said.

"What?" wondered Rowdy, scratching his head.

Then Jasper Zenda rode up, trailing Kuffel's horse by a lariat tied to its bridle. "Found him over by the orchard," Jasper said. "What do you want to do? Should I take him to the stable?"

"No," replied Lance. He walked to the bartender's body and rolled it over and over in the dirt, thus extinguishing a few last sparks on Kuffel's clothing. Then he bent down and lifted the body onto the back of the horse. "Tie him," said

Lance to his cowhands, and they complied, cutting the lariat into short lengths, lashing the beefy Kuffel onto the horse.

"Now," he said, mounting his own horse, "there are two more things you must do for me tonight. First, fire the forge and melt down these surveying devices, then take my wife and daughter and lay their bodies to rest. Bury them here on the ranch, but never tell me—not tonight, not tomorrow, not ever—where you have laid them. Not knowing, I will think that they are everywhere, and so they will be."

He took the reins of Kuffel's horse, touched spurs lightly to the flanks of his own palomino, and moved off slowly toward Black Forks.

An hour before dawn, Lance approached the town. It was a good time. The deep sleep time. Whitlock would have men posted, but they would be hard pressed to stay alert, just beginning to relax after a long night on sentry duty. Sentries were no real problem. Whitlock was. He lived in a hotel room above the saloon.

The town was very quiet, its little scattering of buildings alien and forlorn on the timeless plains. Beyond the town, Lance could barely make out the dark shapes of the soldiers' tents.

Lance dismounted, took up a handful of gravel, and tossed it against an upstairs window. "Hey, Kuff? That you?" Whitlock called immediately, in a hoarse whisper. He must have been getting worried about his henchman's delayed return.

Leaving Kuffel and the horses behind the saloon, Lance entered the building through a rear door, taking care to remain in shadow. He saw the long bar stretching dark along the wall, the door to Whitlock's office at its end, and the staircase coming down. He saw Yellow-teeth coming down the staircase, shirtless, wearing boots, breeches, and a brace of revolvers.

"Boss!" Lance hissed.

Whitlock stopped on the stairway and looked into the darkness. "Kuffel? That you?"

"Yeah."

"Where the hell have you been?" Whitlock asked angrily, hurrying across the saloon toward Lance. "T. R. said everything got balled up out there. He said you might have loused your part. Are they dead? Tell me, for Christ's sake, are the Tallworths dead?"

"No," said Lance, leaping out of the darkness and grabbing Yellow-teeth by the throat.

Whitlock was half-paralyzed by the sight of Lance. He saw the big fist coming toward him. He almost welcomed it.

When Whitlock came back to consciousness, it was not long after dawn. The ground was going by beneath his eyes, and something was thumping steadily at his belly. It took him a few moments to realize he was tied like a sack of potatoes, stomach-down on the back of a horse. The jouncing was painful. It was difficult to breathe. His jaw felt as if it had been broken. Jouncing, gasping, he tried to get his bearings, remembering his encounter with Lance in the saloon. Yes, there was Tallworth, on the horse ahead. It was then that Whitlock noticed a pair of boots that hung down next to him. Another man was slung across the horse, a partner for his last ride.

"Where . . . where are we . . . going?" Whitlock managed, between the whacks to his stomach.

Lance turned in the saddle and sent back a smile that made Whitlock go cold as dead blood.

"Bitterroot Pass," said Lance.

The sun was high by the time Lance reached the pass, but still Lance rode on, far down the pass, westward, until *Ycripsicu* territory was far behind. Mountains rose on either side, and the mouths of blue caverns behind clumps of twisted underbrush. Schuyler Whitlock despaired. Several times he had tried to get a rise out of his riding partner, but there was no response to his anxious questions. He assumed the other man on the horse was Kuffel, but it wasn't until Lance stopped in front of one of the mountain caves that he knew for sure. Lance cut both men free and allowed them to slide down from the horse's back, Whitlock on one side, Kuffel on the other. Whitlock looked through the horse's prancing legs and saw his partner's thick dead face in the dust.

Lance lifted Kuffel, trundled him into the cave, and returned.

Whitlock, who had been trying to free his rope-tied wrists, looked up fearfully. "What are you going to do?" he asked, trying to keep his voice steady. Lance's eyes were frightening, so cold. Whitlock thought he must be mad, and everybody knew you had to stay calm when talking to a madman.

"*Ycripsicu*," Lance said.

It made no sense to Whitlock. That was the thing. Tallworth *was* crazy. Whitlock struggled frantically against his bonds.

"Save your effort. There is one way you might get free, but not now."

Lance bent down and lifted Whitlock to his shoulders, carrying him into the blue coolness of the cave.

"What is . . . what is *ycrip*? Whatever you said?" Whitlock asked.

Lance flopped Whitlock down next to Kuffel's body. "It is a form of revenge meted out to those who love death," answered Lance, in that still, eerie voice. "Through the form of *ycripsicu*, he who has dealt death is made brother forever to the face of his own handiwork."

"What the . . . ?" muttered Whitlock. He had no idea what Lance was talking about.

"There is one chance of your surviving," Lance told him, "and it depends on your answer to this question."

Whitlock was all ears.

226

"Do you wish a gag in your mouth, or shall I break your teeth?"

"What?" Whitlock tried to wriggle and snake away on the floor of the cave. Lance stopped him with a boot planted at the small of his back. "Gag or broken teeth?" Lance asked. "It's very important."

Whitlock felt himself going wild now. Panic was setting in. "Gag?" he asked.

"Very good choice," said Lance, which made no more sense to Whitlock than anything that had happened so far. He watched with mounting horror as Lance gagged him with a neckerchief, then dragged him close to the dead Kuffel. Only when Lance began tying him *to* Kuffel did Whitlock begin to realize what was in store for him.

". . . *brother forever to the face of his own handiwork,"* Lance had said.

Lance was leaving him to die, bound to one who was already dead!

"Now you may contemplate that which you have loved so well," said Lance. "Good-bye."

Whitlock shut his eyes against Kuffel's glassy gaze. He heard Lance's boots on the stone floor of the cave, and then hoofbeats in the pass, and then nothing.

5

Lance was too sad, too weary, to care when a dozen Army men came riding in beneath the High Y gate. Only the stranger on the bay mare beside the colonel roused him to bleak attention. A brash, burly young man with a shock of rust-colored hair, he kept one eye in a squint, as if he were perpetually winking at something.

Lance had ordered his men out onto the range but, too disconsolate over his losses, he had remained behind. In grief deeper than any he had known, Lance lacked the spirit to taste those long restorative days on the plains, to smell the grass and ride in the living wind. Happiness was gone from him now. Pleasure did not exist, nor could it be contemplated. All *Ycripsicu* was the grave of Fawn and Sostana; the revenge against Whitlock had brought only more misery and hopelessness, no peace.

Lance was felling and stacking the blackened timbers of his home when the soldiers and the stranger rode up, halted, and dismounted. The stranger was squinting about, nosy, arrogant, and shameless. He didn't have a care in the world.

Lance mopped the soot from his forehead. "Colonel," he said.

The officer looked at the charred ruins, discomfited as men are in the face of tragedy and heartbreak.

"Heard about your loss," he said. "Mighty sorry."

Through Rowdy and Jasper Zenda, Lance had let it be known that Sostana and Fawn were killed by fire. Disaster was common on the frontier, something to be expected. People thought Lance had been out that night trying to turn the herd into the storm. Bad luck all around. It was the price of life, the way things were.

"Gonna rebuild?" inquired the cocky stranger.

Lance turned to the young man. He had bull-like shoulders and a chin as square and strong as the iron mallet of a sledgehammer. He gave off an aura of energy just about to explode, most likely into mischief, possibly violence. Nothing had happened in his life to make him worry, and the very assurance of his shoulders-back stance suggested that he thought nothing ever would.

"Oh," said the colonel, "excuse me. Tallworth, this is Clint Granger."

Lance's grief-burdened mind recapitulated a few facts: Granger. The railroad. J. J. Granger. St. Paul. Chicago. *Elizabeth*.

He rallied slightly. "Granger," he said, holding out his hand, which the young man shook energetically.

"Pleasure," he said. "Tallworth, we got to talk . . ."

"It'll have to wait," interjected the colonel. "Tallworth, I got to tell you a few things, painful though they might be."

Lance steeled himself. "Go ahead."

The colonel looked at all the men standing around, then looked back at Lance. "Must be a better place to talk than here in the open?"

"Let's go down to the cookhouse, then," Lance suggested. "Cook's out with the roundup, but I know how to fix coffee, anyway."

The colonel ordered his men to water their mounts, then do as they wished, sleep if they wanted. He and Lance started toward the cookhouse. Clint Granger fell in with them, as if it were the most natural thing in the world to do.

"Granger, we're going to talk private business," the officer told him.

Instantly, Clint flared. His face flushed, his eyes glinted

wildly. That immense vitality threatened to boil over. "My pa's a very rich man, and he's got a lot of friends in Washington."

"That may well be, son, but this is my jurisdiction. You go tell my men about your pa. It'll impress some of them, and the rest it'll amuse."

Young though he was, Clint had seldom been spoken to in that manner. The colonel's tone surprised him into acquiescence, if not acceptance. The acceptance of another's will was fundamentally impossible for a Granger.

"Tallworth," said the officer, when he and Lance were seated over steaming coffee at a table in the cookhouse, "I know you've had a hell of a lot to bear, but I wouldn't be doing my job if I didn't talk to you."

"Go on."

"Now, everybody in these parts knows there was bad blood between you and Schuyler Whitlock. Between you and his associate too."

"There was," Lance admitted.

"And Whitlock wanted control over Bitterroot Pass."

"He did."

"So does that young man out there, Clint Granger. And his father. They sent a couple of surveyors out here, but the men disappeared. Know anything about that?"

Bart and Pete. "Why would they have been surveying my land?" he asked.

"I don't know that they were. But you know nothing about them?"

"Only what you've told me. This is dangerous country for those who don't know it."

The colonel sipped coffee thoughtfully. "Ever follow the pass way back into the mountains?" he asked casually.

"Yes."

"Back where those caves are?"

"Yes, I know where the caves are."

"Been there recently?"

230

"Not recently."

The officer shook his head. "You're lucky," he said. "My men were searching for traces of the surveyors—that damn J. J. Granger is powerful enough to get the Army assigned to do his dirty work—and one of the sergeants stumbled into a cave that stank to high heaven. Found two dead men in there. They'd been tied together, apparently, and one of them had tried to chew his arm off in order to get free. I've heard of animals doing that while trying to get out of traps, but this is the first time . . ."

He shook his head.

"Terrible," said Lance. Whitlock had chosen correctly in picking the gag. He had chewed through it, then turned his teeth on his own flesh in a savage frenzy to escape the dead man to whom he was bound.

The colonel gave Lance a hard look. "Who do you think those men were?"

"The two surveyors?"

The colonel kept staring at Lance, right into his eyes. Lance stared back.

"If you're suggesting that I had anything to do with it, we'd best ride to Helena and begin with the proper legal procedures, whatever they are . . ."

The officer sighed, and broke off his intimidating stare.

"No, what's the use. There's no evidence. I've already talked to your men, and you've got a couple of dozen who'll back you in anything. Wish I could say the same for my troops. No"—he finished his coffee—"I'll just file a report. But," he added, standing, "I'd be careful if I were you."

Lance stood too. "How so?"

"Your wife. She was Indian, wasn't she?"

Lance nodded.

"What tribe?"

"Sioux."

"I fought a lot of Sioux. I know a bit about them."

231

He and Lance left the cookhouse and went back out to the ranch yard. Clint Granger saw them and swaggered over.

"Tallworth, can we talk now?"

"Not today. Not ever."

"It's important. It's about right-of-way to the pass. You could make a fortune."

"I don't wish to make a fortune."

Granger gaped. He had never heard *this* from any man, certainly not from a sane man. "I understand," he said, jerking his head toward the ruin of the house. "It'll take a little time to get over . . ."

"I'm not interested," Lance said.

Granger shrugged, undismayed. He would try again. He would be back.

The colonel ordered his men to mount, did so himself, and they rode off, Granger with them, beneath the big gate with the Y above it. Lance saw the colonel glance up at the letter.

Now I have done revenge, he thought. *It was right, but it was a thing of death.* He felt no joy, yet something in his soul was calmed, as if he had accomplished a great responsibility.

* * *

Clint Granger was back on the following day.

"I don't mince words," he told Lance. "Me and my old man want to build a railroad right across this here part of Montana. Now, how about right-of-way? How about kicking in with us?"

Lance, brooding deeply, could not think—and did not want to talk about—railroads, or cattle, or even life. The black spirit had come down upon him, relentless and triumphant. Clint, shrewd son of a shrewd father, saw this and understood. From his saddlebag he withdrew a bottle of

232

good whiskey made in the East, far superior to the ragged corn product of these plains.

"Have some of this," he urged Lance.

Lance laughed, and took the bottle.

"Hell, have a lot. You know what? You're gonna die out here if you don't watch it. The black dog got you by the balls and he ain't gonna let go unless you shake him loose."

Lance looked at Clint, with the bottle in his hand. The bottle was wavering, full of gold, and Clint was wavering behind it, framed by the big black sky. The big sky. Black spirit. Black dog. *Ycripsicu* was a bad dream, and everywhere a grave. Somewhere was a garden in the past, a gatepost, and a girl with auburn hair, deep and without end. But not here, not here . . . Lance laughed.

"Let's you an' me get outta here for a long while," Clint said, squinting shrewdly, winking at Lance, winking at all of life, his rust-colored hair like devil's fire against the burning sky. "Dad would love to meet you. Man like you can rule the West one day. If you got the right partners." Clint laughed and squinted. Why did he do that? Was something wrong with his eye? "Come on, what do you say? You an' me, a lot of whiskey, and the slickest whores money can buy. Come on, what do you say? Let's go to St. Paul. Let's go to Chicago. We'll have a high old time."

Lance laughed some more, and hoisted the wavering bottle, full of gold.

When Rowdy Jenner and the men came back from the roundup, Lance was gone.

"Ain't nothin' changed," said Rowdy. "He'll be back. All's he needs is someone to make his heart beat again. But he'll be back."

Part Five

CHICAGO, ILLINOIS • 1886

1

Alois Smedley introduced J. J. Granger to Elizabeth in the restaurant of the Blackstone Hotel in January of 1886. None of them knew it at the time—save perhaps Granger, who had more than a touch of evil genius in him—but from that moment the auburn-haired beauty and the crude Minnesota tycoon were locked in a complicated, sometimes unreadable duel that would be to the death.

"Well, what the hell have we here!" boomed Granger, clomping through the elegant dining room in his backwoods boots and yanking a chair away from the table. Elizabeth and Smedley had already been seated. Granger's eye, glinting with avarice, amusement, and lust, was fixed on Elizabeth's breasts.

The Blackstone's captain grasped the back of Granger's chair, essaying the ritual of seating.

"Hey, I don't need no help," barked the Minnesotan, half-turning toward the captain. "Hell, I don't even need no help standing *up*!"

He sat down and pulled in his chair, grunting happily at the sight of fine china and expensive silver. "First class, ain'tcha?" he said, ducking his head toward Smedley. His one eye caressed Elizabeth's breasts again, and then he raised it to her face. "Well, and what *do* we have here?" he asked, obviously attracted, carnally and otherwise. "You sure as hell can't be no relative to poor old dead Gustav. He was ugly as sin, God rest his soul. And I see you're lookin' at my gone eye," he added happily.

In truth, Elizabeth could not help noticing the ragged black patch over Granger's left eye. But she'd been looking at the patch no more than at any other part of his astounding appearance. So *this* was an American tycoon? This was the terror of the North Star state, who had congressmen and senators on his payroll, who could buy a whole forest with a squiggle of his pen—he needed only to make an "X"—and who was her competitor in the emerging iron business? Starbane, it was said, was a cultivated man, as well as a competitor. It had seemed so easy, in Oslo, for Elizabeth to suggest driving a wedge between him and Granger. But now Granger was sitting next to her, resembling nothing so much as a human wedge, fashioned of ruthlessness, flesh, and will.

"Guess you wanta know about my gone eye?" he asked jovially, and Elizabeth knew she would hear the story whether she wanted to or not.

"Chippewa arry," Granger declared, banging his fist on the table and looking around for a waiter. "Was just a young pup at the time. Was up in the North Woods, way up around Chrisholm—that's iron country now, hey!—an' was out huntin'. Redskin bastards wasn't even on reservations then . . ." He looked around some more, and banged the table again, catching the eye of several waiters and everyone dining in the place. "Over here, whiskey, on the quick!" Turning back to Elizabeth, he continued. "Well, I was out after deer that day, but a rabbit would've done. Hadn't eaten meat in a week, and that's tough sledding for a red meat eater like me. Had me a deer rifle with high-powered shot, would've punched a hole through three feet of solid oak." Granger paused and chuckled. A waiter, wearing a white coat and an expression of distaste, set a bottle of whiskey and three glasses on the table. Granger grabbed his wrist. "Expect to live long, boy?" he growled.

The waiter, astounded and fearful, glanced at that one baleful yellow eye. "I . . . hope so," he said.

"Then the next time you come over here," commanded Granger, squeezing the waiter's wrist so hard that the poor man let out a whimper, "you come a lot quicker than you did this time, and you come with a great big happy smile on your feeble little face. You understand me?"

The waiter nodded.

"I'll let you go soon's I see that big smile we're all gonna see next time."

The waiter tried for a grin, and failed.

"You can do better than that." J. J. Granger squeezed the man's wrist harder, producing a gasping inhalation of pain and the pitiful parody of a smile.

"That'll do for now," grinned Granger, releasing his prey. "Remember, quick with a grin. Now, where was I?" he asked, turning back to Elizabeth and Smedley, as if nothing had happened.

Elizabeth, however, was stunned, both by the scene she had witnessed, and by J. J. Granger. Why, compared to this rude frontiersman, Uncle Gustav had been as gentle as St. Francis of Assisi. Granger was a barbarian, and he was capable of anything. A person who would gleefully make such a scene in one of Chicago's best restaurants would just as readily demolish a business opponent. Granger had hurt the waiter, who thereafter hustled over with the obsequious attitude of a whipped, grinning dog. But Elizabeth realized that Granger's main goal had been to intimidate her.

"Oh, yeah, I was hunting a deer," Granger continued, "when I heard something in the underbrush. Coulda been fox, coulda been bear. Coulda been beaver, for that matter. But it wasn't none of them things. Lord, no. It was a God-blasted Chippewa with a bow and arry, and he shot the arry straight into my eye. Had to pull the arry out myself, 'cause I was alone in the wilderness, and fix a bandage.

Stumbled back eighteen miles to the camp, bleedin' all the way . . ."

Granger splashed generous quantities of liquor in two of the glasses, handed one to Smedley and took one himself. Looking at Elizabeth questioningly, he gestured with the neck of the whiskey bottle. She declined.

". . . an' you know," he went on, "when I pulled the arry out, my eyeball came right along with it."

He said it very matter-of-factly.

Spare me, Elizabeth thought.

"Want to see the hole?" Granger asked her, lifting his hand to the black patch.

"That's quite all right," Elizabeth said.

Granger laughed, delighted with the effect his tale had aroused, and drank deeply. "Hey, let's get some menus over here," he boomed, waving to his cowed waiter.

"Mr. Granger has had an eventful life, indeed," Smedley interjected with his usual lubricious suavity.

"What, in particular, have you learned from it?" Elizabeth asked Granger, hoping to make conversation and get a bit of insight about the man.

Granger swallowed some more whiskey, neat, and looked directly into her right eye. He looked truly wild, with the glint in his eye, the patch, an unruly shock of salt-and-pepper hair, and a tangled beard of virgin blackness.

"I learned to hate Indians and arrys!" he laughed. "Quickest way to raise my soul to murder is to show me somebody what has Indian blood in them." He stopped laughing. "That's no lie, Miss Rolfson," he said.

Elizabeth believed him.

"Why don't we order and get down to business over the meal?" suggested Alois Smedley. Smedley always kept things going.

The food was hearty but good, juicy dripping slabs of broiled beef, potatoes boiled with onions, tart mashed rutabagas, and a tasty cold stew made of a fruit Elizabeth had never known, cranberries. The men drank whiskey, and Elizabeth had a beer. While they ate, Smedley limned the situation.

"Elizabeth, you're the boss, of course. But here's the deal. J.J. wants to buy us out of the Mesabi."

She looked at Smedley in amazement, then turned to Granger. "But we've only begun to acquire a few leases," she said.

Granger laughed, showing a mouthful of rutabagas and beef. "I'm buyin' off your future," he said. "Look, I don't want to compete with both you *and* Eric Starbane. And, frankly, Rolfson Industries don't have enough of a foothold up there in the iron range to interest me in a merger with you folks."

"Then why deal with us, if we're so powerless?"

"Because I don't want anybody on my flank, goddammit. I got enough trouble fighting over the range with Starbane."

"He's got more leases than you do, isn't that right?" Elizabeth asked.

"Come now . . . " Smedley soothed.

"Naw, that's right," said Granger, giving Elizabeth a glance of respect with his good eye. "And you folks here in Chicago will never catch either one of us. So let me buy up your share. I'll pay you twice what your outlay was. Smedley, here, has shown me the papers. You paid two hundred twenty-five per acre for . . . how many acres you tell me, Alois?"

"Four thousand two hundred and eight."

"All right, let's say four thousand two hundred. At two hundred twenty-five per. So I'll pay you . . . let's see . . . in the direct neighborhood of . . ."

Elizabeth made her own quick calculations. Granger was offering her close to two million dollars! For a small area of land that had scarcely begun to produce iron ore.

"Well, J.J., I must admit that sounds eminently

fair . . ." Smedley began.

"Don't puzzle your pretty little head about it, Miss Rolfson," Granger said, smiling. "That there is a drop in the bucket to a man like me."

"Quite a bucket," Elizabeth observed.

This time Smedley smiled. "Well, let's go ahead and . . ."

"I'd like to think about it," Elizabeth declared, half-afraid Granger was going to reach out and grab her by the wrist, or worse.

"Look," growled Granger, leaning forward, "I told you I got to clear my flank to deal with Starbane." He glared at Smedley. "I thought you told me this was all a formality, Alois? You think I get a kick taking that freezing train down here from St. Paul in the middle of winter?"

"Now, J.J."

Elizabeth had heard Granger's words very clearly. *I thought you told me this was all a formality.* She looked at Smedley. He was cool and unperturbed. A part of his nature. He manifested emotional facades completely antithetical to the situations that produced them. She ought to have suspected skulduggery. And, she realized, she ought to fire him on the spot. But she did not. At the moment, she had neither the knowledge nor the nerve to proceed.

So she let him sit there and proceed to tell her, "All right, Miss Rolfson. As you know, you're the boss." Then he turned to Granger. "She'll think about it, J.J. I'm sure we can come to an accord soon."

"I'll be in town," gruffed the frontier tycoon, "but not too damn long." Then he smiled at Elizabeth, the kind of grin that comes to a cat when it spies a likely canary. "Good thinkin', Miss Rolfson," he said.

When Elizabeth made her first visit to the Rolfson offices the next day, still feeling uncertain about her encounter with

Granger and what to do about it, Alois Smedley did nothing to ease her jitters.

"Well, I believe you have 'gone and done it,'" he observed, somewhat haughtily.

"Pardon me?"

"'Gone and done it.' An American expression. I fear you have fouled up the business with Granger."

"All I said was that I wanted a little time to think his offer over," Elizabeth responded, hating the defensive tone of her voice. "What's so bad about that?"

Smedley, who had been so friendly and cooperative in Norway, and so glibly suave at the Blackstone yesterday, was now displaying another facet of his personality. He was being critical and aggressive. Elizabeth, who had not yet gotten her bearings in this raw new setting, this huge, chaotic semblance of a city at the edge of a wild frontier, felt assurance flowing from her like blood from a wound. That, undoubtedly, was Smedley's intent, but she was powerless to combat it just the same.

"Come into my office and we'll talk," he told her peremptorily. He led her through an impressive antechamber, with a luscious mustard-colored carpet, gleaming mahogany moldings, and a glistening ivory wallpaper that gave the appearance of satin. On the wall was a portrait of Uncle Gustav, flanked by the flags of Norway and the United States. The entryway led directly into a large front office, also richly carpeted, where rows of wide desks attested to the size and industry of Rolfson Industries. Young women worked at the nearest row of desks, with young men in the row directly behind them, and older men back farther still.

"The girls are merely secretaries, of course," sniffed Smedley. "The young men are our executive secretaries. They cannot make decisions, but they are allowed into the company of top managers, those being the older men you see."

Behind the older men was a long wall with one portentous double door directly at its center.

"Let's go back there to my office," commanded Smedley, and started toward the door. He was acting as though this were entirely his terrain, and that he could do anything he pleased here, in any manner he chose.

Elizabeth read the portents in a moment. If she were ever to be respected here as the true head of the company, she would have to dislodge Smedley from that imposing office. He was the only one who had a private office. Even the so-called "top managers" worked side by side at desks, just like the secretaries did.

Elizabeth had also noticed something else. At the moment of her entrance into the room with Smedley, a current of fear had passed through the employees, like a ripple of wind across a field of wheat. The sight of it sent shivers up Elizabeth's spine. What manner of institution had she come here to command? No one was looking at her directly, although she sensed furtive glances, surreptitious peeks. Elizabeth felt as if she were being spied upon in public! She also felt the people at desks along Smedley's course shrink away from him, in a way that combined fear and revulsion.

This would have to stop.

"Mr. Smedley," she said.

He stopped and turned, surprised to see her still standing before the row of secretaries.

"I think this would be a proper time to meet the people who work for me."

Smedley noted the pointed *"for me,"* as she had intended he should, but he was far more discomfited at what he took to be the impropriety of her behavior. A leader did not seek to be familiar *in any way* with the lowly foot-soldiers of his empire! Unthinkable! But if Smedley could muster nothing else, he could always produce the deceptive sheen of savoir faire. It was a part of his deadly charm as much as it was the root of his survival.

"Of course, Miss Rolfson," he oozed, coming back toward her to handle the introductions.

The employees had given no visible signs, but Elizabeth sensed intuitively that she had made a correct move. These people were not afraid of *her*. But they were terrified of Smedley. Even as he took her from desk to desk—"Miss Rolfson, this is Mrs. Pearl, she does our intracity correspondence; Miss Rolfson, this is Miss Tate, she copies records; Miss Rolfson, this is Miss Handley, she works in the file room"—Elizabeth perceived, behind the social facade, a deep hostility toward Smedley that bordered on hatred.

In the case of Miss Handley, the file clerk, that hostility was particularly evident. The girl, a lithe brunette with lovely eyes of chocolate brown, could barely conceal her animosity toward Smedley. But she tried. She had to. Elizabeth, who had already observed the cheap clothing of the other employees, saw that poor Sandra Handley was dressed even more severely. Her long shapeless skirt could not hide cracked, ruined shoes, and her blouse, although fastidiously clean, looked as if it would crumble at the touch. Yet Elizabeth felt a strength, a warmth, in Sandra's quick, shy handshake, and the young girl's eyes met Elizabeth's frankly. Some sort of inquiry there? Some form of request? Sandra Handley kept looking at Elizabeth, even when Smedley had led her on down the row of desks.

Finally, the greetings were completed, and Elizabeth accompanied Smedley into the main office. It was spectacular, and spectacularly expensive, with Gustav Rolfson's penchant for collecting artwork and artifacts clearly evident. Only here, in contrast to the gallery in Oslo, the objects were strange to the eye, almost antediluvian in the impact they aroused, the feeling they evoked.

Smedley laughed when he saw Elizabeth staring at a strange, carved pole. Although there was little outward resemblance, it reminded her of the gargoyles on European cathedrals.

"That's a totem pole," he explained. "The rest of these things are Indian too. Gustav . . . ah, Mr. Rolfson had a feeling for them. That's the reason I never meet with J.J. Granger here in the office. He hates Indians and . . ."

"You've met with Mr. Granger a lot then?"

"Oh, no, no," Smedley replied quickly, smoothly turning her attention to a stone vase of brilliant blue. "This is, for example, a Seminole artifact, perhaps a thousand years old. No one knows how they managed to color the stone with indigo. But they did. This vase is worth thousands of dollars, even now."

Elizabeth wondered how a vase of this value must appear to poor Sandra Handley, who must freeze each day, going to and from work in her threadbare clothing.

"Your uncle certainly did love pretty things," Smedley said. Then, as if the time for pleasantness had been spent, he changed his tone. "Sit down," he commanded. "There are now two major mistakes you have made."

"I'm not aware of . . ."

"There are, I'm afraid, a lot of things you are unaware of. First, yesterday, you committed a possibly irretrievable blunder in turning down Granger's generous offer. . . ."

"I only said I wanted to consider it. People are not especially bighearted, you know, unless they have a motive. . . ."

"Yes, yes," he said impatiently. "And then, just minutes ago, you lowered yourself in the eyes of everyone."

"I did what?" Elizabeth exclaimed.

Smedley was sitting behind a huge desk now, and through the windows behind him Elizabeth could see the expanse of Lake Michigan, blue and vast under a vast blue sky, as if there were no end to America.

"*Lowered* myself?" asked Elizabeth, mystified, from her

chair in front of the desk. *I should be behind the desk*, she thought, but lacked the nerve to address the issue.

"*Never* treat the help with familiarity," Smedley instructed snippily. "Fear is the only technique when it comes to dealing with subordinates. Keep that in mind. You will now have to spend a long time regaining your dignity, after that unfortunate orgy of handshaking."

He is wrong, Elizabeth thought. But she didn't want to pursue the matter now. Smedley, too, was more concerned about something else.

"We have to deal with Granger," he pronounced. "Let me send him a message and indicate our willingness to accept his offer immediately."

This Elizabeth was not prepared to do. Hesitant, but nerved for the moment, she told him what she had decided to attempt.

"I want you to telegraph Eric Starbane," she said, "and ask him if he wishes to make a bid too."

"What?" cried Smedley, astounded.

"As you have stated, Mr. Smedley," responded Elizabeth, clasping her hands together to veil a slight trembling, "you work for me. Perhaps there is a portion of truth, after all, in your manner of dealing with subordinates."

Instantly—too swiftly, in fact—Alois Smedley shifted his tactics. "You're absolutely right, Miss Rolfson," he nodded, smiling. "A telegram will be composed and sent out to St. Paul this very day."

"Good," said Elizabeth, hoping that he could not hear her sigh of relief, but wondering why he had capitulated so readily. Well, her instructions would be followed, and that was the important thing.

"I'd like to see the house this afternoon," she requested. "Would you arrange for a coach?"

"Oh, but I'm afraid that won't be possible," he responded, after a moment's consideration.

"Why not?"

"Well, I've . . . I've taken the liberty of arranging a reception in your honor. At the Merchant's and Manufacturer's Union Club. I think it's important that you meet the men who run things in Chicago, and . . ."

Elizabeth admitted that he was right. The house could wait, for the time being. If she intended to be taken seriously, then it would not do to shrink from the duties required by her new position.

"All right," she agreed, "but until then I *must* see to some shopping. There are things I absolutely have to have if I am going to get through this winter."

"Of course, of *course*," agreed Smedley indulgently.

When she left the main office, leaving Smedley behind the magisterial desk, Elizabeth saw those rows of heads bent over their work. There was no spirit of life in the room, none at all, and the realization depressed her. In surroundings so bright and cheerful, one might have expected at least a sheen of verve, if not contentment. But no. She passed through the workers, toward the door, and none of them raised a head or hand, or gave a word of farewell. The force of this strange ambience struck Elizabeth, and she felt more unsettled than she had upon arriving. Turning at the door, she paused a moment, waiting. Slowly, one by one, the employees ceased what they were doing or what they were pretending to do, and lifted their heads and looked at her.

Behind them, Elizabeth saw the door to the main office ease open perhaps half an inch. She could not see Alois Smedley, but she knew he was there.

"I . . . I want to say that it was a pleasure to meet you," she told them, still angry and smarting over Smedley's denunciation of her friendly behavior, "and I want to get to know all of you well." She paused. They were all staring at her intently. She might as well have been talking in a foreign language they had never heard before. Perhaps she was: the tongue of sincerity, which few in life have mastered. Scanning the room, Elizabeth noticed that Sandra Handley was not at her desk, and that was odd.

"Good-bye, for now," Elizabeth said, leaving the office.

How strange! she was thinking, going down the street. Her American employees had been so long cowed by Gustav, so thoroughly frightened by Alois Smedley, that they seemed incapable of spontaneous behavior. Well, she would make some changes very quickly. Why, if Mr. Starbane was willing to dicker over iron leases, Elizabeth might use such negotiations to ease Smedley aside forthwith. She had already concluded that, being so far behind Granger and Starbane in the iron business, Rolfson Industries ought to turn its attention to other pursuits. She had several of these in mind already.

Just as she left the Rolfson Building, crossing the sidewalk toward the waiting carriage where the uniformed doorman waited, Elizabeth felt a furtive tug on her beaverskin cape.

Elizabeth turned to find Sandra Handley standing at her elbow, shivering in the cold.

"Get away from Miss Rolfson," the doorman commanded, advancing.

"I must talk to you," pleaded Sandra to Elizabeth, her lovely brown eyes full of gloom and fright and desperation. "Please, it'll only take a moment, and . . ."

The doorman reached them and put his big hand on Miss Handley's shivering shoulder. He eyed her with suspicion and malice.

"It's all right," Elizabeth told him, sensing the terrible need that lay behind Sandra's forthright act. "Come," she said to the girl, "let's go back inside where it's warm."

With the doorman looking on in shocked malevolence, Elizabeth led Miss Handley back into the building's granite vestibule, which was only slightly warmer than outside. She pulled off her cloak and wrapped it around the girl's shoulders.

"Why, you'll catch your death . . ."

"No, don't talk, there's so little time," warned Sandra, speaking swiftly in a husky whisper, looking over her shoulder, glancing outside where the big doorman waited, watching.

"What *is* it?" asked Elizabeth. Sandra, the poor thing, seemed beside herself.

"Ma'am, there are terrible things going on," she blurted, fixing her big brown eyes on Elizabeth. The power of utter conviction burned in her gaze.

"Well, tell me. What terrible things?"

"Oh, you ought to *see* the secret files, Ma'am. And Mr. Smedley wants me."

"Wants you?"

"He *wants* me, Ma'am," repeated Sandra Handley, with an emphasis Elizabeth could not misunderstand. "And I don't know what to do. Jobs are hard to come by. My papa died last winter when the flu hit, and now Mama is real sick, and I have four brothers and three sisters to take care of, all younger than me. . . ."

Sandra began to sob, and tried to hide the tears, ashamed of them.

Elizabeth was revolted. Smedley, who had just given her a lecture on familiarity with employees, was making obscene advances on this poor girl. She would settle this with him shortly and not sweetly at all.

"Dry your tears, and go back up to your desk. No one is going to take your job. I promise you. And I'll see that you have no more trouble from Mr. Smedley."

"Oh, Ma'am, thank you, thank you." Sandra wiped her eyes on the sleeve of her pitiful blouse. "But I have to talk to you, Ma'am, about the files. You don't know . . ."

The girl looked somewhat relieved, but her eyes were large and wild, feverish. Elizabeth, for a moment, wondered if Sandra was really telling the truth. Was she showing mere fright, or a sliver of derangement? The two were difficult to tell apart, but still . . .

"You go back up to your desk now."

"No, no, when can we talk? We *must* talk. You don't know . . ."

Sandra Handley was clutching Elizabeth's sleeve now, a resurgence of courage nerving her to press on. Businessmen moving in and out of the building glanced and then gaped.

"Now, now," said Elizabeth, "we can't talk here. Listen, can you come to my hotel tonight? The Blackstone? We'll talk there."

The girl's eyes widened. "Oh, Ma'am, but I couldn't go *there*! They wouldn't let the likes of me in the door."

Sandra was right. Elizabeth's heart went out to the girl. The poor were the poor, in every nation of the earth.

"I shall be outside the hotel waiting for you, then," she offered. "We'll find a warm place to eat and you can tell me . . . what it is you think you have to tell me."

"Oh, but Ma'am, I'm not just whistling Dixie."

"What?" Elizabeth did not understand the phrase. "Look, you'll be able to come at seven o'clock?"

"Yes, indeed. Oh, yes. And thank you, thank you . . ."

Sandra Handley raced back up the stairs to the rows of Rolfson desks.

How very odd, reflected Elizabeth in the coach, on her way to shopping. Many things were happening, and she cursed herself for not understanding what they were. Anger at Smedley mingled with bewilderment over the behavior of Sandra Handley. Well, perhaps tonight it would all be clarified.

When the driver stopped in front of a store with a big sign reading RED RIVER FURRIERS, Elizabeth got down from the carriage and back into the snow and slush and icy wind.

"What is 'Dixie'?" she asked Kohler, her driver.

"The South," he said. "The damn Rebs. My pappy an' his buddies done whipped 'em good."

Yes, their Civil War. It had ended two decades ago. "What does 'whistling Dixie' mean then?" she asked the driver.

"That means talking through your hat."

"Means *what*?" Elizabeth pictured a man addressing the open end of his headpiece.

"It means . . . well, Ma'am, if you'll pardon me, it means shooting the bull."

"I'm afraid I don't grasp it," she said, more mystified than ever. At St. Ada's, her English had been considered excellent. But she could not decipher the connection between whistling and killing a dumb animal.

The driver, trying to find words, grew frustrated. He didn't have that many words to choose from. "You know, Ma'am? Throwing around what the bull produces. What the bull produces out of his . . . out of his *rear end*, Ma'am, if you'll excuse me . . ."

"I *understand*!" cried Elizabeth. "*That* expression must be well nigh universal." Sandra Handley was going to tell her something that was neither worthless nor false.

"Good for you," said Kohler. "Some of you furriners catch on right quick."

2

The Merchant's and Manufacturer's Union Club overlooked the Chicago River. A narrow, three-story building with an elaborate portico and a pink sandstone facade, it appeared outrageously decorative in brawling, workaday Chicago, more unique even than the new opera house, which was considered the wildest architectural whim west of Pittsburgh. To the Union Club repaired the men who had, by virtue of amassing incalculable and virtually untraceable sums of money, acquired power and prestige—and, quite often, notoriety—in the American Midwest. Before luncheon commenced, Smedley sat beside Elizabeth at the head table—she was the honored guest—and pointed out certain men of influence.

"See the man over there? The one with the cream-colored waistcoat? That's Averell Bischofsweisen, the brewer. He arrived in America on a cattle boat from some godforsaken place in Hungary fifteen years ago, and now he has ten million dollars, and a bad case of gout." Smedley laughed. Other people's pains gave him pleasure. "And the man he's talking to, the tall fellow with the bald pate. That's Henry C. Fasching. He's done work for Rockefeller, the oil man. Union busting, breaking heads, and things like that . . ."

Elizabeth stared at Fasching. The man didn't look particularly mean, not mean enough to have done the things Smedley reported. Fasching looked like . . . why, just like any businessman.

". . . and coming in the door now is Travis Chesterfield. He's a character. Very rich, just like everyone who comes to the club. The Chesterfields are the most prosperous landlords in Chicago. 'Show no mercy,' that's their motto. Travis and his son could squeeze blood out of a stone . . ."

"Does Eric Starbane ever come here when he's in Chicago?" asked Elizabeth, curious to know about a competitor, and also subtly reminding Smedley of the telegram he was supposed to send.

"Oh, yes," replied Smedley expansively. "He's been here. Not often, though. He operates mostly out of St. Paul, and sometimes from Duluth. That's the nearest shipping town to the Mesabi Range. Boom town is what it's going to be pretty soon."

He was avoiding the matter of the telegram! "Have you sent that communication?" she demanded.

"I will, I will," he replied apologetically. "It's been drafted according to your instructions, and Miss Handley is seeing to it right now. I do hope she can handle *this* properly, at least," he added casually.

Elizabeth debated whether to bring up the things Sandra Handley had told her about, the alleged "secret files," and Smedley's sexual advances, but decided against it. She would wait until she spoke to the girl this evening.

"What is Eric Starbane like?" she asked the slick-headed executive.

"Starbane? He looks like a big blond god. Norwegian, just like you and your uncle. Gentle in manner, unless provoked, and with a will of iron behind him. Your uncle was obsessed with beating him in business."

"Uncle Gustav was obsessed with other things too," said Elizabeth, thinking of Gustav's preoccupation with the mysterious Gunnarson.

"By the way," said Smedley suddenly, watching her with

a sleepy eye, "Hans told me that Miss Handley bent your ear a bit this morning."

"Bent my ear? And who is Hans?"

"The doorman at our building. He told me Sandra Handley spoke to you. She seemed upset, Hans said."

Smedley still had that sleepy look, as if he didn't really care a fig what Sandra Handley had said. That meant he cared a great deal.

"It was . . . it was unimportant," answered Elizabeth, wishing that she was better at dissembling. There were a lot of skills she would have to learn, and many of them were talents she did not hold in high regard. Yet she had certainly learned, by Smedley's attitude, that Sandra Handley was not just "whistling Dixie." More than that, if even the doorman was instructed to report to Smedley, how many other spies were there?

Most of the Union Club members had arrived and were taking their seats at circular luncheon tables. They jabbered to one another in the hearty, ribald tones of successful males at their ease, waving to Smedley at the head table, and inspecting Elizabeth coolly. She felt as if she were being evaluated, appraised, and weighed pound by pound for value on the marketplace.

"These are busy, rushed men," Smedley explained. "They must hurry back to great affairs . . ."

Like yours with Miss Handley? thought Elizabeth angrily.

". . . so I'll introduce you with a small speech as we lunch, after which you'll meet them one by one. Briefly, of course."

"Of course. It was so kind of you to arrange this."

"Think nothing of it. I'm here to serve you."

"I'm very pleased to hear that."

There was the slightest edge to Elizabeth's voice, and Alois Smedley did not fail to note it.

"I'm sure you are," he replied, with a pointedly neutral intonation.

But he gave a fine little speech. Over a lunch of roast squab stuffed with blueberries and wild rice, Smedley told the businessmen of Chicago all about Elizabeth Rolfson. How much she had loved her dearly departed uncle. How well she had done in "a Swiss school of great repute." How determined she was to be a "good American, and proper epitome of the business profession." How lovely she was. And how he envied the young man who would win her hand.

Elizabeth had to marvel at Smedley's command of the rostrum, his manner of expression and turns of phrase, with appropriate pauses for the laughter he knew would rise to greet his well-chosen witticisms. Smedley might have been an actor. No, he *was* an actor. That was the danger.

"Isn't he a card?" Paul Friedly kept saying. "Isn't Alois a card?" Friedly, the deputy mayor of Chicago, was seated to Elizabeth's right at the head table, to represent the city in greeting her. The Rolfson millions helped to make Chicago rich, and would help to make it richer still.

"He is a card, that's true," observed Elizabeth politely, smiling at the portly deputy mayor. She wanted to add, *He is the Joker*, but decided against it. This was indeed a fine lunch, and everyone was most friendly. But although she felt well physically, Elizabeth experienced a certain mental dizziness, a confusion composed of contradictions that might have been hilarious if the stakes were not so high. Here she was, a newcomer to America. Most immigrants struggled to scrape together pennies for their daily bread, but she was being feted by the mighty of an increasingly important city. She was given this attention because of Rolfson Industries, which she owned, but over which Smedley exercised a sinister and pervasive control. And it was Smedley himself who was standing before all these people, singing her praises. The final irony was that, whatever her beauty and however much Smedley "envied

256

the young man who would win her hand," Elizabeth was already desperately in love and desperately lonely. *What, she thought, forking the tender squab, would saturnine Lance Tallworth think of these men, every one of them powerful and smooth and articulate*? And also portly. For the most part, she had noted, successful American men ran to fat. It was a mark of success that said, *I can afford to eat!*

But the sight of those wide bellies taut against shirtfronts and vests, those fat pink cheeks going round and round as food was consumed, brought to Elizabeth's mind another contradictory image: that of Lance. The hard planes of his body. His strong, dark, hawklike face. Most of all, his mysterious, inexplicable intensity.

This lovely luncheon underscored the anomaly of her position. Elizabeth had everything, but she had nothing, least of all love. The sense of quandary was enhanced still further when Smedley finished speaking. "I have a few things to say," she told him, preparing to get to her feet.

"Oh, no, no," he whispered in hoarse admonishment. "A woman does not stand and address a company of men. It is simply *not done*. Why, it is unusual enough that you are even here in the club! And besides, what would you say? You've never had any training in public address."

Furious, Elizabeth nonetheless held her tongue.

Luncheon concluded with mincemeat pie and the ubiquitous pots of coffee. Then, just as Smedley had said, the great men came up one by one to take her hand in theirs —they did not shake it; they were far too cognizant of her fragile nature for such physical excess! All of them welcomed her to Chicago with expressions of flowery effusiveness: ". . . such a delight to have this vision amongst us . . ." ". . . our city is indeed the recipient of a veritable Helen . . ." All of them were well intentioned and, to their credit, not consciously false. But the elaborate constructions these men had painfully invented for the occasion struck her as hollow and sad, even as she smiled to receive them. Were there but two types of men: those who spoke easily to women, who could use the right words if they chose, but who could not convey true emotion, and those who possessed powerful emotion, but somehow could not—or would not permit themselves—to put it into words?

At this point, her mind on Lance Tallworth again, on his dark reticent intensity, Elizabeth found herself shaking hands with Travis Chesterfield.

". . . overjoyed, I'm sure, to have your beauteous person in our bustling midst . . ." Chesterfield was saying, his big hand wrapped around hers.

"Thank you."

"You must come to see us very soon," he invited eagerly.

Chesterfield was a handsome man, Elizabeth realized. His eyes were cold, but without the hardness of bitter combat. "My son, Booth, would love to meet you," he was telling her, "and you'd be good for him."

Another Harald Fardahl, Elizabeth thought. "Thank you, nice to meet you," she said.

"No, I mean it," he hastened to add. "You and Booth would get along just terrific. I'll have Mrs. Chesterfield whip up an invitation posthaste."

The American idiom! Elizabeth had a brief image of a corseted dowager lashing an embossed calling card. "That would be nice," she murmured.

Then the lunch was over. Smedley helped her on with the beaverskin cape and saw her to the waiting carriage.

"Not bad at all," he said to her. "You certainly impressed Travis Chesterfield. Wouldn't be a bad alliance at that," he added.

"The only alliance I'm interested in today," she snapped, irritated with the arrogant male presumption that she needed to be married off, "is the one between Eric Starbane and that telegram you're going to send. I shall speak to you tomorrow morning. Early."

She actually enjoyed the sight of his thin mouth setting in angry surprise.

When she was out of sight of Smedley and the Union Club, Elizabeth leaned out the window of the coach.

"Kohler," she called to the dour driver, "before you take me back to the Blackstone, I want to drive up past the house."

"The house?" he inquired dully, turning down to look at her from the driver's seat. Was he a dunce, or what? Perhaps looking at horses' backsides for a lifetime did that to one.

"My uncle's house," she told him. "*My* house."

"Oh!" he cried, startled.

"What's the matter?"

"Oh, nothing, Miss Rolfson, nothing," and flicked his whip at the horses.

But after a couple of minutes the carriage stopped. Elizabeth leaned out of the window again and saw Kohler squatting next to the right wheelhorse, his broad blank face twisted into an expression that might have been caused by gas pains, wonder, or genuine interest.

"What is it now?" she asked. His very presence had the effect of making her impatient.

Kohler shook his big head slowly. "Belle lost a shoe, Miss Rolfson. I'm afraid I'll have to get her to the livery right away. To avoid injury."

"Oh, all right. I'll *walk* to the hotel."

"No, no, Ma'am. You don't have to do that. Belle can make it that far. Can't you, Belle, old girl?" He patted the animal's flank as if he were encouraging a comrade.

"I'll see the house another day," Elizabeth told herself as the coach began to move again.

3

The night was twice as cold as the day had been. Elizabeth, bundled in furs, stood outside the Blackstone Hotel, awaiting Sandra Handley. It was already twenty past seven, but perhaps the girl had been delayed. To get here she would have to walk, or spend precious pennies on the streetcar. Elizabeth chastised herself mentally for not having given Miss Handley fare. If Smedley was truly up to no good, and if Sandra Handley could offer evidence to prove it, Elizabeth vowed to reward her generously.

"Sure you don't want to wait inside the lobby?" asked the hotel doorman, for about the tenth time.

Elizabeth shivered, smiled, and said no.

God, the very air was like ice. Wind howled down Chicago's rude streets, whipping clouds of snow against the sides of buildings, drifting into alleyways. In the distance stood the famous Water Tower with its grotesque turrets and useless battlements. A survivor of the Fire of 1871, Elizabeth thought, that might just as well have gone up in smoke. It looked preposterously out of place here in America, this receptacle for water that was supposed to be European, but which looked like nothing Europe had ever produced.

By ten minutes to eight, Elizabeth's toes had become numb, in spite of fur-lined boots, and she gave up. Sandra Handley was wise not to have come out tonight. Leaving the doorman instructions to summon her on the chance that

Sandra did appear, Elizabeth went back into the hotel and up to her suite. Tomorrow she would certainly go to the house and make plans to have it readied. Quickly. Living in a hotel, even a fine one, was adding to her feeling of transiency and impermanence.

Thinking of Miss Handley's remarks about "secret files," Elizabeth went to bed. Sleep did not come easily, although the big bed was warm and comfortable. Smedley's sleek, cultivated, cynical image came to Elizabeth, and the possibility of "secret files" grew rapidly to distinct probability. Yes, Alois was attempting to seduce poor Sandra Handley, and to compromise her at the office as well. He *used* people, Smedley did. He calculated as coldly as ever Uncle Gustav had! Why had Smedley been so agreeable when he was in Norway? The answer was simple. He had wanted Elizabeth to inherit the Rolfson fortune from the start. He had even wanted her to come to America, because she would be inexperienced and ductile. Why on earth would he have wanted choleric Lars Thorsen and crafty Thea Thorsdatter to inherit? They would have fired him forthwith.

Now, though, Smedley was in the driver's seat, behind that big desk. And he knew things. Elizabeth needed him, for now.

In the morning, Elizabeth decided, *I shall give instructions to divide that big office into two chambers!*

Then she slept, but not well.

Suddenly she was awake, cold sunlight glittering in the room. Someone at the door was knocking gently and calling, "Miss Rolfson! Miss Rolfson!"

She had asked to be awakened early.

"Thank you, I'm up," she called. Elizabeth sat up in bed and rubbed the night from her eyes. But before the nocturnal spell was completely gone, it left her an insight shaped by those mysterious processes of the sleeping mind: if Smedley *knew* Sandra Handley had spoken to me, and if he did not *already know* what she might have told me, he would have asked many more questions. Thus, Sandra must have spoken the *absolute* truth!

With a sense of half-fearful anticipation, Elizabeth dressed, breakfasted hurriedly, and descended to the street where Kohler was waiting with the coach.

"Belle is all right today?" Elizabeth asked him.

He looked blank.

"Belle," she repeated. *You dolt*, she thought. "The horse. Has she been reshod?"

"Oh! Belle! Why, of course!"

Something funny about Kohler too, Elizabeth realized, as the big dull-eyed lug helped her into the coach. Then it dawned on her fully: the horse had not thrown a shoe at all. There was some sort of conspiracy afoot to keep her away from Uncle Gustav's house!

Seething, she nerved herself to have it out with Smedley this very day!

Since it was early, there was little traffic, and the carriage rolled quickly southward. Just cross the river, go a bit further, enter the Rolfson Building, and Smedley would find her behind that big desk . . .

The coach stopped. Elizabeth put her head out the window, cold wind stinging her cheeks. "Another shoe, Kohler?" she asked acidly.

But no. A line of hacks and buggies and charabancs was halted in front of her own coach, just at the entrance to the Chicago River Bridge. "What is it?" she asked. She could see a number of Chicago police officers standing on the bridge, looking down at the frozen river.

"Ma'am, I don't know. Something must've happened . . ."

Elizabeth jumped from the coach, and walked toward the bridge, past gawking passengers, bleary-eyed drivers, and stamping, snorting horses. She reached the railing of the bridge.

"Wouldn't look if I was you," warned a policeman.

But Elizabeth looked. On the gray ice of the Chicago River, sprawled almost in an attitude of sleep, was the body of Sandra Handley. One arm lay across her sunken abdomen, the other was outstretched on the ice. Only her fiercely clenched fists, and the horrible grimace of her mouth, belied the posture of rest. Fists and mouth and the thin frozen rivulet of blood that ran from her mouth to the ice and spread there, frozen, in a little pool.

"I told you not to look," said the policeman, a thick, red-faced man bursting with sideburns. "But not to worry. Happens all the time. Obviously a poor girl who couldn't take it anymore. This is a tough town. Look at her shoes."

Through the crack between ruined soles and disintegrating tops protruded Sandra Handley's blue frozen toes.

A squad of police officers were slipping and sliding down the snowy embankment. One carried a folded stretcher, and several others had torches.

"Why the fire?" asked Elizabeth.

"She's frozen to the ice, Ma'am. Driven in when she jumped from the bridge last night. The men have to melt around her a little before they can haul her away."

But she didn't jump! Elizabeth wanted to scream.

When she reached the Rolfson Building, Elizabeth went up to the main office and took her place behind Smedley's big desk. She was furious and frightened, but mostly furious. She would send money to Sandra's family for the funeral, and additional money for support. But first she would find out what Smedley was up to. She began to examine the papers on his desk. He was a neat man, very organized, everything just so. Wondering who had thrown Sandra from the bridge—possibly Alois himself?— Elizabeth riffled through the papers.

Rolfson Industries was involved in many more enterprises than she had surmised. But the stacks of letters, papers, accounts, and cables atop Smedley's desk seemed quite routine.

Outside, in the big open office, Elizabeth could hear the employees arriving for their daily labor. They made a dull, shuffling sound, like people entering a funeral home, or the church of a religion in which they did not believe. There were no sounds of cheerful greeting, and few exclamations of simple recognition. It seemed as if the workers were afraid to speak.

Then, on Smedley's desk, in a big pile of cables, she found the draft of the telegram sent to Eric Starbane. It had been copied in a careful, fine hand. A dead hand, now.

Eric Starbane
312 Summit Ave.
St. Paul, Minnesota

Elizabeth Rolfson, new Directress of Minnesota Mesabi Mining, is offering to you, for immediate sale, all iron mining leases currently held by Rolfson Industries. Section and lot numbers available upon request. Your response, within thirty days, is invited.

(Signed) Alois Smedley
Managing Director
Rolfson Industries
666 North State St.
Chicago, Illinois

In the right-hand corner, in Smedley's hand, was the notation: *Transmitted January 28, 1886.*

Elizabeth sat back in the big leather armchair behind this commanding desk. True, the telegram was cold in tone, but it was a business message; hearts and flowers were not required, nor expected. Now she would wait and see how Starbane responded, and then reevaluate J. J. Granger's offer accordingly.

Next she turned to the drawers of Smedley's desk, expecting to find them locked. They were not. Eight deep sliding repositories opened easily to reveal nothing of note. Stacks of ledgers, bottles of ink, pens, pencils, tablets, stationery, even a Holy Bible occupied Smedley's drawers. But no secret files. Elizabeth checked far back in each of the drawers, even inspected the desk for hidden recesses and false compartments. She had just concluded that there weren't any hiding places when the low solemn buzz of the employees ceased abruptly.

Alois Smedley had arrived.

Elizabeth's first impulse was to slam shut the drawer she was examining and rush for the chair in front of the desk, as if she had been waiting for him. But she quelled that notion, leaning back in the leather chair and waiting instead.

Smedley threw open the door and strode into the room. He was in a hurry, his face fiercely concentrated. And he was more than surprised to see her there. But he masked it.

"Why, good morning, Elizabeth!" He stood there in front of her.

"I have decided to divide this room in two," she said, amazed at how sure her voice sounded. "You'll see to the carpenters? Also, you'll be needing a new desk."

She forced herself to look directly into his eyes, saw the pride and bitter anger there, saw it flare and fade. When he spoke, his tone was smooth and professional. "Of course, Miss Rolfson. It is fitting that you preside here."

"And," Elizabeth went on, still watching him carefully, "summon Miss Handley from her desk, would you please? There are certain things I wish to file."

Smedley's eyes widened ever so slightly in response to her directive, but his face was unreadable. He turned instantly and walked to the doorway, looking out into the front office where rows of heads were bent over desks.

"I'm afraid she's not in yet," he said, turning back to

Elizabeth. "But then, she's never been the most reliable of employees."

What was this? "Why did we retain her then?" she asked.

Smedley shrugged. "She seemed a poor girl. A bit daft, but occasionally a good worker. I hoped she would improve."

He said it matter-of-factly. Elizabeth floundered in suspicion and intent. Had she been wrong? Was she wrong now? Could Sandra Handley have been, as Smedley suggested, "a bit daft"? In that case, the whole of Elizabeth's structure of dark supposition came crashing down.

"If you'll excuse me, Miss Rolfson," Smedley was saying, "I'll go back out front and direct Mr. Tandem, our in-house jack-of-all-trades, to engage a carpenter and redo our offices here."

Smedley was very sure of himself. He had an answer for everything. And, damn, he knew things about various business projects that Elizabeth would have to learn before she chanced running the company on her own. Moreover, Alois appeared genuinely ignorant of Sandra's fate. Could a man involved in murder be *that* good an actor? Particularly the murder of a poor young woman? Elizabeth wanted to believe that a modicum of human decency beat even in the hardest of hearts.

"There is another thing I want to do," Elizabeth said. "I want to visit Uncle Gustav's house. I want to initiate whatever it will take to make the place habitable and move in as soon as possible."

"Fine, fine," Smedley responded, leaving the office to arrange for the carpenters. "You go ahead and do that. Just have Kohler drive you there."

When Smedley had gone, Elizabeth sat at the big desk, confused and fuming. What *was* going on? She bent forward, and looked through everything again, studied lists of numbers, reread business letters, telegrams, memos. Not a thing. It was the desk of a prime businessman, everything in order. *I had better spend several days examining the files*, Elizabeth decided.

A smart rapping sounded at her office door.

"Come in."

One of the top managers, a well-dressed man with a whipped-dog look, Mr. Phineas T. Greenbush, leaned into the room. "Captain O'Riley of the Chicago police to see you, Miss Rolfson. Shall I schedule an appointment or tell him to wait?"

Police. Perhaps O'Riley was here about Sandra Handley. Maybe he would have some answers. "Show the captain in," she told Greenbush.

O'Riley was a thin man of middling height. He would have been totally unprepossessing except for his eyes. Sharp and bright and blue, they saw everything, studied everything. O'Riley's gaze was so intense that it virtually gave off heat. He seemed a bit surprised to see her behind the big desk.

"Miss Rolfson," he said graciously, as she bade him sit down. "I have heard of your arrival in our city, and welcome. This visit of mine, however, is not in the spirit of . . ." His voice trailed off. He had not run out of words, or found difficulty in selecting them. He had chosen to let his sentence hang. He was watching her very closely.

Does he suspect me of a part in Sandra's death! wondered Elizabeth, astonished and hurt. What ought she do now? She knew Sandra was dead, yet had withheld the information from her employees because she wanted to test Alois Smedley. Should she now pretend ignorance of the fact to O'Riley, or speak up? Would the sideburned officer at the bridge railing remember her? Elizabeth felt an obscure guilt, the more pronounced because she was innocent. Or was she? Had not a young woman chanced the bitter night to visit her? Was that not, at the very least, curious?

"I know Miss Handley is dead," she said.

O'Riley seemed a bit amazed at her statement. Elizabeth didn't know why.

"How did you come by this information?" he asked, his blue eyes boring into her.

"On the drive here this morning, my carriage was stopped in traffic at the river bridge. I looked down and saw Sandra dead on the ice."

"And what did you think?" he snapped, as if this conversation had suddenly become an interrogation.

"I thought someone had pushed her," Elizabeth declared.

O'Riley said nothing, thinking for a moment. "Why are you of that opinion?" he asked, softly now.

"Miss Handley was coming to meet me last night, at the Blackstone. We had an appointment. She did not arrive."

"You thought nothing amiss when she did not appear?"

"It was a very cold night. I concluded that she had elected to remain at home."

"If you had been in her home," O'Riley said sadly, "your conclusion might have been altered. It is fully as cold as the streets."

He is a decent man, Elizabeth decided. Still, she did not know his intentions.

"Why was she coming to see you? At your request, or hers?"

"Hers. She said she had something to tell me."

"What?"

"I don't know for sure. It involved the business."

"This business? Rolfson Industries?"

"I think so. Yes."

"What would a filing clerk know that you, the owner, would not know?"

"Captain, as you know, I just arrived in America. In Chicago."

"And why would you, in your position, even choose to listen to a girl like that?"

Elizabeth flared. "What do you mean, 'a girl like that'?"

"My apologies."

"She seemed to be in need of help," Elizabeth offered.

"That is certainly true. As I indicated, I have been to the family home, if such it can be called. Look, Miss Rolfson, I am here because I have to check out the situation. You can understand that. Frankly, she may have jumped or she may have been pushed. I don't know. Her mother is too ill to talk. I doubt she even realizes that her daughter is dead. The eldest son, Todd, blames you for her death."

"Blames *me*? Why?"

"Because his sister went out last night to see you."

"But I . . ."

"I know. But you have to imagine how a boy of thirteen must feel. You have to have seen that pitiful lean-to in which they live out there on the west side, with snow blowing in through the cracks in the walls. He is now the sole support of his mother and those kids."

"I had already decided to make sure they are cared for."

"Thank God for that. Now, do you know anything else about Miss Handley? Any indication of why she wanted to see you in private?"

Elizabeth considered the question. To mention the "secret files" would make her seem like a fool. And there was no substantiation whatever for Sandra's assertion that Alois Smedley had made sexual advances toward her.

"I have no idea," she said.

O'Riley sighed. "You will call me if you think of anything?" he asked. It was more a command than a request.

"Yes."

"All right then, Miss Rolfson." The captain stood, and offered his hand. Elizabeth shook it, and he left. Mr. Phineas Greenbush knocked and edged into the office with a stack of cables.

"Messages, Miss Rolfson."

"Please put them right here on the desk."

He did so, and she scanned them quickly, one by one. None from Eric Starbane. "Thank you, Mr. Greenbush."

When Greenbush had exited, Elizabeth began to go through the telegrams. Most of them were communications of difficulty. A Rolfson steamer carrying bales of cotton had gone aground on a Mississippi sandbar in Cairo, Illinois. A bill would be arriving to cover the costs of dislodging the vessel. A county assessor in Wisconsin was threatening to increase the tax on Rolfson land holdings around Lake Geneva. The Rolfson representative there, Willis Spoonwith, recommended a "gratuity." *Bribe,* corrected Elizabeth. Next she skimmed cables having to do with livery charges in Saginaw, Michigan, rail shipping charges in Cleveland, and the death of an employee, Miles Prewitt, in a fight in a bar in Toledo. Then she read two cryptic messages directly addressed to Alois Smedley.

> CLOSING ON TEN THOUSAND SHORTLY STOP WHAT ARE YOUR INSTRUCTIONS?
>
> > BARNEY JOHNSON
> > HIBBING, MINNESOTA

And:

> GRANGER HAS DECIDED ON RAIL ROUTE THROUGH SOUTHERN MONTANA IN CHALLENGE TO GRAND NORTHERN STOP WILL PROCEED TO ACQUIRE RIGHTS-OF-WAY STOP ADVISE IMMEDIATE DECISION.
>
> > T
> >
> > ST. PAUL, MINNESOTA

Ten thousand? Closing on ten thousand? What did that mean? And who was "T"?

Elizabeth got up and went to the office door. Everyone was busy working. Phineas Greenbush had the desk nearest the door. "Please get me Mr. Smedley at once," she told

270

him. He hurried off, agile and ingratiating as any errand boy. Elizabeth had many questions ready for Smedley when the knock on the door came.

But it was not Smedley. Instead, one of the young women, Clarissa Mellors, announced a caller.

"Mr. Booth Chesterfield to see you, Miss Rolfson. Shall I show him in?"

Booth Chesterfield? Oh, yes, the son of whom Travis Chesterfield had spoken so highly at yesterday's luncheon.

"Please do."

Travis Chesterfield had produced a very handsome son. Dark-haired, broad-shouldered, the young man came in smiling, looking at Elizabeth eagerly. Obviously, his father had awarded Miss Rolfson remarks of high regard. Booth had a strong but as yet somewhat innocent face; his hazel eyes showed intelligence without, however, curiosity. He was a bright, wealthy young man who had looked at the world around him and found it good.

"I do hope I'm not inconveniencing you by showing up here like this," Booth apologized.

"No, not at all. Please sit down."

"Thank you, but I can't stay. Pa's sent me out today to collect the rents on the South Side. That can be pretty tough."

"Collect the rents?"

"Yes. That's our business. We own half of Chicago." His smile was self-deprecating, even modest. "The poorer half," he added. "So I have to make the people pay. It's a hard job, but it's a hard world. That's what Pa says. But what I came about is . . ."

"What happens if the people can't pay?" she asked him, thinking of Sandra Handley's family.

Booth shrugged, looking a little bewildered. "Well, they have to be evicted then," he said, without much appetite for the prospect.

Elizabeth decided that the young man had a soul, but was not yet quite aware of its nature.

"I hope you don't evict anyone today," she told him. "It's very cold."

"I hope not too," he agreed. "But what I came about . . ."

He stumbled, just a bit shyly.

"Yes?" she encouraged.

"I was . . . that is, we were . . . my family was hoping you will be able to join us for dinner next Sunday. At our home. We'll send a coach for you at the Blackstone . . ."

"I'm very happy to accept, thank you, Mr. Chesterfield." It would, indeed, be a pleasure to have the company of a handsome young man her own age, especially on a Sunday, which could be the longest, dullest day of the week. "But I may be living at the mansion by then," she added.

Booth Chesterfield looked a little puzzled at her remark, but made no response. He was just rising to leave when Alois Smedley entered with several tradesmen.

"Booth, my goodness, what a surprise," Smedley boomed. "A pleasure to see you."

"Likewise, Mr. Smedley." Young Chesterfield had excellent manners. "I had heard of Miss Rolfson's arrival, and I wanted to extend a personal greeting."

Elizabeth was not certain, but she thought she saw Smedley give the younger man a wink. Booth left with high hopes for the coming Sunday dinner. After Smedley told the carpenters how the big office was to be divided, he sat down in the chair in front of the desk.

"Our positions are exactly reversed today," he oozed.

"Aren't they? I have some questions."

"I have a very important one first, if you'll permit me?"

"Please go ahead."

"I'm informed a captain of the Chicago police was here a short while ago?"

"Yes. O'Riley. Sandra . . . Miss Handley is dead."

272

Elizabeth watched Smedley's face as carefully as O'Riley had scrutinized her own. He received the news. His eyes widened. He tilted his head to one side, looked back toward the outer office as if such a gesture might summon Sandra back from the dead. "Miss Handley? How?"

"Fell or jumped or was pushed from the Chicago River Bridge."

"Oh, my God," sighed Smedley in a mournful tone, "and only nineteen . . ."

"You knew her age?"

Instantly, he was professional again. "I am a good executive. I keep tabs on most things, even details."

And you like young girls, reflected Elizabeth sourly. If she'd expected Smedley to give himself away, she was mistaken. "Good," she said, "I have some questions for you right now. Who is 'T' and who is Barney Johnson?"

"Cables?" he asked. "May I see them?"

"In a moment."

"Don't you trust me?"

"Frankly, no."

"Those telegrams may be of great importance."

"Quite so, but all I asked was the identity of 'T' and Barney Johnson."

Smedley saw that he had reacted too strongly, and now sought to effect a more insouciant attitude. But Elizabeth could tell he wanted to get his hands on the cables.

"Barney Johnson is our land acquisition agent in the Mesabi," Smedley said casually. "And 'T' is Webster Tuttle. He's a spy. Yes, don't be startled. With millions at stake, do you think a good business strategy would be to venture into the marketplace on a wing and a prayer?"

Elizabeth felt jejune.

"Now, if I may see the cables, please? Things of importance may be transpiring even as we sit here."

Smedley read both cables. His face did not flicker.

273

"What does Johnson mean when he says 'ten thousand'?" Elizabeth wanted to know.

"Oh, nothing much." Smedley smiled tautly. "Only a personal joke. A wager, really."

"Quite a tall wager."

"I agree. But Johnson can afford it, and so can I. As for Webster Tuttle's message, it is quite important. *If* you want the company to go into the railroad business. The West needs more roads, and a great fortune awaits the man . . . ah, the company that builds a railroad to the Pacific to compete with the Grand Northern. Tuttle has learned that J. J. Granger plans to go ahead."

"We dined with Mr. Granger just the other day, and he said nothing."

"It is the nature of business to be deceptive, my dear . . . excuse me, *Miss* Rolfson."

"What do you think? About the railroad?"

"I think Rolfson Industries should stay out of it. We already make considerable profit on our Great Lakes steamers and on Ohio and Mississippi river shipping, and . . ."

"Wait a moment," Elizabeth interrupted. "We are on the verge of retreating from the Mesabi, and now you advocate a similar withdrawal from railroading?"

"Miss Rolfson, we are not prepared . . ."

"I know our accounts as well as you do. I studied them aboard ship while coming here. We are not John D. Rockefeller or Andrew Carnegie, but we are certainly on a par with Eric Starbane and J. J. Granger. Furthermore, railroads are the future. Not river traffic. How many rivers does the American West possess? Not many. Already you suggest withdrawal from the iron range, and I can understand that because we are far behind. Let us get a good price and pour the proceeds into a quest for the railroad!"

Elizabeth had entertained some vague glimmerings along these lines before. But in one of those glorious moments that sometimes arise out of frustration, stress, and simple ambition, she had taken a stand and set herself a mighty course. Yes, she *would* do it! She did *not* like J. J. Granger, not one bit, and if he was going to maneuver her out of iron mines, well, let him sit up there in freezing Minnesota digging ore with pickax and shovel while she sailed out over the Great Plains and across the Rocky Mountains on the . . . what would she call it?

"I want the papers drawn up right away!" she ordered Smedley, still in the expansive grip of a sudden, glorious dream. "I'll call it the Continental Pacific. I want you to get started on this directly. This very afternoon. We'll get those rights-of-way if it's the last thing we do."

"Yes, Miss Rolfson," replied Smedley, "I'll take care of it."

"And don't put the correspondence in secret files," she added, testing him.

"What are you talking about, Miss Rolfson?" he asked.

4.

It was a bright, sun-blasted day, but bitterly cold. Wind slammed against the carriage and shivered the isinglass curtains. Elizabeth sat wrapped in fox furs, holding a small leather purse containing one thousand dollars. She intended to give it to the Handleys, even though Smedley had scoffed, "I don't see what earthly good that'll do. The poor don't know how to handle money. It'll be thrown away and they'll be just as desperate as before." But Elizabeth didn't care what he said. The Handleys needed help, and they must be feeling awful. An item in the Chicago newspaper reported that police were calling Sandra's death "an apparent suicide."

She didn't blame Captain O'Riley. What else was he to think? If only there were some way she herself could learn what had happened to Sandra between the time she'd left her house and the time she'd reached the bridge.

"This must be it," called Kohler from the driver's seat, "but I don't see nobody around."

Elizabeth got out of the coach and looked about the neighborhood. The snow-rutted, snow-drifted street lay like a dangerous ditch between ramshackle rows of squat, teetering shacks. Thin wisps of smoke rose from the tin chimneys of some shacks, but the Handleys' pitiful lean-to just stood there, half-covered by drifts, gray and gloomy and dark. A footpath from the street to the door showed the passage of a few pairs of boots, but that was all.

"The paper said that the funeral would be today . . ." Elizabeth began tentatively.

"Maybe everybody done went out to the cemetery already," Kohler commented. "God, they'd have to blast a grave, this kind of weather."

"I'm going up to the house," Elizabeth decided, and picked her way up the path to the battered door of the shack. It had no proper latch, just a rawhide drawstring, and even the hinges were made of leather, pieces of ragged cowhide nailed to the door and the doorjamb. Tears came to Elizabeth's eyes as she thought of poor, lovely Sandra leaving this stark place, hugging herself against cold and night, going off to meet her death.

Elizabeth knocked on the door. She did not expect an answer, and there was none. Ought she wait for the family to return from the burial? Certainly it would not do to leave the money here.

She loosened the drawstring and pushed the door open slightly. A black pot sat on a cold black stove. Rumpled bedding lay scattered about the dirt floor. A straight-backed wooden chair leaned against the bare plank wall. A man stood next to the chair.

"Come in, Miss Rolfson," said Captain O'Riley, "I was rather expecting you."

Astonished, Elizabeth obeyed.

"Sit down, if you wish."

"No, thank you. What are you. . . ?"

"Doing here? Waiting to see who shows up. Murderers sometimes make an appearance at the funerals of their victims."

"Murder?"

"Yes. I'm convinced it's not a suicide. And I don't believe you're telling me everything you know, either."

"I've told you all I know for sure. My God, you don't think I . . . ?"

"No, Miss Rolfson. You're no murderer, and you're just

as puzzled as I am. You've come with the money, I suppose?"

He was looking at the purse she held.

Elizabeth nodded.

"Best take it, or have it sent, to the Cook County Orphanage."

"What? Why?"

"Actually, the funerals were yesterday. I put the incorrect date in the paper to see if I could lure the killer out here."

"Funerals?" Elizabeth asked, astounded at his use of the plural. "Orphanage?"

"Yes, I'm sorry to say that Mrs. Handley died. A combination of grief, shock, and influenza. The children were sent to the orphanage, all except Todd, the eldest. He ran away. Poor kid. As if Chicago didn't already have a surfeit of waifs and drifters."

Elizabeth felt impotent, useless. She felt a responsibility toward Sandra's family, but all she could do was give money. Truly irreplaceable things cannot be bought.

"I might as well leave then," she said.

O'Riley nodded. "Might as well. But if you think of anything, hear anything, or learn anything about Sandra Handley's last night, please do not hesitate to come to me right away."

"You can count on me," she promised him.

"Take me to Uncle Gustav's house now," she ordered Kohler, when she reached the carriage. She had already decided to have Phineas Greenbush establish a fund for the Handley children, rather than simply hand over money to the orphanage.

Kohler looked surprised. "Why don't I just take you back to the hotel, Ma'am?" he countered.

Elizabeth flared. "Why do you keep finding excuses to keep me from my house? You will take me there and take me there *now*," she commanded, her voice cold and level, "or you've driven Belle for the last time."

Kohler gulped. He was thickheaded but not totally obtuse. Driving a coach was a lot easier than working for a living.

Kohler obeyed. Late in the afternoon, Elizabeth's carriage lurched from the street onto a smooth drive. She looked out to see a hundred-windowed mansion, and a pillar with a Viking on top.

Home, she thought. *Now all I have to do is have it readied.*

The broad circular drive was shoveled clean of snow.

Smoke curled from half a dozen brick chimneys.

Lights blazed behind the glittering windows.

What was going on here? Smedley had clearly told her that the furnaces weren't working, that the house was closed down.

Elizabeth jumped down from the coach and dashed up the wide stone steps. Not bothering to bang the big brass shield-shaped knocker, she pressed down on the ornate doorlatch and rushed into the house. The foyer was floored with sparkling marble slabs reflecting the lights of a massive chandelier. A parlor to the right looked inviting, warmed by a roaring fire in the hearth. Alois Smedley sat contentedly in a soft chair near the fire, slowly puffing a fat cigar.

"Elizabeth!" he cried, startled.

Elizabeth knew at once that Smedley had been living here all along, and had been scheming to continue his occupancy as long as possible.

"Just came over to make sure everything was ready for you," he offered lamely.

"Thank you so much."

"Well, guess I'd best be off now. Do you mind if Kohler drives me?"

"Not in the least," she told him acidly.

Vanessa Royall

* * *

And so Elizabeth had a house and a business to run. But what else did she have? Her nature called to her, especially when she was alone, particularly when she lay awake at night, unable to sleep. Her female nature spoke to her, in fact, in no uncertain terms. *You are being a proper fool*, it told her. *You need love and you have much love to give.*

I will find Lance, she replied, tossing in her lonely bed. He will find me.

Yes, retorted her nature. *Yes, and you grow old. And cold. Soon you will be twenty-two. Twenty-three. Twenty-five. Thirty. You may never see Lance Tallworth again. Forget the emotion. Forget the memory of blinding pleasure. Donnabella Trinacria must be married by now, and expecting her first child. Even Simone and Greta may be wed.*

I want that too, Elizabeth countered, but with Lance.

Stop dreaming. You are a fool.

I am not.

Don't you want a man to pleasure, and to pleasure you? Don't you want children of love from your bodies?

Yes.

Is it enough to live in this great house and go daily to the office and play the part of a great woman?

No.

Then what will you do? Time is passing. You have no one! You hold all men at arm's length.

That's not so! I am friendly to Booth Chesterfield!

True, but your "friendliness" is remote. Does it make either of you happy?

"No," said Elizabeth, when Booth tried to kiss her after Sunday dinner at the Chesterfield house. And over the next month, she continued to discourage him, even as she continued to see him.

"I'm sorry, and I know I'm a disappointment," she told

280

him when he tried to kiss her as they rode home after the Valentine Dance. "I think you're sweet. I really do."

Indeed, Elizabeth did think so. She thought quite highly of him. He was becoming a man with a will of his own, no longer simply an appendage of his landlord father. And Booth showed every sign of becoming a good man too. He had managed to persuade his iron-willed father that summary evictions of destitute tenants not only produced little revenue, but in the long run harmed the Chesterfield reputation. And he was a good listener when Elizabeth talked about her own mercantile problems. Since Eric Starbane had never responded to her telegram, she had gone ahead and sold the iron mining leases to the other Minnesotan, indefatigable J. J. Granger.

"Can you think of it!" she exclaimed to Booth one day. "I sold my leases to a man who drinks his coffee from the saucer!"

"He doesn't!"

"Yes. He pours it from the cup into the saucer, lets it cool a bit, and then slurps it up like a slobbering mutt. Is that an American custom?"

"I hope not," Booth averred. "But he paid you very well."

"That's true," Elizabeth was forced to admit.

And so her relationship with Booth drifted into the spring of 1886, an interaction comprised of companionship, general chatter, and his attempts to evoke affectionate response from her. He was ready to marry her right away. And disappointed when she held out little hope for such a union.

"It is not that I don't care for you . . ." she began.

"You just don't know *what* you want," he observed dourly. "You know what they call you? The Ice Queen. And it has nothing to do with your being from Norway either. Oh, how regally you traipse around in that big office, making decisions about this and that. Hah! Every businessman worth his salt in Chicago knows that Smedley is putting it over on you. 'Yes, Miss Rolfson. No, Miss Rolfson. Absolutely, Miss Rolfson.' And all the while he does what *he* wants, fancy free! You don't even know what goes on in your own company!"

Yes, thought Elizabeth. *I've known it all along. And now everyone else knows too.*

"I just don't know what's going to become of you," Booth concluded grimly. "Of course I care, but there's nothing I can do because there's obviously nothing you want me to do. Or want from me, for that matter. Well, let me tell you this before I say good-bye. There'll come a time in your life too when you'll want someone and that someone won't be there!"

5.

So Elizabeth, furious with herself, went early to her office the next day, determined to have it out with Smedley. But how ought she to proceed? She felt confident of her ability to discharge her crafty tormentor. But then he would simply leave, still knowing all the secrets and strategies with which he had gulled her. No, summarily firing him would not do. First she had to uncover incontrovertible evidence of his chicanery. Thinking of secret files, iron ore, and railroads, Elizabeth stepped down from her carriage in front of the Rolfson Building.

It was very early, and only a few eager souls were on the street. Hans, the big doorman, tipped his cap to her. Kohler, the driver, was making a pretense of getting down from his seat to hold Elizabeth's elbow as she descended. Elizabeth had only a fleeting glance of the man in the dark coat as he raced toward her from the alley at the corner of the building. Still, her mind had the power, in those brief seconds, both to marvel at his speed and to wonder why he flew toward her, before she saw terror in the young face of the stranger whose icy cold hands wrapped themselves around her throat. She felt the desperate shuddering power of his body transmitted to hers, felt the throbbing pulse of his blood in the pressing thumbs that sought her windpipe. She and the stranger were united, two bodies become one for a timeless moment of shaking fury. Making love and dealing death were alike in the frenzy of intimacy. The day grew dark before Elizabeth's eyes, as if a ghostly moon were crossing the path of the sun. The Rolfson Building wavered in sudden shadow. *I am dying*, Elizabeth realized, wondering why she was not seeing the flashing scenes of her life passing before her eyes, scenes everyone was said to experience before death.

Then she was lying on the cold sidewalk, choking. Her throat burned, hot and dry, stung by frosty gulps of air. She still felt around her neck the pressure of clawing hands, even though those hands had been torn away.

Hans and Kohler had her assailant pinned against the side of the carriage. He was sobbing drily, trying to get free. The horses reared and skittered, neighing in alarm.

"You all right, Miss Rolfson?" Hans asked, looking at her.

Elizabeth got up, and nodded. Words would not come yet. She looked at the man who had attacked her. He wasn't a man, she saw now. He was hardly more than a boy. Wearing a threadbare jacket that was much too large for him, patched trousers, and a torn wool cap, he looked like a shivering young tramp, not a murderer.

"I'll go get a policeman," Kohler offered.

"Wait," croaked Elizabeth. Her voice sounded like a death rattle, like a groan from a sepulchre. She stepped toward the boy. His eyes were large and full of fright. She had seen such eyes before.

"Don't get too close to 'im now, Ma'am," warned Hans, who twisted the boy's arm behind his back. His face showed pain, but he did not cry out.

"Don't . . . don't hurt him," Elizabeth managed to say. "Son, why did you . . . why did you want to harm me?"

No answer.

"I'm sure I've never seen you before. Do you know me?"

He nodded, biting his lip to keep from crying out loud. Tears were streaming down his face.

"Let me teach this here kiddo a lesson," growled stupid Kohler, raising his fist.

"Let him alone!" snapped Elizabeth. She was right in front of the boy now. His eyes did look unusually familiar in their size and depth. And in spite of herself, she was drawn to his fury, his desire to destroy her, as surely as she would have been intrigued by someone who wanted to love her.

"What's your name?" she asked.

He returned her gaze with blazing adolescent eyes, the kind of glance that says: *You already know why I am angry, and that only makes me more angry!*

But Elizabeth did not know why. "I'm sure it won't hurt to tell me your name," she said, trying to make her ragged voice soft.

He was still looking at her closely, attempting to decide what to do. Elizabeth couldn't smile, or give that sort of easy signal. The matter was far too serious.

"Who are you?" she tried again.

"Handley," he said, between sobs. "Todd Handley."

Elizabeth knew immediately. The familiar eyes. This was Sandra Handley's brother, who had run away from home to keep from going into the orphanage. Quickly, she glanced at the faces of Hans and Kohler. The driver remained impassive as ever, but she thought she saw Hans give a flicker of recognition when he heard the name "Handley."

"Let him go," she told the men. "Todd, come with me. I'll get you some food."

"What the hell is this deal?" wondered Hans angrily, keeping a grip on the boy.

"What the hell kind of deal is this?" gaped Kohler.

"Let him go," Elizabeth repeated. Todd was looking at her with wonder. His life had been bereft of bright surprises, and this one was far brighter than any he could have imagined.

"Not on your life. . . ." grunted Hans.

"Let him go or you're fired, as of this moment. Both of you."

Hans and Kohler released Todd. The boy stood there, wondering what to do.

"I'm going to have to tell Mr. Smedley about this," Hans grunted.

"Tell him anything you like," snapped Elizabeth. "Tell him I'm thinking of firing him too."

The two lugs looked on in dim astonishment as Elizabeth led Todd Handley into the building. He went with her fearfully, but without protest, all fight gone now. She took him up to her office, and then sent an early-arriving clerk out for breakfast. Todd, whose scrawny frame bespoke infrequent acquaintance with food, devoured boiled eggs, sliced ham, a dozen pieces of bread, and a quart of hot milk.

"Will you tell me why you attacked me?" Elizabeth asked, when the boy showed signs of surfeit.

"On account of my sister." His voice was wary. He was measuring the distance to the door.

"I don't understand."

Tears rose to his eyes again. " 'Cause you musta killed her, or somethin'," he declared, hiding his face behind his hands. "I been lookin' to track you down ever since."

Elizabeth fought back the urge to protest and defend. It was very important that she find out what this was all about.

"I don't understand," she said again.

He wiped his eyes and studied her. She saw in his expression a dawning realization that she was telling the truth, and a horrified remorse at what he had done.

"But . . . but she went out that night to meet you," he faltered, the fine tight world of revenge now coming unglued. "She said she . . ."

"Todd, I want to know who killed your sister as much as you do. Now, start from the beginning, and tell me everything you know. You won't be harmed. I promise you. I know a man, Captain O'Riley of the Chicago police, and he wants to know who killed your sister too."

A surge of hope was unmistakable in the boy's voice. "Then you don't think she . . . ?"

"Killed herself? No. And neither does Captain O'Riley."

Todd Handley's story was not a long one. On the evening of her last night on earth, his older sister Sandra had been nervous and excited. He could tell. She rushed him and the other children through their oatmeal dinner, and was almost snappish with little Tilly, the baby. "That wasn't like her at all," Todd said, "and then she told me she had to go out. To see Miss Rolfson at the Blackstone Hotel. She had mentioned your name before, her new boss, so I knew. I asked her why she had to see you at night. 'Something dangerous at work and it's none of your business,' she told me. I can remember her saying it plain as day. Then she left and I put the little kids to bed. Some of them wouldn't mind me. They only obeyed Sandy. They kept on chattering, bothering poor Ma, and she was sick as a dog. When I finally got them all tucked in, there was a knock on the door. I figured it was Sandy, come back, on account of how cold it was that night. But it wasn't. It was some man come looking for her."

"Some man?"

"Never seen him before nor since."

Elizabeth's mind was racing. "Did men often call on her?"

"Only the boys on the West Side, and I knew them. No, this was a rich man. He had a heavy coat and a fine hat."

"Did you see him clearly?"

"Oh, yes. The light from the lantern shined right in his eyes. I thought of him first thing when . . . when, next day, we found out Sandy was . . . was . . ." He started to cry again.

"That's all right," Elizabeth said. "You cry as long as you want to." She was thinking of notifying Captain O'Riley immediately. "But first tell me one more thing. Would you recognize that man again?"

"Oh, *yes*. I wouldn't forget . . ."

A sudden bustle sounded from the outer office, a flurry of fearful activity. Then the big door swung open, held deferentially by the bowing Phineas T. Greenbush. Alois Smedley strode purposefully into Elizabeth's office. Something important was on his mind.

"Miss Rolfson, Hans just told me . . ."

He stopped, looking at the ragged boy, as if to say: *What on earth is this? What's he doing here? He tried to kill you!*

Elizabeth read his gaze. And she saw, too, the sudden look of horror on young Todd Handley's face, as he recognized the man who had called for his sister on that January night. The boy tensed, ready to flee, yet too paralyzed to move.

"Mr. Smedley," Elizabeth announced casually, "this is Todd Handley. He's going to be our new office boy. We've been needing one. He'll be living with me at my house. Now, have one of the clerks see to getting him decently clothed."

Later that day, she explained the situation to the baffled, still-frightened youth. "Todd, you saw Mr. Smedley at your house on the night Sandra died, and I think he had something to do with her death. In fact, I know he did. But the law does not work according to what you saw and what I might happen to believe. We have to be able to prove it, or Mr. Smedley must be made to admit it. Do you understand?"

"I think so."

"Then we will wait. There is an American phrase I have learned. 'Smoke him out.' We must both be very careful and very clever. We must 'smoke him out.'"

Todd's mouth set tight in resolution. "All right," he agreed.

Elizabeth did not tell him that she would begin an investigation of her own, intent upon unearthing the precise details of Smedley's business chicanery. She would do that, going over every record and transaction. In the meantime, Todd's constant presence would gnaw at Smedley's monumental sangfroid. The reminder of blood on his hands, if not actual guilt for the spilling of that blood, might serve to unnerve him.

She and Todd would have to be very careful, of course. A man who has murdered once will find it more than twice as easy the second time.

Alois Smedley, however, did not rattle. He proved to be as excellent at waiting out Elizabeth's ploy as he had been at covering the tracks of his business machinations. Indeed, he even congratulated Elizabeth on her compassion and charity for taking in and employing "that poor little Handley orphan." "Sandra is looking down upon you from her place in heaven," he oozed, "and thanking you from the bottom of her angel's heart."

For a time, Elizabeth was tempted to write *"Failure"* across the bottom of both her personal and professional ledgers. Smedley brought in a report to the effect that J. J. Granger was making stupendous gains in purchasing rights-of-way across the Dakotas and Montana. No matter the size of the bids authorized by Elizabeth, Granger always seemed able to bid higher. He was even going hell-for-leather against Eric Starbane in the Mesabi, and it was now possible that the ruthless one-eyed manipulator would some day dominate that vast arena too.

Still, as trying as her business affairs were, the matter of her heart was more doleful. A map of Montana yielded no place, town, or city called *Ycripsicu*. Rejecting the idea of hiring a detective to find Lance for her, she began to make plans to go west by rail in the summer. Smedley argued against it, and he didn't even know she would be going there on a matter unrelated to the company! But it was not summer yet, and time weighed heavily upon her.

She received only two invitations over the Easter holiday. One involved a charity dinner given by the United Lutheran Women's Auxiliary Society, and the other a gathering of Grand Army of the Republic veterans.

"Oh, my God," she mourned, "everyone in the city thinks I'm a dowager already." She refused both invitations.

Frustrated and restless, unsure of herself and uncertain of her mood, Elizabeth dressed to the nines, complete with white ermine cape and tiny silver tiara, and had Kohler drive her to the Opera House where a visiting company from New York was doing *Die Fledermaus*. Even if it did not cheer her, at least she would not be sitting at home and brooding about the treadmill of her life.

Elizabeth had seen *Die Fledermaus* performed in Geneva years earlier, and had loved not only the music but the event itself, the costumes, mistaken identities, and generally preposterous story. Tonight, however, her reaction was quite different. A dark mood colored everything. The music wavered. Singers missed notes. In the audience, too, many people coughed. The acting was transparent, the flourishes without lustre.

After several years, the first act ended and the curtain came down. Elizabeth left her seat and went out into the lobby, intending to go home, take a hot bath, and go to bed. Her intention to skip the rest of the opera was doubly strengthened when, with more of the bad luck blighting her, she ran into Travis and Bertha Chesterfield, Booth's parents. Mr. Chesterfield, in white tie, was friendly, but Bertha puckered up her mean little mouth.

"Why, my dear, you're all alone, aren't you?"

I certainly am when I'm with you, Elizabeth thought. "Yes," she answered sweetly.

"How very unfortunate. We're going to the mayor's

house for buffet after the performance. Perhaps we'll see you there?"

"I'm afraid not," Elizabeth smiled.

"Oh, how unfortunate," mourned Mrs. Chesterfield.

"I'm sure Elizabeth has other exciting plans," said her husband, with a kind of hesitant hopefulness.

"Isn't that *grand*, though," observed Bertha, totally unconvinced. "Booth and his fiancée will be at the mayor's," she added.

"How nice," replied Elizabeth. She had to admit that she was mildly curious to know who had caught Booth, or vice versa. She also knew that she did not have to ask.

"Sarah Armour," boasted Mrs. Chesterfield, with all the modesty she could muster. "The family is involved in the processing of . . ."

They kill a lot of cows, Elizabeth thought. If she didn't get out of this Opera House in two minutes she would . . . she didn't know what she would do.

". . . foodstuffs," said Mrs. Chesterfield. "And Sarah is such a . . ."

"Grand," said Elizabeth.

". . . grand girl. I do hope the Armours will invite you to the wedding."

"Everybody's getting married," boomed Mr. Chesterfield, with a wink for Elizabeth.

The second act was announced.

"It's been just *grand* seeing you again," Bertha puckered.

"Happy to have run into you," she told the Chesterfields, "and please give my greetings to Booth."

She couldn't wait to get outside, where the cool spring air was balm. Kohler waited by the coach. She made her way slowly down the steps of the Opera House, feeling blue and alone. It was going to take a lot more than a hot bath to cure her condition.

A man in evening clothes came dashing up the steps, taking them two at a time, his head down.

"Look out!" Elizabeth cried, coming out of her bleak mood too late.

He collided with her, there on the stairs. Elizabeth would have fallen if he hadn't reached out and grabbed hold of her.

"I'm so sorry," he said.

He sounded sorry. He looked sorry. Elizabeth found herself staring into the startlingly deep blue eyes of a very good-looking young man. He had a shining shock of blond hair, wide shoulders, and a woeful expression due to his collision with her.

Elizabeth liked his voice, his manner. *He couldn't be much more than twenty-one*, she thought. *My age.*

She studied him more carefully. Although she had never met him before, Elizabeth sensed a familiarity about him, as if she'd known him for quite some time. It was the most extraordinary sensation, but it was deep and undeniable.

"Oh, forgive me," she stammered. "I didn't mean to stare at you like this."

"I forgive you," he said. "Sure you're all right?" His manner was kindly, but strong at the same time.

"Yes."

Satisfied that she had suffered no harm in their collision, he glanced toward the Opera House. "Leaving so soon?"

"I'm afraid I wasn't getting much out of the performance tonight."

He glanced around. Elizabeth knew he was looking for the escort she didn't have. A woman out in the evening without an escort was . . .

"I'm late," he said. "How far along is it?"

"The second act has begun."

"And you did not care for it?"

"The fault was probably mine."

He looked at her appraisingly, approvingly. Elizabeth was flattered. Again she felt as if she knew him.

"Is that your coach?" he asked. "Let me see you to it."

Elizabeth took his arm and they walked down the steps to the carriage. It felt so natural for him to be taking care of her.

"I know our meeting was rather sudden," he said, "but if I could arrange a proper introduction, I'd like to meet you again."

He helped her into the coach. Elizabeth smiled her thanks. How could she encourage him, when her heart belonged to Lance? If she allowed this young Viking to believe he might pursue her, would he not come to hate her even as Booth Chesterfield had?

"Please?" he asked, before she had a chance to speak. "I'd really like to see you again. My name is Haakon Starbane."

"Starbane?" Was this her business competitor? "Do you know . . . are you kin to Eric Starbane?"

"He's my father. Why?"

Elizabeth sighed. She had met this wonderful man, for whom she'd felt an immediate affinity, and he was the son of her mercantile opponent. "I am Elizabeth Rolfson," she told him. "Of Rolfson Industries. Your father and I . . ."

But Haakon did not seem concerned about business relationships. Something else drew his attention,

"Elizabeth?" he asked, in an odd, wavery voice, pronouncing her name in a manner that, once again, evoked strange feelings in her heart. The way in which he spoke her name was . . . was tender. "Elizabeth *Rolfson*?"

He had stepped back from the coach a pace or two, and was staring at her in a way that was almost frightening. She was quite certain he no longer wanted to see her again, proper introduction or no.

"Good night, Mr. Starbane. I do hope you enjoy what remains of the opera. Kohler!"

The driver cracked his whip, and the carriage moved off into the night.

6

Smedley had grandly announced that he would go to New York over the Easter weekend, on "urgent business."

"We don't have urgent business in New York," Elizabeth had countered, irritated by his increasingly lordly attitude. He had given her a condescending smile and said, "urgent *personal* business," and gone off anyway. After Booth Chesterfield had told her that everyone in Chicago thought she was a fool for letting Smedley run her ragged, Elizabeth had decided to emphasize his subordinate role. This was easier said than done. Smedley did not see himself as anyone's subordinate, certainly not hers.

When Smedley did not come to the office on Easter Monday, however, Elizabeth realized she was glad he was gone. There were a number of things she wanted to investigate, and now she could do so without Smedley breathing down her neck.

"Mr. Greenbush," she called, and Phineas T. stuck his head in the door. "Summon those two land clerks, would you? Detlef and Isbell. They're staying at the Haymarket Hotel. I want to talk to them."

"But . . . but Miss Rolfson, Mr. Smedley spoke with them before he left, and everything's been . . ."

"Mr. Greenbush, summon them. Now. I want to know why we aren't making any headway securing those rights-of-way in South Dakota. All I've gotten from Smedley are excuses and promises. Now, get me Isbell and Detlef, before they start back for Sioux Falls."

"Yes, Miss Rolfson," said Greenbush worriedly.

That was another thing! The employees obeyed her, all right, but they were afraid of Smedley. As long as he was around, she could only pretend to be in charge. But did she know enough about her operations yet to risk firing him? It was an important point, and she thought it over while drinking coffee that Todd Handley brought her. Then she got up and walked over to Smedley's desk. As usual, all the drawers were unlocked. He hid nothing. Or he kept secret files, just as poor Sandra Handley had maintained. The top of his desk was fastidiously neat. Nothing out of order. Then she glanced at his notepad.

- Easter gifts—whiskey for Kohler and Hans
- Cable "T"
- Bottleneck—High Y

It didn't surprise Elizabeth at all that he would buy gifts for Hans the doorman and Kohler. After all, they were Smedley's good and loyal spies, weren't they? And "T" was that spy Smedley employed up in Minneapolis and St. Paul. But about "Bottleneck—High Y" she knew nothing at all. It was just one more thing that he was keeping from her, thereby husbanding his resources of power. Knowledge *is* power, after all.

There was a knock on the door. Isbell and Detlef had made excellent time, which was not like them at all.

"Come in."

"There's a gentleman to see you," Mr. Greenbush faltered. "I told him you were preparing for a meeting, but he insists . . ."

Elizabeth saw Haakon Starbane standing behind Greenbush, his golden hair shining in the morning light. He looked very serious.

"Miss Rolfson, I *must* see you. You'll understand when I've had a chance to explain."

"It's all right, Mr. Greenbush."

Once again that morning, Phineas T. could only worry about the consequences of impropriety. Haakon Starbane entered her office. He could not seem to take his eyes off her, and his stare was unnerving.

"Have you seen enough?" she asked him pointedly, and sat down behind her desk.

He remained standing. "I don't quite know how to begin."

He looked so somber, so *severe*. "Just begin," Elizabeth said, smiling.

"I am studying at the University," he said. "Political science, and I . . ."

For a man who looked so strong and forthright, Elizabeth reflected, he was certainly having trouble expressing himself.

". . . and recently—last week, in fact—I received a long letter from my father. In it, he said that he had learned some time ago of Gustav Rolfson's death. He thought Rolfson Industries were being run by a man named Alois Smedley, but had come across items in the Chicago papers referring to Elizabeth Rolfson . . ."

Elizabeth nodded. "Mr. Smedley would have everyone believe that he is in charge, but that is less true every day, and will soon not be true at all."

He wasn't listening to her. Something else was on his mind. Perhaps he was here as a business emissary, but hadn't the experience to broach the subject properly. She would be direct.

"Both with regard to those mining leases, and now lately in the railroad rights-of-way, I have literally begged your father to go in with me, and in that way we could block Granger. The man is a predator, and he will mar the entire future of the West. . . ." She paused. Now it was Elizabeth's turn to be mystified. Haakon was frowning, as if she were talking about events occurring in another world.

Haakon held up his hand. "One of us is a little confused," he said with a smile. He shook his head, banishing bewilderment. "Father always keeps us well informed, so that if something were to happen to him, Mother and I would be prepared to run the company. Now, you mentioned mining leases you wanted to sell him?"

"Yes, I ordered Mr. Smedley to send your father a telegram to that effect. I *saw* the draft of the message. And your father never had the courtesy to reply, not even to decline . . ."

"Nor did you reply to several messages from us," Haakon responded in gentle accusation, "asking to buy the ten thousand acres then controlled by Rolfson Industries."

"What? Ten thousand? *What*?"

Instantly, yet much too late, Elizabeth understood. Smedley had never showed her Starbane's messages. And he had lied about everything! Now she remembered the telegram to Smedley from "Barney Johnson." CLOSING ON TEN THOUSAND, it had said. Smedley had dismissed the matter as a wager, but that was not at all what it had been. The telegram meant that Rolfson Industries had control of ten thousand acres worth of mining leases.

"I sold almost five thousand acres to Granger," Elizabeth told Haakon.

"No. Granger bragged all over St. Paul and Minneapolis that he had bought ten thousand acres from you. For a song."

He bought ten for the price of five, Elizabeth realized, *because Smedley manipulated everything, with two complete sets of records. Secret files* . . .

"But I'm not here to talk about mining leases, about business. My father sent me here to . . ."

At that moment, Alois Smedley stormed through the door.

297

"What is going on here?" he demanded.

Elizabeth stood up behind her desk and Haakon turned to face Smedley.

"Get out!" Smedley declared, with his usual arrogance.

"I am Haakon Starbane."

Smedley looked from Haakon to Elizabeth, as if trying to gauge how much information they had exchanged. Based upon the information that Phineas T. Greenbush had given him, these two youngsters hadn't had time to exchange much.

"I don't care if you're Eric Starbane," Smedley said. "In fact, I don't care if you're Abe Lincoln returned from the dead. Get out of here."

"Mr. Smedley," said Elizabeth quietly.

He turned to her.

"Please be quiet, Mr. Smedley. I am glad you've returned from New York. I have something to tell you. Mr. Starbane, perhaps we might continue this conversation presently . . ."

"I'll wait outside," said Haakon, glaring at Smedley. He left the office and closed the door behind him.

"Elizabeth, you are a proper fool," said Smedley.

"I won't have you talk to me like that."

"Then I shall have to use words that are more polite. But their meaning will be the same. 'Proper fool.' "

Elizabeth held her temper. "Please explain," she managed. "What have I done wrong this time?"

Invited to accuse, Smedley warmed to the task. "What you have *not* done wrong would be an easier question to answer. Why, I'm tempted to quit and go to work for J. J. Granger!"

"By all means," she retorted.

"What?"

"Go to work for him. Or for anybody else. You are, as of this moment, fired."

Smedley did not seem to believe it.

"I ought to have done it a long time ago," she told him.

Then he recovered himself. "Just fine," he sneered, with such assurance that it seemed he was dismissing her, and not the other way around. "Just fine. By tomorrow morning, my desk will be empty, I'll be gone, and you'll have nothing but problems."

"No. It won't be that way. Ten minutes from now you'll be out of this building, and your desk along with you, if you want it, and I'll be rid of a problem."

For the first time since she'd met him, Smedley's smooth face showed real alarm. This reaction, she knew, had nothing to do with his firing. He had reacted aggressively to that. No, there was something else. . . .

"By the way, how have I been a 'proper fool'?" she asked.

"That's for you to find out, smart girl." He gestured toward his desk. "There's my desk and everything in it."

"Very good."

Smedley started for the door. Elizabeth beat him to it, even opened it for him. He felt compelled to make a final taunt.

"You never *saw* anything!" he declared victoriously.

"I never saw you push Sandra Handley off the bridge," she snapped back, "but that doesn't mean you didn't do it."

"Hah!" he cried, leaving.

The employees in the outer office buzzed frantically as Smedley passed through their midst.

"Mr. Smedley is no longer working for Rolfson Industries," Elizabeth called out to them, while the angry executive was still present. "Mr. Smedley has been discharged."

Smedley heard the burst of applause before he was able to leave the floor.

But Elizabeth knew she had sounded more confident than she actually was. "Todd," she said, after summoning the office boy, "you must leave immediately and follow Mr.

Smedley. Be careful, but don't delay. Find out where he goes, and then come back here. I am going to notify Captain O'Riley right away. I have a suspicion that if Mr. Smedley does anything incriminating, now will be the time. Can you do this for me? Are you afraid?"

The boy thought it over for a second. "Yes," he said. "But I'd better hurry."

After sending another employee for Captain O'Riley, Elizabeth returned to her office and closed her door. She needed some time alone, time to think. She reviewed in her mind all the events of the morning. Then, suddenly, she remembered that Haakon Starbane must still be waiting in the office. She went out and found him standing next to Mr. Greenbush's desk.

"You must excuse me," apologized Elizabeth. "You haven't any idea what's been going on!"

"I'm not so sure about that," he said.

He looked so . . . so *stricken*! She wished he would smile. Now she thought that Eric Starbane *had* sent him here as a business emissary. This was a good day for Haakon to have appeared too. Many things could be cleared up, now that Smedley was gone.

She invited Haakon back into her office, but before they could begin to talk, Captain O'Riley hurried in. He was as lean and dour as ever. "So you finally decided to get rid of Smedley. Why so suddenly?"

"It seemed time."

"Why did you want to see me?"

"Can you watch him, or something? I think . . . I don't know. I sent the Handley boy out after him, to find out where he goes."

"You . . . you what?"

"I said I sent . . ."

"I heard what you said." He got up hastily from the chair in front of her desk. "I hope nothing happens to him.

Smedley is a strong, powerful man. You've struck him where he lives. Such men strike back."

Elizabeth felt guilty and afraid. Everything seemed to get more complicated, no matter what she did. But Todd returned after an hour to say that Smedley had gone first to the telegraph office, and then to lunch at the Tenderloin, a classy restaurant he frequented, where he was fussed and fawned over. Todd did not know to whom Smedley had sent a wire, but he did report that the dismissed executive had ordered rare roast beef and squash.

Elizabeth didn't mind. Todd was safe and O'Riley had been alerted. The boy went back to his duties, and with an apologetic smile Elizabeth turned to Haakon Starbane.

"My father has long been puzzled by the actions of the Rolfson establishment," he said, "but now that I have met Mr. Smedley, many things are explained. Many more things, however, are not. They must be discussed."

"These matters are serious indeed, judged by the look on your face."

He actually smiled, but only a little.

"Shall we go to lunch?" he invited. "What I am about to suggest to you will take time, and . . ."

"Yes? And?"

"And you'll forgive me for saying this—I'm not usually in such a state—but I would very much like a drink of spirits."

* * *

"You've only recently arrived in Chicago, haven't you?" he asked, as they were seated in the Fox Run restaurant. Elizabeth had suggested it because of its proximity to the Rolfson Building, and because it had high-backed booths suitable for private conversation.

"I arrived in January," Elizabeth replied. "And you?"

"This is my last year at the University."

"Do you like it? Political science?"

"Yes. Very much. My father has had to become something of an engineer, what with the mining operation, and business is his background. He wants me to go into public life."

"How do you feel about that?"

"I think it would be exciting. Of course, I wouldn't allow myself to be bought and sold, like some of these congressmen on J. J. Granger's payroll."

"Congressman?" She smiled. "You seek a modest beginning in public life."

"I am a Starbane," he replied, smiling too. "I am expected to aim high."

A waiter appeared. Elizabeth ordered lake trout, and Haakon asked for roast pork.

"I'm trying to decide how to start," he said. "I don't want to alarm you. But my father asked me to see you, and it's very important to all of us."

"If you're suggesting some sort of business alliance against J. J. Granger, I've already said that I'd be pleased . . ."

"It's not that. You are *Elizabeth Rolfson*?"

There it was again. Elizabeth experienced the same tremor at the sound of her name on his lips that she had felt that night outside the Opera House. Why did it seem so natural for him to speak her name? Something in the way he said Eliza*beth* . . .

"I've always thought so. I don't understand . . ."

"Where did you live? Before you came to Chicago?"

"In Norway. That is, I have been at college in Switzerland, but my home is Norway. Uncle Gustav died, and I came here to learn the business."

"Uncle Gustav? He wasn't your father?"

"Oh, no." She was about to tell him about her real father, the hapless Olav, but Haakon pressed on.

302

"Where were you born?" he asked. "What do you remember of your childhood?"

"You are most inquisitive, Mr. Starbane."

"Please. I would not ask these personal questions if the matter were not of extreme importance."

"You've made that point several times. Suppose you simply tell me why you want to know."

Their food was served. Neither made a move to eat.

"All right," he told her. "It's probably the best way. You see, my father and Gustav Rolfson had been enemies since their early years in Norway. Rolfson rooked my father out of his ancestral farm, drove him out of Norway in the most shameless and humiliating fashion. Father came penniless to America, and Rolfson came here a little afterward, rich. They were locked in enmity. I was just a baby when my mother left Rolfson and went to live with my father, who had a daughter by his first marriage . . ."

"I don't see what you're getting at."

Haakon took a deep breath, as if steeling himself for a difficult task. "I think you are that girl, Elizabeth. I think you're my half-sister."

For a moment, Elizabeth did not react at all. Yet before she opened her mind to listen, she already knew that she hoped his words were true. The past, which she had sought for so long, lay now within her grasp, proffered by this very strong and very gentle man. She could not have chosen a better brother, from all the men on earth. Now, too, her earlier reactions made sense. The touch of memory he had evoked in her, that lay just beyond awareness. She felt a strange impulse, full of yearning, born of love and blood, and a desire for comfort and surcease from loneliness.

The little blond boy, long ago, lifting her up to the windowsill. *Can you see? Can you see the boats on the river now, Beth?*

And she had been Beth.

Elizabeth reached out, took his hand, and squeezed it hard. "Tell me everything," she asked.

"All right," he agreed. "Before my father married my mother, he was wed to a Pennsylvania woman named Elaine Nesterling. He had a child by her, you. But Elaine was killed shielding my father from an assassin's bullet . . ."

Elizabeth's head was spinning. Uncle Gustav had told her that her mother had died trying to protect her father from a gunman, but the names he'd used had been Olav and Hilda.

"My father took you and moved to Minnesota. Along with my mother, and me."

"Is your home a big white house overlooking a river?" she asked, scarcely able to believe that she had found the origin of her dream-memory, the lost roots of her past.

"*Windward*," he answered. "On the Mississippi in St. Paul. We have another home, *Bethland*, in Duluth. It's named for . . ."

"Elizabeth? Me?"

Haakon nodded.

"And your mother's name is Kristin?"

"Yes. How did you . . . ?"

"I knew that Uncle Gustav . . ."

"He wasn't your uncle."

"I know that now. I knew he had been married to a woman named Kristin. She was very beautiful . . ."

"She still is."

"But I thought . . . that is, I was told she had left Gustav for a man named Gunnarson."

"That was Rolfson's name for my father. You see, according to tradition, a man's surname was taken from his ancestral land. If he lost the land, he lost his name, and was thereafter called the son of his father, whose name in this case was Gunnar. My father reassumed the name Starbane after he made his fortune in America."

Elizabeth understood. Haakon's father was known as

Starbane here in America, but as Gunnarson to the Norwegians. Proud and bitter, Gustav had been loath to speak of Eric by his rightful name, and Smedley and the Americans knew Eric only as their competitor, Starbane.

"The rivalry between Gustav and my father began with a fight," Haakon was saying. "According to Kristin, Gustav would bear the scar of a riding whip to the end of his days."

"He did."

Elizabeth was silent for a moment. Then she asked: "How . . . how did I come to live with Gustav Rolfson?"

"You were kidnapped and taken from us. Perhaps you were too young to remember. My father suspected Rolfson, and moved heaven and earth to find you, but it was no use. . . ."

Again, Elizabeth sat in silence. She knew it was true, and she was awed by Rolfson's monstrousness. Gustav Rolfson had *almost* achieved what he had set out to do. He had planned to send Elizabeth to America, trained and prepared to wreak vengeance against Eric Starbane. The little girl he had had kidnapped would be Gustav's instrument of revenge against her father, who had stolen Kristin from him.

"I must telegraph my parents immediately," Haakon said.

"I would . . . I would like to go to Minnesota as soon as possible," Elizabeth told him. "If that's all right."

Haakon's embrace was his answer.

7

Haakon took Elizabeth's arm and guided her from the dining room out toward the vestibule of the Fox Run restaurant, from which sounds of a sudden argument erupted.

"I'll eat in any damn restaurant I please and so will my friends," declared a rough masculine voice.

"Please, sir . . ."

"Don't give *me* that 'please, sir' shit! I said I wanted a meal. And I want it now."

Drawn by the racket, Haakon and Elizabeth veered left around the row of potted palms guarding the restaurant entrance and walked into the vestibule.

"Please, sir, we don't want to have you ejected," said the maitre d' soothingly.

"Ejected!" roared his antagonist, a big young bull of a man with a busty young woman clinging to his elbow. "Ejected?" he cried again, most disbelievingly this time. His eyes fell on Haakon and Elizabeth.

"Starbane!" he roared, in half-drunken good nature. "Hey, my good man," he said, turning again to the maitre d', "you have riffraff like Starbane in here, so that means I can get served for sure. Hey, Haakon, come on over here and tell this faded cow's udder who I am, and then we'll have a drink."

"Who *is* that?" Elizabeth whispered. The young man

looked wild and unkempt, although he wore the finest clothing.

"Clint Granger. Let me handle this."

"J.J.'s son? What's wrong with his eye?"

"Nothing. He squints that way trying to ape his father. I don't know why he doesn't wear a patch and be done with it."

The woman attached to Clint's elbow regarded the approach of Haakon and Elizabeth with snooty insouciance. She had very yellow hair piled high and wore a drab brown cloak, beneath which glittered a frilly dress one shade removed from bright red.

"Starbane, by God," roared Clint, exuding fumes of corn liquor as he grabbed Haakon's hand, "what the hell are you doing down here in Chicago? Who's the wench?" He lost his squint for a moment, ogling Elizabeth. The young woman with him pouted theatrically.

"This is my sister, Elizabeth," Haakon offered briefly.

"Say now, ain't that fine. A sister. Didn't know you had a sister. Things is lookin' up. Or things is *goin'* up, if you get my drift."

He yukked hilariously. The girl in the red dress was pleased at Elizabeth's embarrassment. Clint was still pumping Haakon's hand, and holding on tightly. "You know what, Starbane," he accused, with a wave toward the maitre d', "they say me an' my fiancée can't eat here. Me! The son of J. J. Granger! An' have you ever met a more charming an' lovely lady than this here?" Clint swatted his blond companion on the rump. "Me an' her is goin' to get hitched, ain't we, honey? Long about 1917, I figure," he told Haakon from behind his hand, and laughed some more. "Starbane, you get me a table, will you? They'll listen to you, and . . ."

"I thought you Grangers could handle anything," replied Haakon. The last thing he had wanted was a run-in with

Clint Granger, particularly a drunk and obnoxious Clint Granger. He wrenched his hand free.

"Let's go, Haakon," whispered Elizabeth.

"Not till I say so," snapped Clint, revealing quick belligerence. "Don't you Starbanes even want to know what I'm doin' here in town, huh? I figured you'd want to know at least that, since my old man is figurin' to trounce you so good."

Eric shrugged. "So, Clint, tell us what you're doin' in Chicago."

"Nope. No can do. It's a secret," returned Clint, and doubled up in laughter.

Haakon took Elizabeth's arm and they started walking toward the door.

"I didn't *say* you could leave yet," growled Clint, passing from laughter to anger via the quick transmutations of a drunk. He reached out and grabbed Haakon by the shoulder.

"I'll *tell* you what I'm doing down here," he snarled arrogantly. "I'm sewing up the most important right-of-way for Pa's railroad to the West Coast, that's what I'm doin'. I got the contracts here in my pocket"—he patted his breast—"and I got a drunk rancher outside in a cab. As soon as I get him sobered up enough to hold a pen and sign his 'X' like a good boy, well, hell, Pa got the Bitterroot by the balls, pardon me ladies, he got that goddamn High Y bottleneck right on through the Rockies."

"What did you say?" snapped Elizabeth, in a sharp, startled voice.

Clint swayed a little on his feet, and his complaisant companion glanced at him a little warily out of the corners of her eyes. The maitre d' stood looking on now, hoping that Haakon might somehow contrive to get the burly redhead and his whore out of this fine restaurant.

"What's it to you?" Clint demanded of Elizabeth.

Elizabeth was recalling the notation on Smedley's desk pad: "bottleneck" and "High Y."

"You said your father was about to attain something from a rancher?" she prodded. "High Y?"

"High Y," Clint repeated. "Stands for E-crib-see-coo," he added, pronouncing the name carefully for her benefit.

At the mention of this name, Elizabeth's heart stopped. *Ycripsicu.* It had to be. And if it was so, then the rancher that Clint Granger said was outside in a cab must be . . . But Clint continued to talk, oblivious to the effect his words were having.

"It's Injun talk. The rancher told me. Gateway to Bitterroot Pass and the West Coast. I tell you I got him drunk as a skunk in the cab outside—an' I speak the truth when I tell you I kept that pathetic bastard juiced on corn liquor since we left Montana. When he signs that paper in my pocket, that a tricky Chicago lawyer drew up"—here Clint drew a thick forefinger quickly across his throat —"well, it's *adios* Rolfson and it's *adios* Starbane, because J. J. Granger and his empire-building son are coming through."

Clint raised an arm and yanked at the cord of an imaginary train whistle. "*Toot-toot*," he yowled, his exuberant cry echoing all around the restaurant, "*toot-toot.*"

Elizabeth, possessed already of a desperate need to get outside and find the cab Clint had mentioned, nonetheless had to learn something else.

"You'll never beat Rolfson Industries," she told Granger.

"Heh-heh," he cackled shrewdly. "Pa an' me already beat 'em. We had us an inside man. He got fired, but they fired him too late . . ."

Smedley, Elizabeth knew for sure.

". . . an' we got it all, sister."

Clint, hands on hips, postured like a swaying colossus. Once again, Haakon and Elizabeth started for the main door.

"There is one thing you don't have yet," Elizabeth called sweetly to Clint. "That 'X' on the piece of paper."

She ought not to have said it. She was in a hurry to get outside to find the "drunken rancher" in Clint's hired cab, and she fairly pulled Haakon along with her.

"Hold up, Starbane," Clint roared, advancing on the couple and shaking off his "fiancée's" arm. "You don't leave this dump until I get an apology from that tart-tongued sister of yourn!"

"Oh, my goodness," mourned the maitre d'. He had just convinced himself that nothing violent was going to happen.

Haakon, his nerves taut and his patience at an end, turned in the doorway and swung from his heels. Clint was about an inch taller than Haakon, and maybe twenty pounds heavier. Had he been in any condition to fight, there would have been a fierce struggle. But, half-dazed on alcohol, and fogged the other half of the way on drinker's anger, he stumbled right into Haakon's powerful punch. Clint had no chance at all. He snapped out of consciousness as soon as Haakon's fist smashed his face.

"*Now* let's get out of here," Haakon said, rubbing his raw knuckles.

The usual line of horse-drawn hacks was waiting at curbside in front of the Fox Run. Hack drivers saw Elizabeth approaching. Some called out their fares. Others simply watched the beautiful girl in the long flowing cloak, watched with growing wonder as she raced from cab to cab, looking inside. They had never seen anything like it, and were made uneasy by the inexplicable intensity of her strange quest. Most of the cabs, naturally, were empty, but then there was one that was not. Three girls occupied the closed cab of one big hack. They might have been sisters of Clint Granger's companion, whose shrieks of alarm were finally beginning to wane inside the hotel. Two of the sisters were blondes and the third was a copper-redhead.

"Whatcha want, honey?" asked the redhead, as Elizabeth

looked into the cab. "Say, did you see a big guy with kind of a squinty eye in the restaurant?"

"Yes," Elizabeth answered. "He's lying on the floor inside."

One of the blondes laughed. Elizabeth did not laugh. Because, lying on the floor of the cab, in elegant clothes but passed out cold, was Lance Tallworth.

"I want him," Elizabeth told the redhead.

She snickered lewdly. "Honey, if it was up to me, you could have him in a minute. He ain't good for *nothin'*, if you know what I mean. But Clint likes him for some reason, an' we girls ain't supposed to let him out of our sight."

Elizabeth stared at Lance, disbelieving not only the fact that he was here before her eyes, but disbelieving too the sad state in which he appeared. What devastation had taken his weight and color from him? What catastrophe had etched those lines of suffering upon his face? His eyes were closed, as if he were asleep, but the dangerous slackness of his jaw and the pallor of his skin indicated deep malaise, and maybe illness.

"Haakon, please," she called, "come here quickly."

"What's going on? What are you up to?" asked one of the blondes.

"That man on the floor. I'm taking him."

"No, you're not," vowed the redhead.

Haakon approached the cab. "What is it?"

"Clint'll beat us black and blue if we let the rancher out of our sight," said the other blonde.

"*I'll* beat you black and blue," corrected Elizabeth, as she pulled open the door of the cab and climbed inside. The redhead clawed at Elizabeth's hair. She deflected the long fingernails and bent toward Lance. He smelled strongly of liquor and—if there were a scent to it—despair.

"Elizabeth! What in God's name are you doing?" cried Haakon.

One of the blondes fled through the door on the opposite side of the cab.

"Haakon, please, help me. We must get this man out of here. Clint will ruin him."

"*You* get out of here!" ordered the redhead, less sure of herself now that Haakon was present.

"Why on earth are you . . . ?" Haakon began.

"Please. Don't ask questions. It's very important. And look at the state he's in!"

Haakon leaned into the cab and observed. He was thoroughly mystified. Yet he was impressed by Elizabeth's determination to remove the man from the hack. And he wanted to get away from the Fox Run himself, to avoid further difficulty with Clint Granger.

"You'll get in big trouble if you move that man," the redhead whined, making her last effort. The second blonde left the cab and stood on the street, watching.

"Move aside a little," Haakon told Elizabeth. He reached down, eased his hands under Lance's shoulder blades, and pulled him halfway out of the cab. Then he bent over, positioned Lance's weight as best he could, and lifted him onto his shoulders.

"You're gonna be *so* sorry!" bleated the redhead.

Hastily, at a half-trot, with drivers and passersby looking on, Haakon carried the unconscious Lance away.

"Our friend has had a little too much to drink," Elizabeth explained inadequately, as onlookers gaped.

Then they had Lance in Elizabeth's own carriage and the perplexed Kohler was whipping the horses toward the Rolfson mansion. But now it was the Starbane mansion, and always would be.

Lance was sprawled on one of the seats. Elizabeth bent over him, stroking his face, listening half-fearfully to the frighteningly slow beat of his heart.

"Elizabeth, whatever is going on?" asked Haakon. It was almost as if she loved this drunken stranger.

8

Haakon and two of the housemen carried Lance inside and upstairs to a guest bedroom. At times he seemed almost on the verge of consciousness, but always he slipped away.

"I can't explain it all now," Elizabeth told her brother, "but I met this man last year in Geneva. I haven't seen him since then, but I've never felt anything comparable to the way he made me feel, and . . ."

"You're explaining pretty well," he averred. "I understand. How can I help?"

"There's little to be done until the effects of the liquor wear off."

"Was he a drinking man when you knew him?"

"Oh, no." Elizabeth did not want to say that she had known Lance for only a couple of days.

Haakon regarded the big man on the guestroom bed. "Well, I don't know much about these things. Cover him with a lot of blankets. I've heard that sweating helps. I'll go now and telegraph my . . . our parents."

"What will you say?"

"That their daughter seems to live a very interesting life."

"Oh, please."

"They're going to be very happy. Don't worry."

Elizabeth wasn't worried, not about Haakon or Kristin or Eric. But Lance's condition troubled her. She could not imagine what had happened to lure him into this vile and decrepit state. Summoning Jane, her personal maid, they stripped Lance and bathed him, first with alcohol, then with cool water. Jane's eyes widened as she studied the man, narrowed when she observed the way he seemed almost to rise to consciousness, then fall away.

"This isn't good, Ma'am. This isn't good."

Jane was a serious, sometimes doleful girl, moody but competent.

Afternoon passed into evening, then into night. Haakon reappeared.

"I'm to get railroad tickets immediately," he said. "Father and Mother are overjoyed. They can't believe this. Here, look at the telegram they sent." He handed it to her. The words were a blur. ANSWERED PRAYERS . . . MAKE UP FOR LOST YEARS . . . WONDERFUL . . .

And, indeed, it was wonderful. But why did such joy have to be mingled with the sadness she felt about Lance's condition? Beneath blankets now, he was sweating profusely, but that seemed to help as little as the baths had. It seemed that Lance was unable to rise from the strange, eerie lethargy by which he was gripped. Todd Handley hustled around the house, bringing tea and sandwiches to Elizabeth and Jane, and piles of compresses for Lance's forehead.

"I ought to have called a doctor right away," Elizabeth accused herself. "I'll do so now . . ."

Jane, at the bedroom window, looking down toward the city, let out a shriek.

"Fire!" she yelled. "There's a fire in the city!"

Fire, again? Could it be possible that God would allow Chicago to burn a second time?

Elizabeth raced to the window, and so did Haakon and the others. The mansion was close to the lake, and by looking south past the Blackstone, they could see the buildings of the business district. One of the taller structures was afire. It was easy to identify because Elizabeth knew it well, knew its precise relationship to surrounding buildings.

314

"The Rolfson Building is on fire!" she shouted, even as Haakon came to her from behind, grasping her shoulders.

"There's little wind tonight, and that's a blessing," he observed. "It was the awesome wind of Lake Michigan that fanned the flames in 1871."

"But our building is going," Elizabeth cried.

All of them could see, against the night sky, the tongues of fire leaping from the summit of the building, like a flaring torch. And as she watched, Elizabeth felt her initial feeling of loss subside and sink away. What did the building mean to her, anyway? Was it not the grave marker of her past life, the life that had ended today? Was not a new and happy life coming to take the place of the old, with true parents, and a family . . . and Lance?

"That's highly unusual," Haakon observed. "Your building is burning from the top. From your very office, I would guess. See? Only now are the flames beginning to lick their way downward . . ."

"We must go down there!" Elizabeth decided.

"There is little to be done . . ."

"I don't care about that. If the Chicago firemen must risk their lives saving the buildings around mine, then I ought to be there too."

Elizabeth brooked no rationalizations, and grumbling old Kohler hitched fresh horses to the carriage. Giving instructions to Jane regarding Lance's care, she and Haakon and Todd raced toward the fire.

When they reached North State Street, a thousand milling Chicagoans blocked their way, but the mood was one of celebration rather than dismay. "The firemen stopped it from spreadin'!" they cried to one another. "They did their jobs terrific, I'll tell the world!"

Less confident than the mob, they made their way toward the pillar of fire. The heat was raging, even as the Rolfson Building tumbled in blazing beams and fiery ashes to the pavement. A white sheet on the curb opposite the conflagration ballooned and sagged in the air currents created by the fire. When it sagged, the outline of a body could be discerned. Next to the sheet stood Captain O'Riley.

"Who is it?" Elizabeth asked. "Did the fire in my building cause a death?"

O'Riley shrugged, his lean face illuminated in the blaze like a man gazing at a plain of flames beyond the river Lethe. "Only the death of the man who set the fire," he said.

His tale was short, but it bore the accumulated weight of the separate stones that make a mountain. "I had Smedley followed," he said, "from the time he left the telegraph office. I even paid to learn the text of his message. It read: I'M OUT STOP THE END STOP WHAT NOW STOP. And a message came back from St. Paul, Minnesota: NOW DE-STROY WHAT YOU SHOULD NEVER HAVE KEPT."

"Signed 'T'?" asked Elizabeth, to Haakon's confound-ment. He had only a small idea what his new sister might be involved in.

"No," shrugged O'Riley, "it was signed, most unusually, 'In the Land of the Blind.' Do you wish to view Alois Smedley's remains? What remains of his remains. He leaped from the top floor to avoid the flames he set. I myself barely got out alive."

"You were up there?" Elizabeth asked, looking toward the surging funnel of fire that rose where her office had once been.

"I followed Smedley up, after keeping an eye on him all day. But do you know, he didn't enter the Rolfson suite, but rather an empty set of offices adjacent to it."

"All our space was rented," Elizabeth declared.

"This area was not," O'Riley maintained. "Did you ever look?"

"No," she answered sheepishly.

"So I followed him up there," the captain continued, "and observed him moving aside the panels of what proved to be a false wall. Behind that wall, and directly against the

316

section of your office in which the files are kept, Smedley evidently maintained records of his own. He opened drawers and began to remove thick batches of paperwork, lighting and burning the items a few at a time in a metal waste container."

O'Riley shrugged, then continued. "I accosted him. We fought. The container tipped over and the flames spread. I got out. Smedley was trapped. He jumped."

Horrified, Elizabeth glanced from the sheet on the sidewalk to the face of young Todd Handley. He was entranced by the conflagration, and was not listening to her. Nor did she want him to hear. "Sandra Handley told me there were secret files," Elizabeth said. "I always felt that Smedley killed Sandra."

"It seems so, but we'll never know now," O'Riley said. "And with those files gone, there are a lot of things you'll never know."

"I disagree," observed Haakon, on the drive back to the house. Todd was asleep beside them in the carriage and Kohler bobbed and weaved in the driver's seat. Chicago had been saved, but the Rolfson Building was no more.

"Disagree with what?" Elizabeth yawned.

"With what O'Riley said about there being a lot we'll never know. We're already dead certain, for example, who sent Smedley into the building to destroy his true set of files."

"We are?" wondered Elizabeth sleepily.

"In the land of the blind," pronounced Haakon, using the singsong cadence of a childish rhyme. *"In the land of the blind . . ."*

". . . the one-eyed man is king," finished Elizabeth drowsily. *"The one-eyed man is king!"* she repeated, snapping wide awake.

J. J. Granger.

But such knowledge gave her no joy.

"All the evidence is destroyed," she said. "Any fact indicating illegality between Granger and Smedley no longer exists. And so J. J. Granger is far ahead of me in attaining railroad rights-of-way, and all of his gains are strictly legal to the dispassionate eye of the law."

But then she smiled, an exultant, almost triumphant flashing of teeth. She possessed the key to every door.

"Bitterroot Pass!" Elizabeth said.

9

"How come he's not waking up?" worried Jane, the maid, who had risen early to help Elizabeth watch over Lance. "I don't think he looks right, either."

Elizabeth put another wet cloth on her beloved's forehead, and tried not to admit that Jane was right.

Lance lay in the bed, curled almost into a fetal position. Sweat poured from his body, a cold clammy sweat that made Elizabeth uneasy, even though his skin was hot to the touch. Yet he had no temperature, and he did not sniffle or cough, which would have been sure signs of a cold or pneumonia. No, this was something else, and it scared her.

"It's almost dawn now," she said to Jane. "We should have summoned Doctor Eveleth yesterday."

The maid yawned away the last of her sleep and came forward to the bed, knelt down, and looked closely at Lance. She lifted away the damp cloth and touched his forehead. A startled look of awareness appeared on her wide but pretty face.

"No, Miss Rolfson, I wouldn't involve Doc Eveleth, because Mr. Tallworth is in real bad shape. *Real* bad," she repeated somberly.

No! thought Elizabeth. *No, I cannot bear it. To find him after so long, and now this.*

Jane saw her mistress's sudden terror and hastened to elaborate. "Oh, Miss Rolfson, please! Please don't be so alarmed. He's not going to die. It's just that this is real *serious*. Mr. Tallworth isn't just a man who has taken too much alcohol. . . ." She averted her eyes. "He's taken . . . or bèen given . . . other things."

"Other things? What do you mean, 'other things'?"

"Doc Eveleth is going to know, and he might make trouble."

"Doctor Eveleth make trouble? Jane, are you daft? Eveleth is a pillar of Chicago medicine. He'd understand anything."

Jane disagreed. "No, he wouldn't. Not this." She pointed at Lance, who was sweating even more heavily now, and beginning to writhe in the bed. "When he wakes up, he's going to be in hell, and you'd better have something to give him."

Elizabeth stared at her maid in alarm.

"I . . . I had a . . . a friend once," Jane explained. "Anthony. I loved him real lots because he needed me. He needed me when he was"—she nodded toward Lance —"when he was like this. Don't you understand, Miss Rolfson? Mr. Tallworth has been taking dope. Strong dope. The kind that rots your brain if you take it and tortures your body if you don't take it."

Now Elizabeth wished that Haakon had killed Clint Granger at the Blackstone Hotel. Something had happened, somehow. Lance had been deceived, tricked. . . .

"This man is no addict," Elizabeth said. "Anyone can see that." Yet Jane's knowledge might prove useful. Perhaps she was right about not summoning the severe Doctor Eveleth.

Lance stirred. His eyelids flickered.

"If it is true that Mr. Tallworth has been powerfully doped over a period of time," she asked the maid, "what will happen now?"

"He will tremble so hard that the bed will shake, and the floor beneath it. He will be wild-eyed, and recognize no one, and dig his fingernails into his flesh."

"Oh, dear God," Elizabeth cried. "Is there nothing we can do?"

Lance moaned.

"Only two things. Either find some strong dope and give it to him as soon as he is conscious, or tie him to the bed for three or four days until the fury passes. Then he may be all right."

"No," Elizabeth decided. "No," she repeated.

"Oh, please, Miss Rolfson, *please*! I've *seen* it. I've seen how it is."

Lance threw himself upright in bed, his eyes flashing around the room. He hugged himself, shivering. He looked directly at Elizabeth and Jane, without seeing either one of them.

"It's starting," Jane gasped.

"Leave the room and lock the door behind you," Elizabeth commanded.

"No, Ma'am . . ."

"Do as I say. Prepare a pot of tea. Put rum in it. Put a half-bottle of rum in it."

"That won't do, Miss Rolfson . . ."

"Do as you're told!"

Jane hurried out and locked the door. Lance was sweating and shivering and looking around in a jerky, disjointed manner, as if his neck were on a swivel. Elizabeth took a deep breath and sat down on the bed beside him. His eyes were vague and unfocused, but he looked at her. Just looked at her. There was no sign of recognition in his eyes, no expression of any kind on his face.

"Lance," she said. "Lance. I am Elizabeth. *Elizabeth*. Here I am. I love you, Lance," she said, and put her arms around him.

He was shivering very badly, just as Jane had predicted, but he did not resist the embrace.

"I want to help you," she said. "You must let me help you." Then, seeking to test his acuity, and to take his mind off the vile elixir his body would soon be screaming for, she asked him who he was.

A long silence followed. She sensed the rational part of his mind at work behind his black, blasted eyes.

"I . . . I am . . . Sioux," he said falteringly.

To Elizabeth, it sounded like *suuuuuuu*, and her heart fell. What did this mean? But she did not despair.

"Lance. Lance Tallworth," she corrected.

"Lance," he said, with a measure of understanding, although not much. Then suddenly he went into a violent paroxysm, flinging her away, almost flying off the bed. He wound up holding his stomach and moaning. Elizabeth put her arms around him again, wrapping him in the coverlets, repeating his name and hers over and over. Lance just moaned, far away in the hell to which he had been consigned.

Jane knocked, unlocked the door, and entered. She carried a tray with two cups and saucers, a steaming pot of tea, and a bottle full of West Indies rum.

"Pour a cupful and put a lot of rum in it," Elizabeth ordered. Jane did so, and passed the cup to Elizabeth, who lifted it toward Lance's mouth.

But something far down in his eyes caught fire then. He put forward his shaking hand, took the cup, and hurled it against the wall.

"Oh, my God!" cried Jane, leaping away from the bed.

But Elizabeth was of another mind. "No," she cried excitedly, "it's all right. That's how they've given him the dope before. In a cup or glass. He knows that, and he's fighting it. The Grangers are fools. He's fighting them, even in this state. And that's why they never got him to sign those papers. It wouldn't have been with an 'X' either, that's for sure. But he needs something to calm his body now. But how . . . ?"

Then she thought of J. J. Granger, slurping his coffee from a saucer.

"Quick, Jane," she said, while holding Lance on the bed, "pour rum and tea into the saucer. You hold it. Hand me a spoon."

Lance seemed to sense the difference, the kindness and fervent desire to help him. Many spoonsful of rum-flavored tea spilled onto the sheets, onto his chin and chest, but many more he was able to drink. And all the while Elizabeth kept saying: "It's Elizabeth and I love you, Lance. I am Elizabeth and I love you, Lance." At last he relaxed and lay down, shivering, dozing. Half the bottle of rum was gone.

"He is in a very bad state," Jane commented, measuring the bottle.

"No, we spilled a lot. But look, he is somewhat calm."

The maid had to admit that it was true.

"I'll stay with him," Elizabeth vowed. "We will keep up this procedure. It *will* work. He still has the fight in him, and he will be whole again, so help me God!"

For two days the fury raged. Gradually, Elizabeth lessened the proportion of rum to tea until there was very little alcohol at all. Lance drifted in and out of consciousness. He seemed to know that he was in a fight against something evil, and that he was being helped in the struggle. But he had been so walled off from reality by the drugs that the path back was a long one. And still he had those fearsome shivering fits, that made it seem as if some force was trying to shake out his brains and being. When these occurred, Elizabeth took to the bed with him, and held him as tightly as she could, saying, "Lance, Lance, Lance!" over and over.

On the third day, when the fit hit him, she slipped into bed and held him. Soon something fortuitous must happen, or else a doctor must be risked, drugs or no. Lance's body shook and bucked against her own, but she clung to him, offering the living heat of herself to vanquish the clammy coldness that had its hold on him. She watched his face closely as he suffered, searching for some sign that his dreadful condition was improving, but seeing only his twisted expression, and the dull, faraway aspect in his eyes. Then, quite suddenly, as if a dark spirit had fled his body, he shuddered one last time, a great trembling all along his body, and lay still.

"Lance?" she asked softly, assaulted by a great fear. *"Lance?"*

His eyes changed. Elizabeth observed their alteration and it was like standing on a mountain and watching sunlight sweep across the plains below, the movement of a vast golden scythe. Alertness, awareness returned to Lance, like a gift of grace. He recognized her then, but he was very puzzled to see her there in bed with him.

"Elizabeth?" he whispered, his voice strange and dry.

"Yes!" Elizabeth told him, her heart flooding with happiness and relief.

Lance smiled tiredly, then drifted back into his first peaceful sleep in weeks.

In the days that followed, Lance told of everything that had happened to him, of *Ycripsicu* and Fleet Fawn and little Sostana.

"Clint Granger suggested that I accompany him east to St. Paul and Chicago. I'd heard someone named Rolfson in Chicago was interested in railroads, a woman, and I was certain it had to be you. I accompanied Clint in order to get away from my ranch for a time, and the sadness there, as well as to come to Chicago. But he wanted to linger in St. Paul, and there were parties. I drank. There was something in the drink. I kept asking to see J. J. Granger. 'You'll see him when I'm damn good and ready,' Clint told me. 'You got Injun blood in you, an' my pa don't have much truck with your kind.' Soon I found that I needed the dope in my drink. After that, I barely know what happened."

"But you didn't sign the papers he wanted you to," Elizabeth told him.

"Thank God for that. I remember—I think I remember —being in the presence of a bearded, one-eyed monster . . ."

"That would be Granger."

". . . who kept laughing at me and cursing me and trying to put a pen in my hand. This must have happened a dozen times, either on one day, or two different days, or twelve different days. I have no idea. But I kept thinking, 'I must not sign, I must not sign.' And I also kept telling Clint, 'Chicago. Chicago. I'll sign in Chicago.' Maybe he thought that bringing me here would get the signature. I remember the parties and the women and the drinking, but I have no recollection of getting to Chicago at all."

"Well, you did," she said, hugging him, telling him her own story.

"And so you see," she told him, "there will be nothing but happiness for us. You have your life, and I have mine, and we have ours. The Grangers are no threat to us anymore"—how very soon she would rue these bright words—"and I shall build my dream, my railroad into the West, and . . ."

"I do not want the iron horse upon my land," he said matter-of-factly. *"Ycripsicu* is holy ground."

It did not matter. It could be discussed later. Surely he would change his mind. Already he was changing, had changed. Elizabeth allowed herself a small portion of secret pride: she was the one woman in life who held the power to gentle him, a falconer of love thrusting her gloved fist to the heavens, down from which he would come to serve and claim her, both together, both forever.

And when they made love for the first time since Geneva, all the world was swept away. Elizabeth was thrillingly aware of his tall power, of his guarded, mysterious eyes, and the strong arms that had held her in Switzerland, with only a gatepost for a bed.

It did not seem so long ago, and now they had a real bed. So soft and wonderful it was to lie in and entwine, with all of life and time ahead of them. They loved first with their eyes, drinking in the sight of each other. Lance had always held himself aloof from words or gestures that might reveal his soul. But not now. He was telling her with his eyes, and then with his tongue, of need and love and promise.

There in her house in Chicago, with Lake Michigan shining outside, his glance was a wish, her embrace an answer. Elizabeth lost herself in his kiss, remembering his hands as they touched her in all the secret places. Her body throbbed, flowing with desire, as he lingered over buttons, kissing her breasts as silk fell away from flesh. Her body arched with need and she knelt before him, freeing his body in order to possess it for her own. A long kiss of promise and wonder, then he rose upon her and opened her to himself.

Lance was gentle at first, and each approach, each stroke, was almost like a question. Their mouths were as ravenous for each other as their bodies were, but in the fire of their kiss the memory of shared pleasure enhanced the sensation of this ceaseless moment, and all the time they had been apart was as nothing. Elizabeth fitted herself beneath him, moving with him, proudly feeling his urgency throb within her, proud at her ability to make his strong, bronze body tremble in her embrace. Then he grasped her long legs, and drew them up around him, riding her higher, faster now, and Elizabeth's mind faded, grew dreamy and dull as she gasped and moaned, felt her body open and clutch and plunge, only to open and clutch and plunge again, maddened in the pursuit of joy, wanting it now and wanting it forever. Elizabeth felt the pressure building, and no longer possessed enough of her conscious mind to hold on to reality. As if from far away, she felt her body moving faster and faster, and close to her, so close to her, was the sweet body of her beloved, so little known, so well loved, moving into her again and again and again with strokes so powerful they made her gasp, as if in pain, but leaving her wanting another and another and another. And then Elizabeth cried out, holding him inside herself. All sensation lived then for an instant, in the staff and gourd of him throbbing in her body, heavy and hard enough to sire a world. And within the fragile folds of her body, where velvet furrows waited, Elizabeth knew beyond knowing that her womanhood had been touched. If not this time, then soon, soon, she must have the child of this man.

"Now we must prepare to go west to the High Y," she heard him say much later, as they dozed in the afterglow.

"Yes," she said, "and we'll stop in St. Paul along the way. Not only do you have me, I've brought you a whole family too."

It was impossible that there could be this much happiness in one world.

It *was* impossible.

Part Six

MINNESOTA and MONTANA ● 1886–1890

1.

On the morning of her wedding day, Elizabeth Starbane looked down from the back porch of *Windward*, her father's house on the banks of the Mississippi River in St. Paul. It was June 10, 1886, the best day of her life, the best month of her life, the best . . . the best year? Yes, so far. But there would be better years ahead. Each coming year would be better than the one preceding. Elizabeth was certain of it. She felt in love with life itself today, and nothing would be allowed to intrude upon that feeling.

Windward was a wonderful place, with its high white walls, and the tall white pillars and porches on both the street and river sides of the house. From the sunlit porch on which Elizabeth now stood, the brilliant green lawn ran down to the leafy thicket at the river's edge. It was there, all those summers ago, that she had been kidnapped by agents of Gustav Rolfson. She had been snatched while playing along the riverbank with her brother, Haakon, and an Indian called Ned, who was in charge of *Windward*'s stables, and who had loved the children. While Elizabeth felt wholly comfortable in the house, she had not yet been able to bring herself to walk down across the lawn to the riverbank. She knew it was a bit foolish of her, because nothing could happen to her there, but the thicket and the powerful, slowly moving river held a dark memory she did not wish to confront.

Turning away from the riverbank and the dazzling glitter of the sun-drenched prairie beyond it, Elizabeth fairly hugged herself for joy. In only a few hours the wedding ceremony would be held—right here in *Windward*'s vaulting ballroom—and then, after a great celebration to which, it seemed, almost all of Minneapolis and St. Paul had been invited, she and Lance would have the great house to themselves. And the night would be theirs, as well. Haakon was bound for Chicago, to continue his studies; Eric and Kristin were leaving for Duluth, where a new crisis was rising on the iron range.

Rubbish, thought Elizabeth. She did not wish to think of business or the Grangers today, not at all. Just Lance . . . along with Eric and Kristin. *My parents*, she thought, with a tremor. It seemed so wonderful to have parents after such a long time of thinking she had none. It was like the best surprise there ever was.

From her place on the sunny porch, Elizabeth could hear the bustle of preparation inside the great house. The guest list had swollen to include practically every notable in the Upper Midwest. There were, however, two luminaries who had *not* been invited: J. J. Granger and his son, Clint. Eric, with his good nature, his high spirits at Elizabeth's intended marriage, and a measure of shrewdness too, was not averse to inviting the crude pair.

"Look at it this way," he had suggested. "Granger lives right here in St. Paul. He knows about the wedding. A deliberate snub will only make him more acrimonious than he already is. But if he's over here, drinking and feeling good, he might let his tongue slip a little, and we might learn what he's up to."

Eric Starbane and J. J. Granger were virtually at parity

now as regarded control of the iron range. Both dominated outright a commanding majority of stock in their respective mining enterprises. But lately, there had been rumors out of Duluth that J.J. and Clint were seen huddling at the Back Bay Bar in Superior, Wisconsin, with Alvah T. Bascomb. Bascomb, a man with the appearance, instincts, and tenacity of a hyena, was known to have made at least one fortune as an emissary between Andrew Carnegie and John D. Rockefeller.

But Kristin disagreed with Eric's hospitable inclination.

"I won't have J. J. Granger in my house under any circumstances," she cried. "When we first came to St. Paul, he sank the river barge carrying the lumber for our home—I know we can't prove it, but we know he did it—and then we had to buy lumber from him at inflated prices. I won't forget that, and you shouldn't either!"

"Oh, darling, that's long past . . ."

"With J. J. Granger, ten years ago is still right now. And a grudge is as good as forever."

"All right, then," Eric agreed, "no Grangers. I'm sure few of the other guests will miss him."

Elizabeth had smiled, listening to the two of them banter in the gentle good humor born of their years together. Her relationship with Lance was so different, more intense. But then she and Lance were different from the older couple. *Our long separation has just ended*, she thought, *and our life together barely begun*.

Lance and Eric, two strong men, got on well, but his daughter's choice of husband was nonetheless on Eric Starbane's mind. After meeting and speaking with Lance several times, he had asked to see Elizabeth in private.

"I wish you every possible happiness, and that your life not be as torn by separations and disappointments as Kristin's and mine once was. Lance seems a fine man, but very self-contained. Do you think his absorption may grow to trouble you?"

"Oh, no," Elizabeth answered quickly. "He only appears removed. The two of us know each other, and have our ways."

"I'm sure you do," said Eric, smiling. "I only meant . . . well, sometimes silence is hard to interpret."

"Love is a language of many tongues."

"Indeed it is. Oh, by the way, I much prefer Lance to your other suitor."

"What? What other suitor? I don't have . . ."

"I'm teasing," Eric told her. "Clint Granger stopped here at *Windward* a few days ago. He said he had met you in Chicago, and wanted to see you when you arrived. He seems quite taken with you."

"Good Lord," cried Elizabeth, recalling the fight between Haakon and Clint, remembering even more bitterly what Clint had done to Lance. "Even if I see him dead, it will be none too soon!"

Elizabeth, in her turn, had had something to discuss with Eric.

"Tell me about my mother," she said hesitantly. "What was she like? Was she beautiful? Was she . . . ?"

Eric sighed. For a moment, the burden of sad memory came down upon him. "She was very lovely," he said, "and gentle. She loved us both so much. Beautiful too. Like you in many ways, except that her hair was darker. She saved my life the first time by finding me in the woods after the Gettysburg armies had retreated. And she saved it the second time . . ."

"When she stepped in front of the bullet from the gun of Gustav Rolfson's hired assassin."

"Yes. Haakon told you?"

Elizabeth nodded. "Haakon told me also that you tried hard to find me after I was kidnapped—that you always suspected that Gustav Rolfson was responsible."

"Yes, when I learned of a young woman named *Elizabeth* Rolfson, well, I couldn't help but hope. I don't think I could have borne the pain of hope shattered. Haakon himself was rather agitated."

"I know," she said, remembering how severe her brother had been in her office, how stricken he had been to hear her name outside the Opera House.

"What do you plan to do with Rolfson Industries? And that dream railroad of yours? What do you call it?"

"The Continental Pacific. With regard to that, I'm afraid the outlook is not good. Granger was paying Smedley to foul my bids for purchasing rights-of-way from farmers and ranchers. He is far ahead of me in that, and I understand he'll be ready to begin laying track next year. West of the Rockies, in Idaho and Washington, we're doing much better. Mr. Greenbush telegraphed to say our agents are . . ."

"Elizabeth, what does it matter how many rights-of-way Granger holds? *You* have Bitterroot Pass."

Elizabeth shook her head. "No, I don't. Lance seems opposed to a railroad going across his land. *Ycripsicu*, his ranch, is sacred to him. It has something to do with vengeance."

"Sacred?" Eric frowned. "Vengeance?"

"It is an Indian concept, I believe. Something like that. I have not pressed him on it. I think in time he will see . . ."

"In time," Eric echoed, without great enthusiasm. "Anyway, if Granger starts laying track, you can be sure he'll figure out a way to get control of the Bitterroot."

"Never," Elizabeth proclaimed.

"That's my girl," said Eric. "You know, it's going to seem strange. I've just got you back, and already I must give you away!"

2

The Reverend Doctor Estendahl lifted his large head and addressed the assemblage. "We are gathered here today," he intoned, "to join together in the sight of God this man and this woman . . ."

It is happening, thought Elizabeth. Gorgeous banks of fragrant flowers filled the huge parlor of the house, in which the wedding was taking place. Lance stood beside her, like strength itself. He seemed absolutely calm, tremendously self-contained. Only the tiniest quiver along his taut jawline betrayed the intensity of his emotions. Her own emotions were very evident. Her eyes kept blurring.

"Do you take this man to be your lawfully wedded husband?" Reverend Estendahl was asking. "To have and to hold? In sickness and in health? In joy and in . . ."

No sorrow, Elizabeth thought. *No sorrow. We have had enough of that.*

And then Lance was holding her, kissing her as Estendahl had bidden. All she wanted to do was go away with him now, far away to *Ycripsicu* or Geneva or anywhere. But instead she went with him into the ballroom, where the reception was to be held.

The nice little lady who served as society reporter for the St. Paul newspaper would write:

. . . never before has our city witnessed the brightness
and gaiety of so many renowned citizens in celebration
of such a distinguished young couple . . .

It was true. Eric Starbane had "gone all out" for his
daughter's wedding. Three United States senators were
present, and a half dozen congressmen. Fully half the
members of the Minnesota state congress were there with
their wives, and also present were powerful men from as far
away as Kansas City and St. Louis. It was well known by
now that Lance was a rancher by profession, and this
occupation carried with it—to citizens of agrarian Minnesota—the attractive panache suggested by his lean, hard
looks and remote bearing. The women commented with
unbounded admiration on the bride's choice of white satin,
comments that were leavened only infrequently by a little
catty hissing regarding the choice of white.

"If I were so fortunate as to have the company of Mr.
Tallworth for a short time," whispered Mrs. Venable, wife
of Cruzon Venable, speaker of the state house, "I should
wear white too. For surrender!"

"I believe they met in Chicago," opined her companion,
Felicia Watworth, the brewer's hefty wife.

"Oh, no, dear. They met in Geneva. Kristin told me so
herself. Long before poor Elizabeth knew who she was. But
doesn't Mr. Tallworth remind you of someone? I say, but
his looks are striking, aren't they? I wonder what their
children will look like, with her fair face, and his
strong . . ."

"His appearance?" exclaimed Ruta Gerlich, daughter of
Ludlow Gerlich, proprietor of the North Star Iron Foundry.
She had enjoyed a most adequate portion of the roast goose,
quite a lot of the prime rib, and seven glasses of champagne. "Why, don't you know? Mr. Tallworth has Sioux

blood in him. His father was hanged for leading the uprising of 1862!"

"No!" exclaimed the others.

"Yes!" maintained Ruta, who knew her facts. "What an animal he must be."

Mrs. Venable sighed. Her husband, Cruzon, was pompous and portly, more liable to get excited over a joint of cold roast pork than the supple enticements that entered her own mind.

But the wedding was a magnificent success, in spite of carping here and there, and the party roared on through the afternoon and into early evening. In the buzz of a hundred hurried, bibulous conversations, Elizabeth was told:

"Honey, I understand you're involved in something about building a railroad. Don't be silly. Go and have a lot of babies, as the good Lord meant you to do."

"Elizabeth, take a good look at your father and mother now. We all so hope you end up like them."

"I hear you got kind of raked over the coals, down there in Chicago. Man by the name of Smedley, I heard. Too bad, but you got to remember this: the business world is no place for a woman."

"Best thing for a girl like you is a husband that keeps a tight rein. Get my drift?"

"So you're interested in railroads, hey? That's nice. But why don't you just invest in the Grand Northern, like your pa and I did. Heard you already got taken to the cleaners pretty bad, by that fellow Smedley in Chicago . . ."

In response to these comments, which were generally delivered in high good humor mingled with the hilarity of a shrewd, knowledgeable whiskey drinker, Elizabeth reacted invariably with a smile and a pleasant remark. But inwardly she was fuming. Lance, who stood beside her and heard all of the same witticisms, advice, and paternal admonishments, betrayed nothing by his expression, which was cordial but aloof at the same time. But he saw her mood.

"Why do you let them bother you?" he asked once, during a lull in the attention they were receiving.

"Because . . ." she replied, facing the bitter fact, "because my pride has been hurt. I am well educated and I am intelligent. But I was made to look like a fool by Alois Smedley, and *it was my own fault*!"

"So now you want to build the railroad you have planned, and then you will be whole again?"

"Why . . . yes," she said slowly, realizing that he had read her completely.

"I think everyone must at one time or another do something in order to become whole again," he said then, with a significance she did not then understand, "but my ranch is holy ground . . ."

Haakon approached, to offer his congratulations and best wishes. "You've made Father and Mother very happy," Haakon said.

And it was true. Kristin and Eric were dancing now, the elaborate, formalized country dance of their homeland. The crowd of revelers had parted to give them room on the dance floor. Elizabeth could not help but marvel at how beautiful Kristin remained, how strong she had been through all the years of sorrow, how splendid she continued to be. She really did look as young as the girl in the portrait. And Eric, a big man, danced with the grace of a boy. The two were smiling at each other, for all the world to see . . .

A news reporter, in attendance to cover the affair for the Minneapolis paper, would later write—both for publication and affidavit—that the happiness of the day ended without warning.

     . . . thus, having heard a sudden shout from the entrance to the ballroom, this witness did turn away from the dancing couple, and consequently did espy in the ballroom doorway, in attitudes of belligerence and postures of inebriation, two men known to most of the assemblage . . .

"Well, what the hell have we got here, Clint?" roared J. J. Granger, surveying the ballroom with his good eye. He was dressed in an evening coat and light cape for the occasion, but the effect was somewhat mitigated by a revolver thrust into his cummerbund and by the fact that he had eschewed or lost his eyepatch.

"Looks like a wedding, Pa," Clint responded. He too carried a pistol, in a small holster at his belt.

"Wasn't we invited to this here shindig?" J.J. asked theatrically, staggering slightly under the influence of much liquor consumed quite recently.

"I don't think so, Pa," Clint guffawed, swaggering and flexing his big muscles, which rippled beneath his dress coat. He was not nearly as drunk as he'd been at the Fox Run restaurant. "I guess we ain't got the pedigrees *some* people like to admire so much."

The music had ceased. The guests were quieted. Eric had started toward the door to face the Grangers.

"Pedigrees, my ass!" J.J. laughed, regarding everyone sagely from the sunken hollow of the eye an arrow had claimed. "I understand the bride has gone and done got hitched to a red pagan Injun!"

His voice rang through the ballroom, projected as if J.J. had been an orator. Certainly he sought to reach every ear. Nor did he fail.

"Reckon you're right there, Pa," Clint seconded. "Leave it to a Starbane to marry down 'stead of up. 'Cause that's the direction they're headed too."

Haakon was moving forward too, to support his father in the case of a struggle.

"Evenin', J.J., Clint," said Eric. "If you want to be civil, come on in and have a drink."

"We don't want to be civil," Clint laughed, swaying a

little. He had his eyes on Haakon. Time to avenge the one-sided battle in Chicago.

"I never been civil in all my life," boasted J.J. expansively, "so why should I start now. I will take that drink, though, now you mention it."

Haakon stepped up and stood beside Eric. "You both get out," he said, blue eyes blazing.

"Heh-heh," chuckled J.J. "Looka what we got here."

J.J. leaned forward and gave Eric the benefit of his whiskey breath and his good eye. "Think you're better'n us, do you? Sure, I know. But I'm gonna whip you on the iron range and I'm gonna whip you on the rails, and . . ."

"An' we're gonna whip you right now," decided Clint. Bracing himself, he pulled back his fist and shot it forward at Haakon. J.J., in the meantime, drew back his fist to strike Eric.

Neither blow landed. Lance, moving swiftly through the mass of gaping people, suddenly appeared between the Starbanes and the Grangers. Grabbing Clint's flying forearm with one hand, and using his own body for leverage, Lance flipped him and sent him crashing into his father. The procedure was as neat as surgery, and almost as quiet.

When the Grangers untangled themselves, Lance, Haakon, and Eric were standing over them. Lance said nothing, but his eyes riveted Clint, and his eyes were filled with a desire for revenge for what had been done to him with alcohol and drugs.

Clint's eyes returned the hatred, but he saw the odds against him and his father. So did Old J.J. Almost any other man would have been embarrassed, but he wasn't. He knew they didn't like him anyway, neither the Starbanes nor the others. He knew he could buy and sell almost any one of them. So what the hell.

"You let me up," he bargained with Eric, "and I'll find it in my heart to say so long."

"Get up and get out."

"Glad to oblige." He got to his hands and knees, and began to rise. His body was big and strong still, but there was the hint of an old man's stiffness in his movements. Time was passing for him and for them all. Clint, however, figured he had a few good moves remaining. While getting to his feet, his arm snaked out and caught Lance around his knees. One quick pull, and Lance was falling backward. Even while Lance was plunging to the floor, Clint's hand went to the pistol at his belt.

"No!" Kristin cried. *"No!"* shrieked Elizabeth. Cries rose from the guests, and they moved forward or in retreat, depending upon the nature of their personalities.

There was no cause for alarm. Landing lightly as a cat, Lance pushed himself up from the floor with one arm, and catapulted his full weight at top speed into Clint, who was still fumbling with his weapon. Collision of bone and flesh produced a sickening thud, followed by a tremendous crash as Clint Granger once again struck the floor of the ballroom. This time he did not rise, nor did he speak.

"A few of you men come here," Haakon said. "Let's carry him out and dump him in the street."

Eric's counsel prevailed, however, and Clint was borne out to the buggy in which he and his father had arrived, and in which they now departed.

"You're a dead man, Starbane," said J.J. to Eric, before the buggy pulled away from the house.

"You deserve worse, for what you've done to my daughter's wedding," Eric shot back, as angry now as he'd been the day he'd killed the Norwegian sheriff who had come to foreclose on his ancestral home, the corrupt sheriff hired by Gustav Rolfson.

Eric was right too. The celebration could not recover from the damage the Grangers had wrought, although many tried to make it live again. But in the end, it was no use. Darkness fell, and guests departed with wishes for good fortune, with gentle words and smiles, but with none of the high good feelings that usually attend the conclusion of happy events.

"Try not to think about it," Kristin said to Elizabeth, when the guests had all gone. "In the end, the only thing that matters is that you and Lance are happy together. And there are just two people who can win that gift for you."

3

"And now we begin the rest of our lives," Elizabeth whispered, as Lance pulled her down onto the bed.

He said nothing. He was not a man born to make love with words.

Lost in his kiss, held in his embrace, beneath his body, Elizabeth turned to fire and ice, which have a language of their own, a tongue that is not at all difficult to understand. It is the silent speech of a man and a woman alone.

Windward held them, and the June night held *Windward* as Lance and Elizabeth had the world to themselves. Haakon had left for Chicago as planned, while Eric and Kristin were on their way to Duluth. In the morning, Lance and Elizabeth would make their journey to the ranch, to continue the life they were beginning tonight.

Elizabeth would never forget, not ever, nor cease to desire, forever, the triumphant sensation of his long staff coming into her. Her face contorted in the darkness as she took him, a grimace of victorious anticipation. *Oh, you are mine now, come!* Then he was all inside her and she would never let him go. And Lance felt, all about and around the living length of himself, those quivering folds of delight that soothed him everywhere, and maddened him everywhere, a hot enticing kiss that only heaven could have created, that only a creature made of heaven could bestow.

Elizabeth felt his arms about her and the hardness of him inside her and his hungry kiss upon her mouth. He tangled the hair at the back of her neck in one hand, and with the other he stroked delicately the tender petal of flesh that was her whole life now, her life and world threatening to explode like a voluptuous star. Her arms went around him, and her hands caressed his back, tracing his spine down, down, all the way down until she held in her hand the tingling twin crescents of his manhood, and the taut gourd enclosing them. Her fingers were gentle and knowing, and probing and tender and proud. Her fingers were as hungry as her body, as her lips, as hungry as the lips of her body.

Lost in the splendor of her caresses and her kiss, Lance bent over her, kissed her breasts, his own wise touch moving up and down, up and down her inner thighs, his caresses long as forever, even as he stroked her slowly with his body, stroked her with the long length of himself.

And so Lance loved her, each separate thrust an attempt to have her utterly, to bring to both of them and yet to defer forever the ultimate moment of release, a game that can never be won but is never lost. Elizabeth felt herself move slowly around him, as if her body were trying to find a way to take him into herself. And then she felt herself moving more quickly around him, then faster still, until she had lost all control of her movements, of what her body was doing. But she did not care. She barely realized what was happening, so great was the pleasure he gave and she took, the pleasure he took and she gave.

Elizabeth felt her mind fade away and come back, fade away again, only to be stirred back to life by glittering new flickers of pleasure. Then a breathless hollow seemed to glow and grow and spread out beneath her breasts, down through her abdomen as she writhed, spreading downward until every last thought was gone, every last morsel of memory gained in life had fled. Nothing was left of her then except a pulsing petal of sensation. She heard Lance cry, "*Iiiiiiiiiii!*" but could not say whether in agony or affirmation, and then the gorgeous rush took her too. She cried along with him, and felt inside her the pulsing pulsing pulsing spill of him, the flood her body greedily devoured.

And this time she knew for certain. She had no doubt. The tender speech of their flesh, silent though it was, had trembled the spheres of life. And out of the abyss a witness had been summoned, sworn before heaven to attest the love of Elizabeth and Lance.

Much later, while Lance slept, Elizabeth slid out of bed. Exhilarated by the lovemaking, she found herself unable to drift into sleep. Perhaps this was the way it was with her: to be wildly alert after love. Kristin had confided to Elizabeth, several days earlier while wedding preparations were under way, that whenever she and Eric had made love in their early years together, Kristin was stricken afterward by ravenous hunger. "But I didn't want to make myself fat," she'd said, "so in time I managed to content myself with another feast of love." Elizabeth herself had had three such banquets tonight, and for the time being—until dawn—she would content herself with that and let Lance get his rest.

Feeling intently alive and full of joy, she pulled a light cotton robe over her bare, glowing skin and walked to the window. The night, soft and fragrant, was illuminated by moonlight, and the prairies west of the Mississippi lay in shadowed slumber, golden on the hilltops and high ground, blue in the low places, and where the trees were. The great lawn of *Windward* ran down to the thicket by the river, and the Mississippi murmured and gurgled, speaking to life and the night.

The scent of night air was compelling, but something else beckoned Elizabeth too. Her personal odyssey, so intricately bound with this place, bade her now to cut and tie the thread of the past. *That which is over need never be feared again; what has ended can harm one no more.*

Both Lance and Haakon had urged her to banish her fear, forget the riverbank past and the kidnapping. Haakon had even implied that it was silly for her to shiver at lost moments she could barely remember anyway. Yes, he was right, and the night was so gorgeous and so fresh . . .

Elizabeth left the bedroom and descended the sweeping staircase to the main floor. *Windward* was silent, its servants having retired to their quarters under the roof. The ballroom had been cleared and cleaned, with windows flung wide open to air the last whiff of cigar smoke. Elizabeth experienced a kind of sensory postmortem. Her wedding day had come and gone, and it was over. She was no longer Elizabeth Rolfson or Elizabeth Starbane, but a new person known to the world as Mrs. Lance Tallworth. Well, that was all right, that was better than fine.

She walked through the ballroom, opened and passed through the tall screen door that led to the wide porch. Out in the air, the night was even more voluptuous than it had been from the bedroom window. Elizabeth smelled the mingled perfume of grass, lilac, honeysuckle, and willow leaf. Blended thereto was the cool smell of the mighty river that flowed from the trackless north.

I will have done with it, she decided. Stepping down from the white porch with its dignified columns, she walked across dew-wet grass toward the willow thicket and the river, afraid to remember and afraid not to remember the long-ago day on which she had been taken away. Midway across the vast lawn, she turned to look back at *Windward*. A sudden shudder seized her. Time turned backward upon itself. The great house reared into the night sky, dwarfing her just as it had in the lost years, and she felt little and afraid.

But she fought back the feeling. There was no need to be afraid of anything. Within the blue dimness of the willows lurked nothing and no one; beyond the thicket flowed only the river, as it always had and would forever.

Then she went all the way down the lawn. The sharp, slightly bitter scent of the willow leaves flared her nostrils, and the river moved. Here, exactly here, her life had changed. Existence is nothing more than a series of quivering *ifs*. *If* the men had not kidnapped her, life would have been different. *If* they had taken Haakon instead, or her and Haakon both, everything would have changed. But it was useless to think about. The burden of vestigial fear was lifted from her soul. Possessed of a soaring feeling, she stepped into the thicket, pushing aside willow branches as she progressed, and stood at the edge of the river, her toes curling in the cool sand. She sensed it utterly: the living soul of the river, its cold power, and its mystery that embraced the remote, savage heart of the North Country. Back up the lawn, only a hundred yards away, was *Windward*. Behind it lay St. Paul, the city, the capital of this bursting new state. Yet the calm, inexorable power of the river told her that man had merely scratched the surface of this continent. She smelled pine on the river's silver breath, sensed with wonder the uncorrupted, trackless, untamed wilderness through which this river moved and which it owned more fully than man ever would. Born in America and borne back to it on the sea's riding wind, Elizabeth knew this land was more than she would ever need, from here to Montana and onward. She felt a thrilling splendor that was stronger than religion and as powerful as love. It was a sacred moment. She had been wedded again to a force rather than a man, to a power as inexplicable as the man. America. Home.

Sounds now. The river moving in its timeless channel, slipping, hissing, gurgling along the bank. A dog barking somewhere in the city, and a wolf baying in the hills across the river. The soft whisper of willow leaves. The crack of a branch, and the sucking sound of a boot in the riverside mud.

"Ain't right you should be alone on your wedding night, I don't think."

Elizabeth whirled. Moonlight glinted on the knife and on the grinning teeth of Clint Granger.

348

"Understand you grew up in Europe," he snickered softly, raising the knife a little and taking a step toward her. "In Europe, I hear, they got that there 'rights of the *señor*,' where the top man gets the bride, no matter who she marries. Well, let's just say I came here for my 'rights of the *señor*.' "

Elizabeth opened her mouth to scream, but Clint leaped forward. He was on her in a flash, one hand over her mouth. With the other he held the knife to her throat.

"Truth to tell, I came to shove this knife in your half-breed husband, but seein's I'm here, I'll shove somethin' else in you first."

She struggled in his grasp, tried to kick him. But then she felt the point of the knife pricking the flesh of her neck. She ceased to fight, trying furiously to think of a way out. She felt his rude hardness against her thigh.

"Liked you on sight first time I saw you in Chicago," he was saying. "Liked you damn well, too, even if you got the ill-born luck to be a Starbane. Easy now . . ."

The hand that held the knife came clumsily up to her face. With the other, Clint ripped off her cotton robe.

"My God!" he gasped, in honest admiration, "you're even better than I . . ."

Without planning, barely thinking, Elizabeth twisted her head slightly, opened her mouth, and sank her teeth as far as she could into the fleshy heel of his hand. She did not even have to scream. Clint did that for her, much more loudly than she could have, and certainly with enough force to reach the windows of *Windward*.

Clint knew this. "Why you snooty little spitfire!" he snarled, and cuffed her soundly on the side of her head, sending her tumbling into the river. The channel was deep at that place, and Elizabeth, dazed by the blow, went under immediately, gulping water.

She came up the first time, gasping for air, choking and coughing. She saw Clint standing there, grinning at her.

She came up the second time and saw Lance, naked in midair, leaping from the willow thicket toward Clint Granger. Elizabeth choked and took what air she could, fighting the current and the sleepy deadness that invaded her limbs and her brain.

She came up the third time. Lance was holding the knife, squatting over the supine Clint, whose body, naked now too, looked very slack and wide in the moonlight.

Then Lance was in the water and pulling her up. She could hear the servants calling to one another and racing down the lawn toward the river. She heard, above her own wracking, waterlogged gasps, their cries of horror when they reached the riverbank.

Then Lance carried her onto the shore, and she too saw what had elicited their terrified cries.

Clint Granger lay white and dead on the riverbank, beneath the moonlight, his clothing slit from cravat to crotch, his body from jaw to groin.

Grateful as she was to be alive and safe, Elizabeth was nonetheless pierced to the quick by what Lance had done. It was not the fact that Lance had killed Clint that troubled her, but rather the unpremeditated lightning savagery of her husband's assault. He was . . . he was different, much more different, than she had ever supposed. He was—yes, she understood it now—like the river whose spirit had penetrated her soul only moments before, a natural force. In the light of the moon, his face revealed nothing. Elizabeth felt, while he held her cradled in his arms, neither tremble nor tremor. His heart was beating slowly.

"One of you go fetch someone from the law," he said to the servants.

And then, both of them naked, he carried Elizabeth back up across the lawn to *Windward*.

"J. J. Granger was never the same after that," people said later.

"He had good reason," others responded. "How'd you feel if your only son got butchered like a boar?"

J. J. Granger took the matter to court. Lance and Elizabeth's departure for Montana was delayed throughout the summer and early fall of 1886 as they waited for the trial, and as Elizabeth's abdomen began to swell. It was a hot summer of long days and longer evenings, life held in abeyance while the legal machinery of society ground exceedingly fine.

One evening, two weeks after the fateful night, Elizabeth emboldened herself and tried to talk to Lance about what lay within him. They had gone out for a walk along Summit Avenue, down toward the cathedral. Many were out strolling that evening, and Elizabeth could not help but sense in the greetings of those they met a desire to distance themselves as hastily as was tactful.

Did she blame them?

Yes and no.

Even though justified, the killing was a scandal. Irrepressible J. J. Granger had gone into seclusion, something unheard of. A murder trial was forthcoming, with all its attendant haggling and innuendo. And Lance was the eye of gossip's hurricane, which he bore in silence, and which attitude served to distance people the more.

"Naked as a savage," whispered those who were wont to do so, "and he killed poor Clint in the same manner that a savage would gut a deer."

Clint had become "poor Clint." Clint, the rapist boar, had become a gentle "deer," a victim.

Lance's stoic expression did not hide the fact that he yearned for the solace and solitude of the high country. More deeply in love with him than ever, Elizabeth realized that his nature was composed in part of tumultuous passions held barely in check beneath his breast.

"Darling," she commenced, as they walked toward the

351

cathedral in twilight, "I have something to ask you, and I hope you won't mind."

His silence was receptive.

"I . . . I know we are all molded by the lives we have led. And I recognize that you and I are different people. That's one of the reasons we love each other. And I can never really repay you for rescuing me from Clint Granger. Don't mind what others whisper. I don't care about that. But do you think you could"—she hesitated, not quite sure how to phrase it—"do you think a life in which revenge plays such a part . . . do you think that's good?"

"Are you speaking of *Ycripsicu*?" he asked.

"Not the ranch itself, but the name. And what the name signifies."

She had intended to ask him why his attack on Clint had been so ferocious, but realized now that the fury of Lance's assault revealed the depth of his love. Great love. Great rage.

"You are asking me to change the name of my ranch?"

"Would you?"

"Some things must be done," he responded, "if a man is to win respect in life. And if a man is to respect himself."

"But do you think it would be possible for you to. . . ?"

"To renounce my . . . what do you call them? My instincts? Are they mine alone? If something or someone you love were to be destroyed, how do you think you would feel?"

"Yes, I know, darling. And I love you for your passion as much as for your loyalty. But a life in which revenge looms large is not . . ."

"Good?"

"Not . . . not *full*. It cuts you off somewhat. Don't you think it hangs heavy on your heart?"

"I only know that those who have sought to harm me have not been gentle. Nor would they be gentle who might

352

seek to harm you. The enemy must know what lies in wait for him."

"J. J. Granger? They say he is a changed man now."

"No. He is more dangerous now. Time will tell that I am right."

As they strolled along Summit Avenue, a great clattery racket sounded behind them. Turning, they saw a horse-drawn cab jouncing up the street. A passenger seemed to be waving at them. As the cab drew near, Elizabeth recognized the pointed, inquisitive nose of someone from the past.

"Bjorn!" she cried. "Bjorn Tennerson!"

He had emigrated like hundreds of thousands of other Scandinavians.

"Elizabeth Rolfson!" Bjorn exclaimed. "I read about your wedding in the papers. They told me at *Windward* you'd be here!" He walked over and they embraced. Elizabeth introduced Bjorn to her husband.

"He is the man who saved my inheritance," she said. "But I have since discovered that my name was Starbane all along. . . ."

Bjorn looked at her intently, and then turned his gaze to Lance. "You are Tallworth? I have been reading about you in the newspapers too. I am sorry. It is a terrible thing."

Delighted to have come upon her old friend, and to find him as quick-witted and entertaining as ever, Elizabeth invited him back to *Windward* for refreshments. Bjorn listened with interest to her recital of her experiences since coming to America, and offered news of his own. Thea Thorsdatter had managed somehow to escape from prison. She had then contrived to enter the Rolfson mansion in Oslo without being observed, and had sought to escape detection by hiding in the cellar. Her timing was disastrous, however, because shortly after her intrusion Bjorn had had to close and shut the house while he made a long sojourn to Bergen on legal business. The cellar door had also been locked.

"Thea subsisted on champagne and wine for a considerable period of time," Bjorn related, "but in the end she perished. She clawed out her fingernails on the wooden door."

The same wooden door, Elizabeth remembered, *behind which Thea had once locked "the little usurper."*

Still, what a horrible death!

"And what are your plans in America?" she asked Bjorn.

"I have read law for two years and have been admitted to the bar. But it is difficult to get started here."

A possibility began to take shape then in Elizabeth's mind, but it would require thorough consideration and planning. They passed the rest of the evening in pleasant conversation and reminiscence, for which Elizabeth was grateful. Even Lance relaxed in the little lawyer's company, and actually laughed aloud when Bjorn explained that Harald Fardahl, once Elizabeth's feckless suitor, had been jilted in turn by a businessman's daughter, a cabaret dancer, and a tavern maid, after which he entered St. Olav's Monastery to live a life of the cloth.

"But he left after a week," Bjorn related drolly. "In the monastery there was something called the Grand Silence. Harald was prepared to live without women, but not without talking. A month later he was engaged to marry a florist's assistant, although I think she jilted him for a stableboy just before I left for America. . . ."

The trial lasted only a day. On the witness stand, Eric Starbane recounted the appearance of J. J. Granger and his son, Clint, at *Windward* on the day of the wedding. Elizabeth told of Clint's assault upon her. Lance recalled awakening to Clint's howl, realizing that his wife was gone, and going to her rescue.

J. J. Granger, dull of eye and morose of countenance, sat in the courtroom, barely following the proceedings. He had nothing to say.

The jury deliberated for fifteen minutes and found Lance Tallworth not guilty.

Judge Roscoe F. Bullion announced the verdict. But he was a cantankerous old geezer, and he had something on his mind.

"Would the defendant please approach the bench?" he ordered, just before adjourning the proceedings.

Puzzled, Lance stood and walked to a position in front of Judge Bullion.

"The verdict has now been rendered, Mr. Tallworth," rasped Bullion. "The jury has done its duty. But in my official capacity, I feel that I must proffer an admonishment."

Lance seemed to scowl angrily, then collected himself. The spectators quieted. J. J. Granger lifted his head slightly, and played with his eyepatch. *This is unfair!* Elizabeth thought.

"Mr. Tallworth," Bullion began, "this court is always shocked by violence. The jury had to decide on the facts before them, and so they did. But I am an officer in the judiciary of the great state of Minnesota, which I want to keep great, and I made some inquiries about you."

Lance won't be able to take much more of this, Elizabeth thought worriedly.

"Also," the judge continued, "I have reviewed the law. According to the treaty of 1863, signed between your Sioux nation and the government of the United States, you ought right now to be a resident of the Red Lake Indian Reservation. You never received proper papers to leave it and you could be regarded by this court as an outlaw at worst and a vagrant at best . . ."

Lance stood still as stone. In words alone, this robed ancient was tearing asunder the underpinnings of the life he had won for himself.

". . . but I will be charitable," Bullion went on. "Because you have somehow managed to marry into that fine

Starbane family, this court will not arrest you. That is, will not arrest you if, within six months, an attorney of your choice effects and presents to this court evidence that your legal papers for leaving the Red Lake Reservation are complete. . . ."

Elizabeth hoped Lance would not spring forward and attack Judge Bullion. Lance did not.

Afterward, she expected Lance to be bitterly vengeful at the public humiliation Bullion had dealt him. Lance was not.

"Let us leave for Montana as quickly as we can," he said, almost with relief.

"But oughtn't we to speak to Bjorn Tennerson about arranging those papers the judge wanted?" Elizabeth had already decided to offer Bjorn the position formerly held by Alois Smedley.

"No," Lance answered abruptly. "Once out of Minnesota, Bullion has no more jurisdiction over me. I care nothing for the affairs of Red Lake Reservation, or of Minnesota."

Elizabeth felt hurt. Her parents were here. *Windward* was here, and *Bethland* in Duluth, which she wanted one day to see. "But surely we'll wish to return and visit . . ."

"Not I," he replied curtly. "Not after that scene in court."

Elizabeth was sure that he didn't really mean what he'd said.

4

After the trial was over, Lance took his bride to Montana, where Elizabeth fell immediately in love with *Ycripsicu*, with everything about it save its name. She loved the white fences of the corrals, and the low white buildings of the ranch, and the sprawling new house that had been built since the fire. And she loved the rolling plains rising westward to the blue Rockies, and the way the sweeping sky curved down to skim low over the mountain peaks. And quickly, she learned to love with Lance the lonely peace of the high country, where the wind was an endless song. She saw, too, the primal beauty of Bitterroot Pass, and thought she understood why Lance did not want a railroad across his land. So she managed to hold her tongue on the matter of the Continental Pacific. It was not time to talk about that yet. He had his dreams, she had her own. In time, the two dreams would become one as, already, the two of them had become one. Elizabeth bore Lance a daughter in the spring of 1887, and a son in the autumn of 1889. The years were peaceful, joyous. Yet although she did not know why, Elizabeth found herself sensing, anticipating, apprehending some obscure but impending disaster. She fought against the feeling, tried to put it out of her mind. Sometimes she felt that her anxiety was related to the very name of the ranch. Other times she explained the dark feeling of imminence as a result of the youth Gustav Rolfson had stolen from her. Most often, she tried to ignore the feeling. But it would not go away.

Little Selena, with her keen ears, heard the hoofbeats before the rest of them. Two and a half years old now, in October of 1889, she raced to the ranch house window, scrambled up onto a chair she kept there for purposes of observation, and looked out beyond the corrals toward the brown- and gold-colored range. She had her mother's hair and beauty of feature; she had her father's eyes, as intensely black and alive as she was herself.

"It's Rowdy Jenner!" she announced. She had the strong will of both her parents. "It's Rowdy Jenner and he's riding hard."

Lance, seated at the kitchen table and going over the records of another profitable year for the High Y, looked up in surprise. The annual roundup was imminent, but it hadn't begun as yet. And like everybody else, Rowdy wasn't getting any younger. He didn't do much fast riding anymore unless he had to. A range foreman with Rowdy's savvy could always detail some green cowboy to do the hard stuff.

"Maybe one of the men has taken sick," commented Elizabeth. She was seated in a rocking chair in front of a slow fire and nursing dark-haired Jason, born two weeks ago. It was too soon to tell, of course, but Elizabeth was sure she saw, in the infant's watchful eyes, more than a hint of his father's wary indomitability.

"Well," said Lance, "let's hope Rowdy's not bringing trouble. Every year has been better than the last, and I see no reason to . . ."

"Here's Rowdy now," chirped little Selena, hanging on to the curtain with one sturdy fist, "and he doesn't look very happy."

"Please call him Mr. Jenner," corrected Elizabeth. "You know how often you've been told."

"Mr. Jenner looks *real* worried," amended Selena.

Lance got up from the table and closed the big ledger of accounts.

"It's probably nothing," said Elizabeth, as Jason nuzzled and sucked.

The ranch had thrived under Lance's loving direction, with tremendous herds of prize cattle that earned top dollar on the market, and sold for even better money as breeding stock. In Chicago, Bjorn Tennerson had proved an astute manager of Elizstar Industries—Elizabeth herself had chosen the name—and she kept in close touch with him via the special telegraph installed here at the ranch. Lance often joked that Selena had learned Morse code before she'd learned to talk.

J. J. Granger had long been quiescent, brooding over the loss of his beloved son, and Alvah T. Bascomb, the mercantile emissary of hyenalike reputation, had let it be known that Granger was thinking of giving up his plans to build a railroad, and might soon be ready to trade the rights-of-way he had acquired. "What do you want for Christmas?" Lance had asked, a week or so ago. "I've got to go up to Butte anyway, and maybe I'll do some shopping." But Elizabeth had answered: "All I want for Christmas is Bitterroot Pass." Lance had smiled. That was all. But he *had* smiled. And as for the Starbanes, Eric's production of iron ore, by virtue of his command of richer deposits, had considerably outstripped Granger's capacity to produce. "The Granger star is descending," Haakon had written, on his embossed Minnesota state senate stationery.

Rowdy Jenner was banging on the door. Selena raced to let him in, beating her father by a nose. Elizabeth adjusted a corner of Jason's little blue blanket and went on nursing the baby. She regarded Rowdy almost as one of the family. His lean, leathery look, his honesty and loyalty, had long ago won her affection.

"Hey, boss," said Rowdy, standing in the doorway. He

did not lift and tickle Selena as he usually did, and as she expected him to do. "Hey, boss, we got to talk."

Trouble, realized Elizabeth.

"Please come in," Elizabeth offered, wanting to hear what the matter was, and knowing Lance's tendency to try and shield her. It was not that she was unable to bear news of adversity—quite the contrary. Rather, Elizabeth suspected, he did not want her to observe him having to bear adversity.

"Come in, Rowdy, and pour yourself a cup of coffee," Elizabeth said.

"It's *Mr.* Jenner," corrected little Selena, "and you told me so yourself."

But Rowdy was standing there in red bandana, cowhide chaps, and brass spurs, giving Lance a meaningful look.

"I gotta stop by the bunkhouse for something anyway," he suggested with woeful transparency. "Hey, boss, want to walk over there with me?"

"It can't be that bad, can it, Rowdy?" asked Elizabeth.

The foreman just looked sheepish and doleful.

Lance took his hat from a peg at the door, a broad-brimmed hat with a flat, low crown, and prepared to leave with Rowdy.

"I'm coming along!" Selena announced, and dashed to get her own hat, which was a miniature version of her father's.

"No, you're not," he told her, with uncharacteristic severity.

The men left.

"Your father and Mr. Jenner have to talk about something very important," Elizabeth told her daughter, whose little lower lip was thrust out in offended defiance.

Another child might have given way to tears in response to a similar exclusion, but not Selena. She had no time for tears. There was too much to do in life to waste time crying.

"Someday I'm going *everywhere*," she pronounced, "and do everything I want to."

"Some of them North Range Herefords is lookin' mighty funny, boss," Rowdy told Lance when they were outside the ranch house.

"What do you mean, 'funny'?"

"Lookin' a mite sick, that's what I think."

Lance eyed his foreman. "Rowdy, you know more about cattle than I ever will. Tell me what the trouble is."

Rowdy shrugged, the bearer of bad news with no hope of passing the chalice. "Looks like the anthrax to me," he muttered.

Lance straightened. "Anthrax? You're sure."

"Could be wrong, but I doubt it." Rowdy had a hangdog air about him. It was appropriate. He felt terrible, and there was little news he could have brought that would have been worse. Anthrax struck herds of cattle like a plague, and humans could contract it as well, either by eating the meat of infected animals, or simply by being close to sick cattle. Certain symptoms of the disease were much like pneumonia, but anthrax was far more deadly. It was also an economic disaster. The cattle could not be sold for food, nor for breeding, because they would infect other herds. There was only one answer: they had to be shot and buried.

There were on the *Ycripsicu* range, at that time, over eight thousand head of cattle split into three herds roughly equal in size.

"Do you think it's confined to the North Range?" Lance asked.

"Can't tell. Don't know. I saw what I saw and came here fast as I could. Told the boys not to talk about it. If the other ranchers get wind . . ." He spread his hands and shrugged.

"If it is anthrax, we'll have to tell the others anyway. Let's mount up and ride."

A little over an hour later, Lance and Rowdy reached the North Range. Even from a distance, it was easy to tell that tragedy had struck and was spreading. The main herd grazed desultorily under the gaze of a circle of High Y riders, but along the edges of the herd and behind them in the wide valley were the dead and the dying. The dead lay with outstretched heads, lolling tongues, stiff legs, swollen bellies. The dying fell and tried to rise, thrashing about wildly, gasping and choking with an awful hollow sound. The eyes of the dying were wild with panicky incomprehension, almost as if the dumb beasts were capable of being amazed.

Jasper Zenda left the rest of the men and rode over to Lance and Rowdy.

"Looks real bad, boss. They're startin' to fall like flies."

"God *damn*!" said Lance. It was the only time his men were ever to hear him swear.

He and Rowdy rode into the herd, and made a careful inspection of the animals.

"It's anthrax all right, and no mistake," observed Rowdy. "We better get started on shooting this herd, lest a stray goes over to the other ranges and infects them."

Two horsemen appeared then, riding fast from the West Range.

"I'm afraid it's too late for that," said Lance, watching the riders approach. Fast riders generally bear bad news.

So there was no roundup that year. The cattle were shot in groups of a hundred, so they could be buried efficiently. It was better than having carcasses rot in large numbers on the range. Jasper Zenda and several of the men took sick, but Jasper—good old loyal Jasper—was the only one who died. Lance lived out on the range during the killing weeks, so as not to chance carrying the infection to Elizabeth and the children. By mid-November, when the wind from the north had turned cold even during the days, the nightmare was over. *Ycripsicu* lay ruined and blasted under the big sky. The mass graves of cattle pocked the earth like grotesque burial mounds. Lance paid off the men for their season of work, and said he hoped they would be back in the spring. He intended to buy a new herd, he said, and start all over again. At least he would not have to worry about the cattle starving to death during the winter, he said.

Elizabeth knew the depth of her husband's loss, and did not attempt frivolous ploys to cheer him. His financial loss was monumental, but he still owned the land. And she had Elizstar, or forty-two percent of it. They were, in terms of actual worth, wealthy. That fact, however, did little to lift Lance's spirits. Only his little daughter, irrepressible Selena, could bring a genuine light to his eyes that autumn.

"What I can't understand," Lance said to Elizabeth, when he was able to talk about the disaster, "is why our herds were the only ones infected in this part of Montana. It almost seems . . ." His voice trailed off.

". . . as if someone purposely did it?" she finished.

"It could be done. A couple of men could run diseased cattle in with a herd."

"They'd have had to come over a considerable distance, and sick cattle don't travel well. What about those breeding bulls you bought in Butte?"

"Boris and Begonia? They didn't even appear to be sick when we shot them. It was . . . God, what a waste it was."

But Elizabeth had a point. Lance had bought the bulls only weeks before Rowdy first spotted the anthrax.

"Some cattle may be carriers of a disease and never get sick themselves, just like people," Elizabeth said.

They were finishing, with little appetite, the main meal of the day. Traudl, a Norwegian girl from Bismarck hired by Elizabeth, was waiting to clear the table. She seemed a trifle hurt that Lance had not only eaten little of the stuffed pheasant, but hadn't even touched the apple pie with its thick wedge of cheese on top.

In the small office next to the kitchen, the telegraph began to clatter.

"I'll get it," Elizabeth said, rising. Running the telegraph line from Black Forks out to the ranch had been a considerable expense, but it was the only way she could stay in touch with the outside world, especially during the long winter months. Grabbing a pad and pencil, she began to interpret.

"It's from Chicago," she said, listening to the chatter, translating the dots and dashes into words.

> PRICE ELIZSTAR STOCK RISING SLOWLY STEADILY STOP A. T. BASCOMB REQUESTS TO TRAVEL MONTANA SEE YOU PERSONALLY WITH PROPOSAL WILL NOT DEAL WITH ME STOP WIRE DECISION.
>
> B. TENNERSON

"I wonder what this is all about," Elizabeth said. Bascomb, like a hired gunman, served whoever bought his expertise. Rumors circulating a few years earlier to the effect that he was dealing with Granger had never led to anything concrete, at least not that Elizabeth knew about. She was also more curious than elated to learn that Elizstar stock value was on the upswing. The market, in general, had been somewhat stagnant of late. But she wanted to hear what Bascomb had to say. A guest from the outside world would, at the very least, lighten the pall over the ranch brought on by the anthrax epidemic.

ADVISE BASCOMB TO COME IMMEDIATELY, she wired Bjorn. Soon the snow would be flying, and she did not want to have to spend Thanksgiving and Christmas in the company of "the Hyena."

Nor did Alvah T. Bascomb desire to be snowbound on the high plains. He arrived at the ranch two days later, having taken the Grand Northern to Great Falls, and a stagecoach south to Black Forks. There Rowdy Jenner met him with a horse and buggy and brought him out to *Ycripsicu*. Bascomb had not enjoyed the jouncing, and seemed in foul humor when he showed up at the ranch.

Lance invited him into the house and Elizabeth poured a strong drink of whiskey to warm the traveler. Little Jason cried when he saw Bascomb, and even Selena, who was not at all shy, paled a bit when she saw him. For Alvah T. Bascomb did justice to his undesired sobriquet. He had a long, lean body, and a thin yellowish face with a prominent nose. Birth defect or bar brawl had mangled his lips, which were drawn back almost constantly over long yellow teeth. He had a paunch surprisingly protuberant on his thin torso, which gave him the appearance of having recently devoured a small animal.

He drank the whiskey quickly and held out his glass for more.

Jason began to cry again, and Traudl took him away into the bedroom.

Elizabeth poured more whiskey, and the three adults went into the parlor and sat down. The drink had a rapid and salubrious effect on Bascomb, who commented, with rising cheer, on the long coach ride down from Great Falls.

"You people here in southern Montana could certainly use a railroad of your own," he said expansively, while his yellow eyes gave off a cunning glint, "and, matter of fact, that's why I'm here."

"That's why you're here?" asked Lance. "Whom do you represent? Yourself?"

"No, no. I am presently in the service of J. J. Granger."

Lance and Elizabeth exchanged glances.

"Now I know there's been bad blood between J.J. and you folks," Bascomb went on. "I know all about that. But J.J. is first and foremost a businessman, and a damn shrewd one. Also, it's best to have dispassionate representation in these matters. Keeps a lot of excess emotion from getting out of hand, don't you agree?"

He was looking at Lance, as if the comment about "excess emotion" applied particularly to him.

"How's the ranching business going?" Bascomb asked offhandedly. "You know, I don't recollect seeing all that many cattle outside?"

"Don't you now?" Lance said, narrowing his eyes.

"Granger is interested in ranching?" interjected Elizabeth quickly.

"What? Ha-ha. No, of course not. I was just making small talk. No, among other plans he's got in mind, J.J. is interested in railroads."

"You'll get no right-of-way across my ranch," Lance pronounced, "nor will track ever be laid through Bitterroot Pass."

Elizabeth was a little startled at his intransigent tone. She had thought, over the past years, that he'd softened considerably in that opinion.

But Alvah T. Bascomb surprised them both.

"J.J. doesn't want any more rights-of-way. Fact is, he wants to sell the rights-of-way he's already got."

"Say that again," Lance requested.

Bascomb repeated what he'd just said. "He wants to sell."

"Do you mind if I ask why?" Elizabeth wanted to know.

"Not at all. I'd be surprised if you didn't ask. It's quite simple, really. After the tragic death of J.J.'s wonderful son"—he shot Lance a look that was as mocking as a wink—"he took stock and decided the time for his big dreams was past. He's retrenching now, cutting back, pulling in. He's in the autumn of his years, and the shadows are lengthening for him. So he wants to know if you're interested in a business proposition."

He was looking at Elizabeth now. She got up, went into the office, and returned with a map of the northern United States. She tried to appear calm, even indifferent, but inwardly she was tremendously excited. Spreading the map out on the coffee table in front of the three of them, she reviewed her current situation. The Continental Pacific held rights-of-way, by ownership or lease, from Portland, Oregon, to Boise, Idaho, and then northeastward toward the Bitterroot. Track had been laid eastward from Portland, and also a spur line had been laid south from Olympia, Washington, to join the line in Boise. Leases through the Dakotas and most of Montana were controlled by J. J. Granger, although in Minnesota, west of Minneapolis and St. Paul, Elizabeth held over a hundred miles of leases. Since Clint's death, J.J. had mounted not a single operation. Until now.

At one fell swoop, Elizabeth stood on the threshold of achieving her grand design. There was the Bitterroot, of course, but . . .

But at what price?

"As I said," Bascomb explained, "J. J. Granger knows when the race is over. All he wants is a nice little nest egg to live on, something sufficient to let history know he's made a mark on it, you know what I mean?"

"I believe he's already made his mark," Lance said.

Bascomb chuckled appreciatively. "And so have you, my good man. And so have you. I understand you're not legally allowed within the borders of the great state of Minnesota anymore."

"I have spent sufficient time in Minnesota," Lance returned coolly.

"I bet you have! But, be that as it may, let us proceed."

All through the rest of the afternoon and well into the evening, Elizabeth and the Hyena hammered out the deal. Lance was always present, but said little. Now and then Elizabeth looked at him, as if asking his encouragement, his support. And there was love in his eyes, and happiness too, as he saw the extent of her excitement. But *Ycripsicu* lay between them, just as it lay between the two proposed stretches of her Continental Pacific road.

Elizabeth was sure he would soften, now that her great victory was so near. And certainly he did not interfere, or even demur, as she made her plans and parried with Alvah T. Bascomb.

Long after sundown, Traudl served a dinner of rabbit stew in red wine sauce, which the three ate as they negotiated.

"You are speaking of millions of dollars," Elizabeth was telling Bascomb.

"Of course I am. We are talking about rights-of-way over hundreds of miles. The profit you will make on a railroad will very soon exceed the extent of your investment."

"Not that soon."

"But in time."

Bascomb was right. In time, the road would pay. How much time depended on general business conditions, and on the efficiency of the operation itself. The final question was: How badly did she want the road?

Very badly.

"In the manner of payment . . ." she began.

"Cash on the barrelhead," Bascomb cut in. "That's what J.J. told me to tell you. Cash on the barrelhead, or he goes elsewhere with the deal."

"But I thought we might work out a method of payment whereby his remuneration is spread over a period of years. . . ."

Bascomb gave her his high, cackling laugh. "No can do, little lady," he said, with a hint of condescension in his tone. "No can do."

So if that is the way it is, thought Elizabeth, *then that is it*. Her only source of funds in the quantity demanded by Bascomb and Granger was the sale of Elizstar stock, or borrowing money using Elizstar for security. The price of the stock itself had been rising, but the future of the economy as a whole was unreadable.

And so Elizabeth gambled. After a night's sleep, she

awoke early and lay in bed thinking it over. Lance slept beside her, his dark hair down over his forehead and eyes. The ranch house was very quiet, and outside the wind mourned over the plains.

"Darling," Elizabeth whispered, with her lips to his ear. "Wake up. I have to ask you something."

Always a light sleeper, wary even in dreams, Lance opened his eyes. She did not even have to repeat what she had said.

"What is it?" he asked.

"The time has come and I must know. Will you allow me to build across the ranch, or not?"

Lance said nothing, just stared up at the ceiling. Elizabeth sensed torment in him, torment arising from something she either did not know or did not understand.

"What is it? Tell me," she pleaded.

His words were slow in forming. "I know how much all of this means to you, but it is not merely a matter of keeping the earth the way it has been for thousands of years. It is far more than that . . ."

"Tell me, so that I can understand."

"You see, Fawn and Sostana are buried here . . ."

"Yes?"

". . . are buried, according to my instructions, in a grave whose location I do not know and do not wish to know. Thus, they are everywhere, and all of *Ycripsicu* is their grave. That is what I meant when I told you this is sacred ground. They must not be disturbed."

Elizabeth, with her heart going out to him, nonetheless felt that she could work out a solution. "And you never want to know where their graves lie?" she asked.

He nodded. "I want their memories to be everywhere," he said. The next thought was difficult for him to phrase; so much of his harsh past still remained, the past that kept him from giving voice to his most tender reflections. But he said it. "Were it not for Fawn and Sostana, I might not have been capable of the love I was able to feel for you, the love you felt in me and I in you, and the courage to maintain that love over such a long time."

Then they were both silent. Finally, she took his hand under the bedcovers, and held it tightly, felt the answering pressure of his grasp.

"Who buried Fawn and Sostana?" she asked at length.

"Rowdy and Jasper Zenda. I ordered them never to tell me. And now Jasper is dead."

"Rowdy can tell *me* where their grave is located, even though he will never tell you. And wherever it is, I promise you that the railroad will not disturb it, no matter what. That is my vow to you. Can you accept it?"

Elizabeth waited breathlessly for his response. Again she felt the pressure of his grasp. She knew what his answer would be, even as he said it. "Yes, I accept your vow," Lance said. "And now the two of us will end the despicable career of J. J. Granger."

Bold words, but on that cold morning in Montana it seemed that they were true. Every human act, after all, is a gamble, and the race belongs to the swift. While Bascomb wolfed a breakfast of hotcakes, sausages, eggs fried in grease, coffee, and bourbon, Elizabeth was on the telegraph to Bjorn Tennerson in Chicago. Suspecting that Bascomb understood Morse Code, and not wanting him to decipher the clatter of the keys, she closed the office door behind her, and told Traudl to keep Jason in view of the Hyena. Whenever the baby saw the man's yellow face, he let out a shriek. The sounds of Traudl and Selena trying to quiet Jason obscured any telltale rattle the telegraph keys made. Poor little Jason. But someday he would learn how important he had been on this great day in his mother's life.

For several hours, messages were sent and received. Bjorn confirmed that J. J. Granger had indeed sold out his iron mining leases, and now his desire to do the same with his railroad holdings confirmed what Bascomb had said. J. J. Granger was ready to quit. The fact that he had sold the iron leases to Rockefeller-Carnegie and not to Eric Starbane was potentially troublesome to Elizabeth's father, but had no effect on Elizstar. However, the need to sell Elizstar stock in order to buy Continental Pacific rights-of-way required consideration. As Tennerson cabled:

> YOU OWN FORTY-TWO PERCENT CURRENT STOCK STOP CONTROLLING INTEREST STOP TO MEET GRANGER DE-MANDS YOU MUST SELL TWELVE PERCENT STOP WARN THAT PRECIPITATE SALE OF THIS QUANTITY WILL DRIVE STOCK VALUE DOWN TEMPORARILY STOP SUG-GEST STOCK EXCHANGE TO BASCOMB.

But Alvah T. Bascomb would have none of it.

"What the hell does J.J. want Elizstar stock for?" he demanded sarcastically. "He's already got around twenty percent, and it's not earning as much as he wants. No, no, he wants the cash."

Elizabeth was considerably relieved to hear this. J. J. Granger already had too much of Elizstar, in her opinion. That was due to the secret New York stock trading of Smedley. Still, she worried, and cabled Bjorn Tennerson:

> AFTER SALE OF TWELVE PERCENT, AM I STILL IN FIRM CONTROL?

His response was affirmative, as long as the economy remained reasonably strong, and as long as the sale of twelve percent did not lower stock values unduly.

Life was a gamble, always, a trading of one dream for another, of one wish for an even more glittering desire.

Elizabeth made the deal, and bought the rights-of-way. Although as yet unbuilt, her Continental Pacific stretched territorially from St. Paul, Minnesota, to the Pacific Coast.

It was all very exciting, and Elizabeth was euphoric for days. So much work waited to be done, and this prospect too served to buoy her spirits. Only one thing niggled at the back of her mind, a question: *I wonder what J. J. Granger is going to do with all that money?*

5.

Eric Starbane awoke on the last day of his life, and made love to Kristin, his wife, for the last time. They had made love in many places, many moods, many ways, down through the years, but always the rapture recalled for them their first time. The high green meadow above Norway's Sonnendahl Fjord glistened like jade under the June sun, and far below the rocky cliff the fjord was diamond-blue and sparkling. Kristin had given herself there on the soft grass, Eric had taken her. Afterward, they had dived deep into an icy mountain pool and, in an impulsive, eerily beautiful ritual, had bound themselves each to the other. Seeing Kristin's reflection in the water of the shining pool, Eric had scooped it with his hands. "I hold your image," he had said, looking into her eyes, "may I drink now and thus have you, forever to keep?" *Yes*, Kristin had nodded, and then in her turn had made the vow, drunk the pure water, and taken his image unto herself. Then they had made love again, in wonder and affirmation.

Now, in April of 1890, almost thirty years after that first union at Sonnendahl Fjord, they made love for the last time. But, of course, they did not know it then.

For the young, the secrets of a lover's body, the uncharted responses of a beloved's climb to ecstasy, are as delightful as the pure surge of pleasure itself. Each new embrace reveals a surprising monument to wonder, subtle or savage or strange in its enchantment. For the young, life is very long, something with no end of discoveries and no end to itself. But to those who have spent a lifetime in voluptuous conspiracy along the trails of love, few secrets remain. At this point, making love takes on a significance that it never possessed before. The blood is still hot, but no longer does it rush pell-mell as far as it can go. No, now the years have bestowed wisdom and restraint. Lovers know the nature and variations of pleasures to come, but the art of timing makes everything new again. When shall I give her *this*? He is waiting now for *that*, but let him wait and instead kiss him with *the other*.

And in such manner, over a long drowsy time of an April morning, did Eric and Kristin make love. So strange, it seemed like the first time all over again. It always seemed like the first time, the sensation so keen it could not have been real, so readily forgotten that it had to be lived all over again.

"I'd better get up and get dressed," Eric said at last. "I've got a long haul today."

"You're leaving today?" asked Kristin, sitting up in bed. She looked at him with the love she'd always had, and drew her knees up to her chin. "I thought you were going next week."

Eric had been planning a trip to Duluth to meet with Alvah T. Bascomb, representative of the Rockefeller-Carnegie interests. They were asking, again, to buy him out of the Mesabi Range. Now that J. J. Granger had pretty much retreated from the fray of business, Eric had begun to wonder why he ought not to follow suit. He had more than he had ever dreamed. Why not live out his life loving Kristin, and his children, and his grandchildren? Why not spend his time advising Haakon, who was thinking of running for governor someday?

"I decided to go up there early," Eric told his wife as he splashed cold water from the porcelain pitcher into the washbasin, "because Elizabeth and the children are arriving soon for a visit. I want to be back in time for that."

"I'm so glad spring's come," said Kristin, getting out of bed and putting on her robe. She walked to the window and looked down at the Mississippi. In the north, the snows were melting. The river, high and wide, roared past *Windward* day and night, rushing gray waters covering all but the quivering tips of the willows in the thickets at the river's edge. "How must it be in Montana? So remote! But Elizabeth and Lance love it."

"I guess we find what we love, if we're lucky," he said. "I keep looking, of course. Never say die."

"Oh, *you*!" Playfully, she threw a pillow at him. Eric was lathering up to shave just then. The pillow hit him on the back of the neck, not hard but with enough force to send him lurching forward into the shaving mirror that hung on the wall. His forehead struck the mirror smartly, and while Eric was uninjured, the mirror shattered with a crash. There were many minor crashes and pings as the shards fell to the floor.

"Oh, *you*!" Eric retorted, turning to her and laughing, lather all over his face like a foamy beard.

"Seven years bad luck," sighed Kristin, not because she was superstitious—she wasn't—but because she had to pick up the pieces. She would not ask a maid to clean up a mess made out of her own stupidity. And she did not want Eric to step on the broken glass and hurt himself.

After picking up the pieces of the ruined mirror, Kristin went to her dressing room to prepare for the day. Eric finished shaving with the aid of a small mirror balanced on a wire stand. He used a straightedge razor, honed to perfection on a strop at the side of the washbasin, and he never cut himself.

Except this morning.

"Damn!" he muttered, dabbing the red slit. He knew what the trouble was. He didn't really want to travel north at all. Rails would take him all the way—no longer the riverboat-horseback trek of the old days—but he would not be able to get any farther than St. Cloud by nightfall, and then he faced a long second day of train travel through semiwilderness tomorrow. But it was not a wise man who, in 1894, refused to listen to an offer from a representative of Andrew Carnegie and John D. Rockefeller.

That Alvah T. Bascomb must be raking in his full fair share of commissions. Well, he had handled those railroad rights-of-way astutely enough. Money had changed hands, and Elizabeth was ready to begin laying track from St. Paul westward as soon as the ground thawed a little more. That was one of the reasons she—and Selena and Jason—were coming here next week.

Too bad Lance doesn't just clear up that Red Lake business, thought Eric. But he was not one to interfere.

Having completed shaving, he rinsed and folded the razor, and slipped it into his traveling bag. He looked at his reflection in the glass for a moment, pleased with his appearance, which was a little more weathered than it had been thirty years earlier, but which had weathered plenty more than it showed. The only mark was the red razor nick just above his right jawbone. Barely noticeable.

"Cut yourself, I see," commented Kristin at breakfast. They ate lightly these days, toast and cheese with coffee. Eric had a small glass of brandy. "To keep the blood going," he said. "I am fifty, you know."

"When does the train leave?" she asked. "I never recall you cutting yourself before."

"Just before noon. I must stop at the office first. No, I never have cut myself shaving before."

"Well, I hope it doesn't happen again."

"It won't. My hand is steady as a rock. We're still all right. You throw a good pillow for a woman your age."

"For a woman my . . . *what?* I already showed you this morning what a woman my age can do!"

"Is that right? What did you do? At my age, it's getting hard to remember."

"The brain is the only thing you're soft in, then," Kristin retorted.

Eric laughed. "I'm not sure I know what you mean."

"Wait until you come back from your trip and I'll see if I can show you!"

Because Eric and Kristin had been separated for such long periods in the early years of their love, they always made it a point to part affectionately now. But a servant was lackadaisical and tardy in getting Eric's traveling gear packed, and by the time he was ready to leave *Windward*, Kristin was entertaining a few women callers from the Lutheran Church. The Reverend Dr. Estendahl had sent them to solicit funds for the Boers of South Africa, who were facing hard times. All he was able to do was wave to her from the parlor doorway, and she waved back. But that was fine because, after all, this was going to be a short trip.

Horse and carriage took him to his office near the capitol, with its huge gleaming dome and the magnificent gilded horsemen high up on the facade, below the dome. Pioneer and Indian were both commemorated there, the divergent strands of this land's history recognized. In the old days, a thousand years had been an age. Now, in the space of one generation, it was expected that almost everything would change.

Eric began to have an unusual feeling on the drive to his office. It was nothing he could put his finger on precisely, but whatever it was, he had never experienced it before. All of his sensations were at once more keen in perception and less particular in effect. He drove past the cathedral on Summit Avenue, which he had passed almost every day for over twenty years. The colors of the stained-glass windows were richer and more varied than they had ever been, the ornamentation on the stone more intricate, and yet as he

glanced upward, the massive church seemed disquietingly
fragile, a temporary arrangement of form and stone crouch-
ing tentatively on an ancient hill. The grand capitol, too,
seemed wavery and impermanent this morning, and as the
carriage turned east into the morning sun, Eric squinted and
the entire city of St. Paul, proud and buzzing in the bustle
of politics and enterprise, appeared to be nothing more than
an arrangement of props for a play, across the deserted
stage of which he had chanced to wander, not knowing
why. This eerie feeling was so sudden, so strong, that he
looked away from the city and busied himself unnecessarily
in checking his luggage, making sure everything was in
order, though he already knew it was.

Nor did that uncanny, indefinable feeling leave him when
he arrived at his office.

"Mr. Starbane, are you all *right*?" exclaimed Mavis
Youngdahl, his appointments secretary, when Eric entered.

"Why, yes. I think so. Why do you ask?"

Mrs. Youngdahl considered this. "You know," she said
slowly, "I don't know. Maybe *I'm* not myself this morning.
Cut yourself shaving, though."

"First time for everything, unfortunately. What's on the
schedule before I leave for St. Cloud and Duluth?"

He pulled off his coat and sat down behind his desk. It
was not especially large, but was made of the finest teak
obtainable, shipped all the way from Brazil.

"There are some letters you might dictate, if you feel like
it. Alf Spats wants to see you about your stock in the Grand
Northern Railroad. He said to send a messenger to his hotel,
and he can be here in half an hour . . ."

"All right. We'll do that."

". . . and Mr. Webster Tuttle was here, very early. He
didn't stay, though. He said he had a train to catch."

"Tuttle again. I wonder what on earth he wants."

Everybody in Minneapolis knew that Webster Tuttle,
longtime operative or spy for J. J. Granger, was looking for

a job. Tuttle, whose vanity it was to call himself "T" in cryptic correspondence, was no longer needed since J.J. had announced his intention to retire from the fray. Why Tuttle, who had once spied for Granger and Smedley against Elizabeth, would think Eric might have a job for him was a mystery. But lately he had been coming around the office a lot.

"I was noncommittal," Mavis was saying. "I told him you were leaving today for Duluth, and that you'd be back in a week or so."

"Good. Maybe by that time . . ." His voice trailed off.

"Yes?" asked Mavis Youngdahl. Eric was staring into a private middle distance.

"What? Oh, I'm sorry. Strangest thing. I just happened to think of the house I grew up in, back in Norway. Haven't thought of it in years. There was a loose brick in the chimney. I used to keep a few coins hidden behind it. I wonder if they're still there. I wonder who lives in the house now. It was a good house. Stone. Built to last."

"I'm sure it was," agreed Mavis, who looked at him closely. Eric was not much given to reminiscence. He was too alive. Leaving his office and going to her desk, she shivered, although the place was quite warm. Eric was at his desk, as usual, but somehow she had the strangest feeling that he was . . . not there. *Fiddlesticks*, she thought, *I ought to have my head examined!*

A little while later, Alf Spats arrived and closeted himself with Eric. Spats, a thin, mournful man who invariably found the dark side of everything, was entrusted with the care of Eric's stockholdings.

"What's up, Alf?" greeted Eric.

The grim financier entered, trailing his customary cloud of woe and travail. "Thought I'd talk to you before your trip," he said, seating himself gingerly as if his bones might snap. "Grand Northern stock is going up."

Eric owned thirty percent of the Grand Northern. It was the mainstay of his fortune. "So," he said, "that can't hurt."

"The price is going up awfully fast. Big money is buying, but I don't know for sure where it's coming from yet. And that means . . ."

"A raid," Eric finished. The cynical warfare of manipulation. If a raid worked according to plan, it was the quickest tactic to ruin or to acquire a business, or first to ruin it and then to acquire it later on the cheap. Raiders might slowly buy up stock until they gained a controlling interest, or they might fuel a buying panic, forcing the price up, until people were clamoring to own stock, and at this point dump their holdings onto the market and watch the prices plummet out of sight, leaving the target company gasping for life. "Are you sure?" Eric asked.

"Well," said Spats frankly, "a lot of people would say that it's too soon to tell. But not me. Somebody is buying, and buying big."

"Easterners, do you suppose?"

"Could be. Anyway, I aim to find out. Where will you be?"

"Tonight in St. Cloud, upriver. At the Grand Central Hotel. By tomorrow evening, I'll be at *Bethland*, our place in Duluth."

"Thinking of selling your Mesabi business?"

"Not really. But it never hurts to listen to a proposal."

"J. J. Granger did, and it made him a ton of money."

"What's the word on J.J. now? Where is he, anyway?"

Granger, who lived in St. Paul, had not been seen around town for over half a year.

"They tell me he's living in Chicago now. Bought him a big place on Lake Michigan. Got married to a showgirl, is what I heard. Probably she keeps him busy."

"I hope so. Poor old J.J."

"*Poor?* After what he tried to pull . . ."

"I don't know," reflected Eric. "I guess there comes a time when it doesn't pay to be so wary."

"You may be right, but that time hasn't come for me yet. Nor for *you*, either. If there's a full-fledged raid on the Grand Northern, your net worth is going to be just about as frisky as Paulie Wepner on New Year's morning."

Paulie Wepner was a notorious St. Paul inebriate.

"You haven't that much cash on hand, either," Spats added.

"Well, come in when I get back and we'll see what's up," Eric concluded, seeing Alf to the door.

The wiry financier left Eric's office and went out onto the bright street. Nice day. Warm too. But he hadn't even taken off his overcoat when he felt a chill run up his spine. Funny. And he had the absurd feeling that, somewhere, a mighty door had just been blown shut by a terrible wind.

The train to St. Cloud was delayed in St. Paul due to a broken eccentric strap, and it was well after noon when the journey began. St. Cloud was less than a hundred miles north of the capital, but the engine made slow progress. Spring thaw made it prudent to travel slowly. Beneath the pressure of rushing water, embankments might wash away, or whole sections of rail become loosened, disaster for the incautious engineer and his passengers.

Eric, who usually looked forward to trips of any kind, and who enjoyed train travel because it afforded him the opportunity to talk to a variety of people, felt uncharacteristically introspective today. He did not visit the smoking car—the latest touch of elegance on the St. Paul–St. Cloud run—but stayed in his coach seat, watching the land roll along outside the train. Pleasantly, he turned aside an offer of penny-ante poker. Distractedly, he rebuffed the opportunity to enjoy a cigar "made all the way down there in Amazonia, or wherever." Almost curtly, he passed up a chance to share a bottle of good whiskey.

"I'm not myself today," he admitted, looking at his image in the train window.

Facing facts, he realized that he had not wanted to take this trip at all. He had no intention of selling his Mesabi holdings. Although—and now it occurred to him for the first time—he might *have to* sell at least a portion if, as Alf Spats suspected, a raid against the Grand Northern was afoot. *Well, I know raid procedure too*, Eric contented himself, *and there is plenty of time* . . .

In the thick, wavy train windowglass, his image swayed and flowed, as if two images were reflected there, one of them more-or-less his own and a second that was surreal and almost alien.

Eric turned his face away from the glass, away from the empire of endless rolling land that had once thrilled him so much. He felt chilled, although the car was heated, and even as he closed his eyes, trying to rest, he continued to see behind his eyelids the quavery insubstantiality of the phantom face in the train window.

Once in St. Cloud, a burgeoning town of Germans and Swedes, he walked to the Grand Central, "Best Hotel West of Chicago." If it was not that, it was at least a good hotel, and he had a steak dinner alone at the bar. The Grand Central, which catered to the myriad salesmen who had begun to crisscross the Great Plains selling the wares of the civilized East, was invariably crowded. The atmosphere at the bar was expansive, even ribald. But Eric could find in himself no impulse to take part in bonhomie. He could not, for the life of him, understand why he felt so removed from the spirit of adventure and enjoyment that everyone else seemed to possess in such abundance. All he knew was that, tonight, he did not have those things. Even his reflection in the great mirror behind the bar showed an image almost unknown to him. The handsome man in the glass had his features and his coloring and his still-golden hair. Yet in a manner Eric could not understand, that image was only a husk, a shell, all force or character gone from it. Instead of the two faces in the train window, now there was only one. But it was neither his face nor the other.

I'm tired and dull, he told himself, paying his check and walking outside. The air was fresh, and there was a real chill now. Minnesota spring held the vestiges of winter long into April, often into May. Temporarily invigorated by the bracing air, Eric started down toward the river, only a short distance away. Preoccupied without being able to identify the precise cause of his distraction, he turned several times to look back, as if someone were following him. Then he reached the Mississippi, and stood on the high west bank, watching the pounding, tumbling waters, simultaneously excited and stunned by the swirling crash and roar of piled ice crushing to tinder the logs that tossed like toothpicks in the current.

He felt the hands on his shoulder blades and tried to turn. He sensed the rush of air as it enveloped him, and the deafening thunder into which he hurtled. And he saw, not his own image, but the dark face of the other in the river's icy embrace. He raised an arm instinctively, trying to see the bank, to swim there. Then he saw the bank, wild and white through a spray of froth, and saw the dark figure high above. Amazed at the million things living in his mind, even in this instant of doom, Eric thought of everyone he had ever loved. All the way back. His father and mother. Kristin. Elaine. Haakon. Elizabeth. His grandchildren, Selena and Jason. Lance, the dark force who would not be denied. Then he thought of Gustav Rolfson, dead and gone. Adolphus, his father. Clint Granger, gone too. And he saw the face of the man high atop the bank of the river, the face of . . .

Tides of roiling ice came crashing together.

Eric Starbane lived no more.

6

"They found his body in a field about twenty miles south of St. Cloud," Kristin explained. She was dry-eyed. All her tears were gone. "He carried a waterproof wallet, with his papers in it. Otherwise there would have been no way of knowing who he was."

"The ice," she added. "It did terrible damage."

The survivors huddled together at *Windward:* Kristin and Elizabeth, Haakon and Lance. Lance had not hesitated to enter Minnesota again, Judge Roscoe F. Bullion notwithstanding. Only Lance seemed fully to comprehend that death had come, and that it was irrevocable. Selena and little Jason were out on *Windward's* lawn now with a servant.

"You must not think of revenge," Elizabeth had cautioned Lance during their long trek from Montana. "It has no place now."

"Your father did not jump from that riverbank," he returned, with that unnatural remove of his, the still, waiting impassivity that his hidden nature hoarded.

"We must think now of a fitting burial," Kristin said. Well she knew what had ended for her, and she had vowed to see it through with strength. A proud man deserves no less.

The others nodded. Except Lance.

"I must ask you to tell me the details once again," he said quietly.

Elizabeth glanced at him, not quite alarmed but not without concern.

Kristin told him what he wanted to know. Lance listened carefully. The facts were sparse, with the finality of fate, not chance. Eric had journeyed north to meet with Alvah T. Bascomb. When Eric did not arrive in Duluth, Bascomb cabled to see what the matter was. It was then that Kristin had sent out an alarm. Eric was last seen at the Grand Central Hotel in St. Cloud. "It appears as if he went out for a walk, and fell into the river," she concluded. "'What else is there to think?"

"That he was pushed, or knocked unconscious and then thrown in," Lance averred.

"Oh, Lance, darling, we have no way of knowing," Elizabeth said.

"Or of finding out," added Haakon.

Sister and brother could not, at this point, accept the possibility that foul play had been involved. The fact of their father's death was difficult enough to bear without the added burden of knowing that his life had been stolen from them.

But Lance would not so readily let the matter rest.

"Did he see anyone before he left for St. Cloud? Did he have any unusual appointments in the week preceding his departure?"

"Alf Spats was there on that . . . that final day," Kristin managed to say. "I spoke with Mavis Youngdahl, Eric's secretary. Mr. Spats is beyond suspicion. What is on your mind, Lance?"

"Alvah T. Bascomb, for one thing. My cattle die like flies and Alvah T. Bascomb appears at the ranch, offering a deal. Alvah T. Bascomb holds open the offer of another deal, and Eric Starbane dies. But Bascomb, you say, was in Duluth the whole time, and was surprised enough to cable here when Eric did not arrive in Duluth?"

"Yes," Haakon affirmed.

"Unless his 'surprise' was all part of a plan . . ." Lance continued.

"Oh, darling," protested Elizabeth, "you must not begin to think in this way, not without proof . . ."

"Proof," he retorted, almost scornfully and as harshly as he had ever spoken to her. "Proof is something written on the wind, hidden behind frank eyes, concealed within the cadences of speech. Who else did Eric see that last week?" he demanded of Kristin.

"Regular appointments? No one extraordinary. There was one man, Webster Tuttle, who tried to see Eric a number of times. He was there early in the morning of the . . . the last day."

"Webster Tuttle!" cried Elizabeth, with distaste. "Whatever would he want to see Father for?"

"A job, apparently," Haakon said.

"After what he and Smedley and Granger did to me! 'T' indeed! The man should be horsewhipped, and Father ought to have done it. Why, Tuttle was nothing but a conniver and a spy . . ."

"Please don't become agitated, dear," soothed Kristin. "It won't do any good."

"Is there an early train to St. Cloud?" Lance asked abruptly. "One that departs before the train Eric took?"

"Yes," replied Haakon. "What are you driving at?"

"Nothing I can be sure of as yet. Is there any other information you can give me? Anything at all?"

He looked at Kristin and Haakon, who looked at each other.

"Only that Alf Spats was right," Haakon offered slowly. "There is a concentrated raid on Grand Northern Railroad stock. Alf Spats is doing what he can, but since Father's death, his estate has declined three million dollars in value, and the trend continues . . ."

"Elizstar stock is holding, though," commented Elizabeth, trying to provide a note of cheer. "In fact, the price is still rising . . ."

"Wait a minute," exclaimed Haakon, getting up from his chair and pacing back and forth across the finely worked oriental carpet in *Windward*'s front parlor. "Wait a minute. I've been too numb, we've *all* been too numb since Father's death to see the pattern that is right in front of our eyes. Think of it. What is the linchpin of the Starbane fortune? Grand Northern. And how was the raid signaled? By a rise in stock values. Elizabeth, you must telegraph Bjorn Tennerson immediately. I fear we have been royally gulled by the greatest trickster in the Midwest, J. J. Granger, hell-bent on spectacular revenge . . ."

"Granger knows not the first thing of revenge," Lance muttered, "but I do . . ."

"Please, darling," said Elizabeth.

"Yes!" exclaimed Haakon, sure that he was right. "J.J. *could* make a shambles of everything, if now he attacks Elizstar as he has already savaged Grand Northern. Without Elizstar in sound shape, Elizabeth cannot borrow to lay track, buy rolling stock, complete her road. With the Grand Northern stock low, Elizabeth cannot even borrow from the Starbane estate. It is a plan of colossal arrogance and cunning!"

"Now we know why J. J. Granger sold me his rights-of-way," Elizabeth sighed, "and why he sold his share of the iron range."

"To get money for raids on Elizstar and the Grand Northern," Kristin said.

"If all goes according to his plans," commented Haakon, with a discouraged expression, "he can ruin the Continental Pacific utterly, and he might even be able to acquire controlling interest in the Grand Northern . . ."

"And even Elizstar!" Elizabeth realized, with a gasp.

"And father is not here to help us fight." Haakon punched his open palm with a fist, punched it again and again.

They were silent for a long time. A maid brought tea and biscuits, set the tray on a table, and retreated. No one made a move toward the refreshments. A heavy sense of outrage and violation rode the air.

"We must act," Lance said. "I am going to determine the current whereabouts of J. J. Granger."

7

"Ashes to ashes, dust to dust," the Reverend Doctor Estendahl proclaimed. Now and then he glanced up from coffin and text to observe that Lance Tallworth looked exceedingly dangerous today.

Little Selena stood on the grass between her mother and father. It seemed passing strange to her that Grandpa was sleeping in the big bronze box with the shiny handles on its sides. Even more disconcerting was the fact that the bronze box was going to be put into a hole in the ground, and Grandpa was never going to wake up. Selena already held her mother's hand, and now she looked up, reached up, and slipped her other hand into her father's reassuring grip. He was staring far away across the river, and so did she. It was very nice over there, and pretty. Suddenly she knew that everything was going to be all right. In a manner she did not quite understand, but which was otherwise totally plausible, Grandpa would always be able to look out across the river and see the spring trees putting forth their leaves, the grass growing, the changing colors of the seasons as they passed. And so Grandpa would be forever happy.

Yes, she decided, with a pert little nod of affirmation, *that is how it will be*.

Then Reverend Estendahl made the final blessing, and the bronze coffin was lowered by ropes into the earth.

I'll always be able to come here and talk to you, Grandpa, Selena prayed, as hot little tears pooled in the corners of her dark, exquisite eyes. Everyone seemed to be crying now, except Daddy and Grandma. Mama was crying very hard. Selena felt like crying, very much, but Daddy was not and would not. *I won't either*, she told herself. Many, many years later, when the burial of Eric Starbane was the dimmest of memories, Selena would come to know the great bond of blood she shared with her father, come to realize how much they were alike. But all that was for the future. Now she was a little girl, holding hands with her parents and fighting back tears.

Eric's gravesite, selected by Kristin, was in a corner of *Windward*'s lawn, beneath towering maples, on the bank above the Mississippi. "Here we were happiest," she explained after telling the family of her decision, "and this was his home. We all have one place in which we feel most comfortable, one spot of earth to which we belong forever. Some are born to it and know it from the start. Others must find it, as did Eric and I. And so he will remain in the earth he discovered, and which he called home."

Kristin's thoughts, as the coffin was lowered, wandered far from Minnesota clay, back across the years to Lesja in Norway. She had grown up in the same village as Eric, had known him always. But there had come one day when she saw him, really *saw* him, for the first time. That was the day on which she truly began her life. All earlier events were consigned to the murky spheres of fairy tale and myth. On that day, Kristin and some of her school friends played hooky and went into the mountains. Bread and cheese purloined from pantries at home and a stone jug of pale beer made a picnic feast. They trekked high into the hills above Sonnandahl Fjord, and had a happy time eating and drinking and talking about their poor classmates who were "trapped in that dungeon of a schoolroom." They had a very good time until they wondered what punishment they would receive for playing hooky. Pastor Pringsheim, who was in charge of the school, was sure to tell their parents of these scandalous absences, and then . . .

Not feeling as keen as she had at the outset of the day, Kristin had wandered away from the others for a few moments, to be alone and to look down at the majestic fjord. Standing quietly behind a row of pine saplings, she saw a man on horseback ride to a pool among the rocks in the river that cascaded down to the fjord. No, it was not a man. It was Eric Starbane, whom she had always known. Worried about her punishment, she scarcely noticed as he dismounted and drank from the icy pool. But then she saw that he was disrobing for a dive into the pure frigid waters. A glance told her that her friends were still gorging themselves on bread, cheese, and beer. So with a feeling of private excitement she found difficult to fathom or contain, Kristin turned back to see Eric Starbane strip naked under the sun. She had not been mistaken in thinking that a *man* had appeared at the pool. This was not the Eric Starbane she had always known, but instead a tanned demigod whose taut muscles rippled, whose perfect torso gleamed in the sun. Savage and splendid, he poised for the dive, nonchalant in the naturalness of his bearing, the instruments of his manhood heavy and perfect and . . .

He made her gasp.

And then he was gone, down into the pool. Instinctively, Kristin held her breath, kept on holding it.

Finally, he came up, straight up from those pure and icy depths, satyr-son of Neptune shot through with glory.

Kristin knew a delicious flood of heat in her loins.

She barely felt the whipping she received that night.

Not many years thereafter, she made love with Eric on that same meadow above the fjord, and afterward blessed him with the water of the icy pool.

Now, in Minnesota, she walked down the lawn, all the way to the banks of the Mississippi, and from the timeless Father of Waters scooped for Eric her last gift to him. Earth had been thrown over the coffin by then, but she opened her hands and let the water spill out upon his grave.

"This water has known my mortal image," she said, as the others watched, "just as once it held yours. I give it now, not in memory but in promise, until I join you and we have each other, forever to keep."

Warm spring wind moved down the Mississippi Valley, whispering in the bright new leaves of maples as Eric Starbane was laid to rest.

"For this he shall pay," vowed Lance Tallworth that night.

"*Who* shall pay?" Elizabeth pleaded. "*Who?* Don't be thinking of revenge when you don't even know . . . Oh, Lance, darling, we have so many problems already. Don't you understand . . . ?"

"We have but one problem, and his name is Granger."

"You don't know that. At least, no one can prove it."

"Knowledge is its own proof."

"And shouldn't you approach Judge Bullion? I am sure the legal matter about your leaving the reservation can be cleared up easily . . ."

"If I was placed on the Red Lake Reservation against my will, it was my right to leave it. I do not need the law to tell me that I am a free man."

They were lying in bed in the darkness. Elizabeth reached out and touched him. He was there in body, his skin bare and smooth and cool. But she felt, upon touching him, a premonition. He was not here with her. It was another time, and he was gone and far away.

When she awoke in the morning, Lance was not there.

He was not at *Windward*, and no one had seen him leave.

But returning for the noon meal after a morning trying desperately to secure loans from St. Paul banks, Haakon had news. "I talked to Alf Spats. He said that Lance has been asking after Webster Tuttle all around town. Alf said we had better make sure Lance doesn't get himself into big trouble. We've got enough problems already. We'll either have to sell Elizstar stock to save the estate's stake in the Grand Northern, or vice versa."

"We'll do neither!" Elizabeth pronounced.

"And lose both?" Haakon asked, incredulous.

Elizabeth imagined "Uncle" Gustav howling with glee, and J. J. Granger gloating. *Oh, Lance, come home!*

8

Lance Tall One existed in the shadows where time did not show its face. There was no time. There was only now. He simply *was*, becoming a part of the shadows, which he would be for as long as he had to be. Lance Tall One existed for what he had to do, and he would do it whether there was time or not. The white man's mind moved by hours and the brittle hands of clocks. But the ancient Sioux mind *was*, and time did not exist.

J. J. Granger's house near St. Paul was very well guarded. A huge white mansion on the shores of White Bear Lake, northeast of the city, it was built after the ultramodern "Victorian" style, and resembled a castle made of clapboard, with towers and turrets, a profusion of bay windows, and even a widow's walk. Sunlight glittered on the waters of the lake, gleamed on the new paint of the big white house. There were armed guards everywhere.

Granger was afraid. So Lance knew immediately he had had something to do with the murder of Eric Starbane.

Lance took to the woods, watching the house, watching the guards come and go, mulling the conflict to which his life had brought him, seeking to place in balance once and forever the disparate inclinations in his heart. On the one hand, assuming that Granger and Webster Tuttle had conspired to kill Eric Starbane, did they not deserve the summary retribution of *ycripsicu*? And was revenge not more fitting if the two had been devious enough to evade the law? But on the other hand, Lance's heart had been touched indelibly by Elizabeth's love, by Jason and Selena, by Fleet Fawn and Sostana. Lance had been changed by love, but he did not know if he was stronger or weaker than he had been in the past. Was there, in his new life, a place for *ycripsicu*?

If hatred hardens one, does love ennoble? Or does revenge weaken a man, and love make him strong? Or does love make him cease to care about the vigilance that is necessary if he is to be safe from the wicked? Lance struggled with these questions in the woods outside Granger's house, but he came to no conclusions. All he knew was that two evil men had done a terrible thing and no one seemed prepared to do anything about it.

Are you prepared? he asked himself.

Yes.

And if you kill Granger, then what? You do not even know where Tuttle is.

I shall find out.

How?

I shall find out.

But if you kill them both, what will the fact of the killing do to you? Will Elizabeth love you more?

No.

And that is what you desire?

No, but . . .

But?

A great crime cannot go unavenged! A good man cannot be brought down like a stag in the thicket, without the grace of retribution.

And so Lance watched the house and struggled with himself. He began, also, to observe the general pattern of activity around the house. During the day, everything was quiet except for the guards and the arrival and departure of the Western Union messengers on horseback. Granger, locked up here for his own safekeeping, was managing his stock manipulations by telegraph. When evening came, however, gleaming carriages filled with laughing men and women wheeled down the road between the trees and stopped in front of the house. Evidently J.J. felt a need to liven his existence. Gas lamps illuminated the area, and from his place in the trees Lance saw Granger step out of his house to greet the guests. On J.J.'s arm was a beautiful young woman with copper-colored hair, no doubt the Chicago showgirl who had become his new wife.

Lance reflected that J. J. Granger had something to live for again, after the death of his son Clint.

A man who has something to lose . . .

The party lasted, with music and singing and shouting, almost until dawn. Lance ignored it and went to sleep, outside the circle of time.

On the following morning, the Western Union messengers began to appear again, riding their lean, sleek horses through the trees to the house, handing over their messages at the door, and leaving with other messages to be transmitted.

If Granger were masterminding the raids on Elizstar and the Grand Northern, as seemed certain, his mighty machine was fueled by these messages.

Lance licked dew from wet leaves, exhilarated. He seemed to remember being hungry, but that feeling had gone. He watched and he was, that was all.

There were, he observed, three Western Union men. Two were slight, light riders, but the third was a bigger man who rode with an arrogant posture, as if he were meant for better things than delivering telegrams. Lance moved beneath the trees, gained a post next to the road, and waited. One of the small men came and went, and then another. Finally the big man came cantering up the drive, with a message pouch tied to his saddlebag.

Lance sprang from the floor of the forest like a cougar on

the attack, sweeping the messenger off his horse and onto the road. The horse, a dull beast used to the outrages of the city, started and skittered but did not run away. The messenger, knocked breathless by the fall, had no energy to resist Lance, nor even strength to plead for mercy.

Lance bound the man to a tree, affixing also a gag of vines that obstructed the messenger's tongue.

Then he examined the message pouch.

It contained exultant telegrams from Chicago and New York. Just a few more days, one message affirmed, and the Grand Northern would be J. J. Granger's road. Perhaps in a week, another cable suggested, Elizstar would pass from the control of "the half-breed's wife."

It took a moment before Lance realized that he was "the half-breed" and Elizabeth was the "wife."

"No harm will come to you," he told the bound messenger, who had begun to moan and struggle against his bonds. "But if you make a sound from now until nightfall, I will kill you as easily as I blink."

The messenger fell silent.

Lance examined a few remaining items in the pouch. There were several messages for other White Bear Lake residents, and a pad of telegraph paper. There was also a letter, handwritten, sealed, and addressed to Granger. Lance opened it.

> J.J.
> Hot time in the old town tonight. I think we got them where it hurts. I sure appreciate the invitation to your party, and I will be there with bells on. Ya-hoo, as they say in the Wild West.
>
> T.

Webster Tuttle! Lance took the pouch, retrieved the horse, which had begun to chomp tall grass along the roadway, and went into the trees. He studied Tuttle's letter, a crude message in a cruder hand. There was no return address. If Tuttle came here tonight, he and Granger would be together. But that would avail Lance naught, with all the guests and guards around. No, he had to think of something else.

At length, gambling that anything was worth a try, he took a page from the pad, and wrote:

> J.J.
> I must see you alone at once. Everything depends on it.
>
> T.

His handwriting was at least as crude as Tuttle's had been. Resealing the envelope as best he could, he went back to the messenger and stripped him of his clothing. The man protested in a gurgle. Green juice from the gag he was chewing dripped from his chin.

Lance undressed, hid his clothes, and slipped on the messenger's outfit. Then he took the pouch, mounted, and rode up to the house. He assumed a posture of half-sleepy, half-sullen arrogance. Not one of the guards batted an eye as he walked to the door and clanged the knocker.

"Well!" exclaimed the woman who answered his knock, "you're a new one on the job, ain'tcha? And where's Western Union been hidin' you, honey?"

The worst possible situation. Granger's new wife had come to the door. Her voice was only slightly louder than her taste in fashion.

"Who is it, my dear?" called J.J. from a nearby room.

"I don't think you want to know, honeybuns," said the new Mrs. Granger suggestively, with a tone guaranteed to make a man jealous as all get-out.

Lance thought fast. He had observed that every time a messenger appeared, J.J. always had his own missives to dispatch. So his only choices were to remain standing here, waiting for whatever J.J. wanted to send for transmission, or to . . .

"There's a letter in here I was ordered to deliver posthaste," he said quickly, thrusting the pouch at Mrs. Granger. Her red lips opened in an "O" of surprise as the pouch pressed heavily against her belly. "It's a matter of life and death, I was told . . ."

Lance spoke quite loudly, so that J.J. would not miss the message.

"Now I must run," he added. "My partner will be along in a little while."

Lance thought he caught a glimpse of J.J. coming out of his office, and he was sure he heard a call from the doorway as he mounted the horse, but he made it a point to turn away from the house. Arrogantly, he cantered past the bored guards.

When he reached his hiding place in the trees, time had begun to move again. Lance still did not know what he would do, but he would wait to find out.

Less than fifteen minutes after Lance had delivered the messages, Granger's front door opened and J.J. himself came out. Instead of his usual ostentatious haberdashery, Granger wore an old floppy hat and the clothes of a workingman. In the shadow of the hat brim, not even his eyepatch could be seen.

Lance allowed himself a flash of satisfaction. Granger was taking the bait. He would go alone to wherever Tuttle was.

Accordingly, Lance suffered a surge of disappointment when two guards on horseback fell in behind the tycoon. Lance waited five minutes, and then set out after the three, spurring his horse when he saw that they were riding fast.

Where the trail from White Bear Lake joined the main road into St. Paul, Granger and his guards halted. The road was well traveled, with horses, wagons, and buggies, and people on foot trudging along. Lance pulled the Western Union cap low over his face, and slowed his horse. Then J.J. gave his orders. One of the guards headed back to the lake, and the other set off with him toward St. Paul.

Lance followed at a considerable distance, not at all certain that he liked what was happening. The guard would have to be dealt with if Lance were to reach Granger. Moreover, if Webster Tuttle were staying somewhere in the city, there would be too many people around, too much chance of interference, of being observed.

But close to St. Paul, J.J. and his guard trotted their mounts into the quiet little village of Roseville, turned down a side street, and halted next to a small unpainted wooden house. No more than a cabin or shack, it stood behind a thick, untrimmed row of scrub brush. Only the thin wisp of smoke from a tilting chimney pipe gave evidence that the cabin was occupied. Riding about a hundred yards behind the two men, Lance saw them turn in at the cabin and disappear behind the bushes. He rode past, slowed, dismounted, and pulled his horse by the reins into the woods adjacent to the village. Roseville was somnolent on this warm spring morning. A tradesman's wagon rattled across the square. Two women walked toward the general store, carrying baskets, trailed by raggedy towheads in short pants. A dog barked a couple of times and fell silent.

In the shelter of the sweet trees, birds quieted and small unseen animals chittered and fled. The horse was happy to rest and chomp greenery. Through the green leaves, Lance saw the gray cabin, its plank siding warped from rain and weather. His heart was beating slowly and steadily, but a wave of excitement swept over him. His heritage was resurgent: the slow patient stealth of the hunt. At that moment, he truly did not know whether he would kill Granger or not.

If he had the chance.

Leaving the horse tied to a sapling, Lance crept beneath

bushes until he reached the cabin. A single narrow window of discolored glass afforded him a glimpse inside. J. J. Granger, his back to the window, was talking to a slight ferret-faced man. They were seated at a small table. The ferret-faced man looked puzzled, even frightened. J.J. waved his arms in emphatic agitation. The guard slouched next to the door, slurping whatever liquid his canteen contained.

Lance was unarmed. Though he could not tell, he assumed that Granger and Tuttle had weapons. The guard wore a pistol in a holster on his hip.

Acting out of instinct rather than reflecting or deciding, Lance raced around the corner of the cabin and burst into the place, sending the wooden door crashing against the wall. He knew where the guard was standing, and at what height his gun was slung. Lance reached for it as he crashed past the man, yanking the weapon free of its holster. Then he stopped, and leveled the blue muzzle at the furrowed bridge of J. J. Granger's nose.

The guard clawed at his empty holster. Webster Tuttle's mouth was open. Instinctively, J.J. lifted his arms in defense and started to rise.

"Sit down," Lance told him, very quietly. "You know who I am and what I can do."

Granger's good eye bulged. He remembered the sight of his son Clint's body, ripped open on the riverbank. His hard face showed a trace of fear.

"Close the door," Lance told the guard.

The man complied, looking with longing at the green outdoors.

"What the hell is this?" Tuttle faltered, trying to sound outraged.

"Were you in St. Cloud four or five days ago?" Lance demanded of him.

"I . . . hey, what goes on . . . ?" Tuttle blithered.

"I know you were," Lance said.

"You don't know a damn thing," Granger managed, having gathered his courage. "Get out of here and run. The law'll be after you soon enough."

"No, it's you the law will be after," Lance countered.

"What are you up to, anyway, you goddamn Injun?" J.J. barked.

Lance struck him smartly on the side of the head with the pistol barrel. J.J. winced and grunted.

"I am here to avenge the death of Eric Starbane," Lance told him.

"I . . . I didn't have nothin' to do with that," protested J.J., holding one hand to his head. A trickle of blood had begun to seep through his fingers.

"I didn't neither," protested Tuttle, his eyes on the gun.

"You're crazy, Injun. You're barkin' up the wrong tree," J.J. added.

"I don't think so," said Lance.

The guard stood, wary and poised, near the door.

Lance saw now that J.J. and Tuttle were prepared to stick by each other. He knew too that he could not bring himself to kill them until they admitted outright their complicity in Eric's death. Shrewd J.J. sensed Lance's quandary, and saw that, in spite of the gun held no more than six inches from his good eye, he still had a powerful card to play.

"Kill us, you'll never bed that lovely wife of your'n again, Injun. Did you think of that?"

Something to lose. A man with something to lose is a man with a weakness.

"I could kill you and you'd never again bed that new wife of yours either," Lance rejoined. Granger also had that delight to lose.

Tuttle's thin tongue darted from his mouth, and he licked his narrow lips a time or two. "Come on, J.J. Get us out of this."

The guard moved slightly. Lance turned the pistol on

him. J.J. blinked. Lance swung the gun back toward the tycoon.

Granger had decided on a ploy. "Okay, Injun," he admitted, "so you're smart. You tricked me into coming here, and here I am. Now, whatever you may think, I didn't kill Eric Starbane, and neither did Tuttle here, and we don't know nothin' about it. So what can you do? Nothin'. You go on and get the hell out of here, go back to Montana, and we'll forget all about this."

"But you are managing the ruin of Elizstar and the takeover of the Grand Northern, aren't you?"

"Business is business," J.J. smirked.

Lance hit him again with the gun. The smirk disappeared.

Lance looked down at Granger and Tuttle. He could kill them now. It would be so easy. It would be right too. But he thought of Elizabeth, the sad look on her face when she thought of revenge . . .

Then the guard leaped forward, an act either of foolhardy courage or desperation. Granger and Tuttle were no more prepared for the move than Lance was. But Lance had the gun. The guard was in midair, arms outstretched to seize Lance. The pistol cracked, and the guard hurtled past Lance, a human projectile spraying blood from his blasted head. He struck the floor with a shattering thud and lay still. The hot smell of blood and the dry, throat-tightening stench of blue gunpowder filled the cabin.

Neither Tuttle nor Granger spoke now. They knew an Injun who had a taste of blood would always want more, just like a lion.

Lance surprised them. "Tuttle," he ordered, "tie your boss's feet to the table legs. Use the lacings of his boots. Then use his belt to bind his hands to the back of the chair."

Tuttle did as he was told, sweating. J.J. was sweating too. "What are you gonna do, Tallworth?"

"*Mr.* Tallworth to you. Wait and see."

After Granger was bound, Lance fastened Tuttle similarly in a chair on the other side of the little table. The two men, trying not to show fear, watched him. Lance had not killed them. He could have done so. Maybe he wouldn't. Maybe he would leave now. Somehow they could work their way loose . . .

Then Lance lifted the bloody body of the guard, dragged it over to the table, and propped it into a third chair. The guard's ruined head flopped to the side, and he gazed at Granger and Tuttle with a look of tragic accusation. His head lolled and he threatened to fall over. Lance used the guard's holster belt to secure him upright in the chair.

Tuttle looked afraid now. Not afraid as one would be in the presence of mere death, but terrified in the face of possible madness. "What you gonna do now?" he asked, wetting his lips again with that thin serpent's tongue.

Lance smiled. "I am going to wait until you tell me that you killed Eric Starbane on J.J.'s orders. Until you tell me many other things. Then I am going to wait still more, while Mr. Granger speaks. Don't worry. There is plenty of time. Rather, there is no time. I am very patient, and we can remain here for as long as it will take. I see that there is food here," he added, glancing at two shelves of cupboard that ran along one wall.

Tuttle and Granger looked at each other. The horrible insight had come to them simultaneously. They looked at the dead guard, bound to his chair just as they were to theirs. Lance Tallworth was ready to wait *for as long as it took*, while the dead member of this macabre troika progressed into the fate to which all flesh is heir. Right before their eyes! Right under their noses!

"You can't mean this . . ." Granger faltered.

"Oh, but I do," Lance said.

Tuttle began to retch.

"Save your breath for talking," Lance told him.

"You'll . . . you'll smell him *too*!" Granger pointed out, trying to be persuasive.

"I can step outside until you fellows decide to tell me the truth. I can sleep outside."

Webster Tuttle moaned, and looked pleadingly at J.J. *Sleep?* Lance meant to *sleep* here? Overnight? Days might pass. No one but "T" and J.J. knew where Tuttle had holed up. And with the warm spring weather, the guard would reek to high heaven after only a day's time . . .

"I'm sure he won't smell much worse than my anthrax-dead cattle," Lance said, "which is another thing I have been wanting to discuss." He walked over to the cupboard shelves and inspected some of the supplies there. "A jar of canned cauliflower," he said cheerfully, "and canned tomatoes. And here's a tin of dried beef. You fellows aren't getting hungry, are you?"

9

"I don't understand it," Haakon said. "Grand Northern stock is holding steady, and even rising a little. And the raid on Elizstar is clearly over."

He stood on the porch of *Windward*, holding a telegram from Bjorn Tennerson.

"I just don't understand it," he repeated.

Elizabeth and Kristin were with him. They thought that they understood all too well. And while they could not be displeased at this turn of events in business, neither could they contemplate the reason without a sense of foreboding. If J. J. Granger had ceased to move against them, then he was dead. If he was dead, Lance had killed him.

Lance had been gone for three days.

Elizabeth felt tears come to her eyes. Her wild falcon had gone back to his ancient instincts. In stalking Granger, he had sought to revenge Eric Starbane's death. And maybe he had. But he would not be able to get away with it. Either the law would take him, or he would have to flee the law forever.

In either case, any hope of a peaceful, loving life was over.

Haakon saw his mother's burdened expression, noted that his sister was fighting back tears. He knew why.

"It was just Lance's way, that's all," he said, trying to be soothing. "It was his way of helping. We oughtn't to blame him. But we'll have to deal with it now as best we can.

There are the children to think about, Selena and Jason. And then there's the ranch. I suppose you've thought of moving back here to Minnesota?"

"No," said Elizabeth. "I love Montana. And if Lance did what he did to save us, I am going to make sure to hold on to the ranch. Wherever Lance might go in the world, that is where he will come home to in the end."

Little Jason sat gurgling in his high chair that evening, oblivious to tragedy, but Selena, ever perspicacious, regarded the adults carefully.

"Why is everybody so gloomy?" she demanded.

"We're just . . . we're just thinking about important things, honey," said Kristin.

"Is it because Grandpa died? Is that what you're sad about?"

"Well, of course, but . . ."

"It's not because my daddy's gone, is it? Because my daddy's not gone and he's gonna come home. He's gonna come home real soon."

She said it with all the conviction that her young heart held.

Elizabeth could hardly bear to hear it. The evening paper had announced the disappearance of J. J. Granger. "He left three days ago and hasn't returned," his tearful bride had been quoted. "He had a guard, but the man never came back either. I should have gone to the sheriff sooner, but how was I to know? My husband was always going here or there on business, so I just thought . . ."

Elizabeth wondered if killing J. J. Granger had given Lance satisfaction sufficient to bring him a measure of peace. There were certain things that death might give, she admitted, but life was not one of them.

After the children were in bed, Haakon, Kristin, and Elizabeth sat in the parlor, sipping sherry.

"Tomorrow will be better, you'll see," said Kristin, who

had seen so much more of the world's woe than had her children.

"Mother, why don't you go to bed?" Haakon advised. "You look tired and . . ."

"What was that?" exclaimed Elizabeth.

"What?"

"I thought I heard something."

The three quieted, and heard, quite distinctly, the rattle of the door handle on the riverfront side of the house. No one ever entered on that side at night.

Quickly, Haakon sprang up and grabbed a poker from its stand next to the fireplace.

The back door had opened. A cool breeze passed through the house, fluttering curtains and antimacassars.

"Hold it right there, my friend!" threatened Haakon, rushing into the next room, the poker raised. Kristin and Elizabeth were right behind him.

"This door ought to be locked," said Lance Tallworth, standing just inside the doorway. He looked as if he hadn't slept or changed clothes for days. He looked an awful sight. But he was the best thing that Elizabeth had ever seen. She raced to him, and crashed into his embrace. What awful trouble he must be in, to have to steal into the house by darkness. But just now she didn't care, and held him as tightly as she could, felt his strong arms around her.

"Oh, Lance . . ."

"It's all right, my darling. Everything is all right."

They held each other for a long, long time. And all that time Elizabeth didn't think about anything.

"I *told* you my daddy would come home!" cried little Selena victoriously, from the top of the staircase. She rushed down to be hugged too.

Finally, Haakon spoke. "All this is well and good," he said drily. "Lance, in view of what's happened, what are your plans?"

Lance looked up at him, puzzled. "Why, to take my

family back to Montana, of course. That's where we belong."

"To take them . . . where? Just like that? What about J. J. Granger, and all the rest of it?"

Again, Lance appeared to be mystified. "Well, I expect Webster Tuttle will be hanged for killing Eric, and Granger will either be hanged or imprisoned for life. Tuttle was the one who pushed Eric into the river, you see . . ."

The story did not take long to tell. Tuttle and Granger had confessed, had confessed personally to Judge Roscoe F. Bullion. "You might say I arranged it myself," Lance said.

Alvah T. Bascomb, whatever his faults, had had nothing to do with it. And the anthrax had been an act of God.

"In Whom it may be possible at times to believe," Lance told them, lifting Selena into his arms. "We will go back to Montana and start over. I am ready."

"Daddy, you smell funny!" she said.

"The wages of war, darling. It will wash off. It takes a long time, but in the end all the evil things wash off."

"But Lance," asked Kristin, who had been watching and listening with a mingled sense of relief and bewilderment, "why did you come in from the river side? You might just as well have walked in through the front door."

"I visited your husband's grave," he said. "I told him that his enemies had been brought to justice, so that he might know that all is over. So that he may rest in peace."

"Thank you," Kristin said. But then she waited in silence, aware that there was something more that Lance had to say.

"And I went down to the river," Lance said, "to the Father of Waters. And I thanked him that I had been able to overcome my enemies—not just the enemy without, but the enemy within. So that I too may be at peace."

Epilogue–1900

The president of the United States of America, William McKinley, arrived in St. Paul on a golden day in late September. As part of a year-long celebration of the new century, he had elected to travel coast-to-coast by rail, not only to enjoy himself but also to demonstrate how Americans had tamed a continent. And wasn't that true? From the Chesapeake Bay to Puget Sound, from Lake of the Woods to the Gulf of Mexico, from Calais in Maine to Santa Catalina, California, a mighty nation flexed its muscles and looked forward. In Cuba and in the Philippines, American boys had bested the Spaniards. In Minnesota, one of the men who had led those boys, Haakon Starbane, welcomed the president. Haakon, who had served under Theodore Roosevelt at San Juan Hill, was running for the Senate. It was wholly coincidental that McKinley, who was standing for reelection, should be photographed with Haakon, should stay the night at *Windward*, should board the Continental Pacific Clipper for his journey to the West Coast.

Kristin Starbane boarded too. She wanted to see her grandchildren and to see the Pacific. The president responded most warmly to the beautiful widow who had been his hostess—and who was mother of Minnesota's next senator—and asked her to visit with him in his private car.

"Tell me, please," he asked her, "you have seen much of our country. What part do you prefer? Which region?"

"I haven't seen everything," Kristin answered, "but I know that home will always be here in the north."

"Ah!" replied the president.

The Clipper stopped in Black Forks, Montana, to take aboard the Tallworth family. Seldom had the president seen so striking a couple as Lance and Elizabeth. Their son, Jason, studied the president for a long time, and finally smiled and bowed.

"I believe I've been accepted," McKinley said.

He could hardly take his eyes off the Tallworths' daughter, Selena. She was about thirteen or so, McKinley reasoned. Exquisite. Lord help the men when she grew up.

The president asked Mr. and Mrs. Tallworth to remain and have a drink with him in his car as the Clipper pulled out of Black Forks. Well briefed as always, McKinley made small talk.

"This is your ranch, isn't it?" he inquired of Lance, as the train streaked westward.

"Yes, sir."

"Unusual name, I think. What was it again?"

"*Sostana*," Lance answered. "It means 'Peace.'"

McKinley did not fail to notice that the Tallworths exchanged tender glances just then. Ah, to be young . . .

Just before reaching Bitterroot Pass, gateway to the Rocky Mountains, the train, which had been running straight as a plumb line, moved into a long, slow, gentle curve, before returning to its original course and racing through the majestic pass.

"Didn't we detour slightly there?" McKinley wondered. "Any reason why? Plenty of space out here."

"A long time ago . . . " Lance began, but faltered and looked away.

Elizabeth answered the president. "A cowboy named Rowdy Jenner told me this was sacred ground," she said.

"Ah!" observed McKinley.

By the time the Clipper reached the Pacific, everyone was

celebrating. Reporters, photographers, and thousands of citizens swarmed around this mighty train that had come all the way from the Midwest. The Continental Pacific was at once an affirmation and a celebration of destiny. America had, in a word, "arrived."

To delight the public and please the newsmen, McKinley posed with Jason and Selena Tallworth. Camera powder flashed and the crowd cheered. In the distance glittered the Pacific, and the West Coast of America stretched on and on until it disappeared in dazzle and mist.

"Tell me," McKinley asked the children, "what do *you* think? Your grandmother prefers the Upper Midwest, your parents are in love with the high plains. What do you two like?"

Jason and Selena looked out over the ocean, and down along the coast.

"It's really beautiful here," said Selena, with genuine awe in her voice.

"Yes," agreed Jason, "and someday it's going to be all ours."